TALES OF MYSTERY &

General Editor: D...

THE BEAST WITH
FIVE FINGERS
Supernatural Stories

The Beast with Five Fingers

Supernatural Stories
by W. F. Harvey

Selected and introduced by
David Stuart Davies

WORDSWORTH EDITIONS

In loving memory of
MICHAEL TRAYLER
the founder of Wordsworth Editions

I

Readers interested in other titles from
Wordsworth Editions are invited to visit our
website at www.wordsworth-editions.com

For our latest list and a full mail-order service contact
Bibliophile Books, Unit 5 Datapoint,
South Crescent, London E16 4TL
Tel: +44 020 74 74 24 74
Fax: +44 020 74 74 85 89
orders@bibliophilebooks.com
www.bibliophilebooks.com

This edition published 2009 by
Wordsworth Editions Limited
8B East Street, Ware,
Hertfordshire SG12 9HJ

ISBN 978 1 84022 179 4

Typeset in Great Britain by Roperford Editorial
Printed by Clays Ltd, St Ives plc

CONTENTS

INTRODUCTION

Particularly in the early part of the twentieth century there were a number of men who were successful ghost story writers in what one may call an amateur capacity. In other words, they wrote their supernatural tales in their spare time while taking a break from their professional duties. The doyen of this breed was of course M. R. James, who combined a demanding and arduous academic career with very effective forays into the ghost story world. But he was not alone in this practice. There were the Benson Brothers, for example: Robert Hugh Benson was a cleric who turned his hand to a set of unnerving supernatural tales, and Arthur Christopher Benson wrote widely on many other topics, squeezing in a set of ghostly narratives almost as an afterthought. There was also Andrew Caldecott, whose political career saw him rise to great heights, while at the same time he manufactured some very effective and chilling supernatural tales. William Fryer Harvey fits very neatly into this category of part-time scribes of uncanny stories. Apart from M. R. James, who achieved some notoriety in his lifetime and has found many champions of his work since his death, the other writers I have mentioned, including the author of the stories in this collection, were never really part of the mainstream literary world and have to a large extent been forgotten except by the dedicated and knowledgeable fans of the supernatural fiction genre. That is one of the joys and achievements of this Mystery and Supernatural series: we are able to bring these excellent but neglected authors back into print to entertain a new generation of readers. For a long while W. F. Harvey's work has been found only in rare and second-hand bookshops at exorbitant prices. Now you have in your hands a superb collection of the best of his writings.

William Fryer Harvey was born in 1885 of a Yorkshire Quaker family and educated at the Quaker Schools at Bootham, York and Leighton Park, Reading, and afterwards at Balliol College, Oxford.

He took his medical degree at Leeds but, never a robust soul, his training was interrupted by ill health. To help him recover fully, he took a voyage around the world, in the course of which he spent some time in Australia and New Zealand. Clearly the journey broadened his horizons in more ways than one. The range of interesting and idiosyncratic individuals he encountered on this trip fuelled his imagination.

On his return Harvey became interested in the adult education movement, keen to help those whose schooling had not been as efficient and privileged as his own. Harvey assisted at the Working Men's College at Fircroft, near Birmingham. Soon after the outbreak of the First World War, he went with the Friends Ambulance Unit to Flanders. Later he enlisted into the medical service and became a surgeon-lieutenant in the Navy. It was during this period that an incident occurred which changed the course of his life irrevocably. Courageously, Harvey risked his life to carry out an amputation on a stoker petty officer who was trapped in the wrecked and flooded engine room of a destroyer, which was in imminent danger of breaking in two. He carried out the operation successfully, removing the officer's arm, thus releasing him, and allowing the man to be carried to safety. However, after his exertions Harvey collapsed, overcome by the poisonous escaping oil fumes. His lungs never recovered. For the rest of his days he was an invalid and lived very close to death. Following this terrible incident W. F. Harvey was awarded the Albert Medal 'for gallantry at sea' but such was his quiet and unassuming nature that it was only when this award was announced by the authorities, that his family and friends learned of his heroic deed.

After the war, in 1920, Harvey became Warden at Fircroft, but his debilitated condition forced him to resign in 1925. He and his wife lived in Switzerland for a time – the clean air aiding his breathing – but missing England he returned home and died in Letchworth in 1937, at the young age of fifty-two.

W. F. Harvey was by all accounts a fine, gentle and lovable man, and as his war record reveals, he was also courageous but remarkably modest. Yet he found pleasure and success in creating a series of dark, disturbing and frightening tales. Of course it is naïve to expect the writer's character to reflect his writings, and Harvey is a prime example of how dark imaginings can flourish in a creative form beneath a placid and kindly soul. Indeed, his career and his fiction prove quite clearly that in his case at least the imagination is all. As this rich collection of Harvey's works – many out of print for some time – reveals, the man many of his friends regarded as 'saintly', and a fine and gentle character, could plumb the depths of the disturbing to produce tales of a chilling and often horrific and violent nature. And yet paradoxically his work is remarkable for its subtlety and restraint. Like M. R. James he relies on the reader to pick up suggestions from the text to create his own horrid imaginings; but unlike M. R. James his prose is straightforward and quite modern, lacking that pseudo-gothic, academic tone of James and many other ghost story writers of the time.

During his lifetime Harvey penned four collections of stories: *Midnight House* (1910), *The Beast with Five Fingers* (1928), *Moods and Tenses* (1933), and a fourth collection published after his death which I shall deal with later. The tales in this volume have been chosen from all four of these, bringing back into print, for the first time in many years, a number of neglected gems.

'The Beast With Five Fingers', the classic story that heads this selection, is typical of Harvey's smooth and deceptive style, incorporating as it does sly moments of gentle humour amongst the dark and sinister shadows. One of the most effective touches with this particular narrative is the way the author allows the reader to be one jump ahead of the protagonist. While for some time young Eustace Borlsover seems not to be fully aware of the terrible threat that has been unleashed upon him, Harvey enables the reader to be completely cognisant of the danger he is in. When the horror of his situation finally dawns on Eustace, Harvey subtly matches his panic with suspense and dread. 'The Beast with Five Fingers' is beautifully conceived and cinematic in its moments of climax. It is no surprise then that the cinema has used the concept of the spider-like crawling hand in several movies, most notably in Warner's 1945 feature of the same name. The screenplay by Curt Siodmak was supposedly based on Harvey's story but in reality it presented little more than the idea of a sentient hand getting loose in a private library and wriggling in impotent fury when impaled on a letter spike. Another version of the story is found in the horror compendium film, *Dr Terror's House of Horrors* (1964), in which the pompous art critic played by Christopher Lee is pursued by the severed hand of a celebrated painter he has killed. The blackened hand scrabbling its way out of the fire grate is lifted straight from Harvey's tale.

Writers who introduce the work of other writers always seem to strive to find a recurring theme or idea in the oeuvre of their subject. This is not always appropriate and can at times be strained, indicating a desperate need to find links and connections where none exist. In the case of W. F. Harvey, however, if there is one identifying feature in most if not all of his stories it is an exploration of unknown fear – inexplicable dread that takes hold of the consciousness. This is wonderfully demonstrated in 'The Follower', which at first appears to be a slight tale, but which the perceptive reader will find one of the most unnerving stories in the book. It deals with the power of the mind, the tendrils of imagination which can conjure up an all-consuming fear. The subtle warning administered in this tale causes great consternation in the central character, a writer of ghost stories. It forces him to wonder if he had 'got too near the truth' but then to ponder more worryingly, 'What was the truth?'

The force of the creative imagination which also leads on to a probable and unpalatable truth is presented in 'August Heat'. It concerns two men, strangers to each other and yet their individual fates become inextricably entwined. The two men, one snatching an image from nowhere and the other a name, become linked in a nightmare scenario which chillingly Harvey allows the reader to resolve. Indeed Harvey often invites the reader, indirectly, to imagine the final conclusion to his tightly framed tales. A good example of this is the Kafkaesque 'The Man who hated Aspidistras'. We are led to believe that there must be another explanation to the obvious one that is suggested in the early stages of the tale, but Harvey does not provide one and seems to agree with Hamlet that there are more things in heaven and earth than are dreamt of in our philosophy.

There are over forty stories in this collection, and it would be almost impossible and certainly inadvisable to comment on them all in this Introduction. However, while I do not believe that there is a dud present, there are just a few that call out for special mention. Many of the stories are simple in their plot-lines; indeed it could be said that in essence some of them are without a developed plot at all. They are just moments, scenes snatched out of a dark reality and presented in a short, digestible, and carefully crafted form as an unnerving entertainment. We are often left wondering what happens after the final full stop. Just as in 'August Heat', Harvey frequently takes delight in prompting the reader to ponder what would have happened next if he had continued writing. And often at the centre of the story is one rather bewildered character to whom these strange incidents occur, such as the Quaker widow in 'Sarah Bennet's Possession', whose involvement in an apparently harmless parlour game leads to puzzling and creepy consequences. In 'The Tool' the curate narrator discovers to his horror that on a week's walking tour he has somehow mislaid a day – a day when he carried out a most heinous act of which he now has no memory. In these and other tales, Harvey subtly suggests that these things could easily happen to anyone – even the reader. One story which is bound to strike a chord with many readers is 'The Dabblers', a story of school life which blends the innocence and naïveté of childhood with the youthful unfettered cruelties that accompany them.

Unlike many writers of ghost stories, Harvey's subject matter and creative approach to the genre is very varied. He travels many different narrative roads in order to bring the tingle or the chill. Dotted around this collection are stories of pure whimsy where Harvey allows his mind and pen to wander completely away from reality to produce a half-amusing, half-unsettling story. A fine example of this approach is found in 'The Habeas Corpus Club', which features a fantastic establishment patronised by the murdered victims of fiction – those characters whose literary lives have been cut short, usually in the opening chapters of a crime novel, and so have to leave the printed page in a premature, sudden and violent fashion. The story wears a sardonic smile for most of its length but this fades towards the end and is replaced by a cruel smirk in the closing sentences.

An added bonus in this volume is the dozen tales which Harvey entitled *Twelve Strange Cases*. These stories remained in manuscript form, unpublished until some years after his death, eventually appearing in 1951, in the collection *The Arm of Mrs Egan and Other Stories*. The *Twelve Strange Cases* are interrelated stories, being told by a nurse who has witnessed or taken part in these peculiar happenings in the course of her professional duties. Harvey was able to draw on his own medical knowledge and experiences in creating these tales, in which we see the phenomenon of preternatural forces, and the workings of twisted intelligences, of the subconscious, and of sheer eccentricity. As the book flap of the original edition noted:

> [The stories] will arouse a shudder in many who have long since grown tired of the handsome gangster and the clanking ghost . . . Dr Harvey has the gift of seeing through the shadows of a story into the realm of human motives and personality.

Some of these tales involve human villainy rather than that from the supernatural world, but they all possess a satisfying strangeness which intrigues the reader. How wonderful, for example, to begin a story, as Harvey does in 'The Lake', the first of the *Twelve Strange Tales*, with the statement: 'If this story isn't published there is just a chance I may be murdered.' Who cannot wait to read on?

Never have so many of W. F. Harvey's stories been collected in one volume before and it presents a wonderful range of chilling tales, proving not only that this clever author has been unjustly neglected but also that he is one of the masters of the genre.

DAVID STUART DAVIES

THE BEAST WITH
FIVE FINGERS

Supernatural Stories

The Beast with Five Fingers

The story, I suppose, begins with Adrian Borlsover, whom I met when I was a little boy and he an old man. My father had called to appeal for a subscription, and before he left, Mr Borlsover laid his right hand in blessing on my head. I shall never forget the awe in which I gazed up at his face and realised for the first time that eyes might be dark and beautiful and shining, and yet not able to see.

For Adrian Borlsover was blind.

He was an extraordinary man, who came of an eccentric stock. Borlsover sons for some reason always seemed to marry very ordinary women; which perhaps accounted for the fact that no Borlsover had been a genius, and only one Borlsover had been mad. But they were great champions of little causes, generous patrons of odd sciences, founders of querulous sects, trustworthy guides to the bypath meadows of erudition.

Adrian was an authority on the fertilisation of orchids. He had held at one time the family living at Borlsover Conyers, until a congenital weakness of the lungs obliged him to seek a less rigorous climate in the sunny south-west watering-place where I had seen him. Occasionally he would relieve one or other of the local clergy. My father described him as a fine preacher, who gave long and inspiring sermons from what many men would have considered unprofitable texts. 'An excellent proof,' he would add, 'of the truth of the doctrine of direct verbal inspiration.'

Adrian Borlsover was exceedingly clever with his hands. His penmanship was exquisite. He illustrated all his scientific papers, made his own woodcuts, and carved the reredos that is at present the chief feature of interest in the church at Borlsover Conyers. He had an exceedingly clever knack in cutting silhouettes for young ladies and paper pigs and cows for little children, and made more than one complicated wind instrument of his own devising.

When he was fifty years old Adrian Borlsover lost his sight. In a wonderfully short time he adapted himself to the new conditions of life. He quickly learnt to read Braille. So marvellous indeed was his sense of touch, that he was still able to maintain his interest in botany. The mere passing of his long supple fingers over a flower was sufficient means for its identification, though occasionally he would use his lips. I have found several letters of his among my father's correspondence; in no case was there anything to show that he was afflicted with blindness, and this in spite of the fact that he exercised undue economy in the spacing of lines. Towards the close of his life Adrian Borlsover was credited with powers of touch that seemed almost uncanny. It has been said that he could tell at once the colour of a ribbon placed between his fingers. My father would neither confirm nor deny the story.

Adrian Borlsover was a bachelor. His elder brother, Charles, had married late in life, leaving one son, Eustace, who lived in the gloomy Georgian mansion at Borlsover Conyers, where he could work undisturbed in collecting material for his great book on heredity.

Like his uncle, he was a remarkable man. The Borlsovers had always been born naturalists, but Eustace possessed in a special degree the power of systematising his knowledge. He had received his university education in Germany; and then, after post-graduate work in Vienna and Naples, had travelled for four years in South America and the East, getting together a huge store of material for a new study into the processes of variation.

He lived alone at Borlsover Conyers with Saunders, his secretary, a man who bore a somewhat dubious reputation in the district, but whose powers as a mathematician, combined with his business abilities, were invaluable to Eustace.

Uncle and nephew saw little of each other. The visits of Eustace were confined to a week in the summer or autumn – tedious weeks, that dragged almost as slowly as the bath-chair in which the old man was drawn along the sunny sea-front. In their way the two men were fond of each other, though their intimacy would, doubtless, have been greater, had they shared the same religious views. Adrian held to the old-fashioned evangelical dogmas of his early manhood; his nephew for many years had been thinking of embracing Buddhism. Both men possessed, too, the reticence the Borlsovers had always shown, and which their enemies sometimes called hypocrisy. With Adrian it was a reticence as to the things he had left undone; but with Eustace it seemed that the curtain which he was so careful to leave undrawn hid something more than a half-empty chamber.

Two years before his death Adrian Borlsover developed, unknown to himself, the not uncommon power of automatic writing. Eustace made the discovery by accident. Adrian was sitting reading in bed, the forefinger of his left hand tracing the Braille characters, when his nephew noticed that a pencil the old man held in his right hand was moving slowly along the opposite page. He left his seat in the window and sat down beside the bed. The right had continued to move, and now he could see plainly that they were letters and words which it was forming.

'Adrian Borlsover,' wrote the hand, 'Eustace Borlsover, Charles Borlsover, Francis Borlsover, Sigismund Borlsover, Adrian Borlsover, Eustace Borlsover, Saville Borlsover. B for Borlsover. Honesty is the Best Policy. Beautiful Belinda Borlsover.'

'What curious nonsense!' said Eustace to himself.

'King George ascended the throne in 1760,' wrote the hand. 'Crowd, a noun of multitude; a collection of individuals. Adrian Borlsover, Eustace Borlsover.'

'It seems to me,' said his uncle, closing the book, 'that you had much better make the most of the afternoon sunshine and take your walk now.'

'I think perhaps I will,' Eustace answered as he picked up the volume. 'I won't go far, and when I come back, I can read to you those articles in *Nature* about which we were speaking.'

He went along the promenade, but stopped at the first shelter, and, seating himself in the corner best protected from the wind, he examined the book at leisure. Nearly every page was scored with a meaningless jumble of pencil-marks; rows of capital letters, short words, long words, complete sentences, copy-book tags. The whole thing, in fact, had the appearance of a copy-book, and, on a more careful scrutiny, Eustace thought that there was ample evidence to show that the handwriting at the beginning of the book, good though it was, was not nearly so good as the handwriting at the end.

He left his uncle at the end of October with a promise to return early in December. It seemed to him quite clear that the old man's power of automatic writing was developing rapidly, and for the first time he looked forward to a visit that would combine duty with interest.

But on his return he was at first disappointed. His uncle, he thought, looked older. He was listless, too, preferring others to read to him and dictating nearly all his letters. Not until the day before he left had Eustace an opportunity of observing Adrian Borlsover's new-found faculty.

The old man, propped up in bed with pillows, had sunk into a light sleep. His two hands lay on the coverlet, his left hand tightly clasping his right. Eustace took an empty manuscript-book and placed a pencil within reach of the fingers of the right hand. They snatched at it eagerly, then dropped the pencil to loose the left hand from its restraining grasp.

'Perhaps to prevent interference I had better hold that hand,' said Eustace to himself, as he watched the pencil. Almost immediately it began to write.

'Blundering Borlsovers, unnecessarily unnatural, extraordinarily eccentric, culpably curious.'

'Who are you?' asked Eustace in a low voice.

'Never you mind,' wrote the hand of Adrian.

'Is it my uncle who is writing?'

' "O my prophetic soul, mine uncle!" '

'Is it anyone I know?'

'Silly Eustace, you'll see me very soon.'

'When shall I see you?'

'When poor old Adrian's dead.'

'Where shall I see you?'

'Where shall you not?'

Instead of speaking his next question, Eustace wrote it: 'What is the time?'

The fingers dropped the pencil and moved three or four times across the paper. Then, picking up the pencil, they wrote: 'Ten minutes before four. Put your book away, Eustace. Adrian mustn't find us working at this sort of thing. He doesn't know what to make of it, and I won't have poor old Adrian disturbed. Au revoir!'

Adrian Borlsover awoke with a start.

'I've been dreaming again,' he said; 'such queer dreams of leaguered cities and forgotten towns. You were mixed up in this one, Eustace, though I can't remember how. Eustace, I want to warn you. Don't walk in doubtful paths. Choose your friends well. Your poor grandfather . . . '

A fit of coughing put an end to what he was saying, but Eustace saw that the hand was still writing. He managed unnoticed to draw the book away. 'I'll light the gas,' he said, 'and ring for tea.' On the other side of the bed-curtain he saw the last sentences that had been written.

'It's too late, Adrian,' he read. 'We're friends already, aren't we, Eustace Borlsover?'

On the following day Eustace left. He thought his uncle looked ill when he said goodbye, and the old man spoke despondently of the failure his life had been.

'Nonsense, uncle,' said his nephew. 'You have got over your difficulties in a way not one in a hundred thousand would have done. Everyone marvels at your splendid perseverance in teaching your hand to take the place of your lost sight. To me it's been a revelation of the possibilities of education.'

'Education,' said his uncle dreamily, as if the word had started a new train of thought. 'Education is good so long as you know to whom and for what purpose you give it. But with the lower orders of men, the baser and more sordid spirits, I have grave doubts as to its results. Well, goodbye, Eustace; I may not see you again. You are a true Borlsover, with all the Borlsover faults. Marry, Eustace. Marry some good, sensible girl. And if by any chance I don't see you again, my will is at my solicitor's. I've not left you any legacy, because I know you're well provided for; but I thought you might like to have my books. Oh, and there's just one other thing. You know, before the end people often lose control over themselves and make absurd requests. Don't pay any attention to them, Eustace. Goodbye!' and he held out his hand. Eustace took it. It remained in his a fraction of a second longer than he had expected and gripped him with a virility that was surprising. There was, too, in its touch a subtle sense of intimacy.

'Why, uncle,' he said, 'I shall see you alive and well for many long years to come.'

*　　*　　*

Two months later Adrian Borlsover died.

Eustace Borlsover was in Naples at the time. He read the obituary notice in the *Morning Post* on the day announced for the funeral.

'Poor old fellow!' he said. 'I wonder whether I shall find room for all his books.'

The question occurred to him again with greater force when, three days later, he found himself standing in the library at Borlsover Conyers, a huge room built for use and not for beauty in the year of Waterloo by a Borlsover who was an ardent admirer of the great Napoleon. It was arranged on the plan of many college libraries, with tall projecting bookcases forming deep recesses of dusty silence, fit graves for the old hates of forgotten controversy, the dead passions of forgotten lives. At the end of the room, behind the bust of some unknown eighteenth-century divine, an ugly iron corkscrew stair led to a shelf-lined gallery. Nearly every shelf was full.

'I must talk to Saunders about it,' said Eustace. 'I suppose that we shall have to have the billiard-room fitted up with bookcases.'

The two men met for the first time after many weeks in the dining-room that evening.

'Hallo!' said Eustace, standing before the fire with his hands in his pockets. 'How goes the world, Saunders? Why these dress togs?' He himself was wearing an old shooting-jacket. He did not believe in mourning, as he had told his uncle on his last visit; and, though he usually went in for quiet-coloured ties, he wore this evening one of an ugly red, in order to shock Morton, the butler, and to make them thrash out the whole question of mourning for themselves in the servants' hall. Eustace was a true Borlsover. 'The world,' said Saunders, 'goes the same as usual, confoundedly slow. The dress togs are accounted for by an invitation from Captain Lockwood to bridge.'

'How are you getting there?'

'There's something the matter with the car, so I've told Jackson to drive me round in the dogcart. Any objection?'

'Oh, dear me, no! We've had all things in common for far too many years for me to raise objections at this hour of the day.'

'You'll find your correspondence in the library,' went on Saunders. 'Most of it I've seen to. There are a few private letters I haven't opened. There's also a box with a rat or something inside it that came by the evening post. Very likely it's the six-toed beast Terry was sending us to cross with the four-toed albino. I didn't look because I didn't want to mess up my things; but I should gather from the way it's jumping about that it's pretty hungry.'

'Oh, I'll see to it,' said Eustace, 'while you and the captain earn an honest penny.'

Dinner over and Saunders gone, Eustace went into the library. Though the fire had been lit, the room was by no means cheerful.

'We'll have all the lights on, at any rate,' he said, as he turned the switches. 'And, Morton,' he added, when the butler brought the coffee, 'get me a screwdriver or something to undo this box. Whatever the animal is, he's kicking up the deuce of a row. What is it? Why are you dawdling?'

'If you please, sir, when the postman brought it, he told me that they'd bored the holes in the lid at the post office. There were no breathing holes in the lid, sir, and they didn't want the animal to die. That is all, sir.'

'It's culpably careless of the man, whoever he was,' said Eustace, as he removed the screws, 'packing an animal like this in a wooden box with no means of getting air. Confound it all! I meant to ask Morton to bring me a cage to put it in. Now I suppose I shall have to get one myself.'

He placed a heavy book on the lid from which the screws had been removed, and went into the billiard-room. As he came back into the library with an empty cage in his hand, he heard the sound of something falling, and then of something scuttling along the floor.

'Bother it! The beast's got out. How in the world am I to find it again in this library?'

To search for it did indeed seem hopeless. He tried to follow the sound of the scuttling in one of the recesses, where the animal seemed to be running behind the books in the shelves; but it was impossible to locate it. Eustace resolved to go on quietly reading. Very likely the animal might gain confidence and show itself. Saunders seemed to have dealt in his usual methodical manner with most of the correspondence. There were still the private letters.

What was that? Two sharp clicks and the lights in the hideous candelabras that hung from the ceiling suddenly went out.

'I wonder if something has gone wrong with the fuse,' said Eustace, as he went to the switches by the door. Then he stopped. There was a noise at the other end of the room, as if something was crawling up the iron corkscrew stair. 'If it's gone into the gallery,' he said, 'well and good.' He hastily turned on the lights, crossed the room, and climbed up the stair. But he could see nothing. His grandfather had placed a little gate at the top of the stair, so that children could run and romp in the gallery without fear of accident. This Eustace closed, and, having considerably narrowed the circle of his search, returned to his desk by the fire.

How gloomy the library was! There was no sense of intimacy about the room. The few busts that an eighteenth-century Borlsover had brought back from the grand tour might have been in keeping in the old library. Here they seemed out of place. They made the room feel cold in spite of the heavy red damask curtain and great gilt cornices.

With a crash two heavy books fell from the gallery to the floor; then, as Borlsover looked, another, and yet another.

'Very well. You'll starve for this, my beauty!' he said. 'We'll do some little experiments on the metabolism of rats deprived of water. Go on! Chuck them down! I think I've got the upper hand.' He turned once more to his correspondence. The letter was from the family solicitor. It spoke of his uncle's death, and of the valuable collection of books that had been left to him in the will.

There was one request [he read] which certainly came as a surprise to me. As you know, Mr Adrian Borlsover had left instructions that his body was to be buried in as simple a manner as possible at Eastbourne. He expressed a desire that there should be neither wreaths nor flowers of any kind, and hoped that his friends and relatives would not consider it necessary to wear mourning. The day before his death we received a letter cancelling these instructions. He wished the body to be embalmed (he gave us the address of the man we were to employ – Pennifer, Ludgate Hill), with orders that his right hand should be sent to you, stating that it was at your special request. The other arrangements about the funeral remained unaltered.

'Good Lord,' said Eustace, 'what in the world was the old boy driving at? And what in the name of all that's holy is that?'

Someone was in the gallery. Someone had pulled the cord attached to one of the blinds, and it had rolled up with a snap. Someone must be in the gallery, for a second blind did the same. Someone must be walking round the gallery, for one after the other the blinds sprang up, letting in the moonlight.

'I haven't got to the bottom of this yet,' said Eustace, 'but I will do, before the night is very much older'; and he hurried up the corkscrew stair. He had just got to the top, when the lights went out a second time, and he heard again the scuttling along the floor. Quickly he stole on tiptoe in the dim moonshine in the direction of the noise, feeling, as he went, for one of the switches. His fingers touched the metal knob at last. He turned on the electric light.

About ten yards in front of him, crawling along the floor, was a man's hand. Eustace stared at it in utter amazement. It was moving quickly in the manner of a geometer caterpillar, the fingers humped up one moment, flattened out the next; the thumb appeared to give a crablike motion to the whole. While he was looking, too surprised to stir, the hand disappeared round the corner. Eustace ran forward. He no longer saw it, but he could hear it, as it squeezed its way behind the books on one of the shelves. A heavy volume had been displaced.

There was a gap in the row of books, where it had got in. In his fear lest it should escape him again, he seized the first book that came to his hand and plugged it into the hole. Then, emptying two shelves of their contents, he took the wooden boards and propped them up in front to make his barrier doubly sure.

'I wish Saunders was back,' he said; 'one can't tackle this sort of thing alone.' It was after eleven, and there seemed little likelihood of Saunders returning before twelve. He did not dare to leave the shelf unwatched, even to run downstairs to ring the bell. Morton, the butler, often used to come round about eleven to see that the windows were fastened, but he might not come. Eustace was thoroughly unstrung. At last he heard steps down below.

'Morton!' he shouted. 'Morton!'

'Sir?'

'Has Mr Saunders got back yet?'

'Not yet, sir.'

'Well, bring me some brandy, and hurry up about it. I'm up in the gallery, you duffer.'

'Thanks,' said Eustace, as he emptied the glass. 'Don't go to bed yet, Morton. There are a lot of books that have fallen down by accident. Bring them up and put them back in their shelves.'

Morton had never seen Borlsover in so talkative a mood as on that night. 'Here,' said Eustace, when the books had been put back and dusted, 'you might hold up these boards for me, Morton. That beast in the box got out, and I've been chasing it all over the place.'

'I think I can hear it clawing at the books, sir. They're not valuable, I hope? I think that's the carriage, sir; I'll go and call Mr Saunders.'

It seemed to Eustace that he was away for five minutes, but it could hardly have been more than one, when he returned with Saunders. 'All right, Morton, you can go now. I'm up here, Saunders.'

'What's all the row?' asked Saunders, as he lounged forward with his hands in his pockets. The luck had been with him all the evening. He was completely satisfied, both with himself and with Captain Lockwood's taste in wines. 'What's the matter? You look to me to be in an absolutely blue funk.'

'That old devil of an uncle of mine,' began Eustace – 'Oh, I can't explain it all. It's his hand that's been playing Old Harry all the evening. But I've got it cornered behind these books. You've got to help me to catch it.'

'What's up with you, Eustace? What's the game?'

'It's no game, you silly idiot! If you don't believe me, take out one of those books and put your hand in and feel.'

'All right,' said Saunders; 'but wait till I've rolled up my sleeve. The accumulated dust of centuries, eh?' He took off his coat, knelt down, and thrust his arm along the shelf.

'There's something there right enough,' he said. 'It's got a funny, stumpy end to it, whatever it is, and nips like a crab. Ah! no, you don't!' He pulled his hand out in a flash. 'Shove in a book quickly. Now it can't get out.'

'What was it?' asked Eustace.

'Something that wanted very much to get hold of me. I felt what seemed like a thumb and forefinger. Give me some brandy.'

'How are we to get it out of there?'

'What about a landing-net?'

'No good. It would be too smart for us. I tell you, Saunders, it can cover the ground far faster than I can walk. But I think I see how we can manage it. The two books at the ends of the shelf are big ones, that go right back against the wall. The others are very thin. I'll take out one at a time, and you slide the rest along, until we have it squashed between the end two.'

It certainly seemed to be the best plan. One by one as they took out the books, the space behind grew smaller and smaller. There was something in it that was certainly very much alive. Once they caught sight of fingers feeling for a way of escape. At last they had it pressed between the two big books.

'There's muscle there, if there isn't warm flesh and blood,' said Saunders, as he held them together. 'It seems to be a hand right enough, too. I suppose this is a sort of infectious hallucination. I've read about such cases before.'

'Infectious fiddlesticks!' said Eustace, his face white with anger; 'bring the thing downstairs. We'll get it back into the box.'

It was not altogether easy, but they were successful at last. 'Drive in the screws,' said Eustace; 'we won't run any risks. Put the box in this old desk of mine. There's nothing in it that I want. Here's the key. Thank goodness there's nothing wrong with the lock.'

'Quite a lively evening,' said Saunders. 'Now let's hear more about your uncle.'

They sat up together until early morning. Saunders had no desire for sleep. Eustace was trying to explain and to forget; to conceal from himself a fear that he had never felt before – the fear of walking alone down the long corridor to his bedroom.

* * *

'Whatever it was,' said Eustace to Saunders on the following morning, 'I propose that we drop the subject. There's nothing to keep us here for the next ten days. We'll motor up to the Lakes and get some climbing.'

'And see nobody all day, and sit bored to death with each other every night. Not for me, thanks. Why not run up to town? Run's the exact word in this case, isn't it? We're both in such a blessed funk. Pull yourself together, Eustace, and let's have another look at the hand.'

'As you like,' said Eustace; 'there's the key.'

They went into the library and opened the desk. The box was as they had left it on the previous night.

'What are you waiting for?' asked Eustace.

'I am waiting for you to volunteer to open the lid. However, since you seem to funk it, allow me. There doesn't seem to be the likelihood of any rumpus this morning at all events.' He opened the lid and picked out the hand.

'Cold?' asked Eustace.

'Tepid. A bit below blood heat by the feel. Soft and supple too. If it's the embalming, it's a sort of embalming I've never seen before. Is it your uncle's hand?'

'Oh yes, it's his all right,' said Eustace. 'I should know those long thin fingers anywhere. Put it back in the box, Saunders. Never mind about the screws. I'll lock the desk, so that there'll be no chance of its getting out. We'll compromise by motoring up to town for a week. If we can get off soon after lunch, we ought to be at Grantham or Stamford by night.'

'Right,' said Saunders, 'and tomorrow – oh, well, by tomorrow we shall have forgotten all about this beastly thing.'

If, when the morrow came, they had not forgotten, it was certainly true that at the end of the week they were able to tell a very vivid ghost story at the little supper Eustace gave on Hallowe'en.

'You don't want us to believe that it's true, Mr Borlsover? How perfectly awful!'

'I'll take my oath on it, and so would Saunders here; wouldn't you, old chap?'

'Any number of oaths,' said Saunders. 'It was a long thin hand, you know, and it gripped me just like that.'

'Don't, Mr Saunders! Don't! How perfectly horrid! Now tell us another one, do! Only a really creepy one, please.'

'Here's a pretty mess!' said Eustace on the following day, as he threw a letter across the table to Saunders. 'It's your affair, though. Mrs Merrit, if I understand it, gives a month's notice.'

'Oh, that's quite absurd on Mrs Merrit's part,' replied Saunders. 'She doesn't know what she's talking about. Let's see what she says.'

Dear Sir [he read], This is to let you know that I must give you a month's notice as from Tuesday, the 13th. For a long time I've felt the place too big for me; but when Jane Parfit and Emma Laidlaw go off with scarcely as much as an 'If you please', after frightening the wits out of the other girls, so that they can't turn out a room by themselves or walk alone down the stairs for fear of treading on half-frozen toads or hearing it run along the passages at night, all I can say is that it's no place for me. So I must ask you, Mr Borlsover, sir, to find a new housekeeper, that has no objection to large and lonely houses, which some people do say, not that I believe them for a minute, my poor mother always having been a Wesleyan, are haunted.

Yours faithfully,
ELIZABETH MERRIT

P.S. – I should be obliged if you would give my respects to Mr Saunders. I hope that he won't run any risks with his cold.

'Saunders,' said Eustace, 'you've always had a wonderful way with you in dealing with servants. You mustn't let poor old Merrit go.'

'Of course she shan't go,' said Saunders. 'She's probably only angling for a rise in salary. I'll write to her this morning.'

'No. There's nothing like a personal interview. We've had enough of town. We'll go back tomorrow, and you must work your cold for all its worth. Don't forget that it's got on to the chest, and will require weeks of feeding up and nursing.'

'All right; I think I can manage Mrs Merrit.'

But Mrs Merrit was more obstinate than he had thought. She was very sorry to hear of Mr Saunders's cold, and how he lay awake all night in London coughing; very sorry indeed. She'd change his room for him gladly and get the south room aired, and wouldn't he have a hot basin of bread and milk last thing at night? But she was afraid that she would have to leave at the end of the month.

'Try her with an increase of salary,' was the advice of Eustace.

It was no use. Mrs Merrit was obdurate, though she knew of a Mrs Goddard, who had been housekeeper to Lord Gargrave, who might be glad to come at the salary mentioned.

'What's the matter with the servants, Morton?' asked Eustace that evening, when he brought the coffee into the library. 'What's all this about Mrs Merrit wanting to leave?'

'If you please, sir, I was going to mention it myself. I have a confession to make, sir. When I found your note, asking me to open that desk and take out the box with the rat, I broke the lock, as you told me, and was glad to do it, because I could hear the animal in the box making a great noise, and I thought it wanted food. So I took out the box, sir, and got a cage, and was going to transfer it, when the animal got away.'

'What in the world are you talking about? I never wrote any such note.'

'Excuse me, sir; it was the note I picked up here on the floor on the day you and Mr Saunders left. I have it in my pocket now.'

It certainly seemed to be in Eustace's handwriting. It was written in pencil, and began somewhat abruptly.

'Get a hammer, Morton,' he read, 'or some other tool, and break open the lock in the old desk in the library. Take out the box that is inside. You need not do anything else. The lid is already open. Eustace Borlsover.'

'And you opened the desk?'

'Yes, sir; and as I was getting the cage ready, the animal hopped out.'

'What animal?'

'The animal inside the box, sir.'

'What did it look like?'

'Well, sir, I couldn't tell you,' said Morton, nervously. 'My back was turned, and it was half-way down the room when I looked up.'

'What was its colour?' asked Saunders. 'Black?'

'Oh no, sir; a greyish white. It crept along in a very funny way, sir. I don't think it had a tail.'

'What did you do then?'

'I tried to catch it; but it was no use. So I set the rat-traps and kept the library shut. Then that girl, Emma Laidlaw, left the door open when she was cleaning, and I think it must have escaped.'

'And you think it is the animal that's been frightening the maids?'

'Well, no, sir, not quite. They said it was – you'll excuse me, sir – a hand that they saw. Emma trod on it once at the bottom of the stairs. She thought then it was a half-frozen toad, only white. And then Parfit was washing up the dishes in the scullery. She wasn't thinking about anything in particular. It was close on dusk. She took her hands out of the water and was drying them absent-minded like on the roller towel, when she found she was drying someone else's hand as well, only colder than hers.'

'What nonsense!' exclaimed Saunders.

'Exactly, sir; that's what I told her; but we couldn't get her to stop.'

'You don't believe all this?' said Eustace, turning suddenly towards the butler.

'Me, sir? Oh no, sir! I've not seen anything.'

'Nor heard anything?'

'Well, sir, if you must know, the bells do ring at odd times, and there's nobody there when we go; and when we go round to draw the blinds of a night, as often as not somebody's been there before us. But, as I says to Mrs Merrit, a young monkey might do wonderful things, and we all know that Mr Borlsover has had some strange animals about the place.'

'Very well, Morton, that will do.'

'What do you make of it?' asked Saunders, when they were alone. 'I mean of the letter he said you wrote.'

'Oh, that's simple enough,' said Eustace. 'See the paper it's written on? I stopped using that paper years ago, but there were a few odd sheets and envelopes left in the old desk. We never fastened up the lid of the box before locking it in. The hand got out, found a pencil, wrote this note, and shoved it through the crack on to the floor, where Morton found it. That's plain as daylight.'

'But the hand couldn't write!'

'Couldn't it? You've not seen it do the things I've seen.' And he told Saunders more of what had happened at Eastbourne.

'Well,' said Saunders, 'in that case we have at least an explanation of the legacy. It was the hand which wrote, unknown to your uncle, that letter to your solicitor bequeathing itself to you. Your uncle had no more to do with that request than I. In fact, it would seem that he had some idea of this automatic writing and feared it.'

'Then if it's not my uncle, what is it?'

'I suppose some people might say that a disembodied spirit had got your uncle to educate and prepare a little body for it. Now it's got into that little body and is off on its own.'

'Well, what are we to do?'

'We'll keep our eyes open,' said Saunders, 'and try to catch it. If we can't do that, we shall have to wait till the bally clockwork runs down. After all, if it's flesh and blood, it can't live for ever.'

For two days nothing happened. Then Saunders saw it sliding down the banister in the hall. He was taken unawares and lost a full second before he started in pursuit, only to find that the thing had escaped him. Three days later Eustace, writing alone in the library at night, saw it sitting on an open book at the other end of the room. The fingers crept over the page, as if it were reading; but before he had time to get up from his seat, it had taken the alarm, and was pulling itself up the curtains. Eustace watched it grimly, as it hung on to the cornice with three fingers and flicked thumb and forefinger at him in an expression of scornful derision.

'I know what I'll do,' he said. 'If I only get it into the open, I'll set the dogs on to it.'

He spoke to Saunders of the suggestion.

'It's a jolly good idea,' he said; 'only we won't wait till we find it out of doors. We'll get the dogs. There are the two terriers and the under-keeper's Irish mongrel, that's on to rats like a flash. Your spaniel has not got spirit enough for this sort of game.'

They brought the dogs into the house, and the keeper's Irish mongrel chewed up the slippers, and the terriers tripped up Morton, as he waited at table; but all three were welcome. Even false security is better than no security at all.

For a fortnight nothing happened. Then the hand was caught, not by the dogs, but by Mrs Merrit's grey parrot. The bird was in the habit of periodically removing the pins that kept its seed- and water-tins in place, and of escaping through the holes in the side of the cage. When once at liberty, Peter would show no inclination to return, and would often be about the house for days. Now, after six consecutive weeks of captivity, Peter had again discovered a new way of unloosing his bolts and was at large, exploring the tapestried forests of the curtains and singing songs in praise of liberty from cornice and picture-rail.

'It's no use your trying to catch him,' said Eustace to Mrs Merrit, as she came into the study one afternoon towards dusk with a step-ladder. 'You'd much better leave Peter alone. Starve him into surrender, Mrs Merrit; and don't leave bananas and seed about for him to peck at when he fancies he's hungry. You're far too soft-hearted.'

'Well, sir, I see he's right out of reach now on that picture-rail; so, if you wouldn't mind closing the door, sir, when you leave the room, I'll bring his cage in tonight and put some meat inside it. He's that fond of meat, though it does make him pull out his feathers to suck the quills. They do say that if you cook – '

'Never mind, Mrs Merrit,' said Eustace, who was busy writing; 'that will do; I'll keep an eye on the bird.'

For a short time there was silence in the room.

'Scratch poor Peter,' said the bird. 'Scratch poor old Peter!'

'Be quiet, you beastly bird!'

'Poor old Peter! Scratch poor Peter; do!'

'I'm more likely to wring your neck, if I get hold of you.' He looked up at the picture-rail, and there was the hand, holding on to a hook with three fingers, and slowly scratching the head of the parrot with the fourth. Eustace ran to the bell and pressed it hard; then across to the window, which he closed with a bang. Frightened by the noise, the parrot shook its wings preparatory to flight, and, as it did so, the fingers of the hand got hold of it by the throat. There was a shrill scream from Peter, as he fluttered across the room, wheeling round in circles that ever descended, borne down under the weight that clung to him. The bird dropped at last quite suddenly, and Eustace saw fingers and feathers rolled into an inextricable mass on the floor. The struggle abruptly ceased, as finger and thumb squeezed the neck; the bird's eyes rolled up to show the whites, and there was a faint, half-choked gurgle. But, before the fingers had time to loose their hold, Eustace had them in his own.

'Send Mr Saunders here at once,' he said to the maid who came in answer to the bell. 'Tell him I want him immediately.'

Then he went with the hand to the fire. There was a ragged gash across the back, where the bird's beak had torn it, but no blood oozed from the wound. He noted with disgust that the nails had grown long and discoloured.

'I'll burn the beastly thing,' he said. But he could not burn it. He tried to throw it into the flames, but his own hands, as if impelled by some old primitive feeling, would not let him. And so Saunders found him, pale and irresolute, with the hand still clasped tightly in his fingers.

'I've got it at last,' he said, in a tone of triumph.

'Good, let's have a look at it.'

'Not when it's loose. Get me some nails and a hammer and a board of some sort.'

'Can you hold it all right?'

'Yes, the thing's quite limp; tired out with throttling poor old Peter, I should say.'

'And now,' said Saunders, when he returned with the things, 'what are we going to do?'

'Drive a nail through it first, so that it can't get away. Then we can take our time over examining it.'

'Do it yourself,' said Saunders. 'I don't mind helping you with guinea-pigs occasionally, when there's something to be learned, partly because I don't fear a guinea-pig's revenge. This thing's different.

'Oh, my aunt!' he giggled hysterically, 'look at it now.' For the hand was writhing in agonised contortions, squirming and wriggling upon the nail like a worm upon the hook.

'Well,' said Saunders, 'you've done it now. I'll leave you to examine it.'

'Don't go, in heaven's name! Cover it up, man; cover it up! Shove a cloth over it! Here!' and he pulled off the antimacassar from the back of a chair and wrapped the board in it. 'Now get the keys from my pocket and open the safe. Chuck the other things out. Oh, Lord, it's getting itself into frightful knots! Open it quick!' He threw the thing in and banged the door.

'We'll keep it there till it dies,' he said. 'May I burn in hell, if I ever open the door of that safe again.'

* * *

Mrs Merrit departed at the end of the month. Her successor, Mrs Handyside, certainly was more successful in the management of the servants. Early in her rule she declared that she would stand no nonsense, and gossip soon withered and died.

'I shouldn't be surprised if Eustace married one of these days,' said Saunders. 'Well, I'm in no hurry for such an event. I know him far too well for the future Mrs Borlsover to like me. It will be the same old story again; a long friendship slowly made – marriage – and a long friendship quickly forgotten.'

But Eustace did not follow the advice of his uncle and marry. Old habits crept over and covered his new experience. He was, if anything, less morose, and showed a greater inclination to take his natural part in country society.

Then came the burglary. The men, it was said, broke into the house by way of the conservatory. It was really little more than an attempt, for they only succeeded in carrying away a few pieces of plate from the pantry. The safe in the study was certainly found open and empty, but, as Mr Borlsover informed the police inspector, he had kept nothing of value in it during the last six months.

'Then you're lucky in getting off so easily, sir,' the man replied. 'By the way they have gone about their business I should say they were experienced cracksmen. They must have caught the alarm when they were just beginning their evening's work.'

'Yes,' said Eustace, 'I suppose I am lucky.'

'I've no doubt,' said the inspector, 'that we shall be able to trace the men. I've said that they must have been old hands at the game. The way they got in and opened the safe shows that. But there's one little thing that puzzles me. One of them was careless enough not to wear gloves, and I'm bothered if I know what he was trying to do. I've traced his finger-marks on the new varnish on the window-sashes in every one of the downstairs rooms. They are very distinctive ones too.'

'Right hand or left or both?' asked Eustace.

'Oh, right every time. That's the funny thing. He must have been a foolhardy fellow, and I rather think it was him that wrote that.' He took out a slip of paper from his pocket. 'That's what he wrote, sir: "I've got out, Eustace Borlsover, but I'll be back before long." Some jailbird just escaped, I suppose. It will make it all the easier for us to trace him. Do you know the writing, sir?'

'No,' said Eustace. 'It's not the writing of anyone I know.'

'I'm not going to stay here any longer,' said Eustace to Saunders at luncheon. 'I've got on far better during the last six months than I expected, but I'm not going to run the risk of seeing that thing again. I shall go up to town this afternoon. Get Morton to put my things together, and join me with the car at Brighton on the day after tomorrow. And bring the proofs of those two papers with you. We'll run over them together.'

'How long are you going to be away?'

'I can't say for certain, but be prepared to stay for some time. We've stuck to work pretty closely through the summer, and I for one need a holiday. I'll engage the rooms at Brighton. You'll find it best to break the journey at Hitchin. I'll wire to you there at the Crown to tell you the Brighton address.'

The house he chose at Brighton was in a terrace. He had been there before. It was kept by his old college gyp, a man of discreet silence, who was admirably partnered by an excellent cook. The rooms were on the first floor. The two bedrooms were at the back, and opened out of each other. 'Mr Saunders can have the smaller one, though it is the only one with a fireplace,' he said. 'I'll stick to the larger of the two, since it's got a bathroom adjoining. I wonder what time he'll arrive with the car.'

Saunders came about seven, cold and cross and dirty. 'We'll light the fire in the dining-room,' said Eustace, 'and get Prince to unpack some of the things while we are at dinner. What were the roads like?'

'Rotten. Swimming with mud, and a beastly cold wind against us all day. And this is July. Dear Old England!'

'Yes,' said Eustace, 'I think we might do worse than leave Old England for a few months.'

They turned in soon after twelve.

'You oughtn't to feel cold, Saunders,' said Eustace, 'when you can afford to sport a great fur-lined coat like this. You do yourself very well, all things considered. Look at those gloves, for instance. Who could possibly feel cold when wearing them?'

'They are far too clumsy, though, for driving. Try them on and see'; and he tossed them through the door on to Eustace's bed and went on with his unpacking. A minute later he heard a shrill cry of terror. 'Oh, Lord,' he heard, 'it's in the glove! Quick, Saunders, quick!' Then came a smacking thud. Eustace had thrown it from him. 'I've chucked it into the bath-room,' he gasped; 'it's hit the wall and fallen into the bath. Come now, if you want to help.' Saunders, with a lighted candle in his hand, looked over the edge of the bath. There it was, old and maimed, dumb and blind, with a ragged hole in the middle, crawling, staggering, trying to creep up the slippery sides, only to fall back helpless.

'Stay there,' said Saunders, 'I'll empty a collar-box or something, and we'll jam it in. It can't get out while I'm away.'

'Yes, it can,' shouted Eustace. 'It's getting out now; it's climbing up the plug-chain. – No, you brute, you filthy brute, you don't! – Come back, Saunders; it's getting away from me. I can't hold it; it's all slippery. Curse its claws! Shut the window, you idiot! It's got out!' There was the sound of something dropping on to the hard flag-stones below, and Eustace fell back fainting.

*   *   *

For a fortnight he was ill.

'I don't know what to make of it,' the doctor said to Saunders. 'I can only suppose that Mr Borlsover has suffered some great emotional shock. You had better let me send someone to help you nurse him. And by all means indulge that whim of his never to be left alone in the dark. I would keep a light burning all night, if I were you. But he must have more fresh air. It's perfectly absurd, this hatred of open windows.'

Eustace would have no one with him but Saunders. 'I don't want the other man,' he said. 'They'd smuggle it in somehow. I know they would.'

'Don't worry about it, old chap. This sort of thing can't go on indefinitely. You know I saw it this time as well as you. It wasn't half so active. It won't go on living much longer, especially after that fall. I heard it hit the flags myself. As soon as you're a bit stronger, we'll leave this place, not bag and baggage, but with only the clothes on our backs, so that it won't be able to hide anywhere. We'll escape it that way. We won't give any address, and we won't have any parcels sent after us. Cheer up, Eustace! You'll be well enough to leave in a day or two. The doctor says I can take you out in a chair tomorrow.'

'What have I done?' asked Eustace. 'Why does it come after me? I'm no worse than other men. I'm no worse than you, Saunders; you know I'm not. It was you who was at the bottom of that dirty business in San Diego, and that was fifteen years ago.'

'It's not that, of course,' said Saunders. 'We are in the twentieth century, and even the parsons have dropped the idea of your old sins finding you out. Before you caught the hand in the library, it was filled with pure malevolence – to you and all mankind. After you spiked it through with that nail, it naturally forgot about other people and concentrated its attention on you. It was shut up in that safe, you know, for nearly six months. That gives plenty of time for thinking of revenge.'

Eustace Borlsover would not leave his room, but he thought there might be something in Saunders's suggestion of a sudden departure from Brighton. He began rapidly to regain his strength.

'We'll go on the 1st of September,' he said.

*   *   *

The evening of the 31st of August was oppressively warm. Though at midday the windows had been wide open, they had been shut an hour or so before dusk. Mrs Prince had long since ceased to wonder at the strange habits of the gentlemen on the first floor. Soon after their arrival she had been told to take down the heavy window curtains in the two bedrooms, and day by day the rooms had seemed to grow more bare. Nothing was left lying about.

'Mr Borlsover doesn't like to have any place where dirt can collect,' Saunders had said as an excuse. 'He likes to see into all the corners of the room.'

'Couldn't I open the window just a little?' he said to Eustace that evening. 'We're simply roasting in here, you know.'

'No, leave well alone. We're not a couple of boarding-school misses fresh from a course of hygiene lectures. Get the chessboard out.'

They sat down and played. At ten o'clock Mrs Prince came to the door with a note. 'I am sorry I didn't bring it before,' she said, 'but it was left in the letter-box.'

'Open it, Saunders, and see if it wants answering.'

It was very brief. There was neither address nor signature.

'Will eleven o'clock tonight be suitable for our last appointment?'

'Who is it from?' asked Borlsover.

'It was meant for me,' said Saunders. 'There's no answer, Mrs Prince,' and he put the paper into his pocket.

'A dunning letter from a tailor; I suppose he must have got wind of our leaving.'

It was a clever lie, and Eustace asked no more questions. They went on with their game.

On the landing outside Saunders could hear the grandfather's clock whispering the seconds, blurting out the quarter-hours.

'Check,' said Eustace. The clock struck eleven. At the same time there was a gentle knocking on the door; it seemed to come from the bottom panel.

'Who's there?' asked Eustace.

There was no answer.

'Mrs Prince, is that you?'

'She is up above,' said Saunders; 'I can hear her walking about the room.'

'Then lock the door; bolt it too. Your move, Saunders.'

While Saunders sat with his eyes on the chessboard, Eustace walked over to the window and examined the fastenings. He did the same in Saunders's room, and the bath-room. There were no doors between the three rooms, or he would have shut and locked them too.

'Now, Saunders,' he said, 'don't stay all night over your move. I've had time to smoke one cigarette already. It's bad to keep an invalid waiting. There's only one possible thing for you to do. What was that?'

'The ivy blowing against the window. There, it's your move now, Eustace.'

'It wasn't the ivy, you idiot! It was someone tapping at the window'; and he pulled up the blind. On the outer side of the window, clinging to the sash, was the hand.

'What is it that it's holding?'

'It's a pocket-knife. It's going to try to open the window by pushing back the fastener with the blade.'

'Well, let it try,' said Eustace. 'Those fasteners screw down; they can't be opened that way. Anyhow, we'll close the shutters. It's your move, Saunders. I've played.'

But Saunders found it impossible to fix his attention on the game. He could not understand Eustace, who seemed all at once to have lost his fear. 'What do you say to some wine?' he asked. 'You seem to be taking things coolly, but I don't mind confessing that I'm in a blessed funk.'

'You've no need to be. There's nothing supernatural about that hand, Saunders. I mean, it seems to be governed by the laws of time and space. It's not the sort of thing that vanishes into thin air or slides through oaken doors. And since that's so, I defy it to get in here. We'll leave the place in the morning. I for one have bottomed the depths of fear. Fill your glass, man! The windows are all shuttered; the door is locked and bolted. Pledge me my Uncle Adrian! Drink, man! What are you waiting for?'

Saunders was standing with his glass half raised. 'It can get in,' he said hoarsely; 'it can get in! We've forgotten. There's the fireplace in my bedroom. It will come down the chimney.'

'Quick!' said Eustace, as he rushed into the other room; 'we haven't a minute to lose. What can we do? Light the fire, Saunders. Give me a match, quick!'

'They must be all in the other room. I'll get them.'

'Hurry, man, for goodness' sake! Look in the bookcase! Look in the bath-room! Here, come and stand here; I'll look.'

'Be quick!' shouted Saunders. 'I can hear something!'

'Then plug a sheet from your bed up the chimney. No, here's a match!' He had found one at last, that had slipped into a crack in the floor.

'Is the fire laid? Good, but it may not burn. I know – the oil from that old reading-lamp and this cotton wool. Now the match, quick! Pull the sheet away, you fool! We don't want it now.'

There was a great roar from the grate, as the flames shot up. Saunders had been a fraction of a second too late with the sheet. The oil had fallen on to it. It, too, was burning.

'The whole place will be on fire!' cried Eustace, as he tried to beat out the flames with a blanket. 'It's no good! I can't manage it. You must open the door, Saunders, and get help.'

Saunders ran to the door and fumbled with the bolts. The key was stiff in the lock. 'Hurry,' shouted Eustace, 'or the heat will be too much for me.' The key turned in the lock at last. For half a second

Saunders stopped to look back. Afterwards he could never be quite sure as to what he had seen, but at the time he thought that something black and charred was creeping slowly, very slowly, from the mass of flames towards Eustace Borlsover. For a moment he thought of returning to his friend; but the noise and the smell of the burning sent him running down the passage, crying: 'Fire! Fire!' He rushed to the telephone to summon help, and then back to the bathroom – he should have thought of that before – for water. As he burst into the bedroom there came a scream of terror which ended suddenly, and then the sound of a heavy fall.

* * *

This is the story which I heard on successive Saturday evenings from the senior mathematical master at a second-rate suburban school. For Saunders has had to earn a living in a way which other men might reckon less congenial than his old manner of life. I had mentioned by chance the name of Adrian Borlsover, and wondered at the time why he changed the conversation with such unusual abruptness. A week later Saunders began to tell me something of his own history; sordid enough, though shielded with a reserve I could well understand, for it had to cover not only his failings, but those of a dead friend. Of the final tragedy he was at first especially loath to speak; and it was only gradually that I was able to piece together the narrative of the preceding pages. Saunders was reluctant to draw any conclusions. At one time he thought that the fingered beast had been animated by the spirit of Sigismund Borlsover, a sinister eighteenth-century ancestor, who, according to legend, built and worshipped in the ugly pagan temple that overlooked the lake. At another time Saunders believed the spirit to belong to a man whom Eustace had once employed as a laboratory assistant, 'a black-haired, spiteful little brute,' he said, 'who died cursing his doctor, because the fellow couldn't help him to live to settle some paltry score with Borlsover.'

From the point of view of direct contemporary evidence, Saunders's story is practically uncorroborated. All the letters mentioned in the narrative were destroyed, with the exception of the last note which Eustace received, or rather which he would have received, had not Saunders intercepted it. That I have seen myself. The handwriting was thin and shaky, the handwriting of an old man. I remember the Greek 'e' was used in 'appointment'. A little thing that amused me at the time was that Saunders seemed to keep the note pressed between the pages of his Bible.

I had seen Adrian Borlsover once. Saunders I learnt to know well. It was by chance, however, and not by design, that I met a third person of the story, Morton, the butler. Saunders and I were walking in the Zoological Gardens one Sunday afternoon, when he called my attention to an old man who was standing before the door of the Reptile House.

'Why, Morton,' he said, clapping him on the back, 'how is the world treating you?'

'Poorly, Mr Saunders,' said the old fellow, though his face lighted up at the greeting. 'The winters drag terribly nowadays. There don't seem no summers or springs.'

'You haven't found what you were looking for, I suppose?'

'No, sir, not yet; but I shall some day. I always told them that Mr Borlsover kept some queer animals.'

'And what is he looking for?' I asked, when we had parted from him.

'A beast with five fingers,' said Saunders. 'This afternoon, since he has been in the Reptile House, I suppose it will be a reptile with a hand. Next week it will be a monkey with practically no body. The poor old chap is a born materialist.'

Midnight House

I had often seen the name on the ordnance map, and had as often wondered what sort of a house it was.

If I had had the placing, it should have been among pine woods in some deep, waterless valley, or else in the Fens by a sluggish tidal river, with aspens whispering in a garden half choked by poisonous evergreens.

I might have placed it in a cathedral city, in a sunless alley overlooking the narrow strip of graveyard of a church no longer used; a house so surrounded by steeple and belfry that every sleeper in it would wake at midnight, aroused by the clamorous insistence of the chimes.

But the Midnight House of cold reality, that I had found by chance on the map when planning a walking tour that never came into being, was none of these. I saw no more than an inn on an old coaching road that crossed the moors as straight as an arrow, keeping to the hill-tops, so that I guessed it to be Roman.

Men have a certain way of living in accordance with their name that one often looks for in vain with places. The Pogsons will never produce a poet, whatever may be the fame they may achieve as lawyers, journalists, or sanitary engineers; but Monckton-in-the-Forest, through which I passed last week, is a railway junction and nothing more, in the middle of a bare plain; not a stone remains of the once famous priory that gave to the place its name.

I expected then to be disappointed, but for some reason or other I made a resolve, if ever chance should leave me within twenty miles of the inn, to spend a night in Midnight House.

I could not have chosen a better day. It was late in November and warm – too warm I had found for the last five-mile tramp across the heather. I had seen no one since noon, when a keeper on the distant skyline had tried in vain to make me understand that I was trespassing; and now at dusk I stood again on the high road with Midnight House below me in the hollow.

It would be hard to picture a more desolate scene – bare hills rising on every side to the dull, lead sky above; at one's feet heather, burnt black after last spring's firing, broken in places by patches of vivid emerald that marked the bogs.

The building of stone, roofed with heavy, lichen-covered flags, formed three sides of a square, the centre of which was evidently used as a farmyard.

Nowhere was there sign of life; half the windows were shuttered, and, though the dim light of afternoon was fast waning, I saw no lamp in the tap-room, by the door which overlooked the road.

I knocked, but no one answered; and, growing impatient at the delay, walked round to the back of the house, only to be greeted by the savage barking of a collie, that tugged frantically at the chain which fastened it to the empty barrel that served it as kennel. The noise was at any rate sufficient to bring out the woman of the house, who listened stolidly to my request for a night's lodging, and then to my surprise refused me.

They were busy, she said, and had no time to look after visitors. I was not prepared for this. I knew that there were beds at the inn; it was used at least once a year by the men who rented the shooting, and I had not the slightest inclination for another ten-mile tramp along roads I did not know. A drop of rain on my cheek clenched the matter; grudgingly the woman saw reason in my arguments and finally consented to take me in. She showed me into the dining-room, lit the fire, and left me with the welcome news that the ham and eggs would be ready in half an hour's time.

The room in which I found myself was of some size, panelled half-way up to the ceiling, though the natural beauty of the wood had been recently spoiled by a coat of drab-coloured paint.

The windows were, as usual, firmly shut; and from the musty smell I gathered that it was little used. Half a dozen sporting prints hung on the walls; over the mantelpiece was a cheap German engraving representing the death of Isaac; on the sideboard were two glass cases, containing a heron and two pied blackbirds, both atrociously stuffed; while above that piece of hideous Victorian furniture, two highly coloured portraits of the Duke and Duchess of York gazed smilingly upon the patriarch.

Altogether the room was not a cheerful one, and I was relieved to find a copy of *East Lynne* lying on the horsehair sofa. Most inns contain the book; the fourteen chapters which I have read represent as many evenings spent alone in wayside hostelries.

Just before six the woman came in to lay the table. From my chair in the shadow by the fireside I watched her unobserved. She moved slowly; the simplest action was performed with a strange deliberation, as if her mind, half bent upon something else, found novelty in what before was commonplace. The expression of her face gave no clue to her thoughts. I saw only that her features were strong and hard.

As soon as the meal was upon the table she left the room, without having exchanged a word; and feeling unusually lonely, I sat down to make the best of the ham and eggs and the fifteenth chapter of *East Lynne*.

The food was good enough, better than I had expected; but for some reason or other my spirits were no lighter when, the table having been cleared, I drew up my chair to the fire and filled my pipe.

'If this house is not already haunted,' I said to myself, 'it is certainly time it were so,' and I began to pass in review a whole procession of ghosts without finding one that seemed really suited to the place.

At half-past nine, and the hour was none too soon, the woman reappeared with a candle, and intimated gruffly that she would show me my room. She stopped opposite a door at the end of a corridor to the left of the stair head. 'You had better wedge the windows, if you want to sleep with them open; people complain a deal about their rattling.' I thanked her and bade her good night.

I was spared at least the horror of a four-poster, though the crimson-canopied erection, which occupied at least a quarter of the room, seemed at first sight to be little better. There was no wardrobe, but in its place a door, papered over with the same material as the walls and, at first sight, indistinguishable from them, opened into a closet, empty save for a row of hooks and lighted by a single window.

I noticed that neither of the doors had keys, and that a red velvet bell-pull by the bed was no longer fastened to its wire, but hung useless from a nail driven into one of the beams of the ceiling.

I am in the habit of securely bolting my door whenever I spend a night away from home, a piece of common prudence which nothing less than an awful fright from a sleep-walker taught me twenty years ago.

To do so was on this occasion impossible, but I dragged a heavy chest across the door which led into the passage, placing the water-jug against the inner one, in case the wind should blow it open in the night: then, after wedging the window with my pocket-knife, I got into bed, but not to sleep. Twice I heard the clock outside strike the hour, twice the half-hour, yet, late as it was, the house seemed still awake. Distant footsteps echoed down the stone passages; once I caught the crash of broken crockery – never the sound of a voice. At length I fell asleep, with the same feeling of unaccountable depression that had dogged me since sundown still upon me.

I had in truth walked far too far that day to receive the inestimable boon of the weary, a dim consciousness of annihilation. Instead I tramped again over dream moors with a Baedeker in my hand, trying in vain to find the valley of the shadow.

I came at last to a mountain tarn, filled with brown peat water; on the marge a huge ferry-boat was drawn up, on which crowds of men, women, and children were embarking. The boat at last was full and we were putting off, the heavy sails filling before a wind which never ruffled the surface of the water, when someone cried that there was still another to come, pointing as he spoke to an old man who stood on the shore madly gesticulating. An argument followed, some in the boat saying that it was too late to put back, others that the man would perish with cold if we left him there on the shelterless moor. But we were too eager to see the valley of the shadow, and the steersman held on his course. As we left him, a sudden change came across the old man's features; the mask of benevolence vanished; we saw only a face of such utter malignancy that the children in fright ran whimpering to their mothers.

In the boat they whispered his name, how that he was a man for ever seeking to gain entrance to the ferry, that he might accomplish some awful purpose, and in joy at our escape a strange song was raised, which rose and fell like the music of a running stream.

I was awakened by the sound of rain upon the window; the water in the brook outside had already risen and was making itself heard, but with a sound so soothingly monotonous that I was soon asleep again.

Again I dreamed. This time I was a citizen of a great leaguered city. The once fertile plain that stretched from the walls to the dim horizon lay ravaged by the armies that had swept over it. The sun was sinking as a crowd of half-starved wretches came to the western gate, clamouring to come in. They were the peasants, caught between the besieging hosts and the frowning barriers of the city that had no food for mouths other than its own. As I stood at the postern to the right of the main gate with a little knot of companions, a man approached who at once attracted our attention. He was a huge fellow, in the prime of life, straight as a tree, and strong enough to carry an ox. He came up to our leader and asked to be let in. 'I have travelled day and night for twelve months,' he said, 'that I might fight by your side.' The last sally had cost us dear and we were short of men such as he. 'Come in and welcome,' said the captain of the guard at last. He had already taken a key from his breast and was unlocking the postern, when I cried out. Something in the man's face I had recognised; it was that of the old man who had tried to get into the ferry. 'He's a spy!' I shouted. 'Lock the gates, for God's sake! Shut the window, or he'll climb in!'

I jumped out of bed with my own words ringing in my ears. Some window at any rate required shutting; it was the one in the cupboard opening out of my room. Wind had come with the rain and the sash had been loosened. The air was no longer close and the clouds were lifting, scudding over the moon. I craned out my neck, drinking in the cool night air. As I did so, I noticed an oblong patch of light on the roadway; it came from an upper window at the opposite end of the building; now and then the patch was crossed by a shadow. The people of the inn kept strangely late hours.

I did not at once go back to bed, but, stiff and sore, drew up a chair to the window with pillows and a couple of blankets, and there I sat for fully half an hour, listening to the howling of the dog, a wail of utter weariness far too dismal for the moon alone to have awakened. Then it suddenly turned into an angry growl, and I caught the sound of distant hoofs upon the road. At the same time the shadow reappeared upon the blind, the window was pulled up, and the hard, sour face of my landlady peered out into the darkness.

Evidently she was expecting someone. A minute later a horse, that had been hard ridden, drew up steaming before the door; its rider dismounted.

'Leave the beast to me,' said the woman from the window, in a voice hardly raised above a whisper. 'I'll see that it's made all right in the stable. Come straight upstairs; it's the third room on the right.'

The man took up what seemed to be a heavy bag and, leaving his horse, passed on up the stair. I heard him stumble at the step on the landing and swear beneath his breath. Just then the clock struck three. I began to wonder if any mischief were brewing in Midnight House.

I have only the vaguest recollection of what happened between then and dawn. My attempts to obtain sleep were not as great as the struggles I made to free myself from the awful nightmares that took possession of me as soon as I began to lose consciousness. All I knew was that there was a spirit of evil abroad, an ugly, horrible spirit, that was trying to enter the house; and that everyone seemed to be blind to its true nature, seemed to be helping it to gain its end. That was the lurid background of my dreams. One thing alone I remember clearly, a long-drawn-out cry, real and no wild fantasy, that came out of the night to die away into nothingness.

When I got up in the morning soon after nine, I had a splitting headache that made me resolve to be less ready in future to sample strange beds and stranger inns.

I entered the dining-room to find myself no longer alone. A tall, middle-aged man, with a look about him as if he had passed anything but a restful night, was seated at the table. He had just finished breakfast, and rose to go as I took my place. He wished me a curt good morning and left the room. I hurried over my meal, paid my bill to the same impassive-faced woman, the only occupant of the house I had seen, and shouldering my rucksack, set out along the road. I walked on for two miles, until I had nearly reached the summit of a steep incline, and was hesitating over which of three roads to take, when, turning round, I saw the stranger approaching.

As soon as his horse had overtaken me I asked him the way.

'By the by,' I said, 'can you tell me anything about that inn? It's the gloomiest house I ever slept in. Is it haunted?'

'Not that I know of. How can a house be haunted when there are no such things as ghosts?'

Something in the ill-concealed superiority of the tone in which he replied made me look at him more closely. He seemed to read my thoughts. 'Yes, I'm the doctor,' he said, 'and precious little I get out of the business, I can tell you. You are not looking out for a quiet country practice yourself, I suppose? I don't think a night's work like this last's would tempt you.'

'I don't know what it was,' I said, 'but, if I was to hazard a guess, I should say some singularly wicked man must have died in the inn last night.'

He laughed out loud. 'You're rather wide of the mark, for the fact is I have been helping to usher into the world another pretty innocent. As things turned out, the child did not live above half an hour, not altogether to the mother's sorrow, I should judge. People talk pretty freely in the country. There's nothing else to do; and we all know each other's affairs. It might have come into the world in better circumstances, certainly; but after all is said and done, we shan't have much to complain of if we can keep the birth-rate from falling any lower. What was it last year? Some appallingly low figure, but I can't remember the actual one. Yes, I've always been interested in statistics. They can explain nearly everything.'

I was not quite so sure.

The Dabblers

It was a wet July evening. The three friends sat around the peat fire in Harborough's den, pleasantly weary after their long tramp across the moors. Scott, the ironmaster, had been declaiming against modern education. His partner's son had recently entered the business with everything to learn, and the business couldn't afford to teach him. 'I suppose,' he said, 'that from preparatory school to university, Wilkins must have spent the best part of three thousand pounds on filling a suit of plus-fours with brawn. It's too much. My boy is going to Steelborough grammar school. Then when he's sixteen I shall send him to Germany so that he can learn from our competitors. Then he'll put in a year in the office; afterwards, if he shows any ability, he can go up to Oxford. Of course he'll be rusty and out of his stride, but he can mug up his Latin in the evenings as my shop stewards do with their industrial history and economics.'

'Things aren't as bad as you make out,' said Freeman, the architect. 'The trouble I find with schools is in choosing the right one where so many are excellent. I've entered my boy for one of those old country grammar schools that have been completely remodelled. Wells showed in *The Undying Fire* what an enlightened headmaster can do when he is given a free hand and isn't buried alive in mortar and tradition.'

'You'll probably find,' said Scott, 'that it's mostly eyewash; no discipline, and a lot of talk about self-expression and education for service.'

'There you're wrong. I should say the discipline is too severe if anything. I heard only the other day from my young nephew that two boys had been expelled for a raid on a hen-roost or some such escapade; but I suppose there was more to it than met the eye. What are you smiling about, Harborough?'

'It was something you said about headmasters and tradition. I was thinking about tradition and boys. Rum, secretive little beggars. It seems to me quite possible that there is a wealth of hidden lore passed on from one generation of schoolboys to another that it might be well worth while for a psychologist or an anthropologist to investigate. I remember at my first school writing some lines of doggerel in my books. They were really an imprecation against anyone who should steal them. I've seen practically the same words in old monkish manuscripts; they go back to the time when books were of value. But it was on the fly-leaves of Abbott's *Via Latina* and Lock's *Arithmetic* that I wrote them. Nobody would want to steal those books. Why should boys start to spin tops at a certain season of the year? The date is not fixed by shopkeepers, parents are not consulted, and though saints have been flogged to death I have found no connection between top whipping and the church calendar. The matter is decided for them by an unbroken tradition, handed down, not from father to son, but from boy to boy. Nursery rhymes are not perhaps a case in point, though they are stuffed with odd bits of folklore. I remember being taught a game that was played with knotted handkerchiefs manipulated by the fingers to the accompaniment of a rhyme which began: 'Father Confessor, I've come to confess.' My instructor, aged eight, was the son of a High Church vicar. I don't know what would have happened if old Tomlinson had heard the last verse.

> 'Father Confessor, what shall I do?'
> 'Go to Rome and kiss the Pope's toe.'
> 'Father Confessor, I'd rather kiss you.'
>   'Well, child, do.'

'What was the origin of that little piece of doggerel?' asked Freeman. 'It's new to me.'

'I don't know,' Harborough replied. 'I've never seen it in print. But behind the noddings of the knotted handkerchiefs and our childish giggles lurked something sinister. I seem to see the cloaked figure, cat-like and gliding, of one of those emissaries of the Church of Rome that creep into the pages of George Borrow – hatred and fear masked in ribaldry. I could give you other examples, the holly and ivy carols, for instance, which used to be sung by boys and girls to the accompaniment of a dance, and which, according to some people, embody a crude form of nature worship.'

'And the point of all this is what?' asked Freeman.

'That there is a body of tradition, ignored by the ordinary adult, handed down by one generation of children to another. If you want a really good example – a really bad example I should say, I'll tell you the story of the Dabblers.' He waited until Freeman and Scott had filled their pipes and then began.

'When I came down from Oxford and before I was called to the Bar, I put in three miserable years at school teaching.'

Scott laughed.

'I don't envy the poor kids you cross-examined,' he said.

'As a matter of fact, I was more afraid of them than they of me. I got a job as usher at one of Freeman's old grammar schools, only it had not been remodelled and the headmaster was a completely incompetent cleric. It was in the eastern counties. The town was dead-alive. The only thing that seemed to warm the hearts of the people there was a dull smouldering fire of gossip, and they all took turns in fanning the flame. But I mustn't get away from the school. The buildings were old; the chapel had once been the choir of a monastic church. There was a fine tithe barn, and a few old stones and bases of pillars in the headmaster's garden, but nothing more to show where monks had lived for centuries except a dried-up fish pond.

'Late in June at the end of my first year, I was crossing the playground at night on my way to my lodgings in the High Street. It was after twelve. There wasn't a breath of air, and the playing fields were covered with a thick mist from the river. There was something rather weird about the whole scene; it was all so still and silent. The night smelt stuffy; and then suddenly I heard the sound of singing. I don't know where the voices came from nor how many voices there were, and not being musical I can't give you any idea of the tune. It was very ragged with gaps in it, and there was something about it which I can only describe as disturbing. Anyhow I had no desire to investigate. I stood still for two or three minutes listening and then let myself out by the lodge gate into the deserted High Street. My bedroom above the tobacconist's looked out on to a lane that led down to the river. Through the open window I could still hear, very faintly, the singing. Then a dog began to howl, and when after a quarter of an hour it stopped: the June night was again still. Next morning in the masters' common room I asked if anyone could account for the singing.

' "It's the Dabblers," said old Moneypenny, the science master, "they usually appear about now."

'Of course I asked who the Dabblers were.

' "The Dabblers," said Moneypenny, "are carol singers born out of their due time. They are certain lads of the village who, for reasons of their own, desire to remain anonymous; probably choirboys with a grievance, who wish to pose as ghosts. And for goodness' sake let sleeping dogs lie. We've thrashed out the Dabbler controversy so often that I'm heartily sick of it."

'He was a cross-grained customer and I took him at his word. But later on in the week I got hold of one of the junior masters and asked him what it all meant. It seemed an established fact that the singing did occur at this particular time of the year. It was a sore point with Moneypenny, because on one occasion when somebody had suggested that it might be boys from the schoolhouse skylarking he had completely lost his temper.

' "All the same," said Atkinson, "it might just as well be our boys as any others. If you are game next year we'll try to get to the bottom of it."

'I agreed and there the matter stood. As a matter of fact when the anniversary came round I had forgotten all about the thing. I had been taking the lower school in prep. The boys had been unusually restless – we were less than a month from the end of term – and it was with a sigh of relief that I turned into Atkinson's study soon after eight to borrow an umbrella, for it was raining hard.

' "By the by," he said, "tonight's the night the Dabblers are due to appear. What about it?"

'I told him that if he imagined that I was going to spend the hours between then and midnight in patrolling the school precincts in the rain, he was greatly mistaken.

' "That's not my idea at all," he said. "We won't set foot out of doors. I'll light the fire; I can manage a mixed grill of sorts on the gas ring and there are a couple of bottles of beer in the cupboard. If we hear the Dabblers we'll quietly go the round of the dormitories and see if anyone is missing. If they are, we can await their return."

'The long and short of it was that I fell in with his proposal. I had a lot of essays to correct on the Peasants' Revolt – fancy kids of thirteen and fourteen being expected to write essays on anything – and I could go through them just as well by Atkinson's fire as in my own cheerless little sitting-room.

'It's wonderful how welcome a fire can be in a sodden June. We forgot our lost summer as we sat beside it smoking, warming our memories in the glow from the embers.

' "Well," said Atkinson at last, "it's close on twelve. If the Dabblers are going to start, they are due about now." He got up from his chair and drew aside the curtains.

' "Listen!" he said. Across the playground, from the direction of the playing-fields, came the sound of singing. The music – if it could be called such – lacked melody and rhythm and was broken by pauses; it was veiled, too, by the drip, drip of the rain and the splashing of water from the gutter spouts. For one moment I thought I saw lights moving, but my eyes must have been deceived by reflections on the window pane.

' "We'll see if any of our birds have flown," said Atkinson. He picked up an electric torch and we went the rounds of the dormitories. Everything was as it should be. The beds were all occupied, the boys all seemed to be asleep. It was quarter-past twelve by the time we got back to Atkinson's room. The music had ceased; I borrowed a mackintosh and ran home through the rain.

'That was the last time I heard the Dabblers, but I was to hear of them again. Act II was staged up at Scapa. I'd been transferred to a hospital ship, with a dislocated shoulder for X-ray, and as luck would have it the right-hand cot to mine was occupied by a lieutenant, R.N.V.R., a fellow called Holster, who had been at old Edmed's school a year or two before my time. From him I learned a little more about the Dabblers. It seemed that they were boys who for some reason or other kept up a school tradition. Holster thought that they got out of the house by means of the big wistaria outside B dormitory, after leaving carefully constructed dummies in their beds. On the night in June when the Dabblers were due to appear it was considered bad form to stay awake too long and very unhealthy to ask too many questions, so that the identity of the Dabblers remained a mystery. To the big and burly Holster there was nothing really mysterious about the thing; it was a schoolboys' lark and nothing more. An unsatisfactory act, you will agree, and one which fails to carry the story forward. But with the third act the drama begins to move. You see I had the good luck to meet one of the Dabblers in the flesh.

'Burlingham was badly shell-shocked in the war; a psychoanalyst took him in hand and he made a seemingly miraculous recovery. Then two years ago he had a partial relapse, and when I met him at Lady Byfleet's he was going up to town three times a week for special treatment from some unqualified West End practitioner, who seemed to be getting at the root of the trouble. There was something extraordinarily likeable about the man. He had a whimsical sense of humour that must have been his salvation, and with it was combined a capacity for intense indignation that one doesn't often meet with these days. We had a number of interesting talks together (part of his regime consisted of long cross-country walks, and he was glad enough of a companion) but the one I naturally remember was when in a tirade against English educational methods he mentioned Dr Edmed's name – "the head of a beastly little grammar school where I spent five of the most miserable years of my life." '

' "Three more than I did," I replied.

' "Good God!" he said, "fancy you being a product of that place!"

' "I was one of the producers," I answered. "I'm not proud of the fact; I usually keep it dark."

' "There was a lot too much kept dark about that place," said Burlingham. It was the second time he had used the words. As he uttered them, "that place" sounded almost the equivalent of an un-namable hell. We talked for a time about the school, of Edmed's pomposity, of old Jacobson the porter – a man whose patient good humour shone alike on the just and on the unjust – of the rat hunts in the tithe barn on the last afternoons of term.

' "And now," I said at last, "tell me about the Dabblers."

'He turned round on me like a flash and burst out laughing, a high-pitched, nervous laugh that, remembering his condition, made me sorry I had introduced the subject.

' "How damnably funny!" he said. "The man I go to in town asked me the same question only a fortnight ago. I broke an oath in telling him, but I don't see why you shouldn't know as well. Not that there is anything to know; it's all a queer boyish nightmare without rhyme or reason. You see I was one of the Dabblers myself."

'It was a curious disjointed story that I got out of Burlingham. The Dabblers were a little society of five, sworn on solemn oath to secrecy. On a certain night in June, after warning had been given by their leader, they climbed out of the dormitories and met by the elm-tree in old Edmed's garden. A raid was made on the doctor's poultry run, and, having secured a fowl, they retired to the tithe barn, cut its throat, plucked and cleaned it, and then roasted it over a fire in a brazier while the rats looked on. The leader of the Dabblers produced sticks of incense; he lit his own from the fire, the others kindling theirs from his. Then all moved in slow procession to the summerhouse in the corner of the doctor's garden, singing as they went. There was no sense in the words they sang. They weren't English and they weren't Latin. Burlingham described them as reminding him of the refrain in the old nursery rhyme:

> There were three brothers over the sea,
> *Peri meri dixi domine.*
> They sent three presents unto me,
> *Petrum partrum paradisi tempore*
> *Peri meri dixi domine.*

' "And that was all?" I said to him.

' "Yes," he replied, "that was all there was to it; but – "

'I expected the but.

' "We were all of us frightened, horribly frightened. It was quite different from the ordinary schoolboy escapade. And yet there was fascination, too, in the fear. It was rather like," and here he laughed, "dragging a deep pool for the body of someone who had been drowned. You didn't know who it was, and you wondered what would turn up."

'I asked him a lot of questions but he hadn't anything very definite to tell us. The Dabblers were boys in the lower and middle forms and with the exception of the leader their membership of the fraternity was limited to two years. Quite a number of the boys, according to Burlingham, must have been Dabblers, but they never talked about it and no one, as far as he knew, had broken his oath. The leader in his time was called Tancred, the most unpopular boy in the school, despite the fact that he was their best athlete. He was expelled following an incident that took place in chapel. Burlingham didn't know what it was; he was away in the sick-room at the time, and the accounts, I gather, varied considerably.'

Harborough broke off to fill his pipe.

'Act IV will follow immediately,' he said.

'All this is very interesting,' observed Scott, 'but I'm afraid that if it's your object to curdle our blood you haven't quite succeeded. And if you hope to spring a surprise on us in Act IV we must disillusion you.' Freeman nodded assent.

' "Scott who Edgar Wallace read," ' he began. 'We're familiar nowadays with the whole bag of tricks. Black Mass is a certain winner; I put my money on him. Go on, Harborough.'

'You don't give a fellow half a chance, but I suppose you're right. Act IV takes place in the study of the Rev. Montague Cuttler, vicar of St Mary Parbeloe, a former senior mathematics master, but before Edmed's time – a dear old boy, blind as a bat, and a Fellow of the Society of Antiquaries. He knew nothing about the Dabblers. He wouldn't. But he knew a very great deal about the past history of the school, when it wasn't a school but a monastery. He used to do a little quiet excavating in the vacations and had discovered what he believed to be the stone that marked the tomb of Abbot Polegate. The man, it appeared, had a bad reputation for dabbling in forbidden mysteries.'

'Hence the name Dabblers, I suppose,' said Scott.

'I'm not so sure,' Harborough answered. 'I think that more probably it's derived from diabolos. But, anyhow, from old Cuttler I gathered that the abbot's stone was where Edmed had placed his summerhouse. Now doesn't it all illustrate my theory beautifully? I admit that there are no thrills in the story. There's nothing really supernatural about it. Only it does show the power of oral tradition when you think of a bastard form of the black mass surviving like this for hundreds of years under the very noses of the pedagogues.'

'It shows too,' said Freeman, 'what we have to suffer from incompetent headmasters. Now at the place I was telling you about where I've entered my boy – and I wish I could show you their workshops and art rooms – they've got a fellow who is – '

'What was the name of the school?' interrupted Harborough.

'Whitechurch Abbey.'

'And a fortnight ago, you say, two boys were expelled for a raid on a hen roost?'

'Yes.'

'Well, it's the same place that I've been talking about. The Dabblers were out.'

'Act V,' said Scott, 'and curtain. Harborough, you've got your thrill after all.'

Unwinding

Like many other bachelors of forty, I have a horror of parlour games.

My worst nightmare – for I have unfortunately a whole dream stable full of them, is to be pursued down endless corridors by a maiden lady who wishes me to join herself and two elder sisters at Halma.

After Halma, and a game I played one evening fifteen years ago, called 'Ludo', my pet aversion is 'Unwinding'.

What are the rules? Why, simplicity itself! Someone thinks of ham and eggs; that reminds me of my landlady, and she in return reminds my neighbour of Sarah Gamp; and so you proceed until you arrive at the north pole or some other equally remote point, when you unwind, going through all the nonsense again backwards way.

The game, however, has one advantage; you see the curious way in which some people's memories work.

And with this as an introduction I will tell you the only story I know about a parlour game.

If you are a naturalist you may be acquainted with the name of Charles Thorneycroft, the author of the three-volume treatise on British spiders; his name also figures in the clergy list as vicar of Willeston Parva, but it is to the former fact that he owes the five lines in last year's edition of Who's Who.

Though he is almost an old man now, his friends hardly notice the change, for he has always had an old man's characteristics, a certain garrulity in anecdote, great mismanagement in business affairs, coupled with an extreme degree of absentmindedness.

For twenty years the Reverend Charles Thorneycroft has held the living of Willeston Parva, declining all offers of preferment; for Willeston Fen lies in the borders of his parish, and Willeston Fen is one of the few remaining breeding grounds of two species of butterfly that are rapidly becoming extinct.

Besides his spiders and his library, the vicarage is large enough to give shelter to Mrs Thorneycroft and her three daughters, charming girls in spite of the atmosphere of mixed hockey and parish small talk in which they live.

Last year my customary visit to Willeston coincided with Millicent's second birthday party. By that I do not mean that Millicent, in clerical parlance, was standing upon the threshold of her second year, for she was fifteen, and very proud of the fact.

But it was her overflow party, when her grown-up friends were called in to eat of the fragments that remained.

The arrangement was excellent, for the guests on the first occasion, with girlish indiscretion, devoured everything that was indigestible, leaving to their elders on the following day a safe if uninteresting repast.

On this occasion the party consisted entirely of men. There was Dr Philpots, an old-fashioned homoeopath; Mr Greatorex, who farmed a couple of thousand acres Fenchurch way, and who drove tandem to the delight of all Fenchurch children; and Captain Dawson.

These three were old friends and had come to Millicent's second birthday party for years in succession. It was this that made her two sisters object to the proposal to ask Mr Cholmondley of Oldbarnhouse.

As Madge said, Mr Cholmondley was a newcomer. He never came to church; their father and he had never met.

According to Laura, the upholder of propriety, who went with her mother to pay calls, he was a mere nobody, in spite of his aristocratic name. She, for one, thought him uneducated, but as it was not her birthday party, she forbore to interfere.

And so Millicent, actuated a little by pity for the lonely gentleman, and largely by obstinacy, invited Mr Cholmondley.

At the last moment she almost hoped he would refuse, but to her own and everyone else's surprise, he accepted, and his present won her heart at once.

The guests assembled late in the afternoon, and as the evening was warm we were on the lawn playing croquet until within half an hour of supper; but when the captain twice in succession sent black spinning into a clump of geraniums under the impression that it was his partner's ball, we had to admit that it was too dark to continue.

'Let's fill up the time by playing at Unwinding,' said Millicent. 'It's perfectly simple; we can wind until supper's ready, and unwind afterwards.'

Laura said the game was silly, Madge that it was quite nice, and as no other suggestions were forthcoming, we began to wind. I forget most of the string of nonsense we concocted, but I remember that from Irving we went to Hamlet, from Hamlet to Champainbury, a little village on the other side of the parish, then to champagne and from champagne to luxury.

Dr Philpots, who, when not fully absorbed in homoeopathy, was apt to fall back on Socialism, declared that luxury reminded him of first-class railway carriages.

The vicar, deep in an article in *Nature*, had not been listening.

'What is it?' he said. 'Oh, first-class railway carriages! First-class railway carriages remind me of murder! An admirable criticism of the whole question,' he went on, 'I only hope Fortescue will have sufficient sense of decency to read it.'

Needless to say, we passed over Fortescue's shortcomings, to in-quire how he had got the idea of murder into his head. There was really no connection between the two things at all.

But the vicar's opinion was not to be shaken. 'Whenever I see a first-class railway carriage I think of murder. I'll tell you why when we go into supper.'

'It's like this,' he said as soon as we were seated. 'About ten years ago I had to travel down from London by the last train on Saturday night. The day had been tiring, and as the Sunday's sermon was still unprepared, I departed from my usual habit, and took my seat in an empty first-class compartment.

'I wrote undisturbed for an hour and a half, until the sudden grinding of brakes, and the flash of red and green signal lamps, informed me of the fact that we had reached Marshley junction.

'One or two people got out, but it seemed as if I were to have the carriage to myself again. The guard had blown his whistle, and we had begun to move, when the train from Saunchester drew up. I put my head out of the window to see if there was anyone who had been rash enough to risk the connection. Yes, almost before the train had stopped, a door was thrown open, and a man rushed across the platform.

'The carriage I was in was the last in my train. He had just time to open the door of my compartment, when the guard shouted to him to stand clear. He flung himself down in the corner, panting. "That was touch and go," I said. "It was lucky for you the door was not locked." He assented, and I went on with my work, only noting that the man looked very pale. When I had finished the page I was writing, I chanced to look on the floor. "If you don't mind," I said to my companion, "we will have the window raised. The rain seems to be getting in." It was trickling across the floor, making its way along a crack in the oilcloth. But though I had closed the window, the little stream still ran on. I am shortsighted, and it took me twice as long as it would have done another to realise that it was not water but blood. It was dripping from a wound in the hand of the man who sat opposite me.

' "It's a nasty cut," he said, as his eyes caught mine. "Could you bind it up for me? You will find a handkerchief in my coat pocket. There was a drunken man in my carriage. He filled himself with whisky, and then smashed the bottle, and when it came to a free fight, I fell and cut myself. There's something to be said for the teetotaller's point of view after all.

' "That's better," he said, as I finished tying the bandage. "It's exceedingly kind of you to have put yourself to so much trouble. I'm afraid I shall have ruined this suit, and as bad luck would have it, it's new today."

'We were silent some time, while the stranger wiped the mist from the pane with the window sash.

' "Yes," he said, "drunkenness is a horrible thing, but I doubt very much whether prohibition would have the effect so many people think." He went on to talk of America, which he seemed to know. I turned the conversation on to the question of mob law and its relation to crime.

' "It's useless," I remember him saying, "to think that violence can suppress violence. In most cases I think that even the compulsory detention of criminals in prisons and reformatories defeats its own object. A man's conscience, though it may permit a crime, may be trusted to cause him more discomfort than all your dark cells and strait waistcoats. But, of course, I may be prejudiced."

'He kept me busily engaged in talk, until we reached the next station. Lowering the window before the train stopped he looked out upon the platform. "My brother ought to be here to meet me," he said, "but I don't see him anywhere. Good night, sir!"

'My first feeling, after he had gone, was one of curiosity as to his profession. In spite of his talk, he seemed hardly a gentleman. I finally docketed him as a newspaper reporter. I went on with my writing, but broke off a minute later. "What a curiously disagreeable fellow his brother must be," I said to myself. "He seemed actually relieved to find that he was not on the platform to meet him."

'Next morning the papers were full of an awful murder committed on the line. The body of an old gentleman horribly mutilated had been found in a compartment on the 10.30 train from Saunchester. There was every sign of a desperate struggle, and a handbag and pocket-book found under the seat had evidently been rifled. No clue to the identity of the murderer had been observed.

'I thought little of the matter at the time. It was not till late in the day that I realised that it was the 10.30 from Saunchester that had steamed into Marshley station just as we were leaving. Immediately following this, came the thought that the stranger who had entered my carriage was the murderer. I dismissed the idea as preposterous, as unjust to a man of whom I knew no ill, but try as I would, it came back again and again until finally I had to receive it, and to fashion some sort of lurid story around my fellow-traveller.

'As the months went by, I felt at times that I ought to communicate my suspicions to the police, but I comforted myself with the belief that they would probably know as much as I did. I agreed with the stranger's theory that conscience is the best of sleuth-hounds, and so I let the matter rest. But whenever I think of first-class railway carriages, I think of murder. The two things are linked together in my brain as closely as two things can be.'

Supper finished, we separated, some of the men strolling on to the veranda for a smoke, while the rest of us went back to the drawing-room.

The vicar showed us some spiders he had received that morning from a friend in Brazil. He was all enthusiasm, but we were relieved when he left us at last to hunt some reference in his paper-backed German books.

'Let's unwind!' said Millicent. 'Never mind father and the others. They can join in later.' So we began. We started with three lives each, which when exhausted, were liable to be extended, after the merciful manner of old ladies and children. After we had been un-winding for five minutes, the vicar came in with his book, his five fingers marking the places of the references.

'The tower of London,' said Laura, 'reminds me of Richard the Third.

'Richard the Third,' said Millicent, 'reminds me of murder.'

'Murder,' said her mother, 'reminds me of first-class railway carriages.'

It was the vicar's turn, but he was deep in his book. 'Wake up, father!' said Madge. 'What do first-class railway carriages remind you of?'

'Mr Cholmondley,' said the vicar, and went on with his reading.

Madge shook the old gentleman, and took his book away. 'Now, father,' she said, 'do play properly! You've lost five lives already. What do first-class railway carriages remind you of? You can have till we count ten.'

The vicar took off his spectacles, and wiped them carefully. Then with a little nervous smile he had when he thought that his daughters were not treating him with respect that was his due before company, he said: 'Murder.'

'Oh, dear! I'm afraid he's hopeless,' said Millicent to the gentlemen who just then came in from their smoke. 'Here's papa saying that first-class railway carriages remind him of Mr Cholmondley, and then that they remind him of murder.'

'Yes, Mr Cholmondley,' said her mother, 'you will have to defend yourself. Why, he isn't here! Hasn't he finished his cigar?' she asked of Greatorex.

'We thought he was in here with you,' he replied. 'I haven't seen him since supper.'

There was silence for a minute, broken by a knocking at the door. The maid came in with a note. It was from Cholmondley, apologising for running off without saying goodbye. He had had a telegram from his mother, who was dying in the south of France, and had been obliged to catch the earliest train.

'Poor man!' said the vicar's wife, 'I remember now how silent he was during supper. Our careless talk must indeed have been a trial to him!' and she began to discuss with Greatorex the insanitary conditions of all continental hotels.

But the vicar sat in his armchair; his book on spiders had dropped unheeded to the floor. He was gazing into the fire with an expression of utter incredulity.

Mrs Ormerod

Agatha, my dear, you are a saint with your letters. They come every month as regularly as the tradesmen's bills, and mine to you are hardly more frequent than the demands for Poor Rate. They have to be long to restore British credit. Tonight I'm blissfully free; Bill has unexpectedly been called down to address a meeting of local bigwigs in his constituency, so you can picture me feeling all good inside – it isn't the cook's night out – chair drawn up to a blazing fire, coffee on the table beside me, and a fountain pen filled to capacity, which explains the blot.

I'm a pig I suppose to mention November luxuries like this when I remember how impossible you find the problem of maids. You ought to edit a new *Famous Trials* series. If you do I have a contribution to make. So here goes.

When you were last in England I think you met the Inchpens when they called one afternoon, though I expect you've forgotten all about it. Aleck Inchpen was a medical missionary in equatorial Africa, tall, thin, stooping, dreadfully shortsighted, with a wisp of a beard; rather a big bug in the anthropological way, but a perfect dear. His wife was at the Royal Free with Nell Butterworth. You would never imagine she was a doctor. She rescues wasps from marmalade and puts them on the window-sill with a saucer of water for their wash and brush up. She reminds me rather of the French mistress at St Olave's and the strange thing is I like her enormously. These two have faced innumerable hardships, have lived alone hundreds of miles away from other white people, have adopted I don't know how many black twins who would otherwise have been left to die, twins apparently being unlucky, and have now come back to England, where Aleck is to write an epoch-making work on native psychology in the intervals of going round as a deputation – a ghastly job – lantern slides, curios, silver collection, vicar in the chair, reluctant hospitality, and third-class railway fares. His wife is more or less crippled with rheumatoid arthritis, and her chief trouble is that she doubts if they are justified in having a joint income of five hundred a year with permission to live in a dilapidated house that is far too big for them and would give anyone else the fidgets.

Two more helpless, lovable babes you never saw.

I spent a long weekend with them in September. I wasn't exactly asked, in fact I fished for the invitation because I had a sort of feeling in my bones that I could help them. Be warned by me. If you ever meet any saints, take from them all that they can give you, but never interfere with them. The repercussions are simply awful.

If I had been wise I would have seen from Mary Inchpen's letter that she wasn't altogether anxious for me to come, but she warned me about the inconveniences of the simple life, and that put me on my mettle. Their cook-housekeeper, Mrs Ormerod, was kind but slow and not used to visitors, and with a house like theirs that was really far too big for them it was impossible to keep things as nice as she would wish. I would have to make allowances for Mrs Ormerod, who was one of those good women who were never properly appreciated. Reading between the lines, I came to the conclusion that Mrs Ormerod was a dragon. I rather fancied myself as a fighter of dragons.

Viner's Croft was a derelict farmhouse. I didn't tell the Inchpens what train I was coming by because I didn't want to be met by Aleck in the second-hand car he had bought. (He is constitutionally incapable of managing a car.) So the carrier drove me from the station in his Ford along twisting lanes. Whenever the road forked we took the worst turning, and by the time he had deposited me at the foot of the hollow in which Viner's Croft is tucked away I was thinking of your impassable seas of mud.

The door was opened by an unpleasant-looking little boy. He gazed at me through his spectacles with half-open mouth – I could have boxed his ears – and then saying that he would fetch his mother, left me on the mat. I waited for three minutes and then Mrs Ormerod, the housekeeper, appeared.

Agatha, my dear, if you rolled all your *Famous Trials* into one you wouldn't have the faintest idea of that abominable woman.

At first sight I put her down as about fifty, but I expect she was a good deal older than that. Anyhow her hair was dyed and her teeth were false. I've no objection to people improving their looks; on the contrary I'm grateful to them – but hair of a canary yellow and a cameo brooch of a disconsolate female weeping over an urn! She was dressed in a sickly sort of sea-green robe, with white cuffs turned up from podgy wrists, and she wore a girdle from which was suspended a bunch of keys. Round her neck hung a chain, and from it dangled a curious jade ornament that I found out to be a whistle.

I gave my name and said that I believed I was expected.

'I believe you are,' said Mrs Ormerod. She looked me up and down in the way she might have done a truant kitchen-maid arriving home an hour late after her evening out. And then she winked at me. At least an ordinary lay person would have called it a wink – 'habit spasm' is the term the Inchpens use. Her left eyelid quivered and then suddenly closed. I felt rather like a mouse looking at a gorged owl that was too lazy to pounce before dusk. Mrs Ormerod blew her whistle, the small boy came trotting down the corridor and seized my bag, while I followed the housekeeper the length of the rambling house to the drawing-room and safety.

Mary Inchpen gave me the warmest of welcomes. She is an enfolding sort of person, and wraps herself round you in a way that I could never put up with from anyone else. Aleck, I found, was spending the day in Maldon and wouldn't be back before evening, so we had tea by ourselves. She wasn't at all well, and had to walk with a stick, but she insisted on taking me all round the house before it was too dark. It's a regular rabbit-warren of a place, with steps up and steps down, and only half the rooms are furnished. The rest are filled with lumber which Mary is gradually sorting out, so that Aleck will be able to unpack his great cases of curios from Africa – not the sort of things to dream about from what little I saw of them. There is no gas, of course, only oil lamps, and the water has to be pumped until the well goes dry, after which they depend on big water-butts, all green and slimy.

Mary was rather fidgety until Aleck got back safely just before supper time. However it seemed that he had only run over a chicken and scraped a little paint from the mudguard in passing a wagon. Anyone might do that in these narrow lanes. After supper Aleck disappeared for a quarter of an hour. He did this after every meal. I thought at first it was to smoke a cigarette in peace, but before I left I found he used to help Mrs Ormerod to wash up.

We went to bed early. I'm a shocking sybarite in many ways and even in September I'm dependent on a hot-water bottle. When I unpacked my things I placed mine in a conspicuous position on the bed, where its leanness asked to be filled. Of course it wasn't. The sheets had been turned down, the blinds drawn and the bottle hung on a hook on the door. If Mrs Ormerod hadn't taken my hint I most certainly was not going to take hers, even if it meant a journey down to the kitchen with a candle that as likely as not would blow out on the way. I got there at last, knocked at the door and was told to come in.

Mrs Ormerod was seated in a comfortable armchair before the fire, busy sewing. I asked for some hot water. The kettle it appeared had already been removed from the fire, but if I cared to wait I was at liberty to do so. No apologies, no attempt to set me at my ease, not even a chair was offered me. So I sat down and waited while Mrs Ormerod went on with her sewing – rather a striking piece of embroidery that might have been an altar-cloth. Long before the kettle boiled my patience was worn out. I filled the bottle myself at last with water that was little more than tepid, but not nearly so tepid as the good night I gave her.

'Good night,' said Mrs Ormerod without getting up from her chair. And then her left eye winked at me. I can see it now. 'Curse you,' it said, 'for a meddlesome Matty and maker of extra work, and if you think that you are going to get anything out of me you are mightily mistaken.'

I stayed four days at Viner's Croft. One would have been enough to show me that Mrs Ormerod was not only the Inchpens' house-keeper but their manageress. She had them completely under her thumb. Aleck cleaned the boots and the knives while Mary had the beastly business of trimming lamps; and all the time there was that objectionable little boy Simon, who could have done it perfectly well, instead of which Mary gave him lessons on the pianoforte, and every day for an hour Aleck taught him, at his or Mrs Ormerod's request, Latin! I suppose she had some idea of his going into the Church, when the most he could look for would be to get a job as a barber's assistant. I thought at first that he was Mrs Ormerod's own child until Mary told me that she had adopted him. She had adopted others as well, but had been sadly disappointed in them.

'Poor Mrs Ormerod,' said Mary. 'She has passed through deep waters.'

I dare say she had, but she was on dry land now and looked as if she thoroughly appreciated the fact.

I don't want to do Mrs Ormerod injustice. She had her points. She was scrupulously clean, and an excellent cook. She had typed out the manuscript of Aleck's new book, and was interested in it too. She knew how to make that child obey her. When she whistled he dropped whatever he was doing and made a beeline for her. But fancy whistling for a child! It makes me sick to think of it.

I lay awake at night pitying the Inchpens, exasperated with them, and wondering all the time how I could free them from the incubus of Mrs Ormerod.

I have a theory of my own that good attracts evil. It shows it up of course and draws attention to it. The Inchpens always convinced me of selfishness – but it goes beyond that. Really good people, saint-like people, act as magnets to those who have more than a streak of the devil in them. That's why they have adventures and meet with folk that you or I seldom see. That's why Mrs Ormerod stays on with them, horrible parasite that she is.

You may say I was making a fuss about nothing. Here was a woman capable enough at her job and two kindly souls who seemed content to ignore what to me appeared impudence. But did Aleck really enjoy cleaning the knives and making his wife's early morning cup of tea? And wasn't Mary at heart humiliated when she half apologised one day for there being visitors to lunch, to say nothing of her seeing that woman going about the house with her keys hanging at her girdle? Of course she was. I know when people are unhappy, and I under-stand Mary's jargon. When she says she has much to be thankful for and is greatly blessed, she means that things are pretty bad, but they might be worse.

So, greatly daring, on the third morning of my stay at Viner's Croft I tackled Mary and without beating about the bush told her that I thought she ought to get rid of Mrs Ormerod. She was almost annoyed.

'Why do all my friends say that?' she exclaimed. 'It almost makes me afraid of asking them to stay here. You none of you really know Mrs Ormerod. In some ways she isn't an easy person to live with; like many sensitive people she takes offence very readily. She knows that she is capable and likes to have things in her own hands. We ought not to judge her. She has had a very unhappy life. That affliction of the eye means that she is debarred from positions of responsibility that her abilities would otherwise entitle her to and has to be content instead with an absurdly low salary. It isn't as if Aleck and I weren't used to living with queer people. You should have seen some of my African lady helps. And if we can't put up with Mrs Ormerod, who can? It's a challenge – no, I don't mean that, it's a privilege to help one whose good qualities make it difficult to help.'

I had to leave it at that. The befogged perversity of Mary was impenetrable. There remained Aleck.

With the natural desire to postpone an unpleasant task I had already left things rather late and now it was almost laughable to see the anxiety with which Mary tried to guard against the possibility of my being left alone with her husband. While I shadowed Aleck, Mary shadowed me, and betwixt and between were Mrs Ormerod and the boy. I had at last to feign a headache, to lie on my bed for half an hour, and then when I had seen Simon go off to feed the fowls I slipped quietly downstairs and made my way to Aleck's study.

There I had it out with him.

I didn't waste any time over preliminaries but came straight to the point, which wasn't Mrs Ormerod but Mary. I told him – which was perfectly true – that she seemed to me to be thoroughly run down and despite the country air not nearly so well as when I saw her in town.

He agreed. 'I am afraid it is my fault,' he said. 'This deputation work takes up a lot of time, and then there is my book as well. Mary is too much alone. Perhaps I ought to speak to Mrs Ormerod. She once half suggested that she should share our meals. I expect we ought to have treated her more as one of the family, but as one gets older one sets a higher value on privacy and we have been accustomed all our lives to live alone. How would it be if I asked Mrs Ormerod and Simon to have lunch with us – we might all have it in the kitchen – and then if the plan succeeded we might extend it to other meals? I am at times conscious that we are a divided household.'

I could have shaken the man for his obtuseness.

'Aleck,' I said, 'just listen to me. You are living in a fool's paradise, and Mrs Ormerod is the serpent. If you really care for your wife's peace of mind, not to mention your own, you have just got to get rid of the woman. She makes Mary's position impossible. In all sorts of ways she humiliates her. She can't even go into her own kitchen. Only yesterday when we were picking up windfalls in the orchard she told me how much she would have enjoyed making jam, but Mrs Ormerod liked to make it in her own time and in her own way. And I believe that Mary would gladly have typed out your manuscript for you. Why ever didn't you suggest it to her?'

Aleck pulled off his spectacles and wiped them nervously.

'Perhaps I ought to have done,' he said, 'but Mrs Ormerod volunteered, and the book, my dear, the book is not exactly pleasant reading. I don't quite know whether Mary would have liked it. Of course I realise that Mrs Ormerod is – what shall I say? – a rather queer woman, and one doesn't see all her good qualities at first. But I believe she is devoted to the boy. It would be difficult for her to find a home for him. One mustn't always do the easiest thing.'

'Aleck,' I said, 'whether you like it or not, you are doing the easiest thing in letting matters drift like this. Mary won't give Mrs Ormerod notice. She is not well enough to face up to it. But you are. The truth of the matter is that you are frightened of Mrs Ormerod. She may be, as you say, a rather queer woman. Don't think about that, but concentrate on the fact that she is intensely selfish, thoroughly uncongenial, and is getting on your wife's nerves. Give her notice today while I'm with you. She will turn on me, and there will be an unholy row, but from the affection I have for you both I'm prepared to stand the racket.'

He fidgeted with a paper knife.

'I am willing to admit that there may be something in what you say and I'm grateful for your speaking out like this. You mustn't be dragged into any quarrel though, and in any case a matter of this magnitude can't be decided upon in a hurry. I shall sleep on it and let you know my final decision before you leave.'

You can imagine, my dear, that our last evening together was not one of the brightest and best. Aleck and Mary were glum, and since I didn't know what the silence might bring forth I had my work cut out in filling in the gaps in the conversation with the most awful rubbish. At last I pleaded my headache – by this time it was real enough – and the fact that I was leaving first thing in the morning – as an excuse for bed.

After my first unsuccessful attempt to get a hot-water bottle I had not bothered about it. After all, the nights were not cold. Really I supposed I funked going down to the kitchen to face Mrs Ormerod. You can imagine then my surprise when she knocked at my bedroom door with my bottle in her hand, filled and gloriously hot.

'I thought perhaps you would like it tonight,' she said. 'They are comforting if you chance to wake in the early hours.' Then came the wink. 'Good night!'

I wondered as I lay in bed if she thought I might, after all, be worth propitiating. But I didn't wonder any longer when I woke up about two to find the blessed thing had leaked and had soaked the bedclothes and mattress. It was a new bottle, too. By the light of my candle I surveyed the damage. I could see no puncture, so I unscrewed the stopper. The rubber washer was torn, and of course Mrs Ormerod had torn it. She must have gone to sleep chuckling. I remembered her 'if you chance to wake in the early hours'. That wink of hers, like a witty man's stutter, was her way of pointing her remarks. I wondered if she were awake then and if Aleck and Mary were letting their minds wander along the dark passages of Viner's Croft in search of peace. I wondered if I should have the courage to ring the bell and summon Mrs Ormerod from the vasty deep. But Mary might come instead, Mary who had lived for months in rain-sodden huts in tropical Africa. Pioneers! O Pioneers! I fixed up some sort of bed on the hardest of sofas and, with the candle still burning to comfort me, fell at last into a restless, aching sleep.

It was half-past six when I awoke to gaze with gathering resent-ment upon the disorder of my room. In less than three hours Viner's Croft would see me no more. There was satisfaction in that. Why not anticipate my return to civilisation and ring for an early morning cup of tea? Such a demand would annoy Mrs Ormerod very much and I wanted to annoy her. I gave a tug at the old-fashioned bell-pull and waited. Silence for five minutes and then a pad, pad along the corridor and a knock at the door.

'Come in!' I said.

Enter Mrs Ormerod in a mauve wrapper and bedroom slippers, registering injured innocence and anxious solicitude except for the left eye, which was wholly malevolent.

'I am most awfully sorry to trouble you,' I said, 'but do you think you could get me a cup of tea? I've been lying awake for hours; the bottle leaked in the night and I'm chilled to the bone.'

'I'll light the fire at once and put the kettle on. No trouble I assure you' (wink), 'most unforeseen.'

The boy Simon brought up the tea, very weak and barely tepid. He held it out to me with a sickly grin and then darted off, leav-ing the door open. Mrs Ormerod had whistled for him. I didn't drink it. For all I knew it might have been doctored – poison she wouldn't have dared to try. It went out of the window to water the Michaelmas daisies.

Breakfast. A lively meal. Aleck jocular over his porridge and Mary finding it hard to express her gratitude for the four delightful days I had given them. Did I want to say goodbye to Mrs Ormerod? Oh, I had already seen her that morning, and Simon too! She didn't want to hurry me, but she always insisted on Aleck taking plenty of time when he drove to the station, and – in a whisper to me – 'You won't talk to him while he's driving, will you? He's rather shortsighted and the car requires all his attention.'

Dear Mary! How easy it was to see through her. She thought that I thought that the time for the great tête-à-tête had arrived.

I said very little to Aleck; his spirits were boisterously high and I could see that he had come to some decision, though it wasn't until the train was moving off from the platform that he told me that as soon as he got back to Viner's Croft he was going to give a month's notice to Mrs Ormerod.

Did he do it? No, my dear. In this queer world, this very queer world, there's many a slip 'twixt cup and lip. What exactly happened I never heard either from Aleck or Mary. There came rumours, and for my own peace of mind I wrote to Mrs Wilson, the vicar's wife, whom I had met at lunch at Viner's Croft.

Aleck on his way back from the station had run into Simon and had half killed the boy. It seems that he had been standing by the roadside, a hundred yards from the house, waiting for the car, when, hearing Mrs Ormerod's whistle, he darted across the road and the mudguard caught him in the back. They think that it is quite likely he will live, but it will be months before he can be moved. 'How fortunate,' wrote Mrs Wilson, 'that the Inchpens are both doctors. Poor Simon has given Mary a new object in life. She lives for the day when he will be well enough to go with his mother to the sea. But he is horribly frail, and though I've never breathed it to Mary, I fear he will never leave the house. The strange Mrs Ormerod bears up wonderfully.'

Cheer up, Agatha. You have never had to deal with a woman like that. She can't really touch the Inchpens; they are too good. But ordinary mortals like you and me? Ugh! I shall dream of Mrs Ormerod tonight.

Double Demon

George Cranstoun put down the newspaper to watch more closely the two women who sat in the shade of the cedar on the far side of the lawn.

He had decided that the time had come to inform them of his decision. Its success would depend on his reading of their characters. Were they, in a word, capable of entertaining the idea of murder? He thought they were.

He looked at his sister Isobel reclining on her chaise-longue, sixty years old, very much an invalid, an aristocrat to her fingertips, used to giving orders, relentless, not unconventional but above conventions, a woman who could keep a secret and proud, devilishly proud. Unprincipled?

Well, if to stick at nothing for a principle was that, he supposed she was. The good name of the family was what Isobel cared for most in the world. Provided that were safe she could be trusted to keep silent.

And Judith? A beautiful woman, Judith. More beautiful since his sister had persuaded her to stop wearing her nurse's uniform. Clever, too, as clever as they make them, and a born actress. She knew how to get her own way right enough and had patience to wait for it. A hard, unscrupulous woman. Isobel had made a mistake in keeping her on when she had really no need for a full-time nurse. Half nurse, half companion was an obviously unsatisfactory arrangement. They were bound to get on each other's nerves.

He wondered sometimes if Judith shared a secret with his sister, and that Isobel hated her for this. So much the better if it were so. It would make his task easier.

There was a movement of the chairs on the other side of the lawn. Isobel was going in to rest. Judith picked up the books and cushions and followed her.

George lit a cigarette. It was hot in the garden, infernally hot. From where he sat in the old stone summerhouse his eye took in the long low front of Cranstoun Hall with its white portico. There were too many trees about the house, he told himself. They shut it in on every side except where the gardens sloped down to the park with its lake and templed island. All right perhaps in spring, but in late July the deep green of the foliage was too sombre. Far too many flies about too. A wind ought to blow through the place and there was no breath of wind.

Ah, there was Judith!

He got up and crossed the lawn to meet her.

'What about a stroll in the rock garden?' he said. 'There's something I want to talk to you about.'

'I don't mind where I go as long as you give me a cigarette. What's the matter, George? You've been moody all day. Is anything worrying you?'

'You can't expect me to be my brightest and best in this infernal heat, but what I've got to say is important, damned important, and you've got to listen. I've loved you now – how long? We can't marry; as things are at present, there's no chance of it.'

Judith gave him a curious smile.

'Have I said I wanted to marry you, George?'

'Not in so many words, but we understand each other very well. You've made it clear that you don't want to flirt with me. That's policy.'

'Well, perhaps it is.'

'Anyhow I love you.'

'And if I say that I don't love you?'

'Policy again. You sympathise with me, don't you?'

'I'm awfully sorry for you.'

'But you do sympathise. You understand me better than I do myself. And I've kissed you, not nearly as many times as I want to and as I hope to do, and you've put up with it. Now let's be frank. You are poor, ambitious, unscrupulous. (I know all about your going through my letters.) You've played up to Isobel, making out that she is far worse than she is so that you could keep your job.

'I want you badly and since it's the only way, we must marry. You'd like the job of running this place, and you'd do it damned well. You would make an excellent hostess. Isobel has lost all interest in that side of things, with the result that we are shunned as if we had the plague. We could travel too and rent a villa on the Riviera. You'd enjoy a flutter at Monte Carlo.

'All this to me is a delightful prospect. But I can't marry you while Isobel lives. She treats me like a boy. You know my father left me practically nothing. She got everything; she's rolling in money, and I'm her dependant. She's so madly jealous of me that I can't even invite my friends here without first asking her leave. She grudges me any new acquaintance I might make. She barely lets me out of her sight. You agree?'

They had reached the rock garden. Judith sat down on a seat by the side of a miniature cascade, dabbling her fingers in the cool water.

'You've put the case very clearly, George, but it doesn't seem to get us much further.'

'Exactly. We are up against a dead wall. Isobel must go. She's been ill now for months. She can't get much pleasure out of life. Years ago she tried to commit suicide – news to you, but it's true all the same. We can get a great deal of pleasure out of life on certain conditions. I shall help her to go.'

'How?' said Judith, still dabbling her fingers in the cool water of the cascade.

George lowered his voice as he told her how.

'And when?' asked Judith.

George told her when.

'And you'll swear,' she said after a pause, looking him straight in the eyes, 'that it won't be before?'

'Yes, I swear it won't. It may be later because it depends on a number of things. But it won't be before.'

'And Isobel won't suspect?'

'No, I shall tell her a story about you. She'll think it's you I am going to put out of the way. There's something secretive about Isobel, something she wishes to hide from me, and I think I know what it is. She's jealous of you, she hates you. As I said, she has never got much out of life and you, the daughter of a clerk in Balham, have, and are going to get more.

'So now you know all about it, my beautiful Judith,' he went on. 'In a year's time you'll hardly know this place. We shall be entertaining the gayest of house parties and you doubtless will be flirting with someone a little more presentable than your friend Dr Croft. It appeals to you? I see it does. Well, all you have to do is to keep quiet and leave the rest to me. If you have finished washing your hands we will go back to the house.'

Dinner that evening was more than usually silent. Judith complained of a headache. Nurse companions are not expected to suffer from headaches. 'Too long an exposure to the sun, my dear,' said Miss Cranstoun acidly. 'You should wear a hat.' George did little to keep the conversation going. His interest centred in the decanter.

They adjourned to the library. Judith, refusing coffee, made letter-writing an excuse for an early withdrawal, and the two Cranstouns, brother and sister, were left alone.

'George,' said Isobel, 'you drank far too much at dinner. You know very well you are supposed to be on a definite regimen. If you can't keep to the amount stipulated we shall have to give up wine altogether. I don't want to do that. The servants will draw their own conclusions, but you can't go on as you have been doing.'

'Don't be a fool, Isobel,' George replied. 'For a clever woman your obtuseness sometimes amazes me. You keep me on the leash, you treat me as a boy, you give me no responsibility, and then expect me to find complete satisfaction in life. But I'm not going to quarrel with you. I have other far more important things to talk about. If I told you I wanted to marry that Wentworth girl what would you say?'

'Impossible, George. You hardly know her.'

'That's not my fault. You take such precious care nowadays to prevent our making new friends. You have no objection to her family?'

'Of course not. They are as old as ours. But you can't marry her.'

'I'm inclined to agree with you. Judith, for one, would prevent it.'

'Judith? What on earth has she got to do with it?'

'More than you think. Judith is a very clever woman and her chief cleverness is in hiding her cleverness. You made a big mistake, Isobel, in keeping her on so long. There was really no need.'

'I've certainly been much better the last month, but I'm not well.'

'She sees to that.'

'Now what exactly do you mean, George?'

'I'm suggesting that Judith, who after all has ample opportunities, takes care, to put it mildly, that your progress should not be too rapid. Do you like her?'

'She is a competent nurse.'

'And as a competent nurse she knows the value of drugs. Of course you don't like her, Isobel. You know she gets on your nerves, you know you hate the way she orders the servants about and treats the place as if it belonged to her. She thinks it will some day. I suppose you haven't noticed that she's been setting her cap at me?'

'I don't believe it.'

'It's true none the less. At first I rather liked the girl, but when I found that she had been tampering with my letters and was proposing to use blackmail, if necessary, for a lever, I revised my opinion. I can't afford to be blackmailed, Isobel. We can't afford it.'

'But George, she has nothing to go on.'

'I wish I could think that. You remember that keeper, Carver, whose daughter worked in the dairy? He bought a pub down in Wilton. That's settled all right, I fancy. She won't get much change out of him. But there are other things too. And it seems that my father . . . Well, anyhow, for the sake of the family's good name I've decided that we shan't be troubled with Judith much longer.'

'I engaged her, George, and it is I who shall dismiss her.'

'I wasn't thinking of dismissing her, not in your way.' He cast a glance behind his shoulder and drew his chair nearer to his sister's. 'What I really was thinking of was — '

'And why, George,' said his sister at last, 'do you tell me this?'

'Partly because your help is necessary; much more because I have no wish to go through life with an unshared secret. Yours is a stronger character than mine. We shall need each other's support in the future even more than we have done in the past.'

'But Judith; won't she suspect?'

'No. That will be the last thing she will dream of doing.' He told her why.

'And, George,' said Miss Cranstoun faintly, 'it's a thing I ought to know, it's an awful thing to ask, but . . . when?'

George told her when.

'And now,' he said, 'I'll say good night. There are one or two things I want to do.'

George Cranstoun locked the door of his room, and taking a key from his pocket unlocked a cupboard. He took down a bottle of whisky from the shelf, poured himself out a stiff peg, and drew a pack of patience cards from a drawer in the writing desk. Things on the whole had gone very well. He had been right in his surmise. Judith and Isobel were capable of entertaining the idea of murder. Altogether an intriguing situation.

Very carefully he put out the cards and began his game of Double Demon. It would be a good omen if luck were with him tonight. Eleven o'clock struck, twelve o'clock. The cards would not come out. Half an hour after midnight he went to bed, and when the clock struck one he was sound asleep.

But when the clock struck one Isobel Cranstoun was wide awake. She had locked her bedroom door. Judith Fuller was wide awake. She, too, had locked her bedroom door, but the communicating door between Isobel's room and Judith's was unlocked, unbolted.

George Cranstoun smiled in his sleep.

*   *   *

In the garage at Cranstoun Hall there were three cars, the Daimler, an Austin Seven, and a capacious bus-like vehicle built to old Mr Cranstoun's orders, which, despite the fact that it was supposed to serve a number of useful purposes, was seldom used. George told the chauffeur that it would be wanted early in the afternoon to go into Totbury. Miss Cranstoun had arranged for the indoor and outdoor staff to visit the County Show. They were not perhaps as appreciative as they might have been had the notice been longer. McFarlane would have liked more time to overhaul the engine, the upper housemaid might have arranged for her new dress to have been delivered earlier; the cook, had she known, would have arranged to meet her cousin; Mr Brown, the head gardener, had some job or other that wanted doing while the fine weather held.

*   *   *

It was, however, characteristic of Miss Cranstoun to make a sudden decision to arrange for other people's pleasure, and Totbury Show had many attractions. Only Woodford the butler, and Mrs Carlin the housekeeper, chose to remain behind. Mr George, said Miss Cranstoun, had planned a picnic tea on the island in the lake. They would want only a cold supper.

George spent the morning down by the boathouse, while his sister and Judith took advantage of his absence to hurry over the packing that was necessary for his journey. Each was conscious of a certain restraint, and they worked in silence.

George removed the padlock from the bar that locked the boathouse and got out the punt. It was a good punt, though it badly needed a coat of varnish. The punt was provided with two poles. One was all that would be required, and one paddle. The second pole and paddle he placed in the corner of the boathouse. He brought out cushions from the locker and placed them in the sun to air; then getting into the punt he kept along the reed-fringed side of the lake until he was opposite the island. The island with its solitary poplar and grey stone temple almost hid the hall. Almost but not quite. He could still see the upper rooms of the east wing and the end of the terrace walk. The risk was negligible. From the bank to the island, from the island to the bank, four times he made the double journey, on each occasion varying his approach. Finally, he fixed on his course; the lake was deep enough there and the bottom muddy. It would all happen in the most natural way. Judith, seated at the far end of the punt, would like to try her hand with the pole. Isobel would say that it wasn't really safe to change places out in the lake. They had better wait until they reached the island. But, of course, it would be quite safe if they didn't hurry over it. And then he would lose hold of the pole just as Judith was creeping along, there would be a sudden lurch, and . . . George Cranstoun remembered the pictures he had seen of methods of rescuing the drowning. The method that appealed to him most was that in which the rescuer, swimming on his back supported the head of the drowning person with his hands and held it just above the level of the water. In this case it would be just below.

A gallant attempt at a double rescue.

George Cranstoun smiled.

An early lunch. Then the departure of the bus for Totbury. At half-past two the unexpected arrival of Dr Croft and another doctor to see Isobel. Judith, of course, has to be present at the interview.

'But why are they so long about it?' thinks George, as he paces the terrace. 'There's nothing much the matter with Isobel.' He had heard nothing about getting a second opinion. The absurd secretiveness of women. Anyhow, he might as well fill in time by carrying down a few extra cushions to the boathouse.

What was Woodford doing hurrying after him like that, poor old Woodford with that hangdog face of his?

Dr Croft would like a word with him in the library? To blazes with Dr Croft, but he supposed he would have to see the man.

In the library with his back to the empty fireplace, stood Dr Croft. He did not appear to be at ease, and glanced up at his companion as if he expected him to take the lead. 'Dr Hoylake,' he said stiffly. 'I don't think you have met him before.'

George Cranstoun nodded. He was not interested in Dr Hoylake.

'It's like this, Mr Cranstoun,' Dr Croft went on. 'We've been having a long talk with Miss Cranstoun, and we have come to the conclusion, and Dr Hoylake agrees, that for the good of everybody, and not least for your own good, we shall have to make a rather serious break in your life's routine. I don't think it need be for long. Dr Hoylake, perhaps you would like to explain?'

Dr Hoylake spoke with slowness and deliberation. George Cranstoun realised what he was saying. He found the idea curiously interesting. It explained much.

As he listened he looked out of the window, across the gardens, across the park, to the lake and the boathouse. Somebody, probably Jackson the head keeper, was quietly putting the punt away.

'Safe for the time being under lock and key,' said George Cranstoun. 'Well, gentlemen, shall we go?'

The Tool

I like the long south corridor, with its light-coloured walls and low windows looking on to the garden. I do my writing there, for it is very quiet, especially when Jellerby is off colour and is obliged to keep to his room. He calls himself a Social Democrat, and is eloquent on the rights of man – a wonderfully fluent speaker, with facts and figures at his fingertips to drive home every argument. But one tires of that sort of thing very easily. Of the two I would rather listen to Charlie Lovel recite his endless pedigree, as he sits dribbling over his knitting.

I cannot help smiling to myself when I think of yesterday's sermon. Canon Eldred was the preacher, and was obviously ill at ease, as indeed I should have been in similar circumstances. He has a red cheerful face, with comfortable folds of flesh about the chin; a typical healthy-minded Philistine, whom it did one good to see. However, he was there to speak to us. He took as his theme the Duty of Cheerfulness. The subject was excellent, and what he said was to the point; but I could not help wondering whether he had the slightest idea of the condition of those whom he addressed. Evidently he realised our need, but there was a tendency to regard us less as men than as children. He spoke incautiously of the man in the street, and, in so doing, showed the falsity of his position. We have no use for arguments calculated to satisfy the ordinary man, since we are extra-ordinary men in an extraordinary position.

No, 'the man in the street' was, to say the least of it, a most unhappy phrase!

I should like to tell Canon Eldred my own story. He told us that next week he was going away to enjoy a well-earned holiday. Two years ago I was taking my summer holiday too. Autumn holiday it was, in fact, for our vicar – I was senior curate at the time in a big working-class parish in the north of England – had gone off to the sea with his children in July, and Legge, my junior, had claimed August for the Tyrol.

I had made no definite plans for myself that year. Something, I felt sure, would turn up, and if all my friends were booked elsewhere, I knew that I could depend on ten days at my uncle's place in Devonshire, or a fortnight of fresh air and plain living on Bob's disreputable old ketch. But somehow everything fell through. My uncle, who was beginning to be troubled about death duties, had let the shooting for the first time in fifty years; Bob was busy running his craft aground on Danish shoals, and I was left to my own resources. I set off finally at twelve hours' notice on a ten days' walking-tour, determined to hunt out some weatherproof barn within easy distance of a river or the sea, where Legge and I could take our boys to camp at Easter.

I left on a Monday (and I would have Canon Eldred, if he ever reads this, note the date, because the dates are an important part of my narrative) and Legge came with me to the station, for I had several matters to arrange with him connected with the parish work. I took a ten days' ticket. It was stamped 22nd September, and, as I said, the 22nd was a Monday.

That night I slept at Dunsley. It was the end of the season. Nearly all the visitors had left the place, but the harbour was jammed with the herring fleet, storm-bound for over three days, and all the alleyways in the old town were crowded with fishermen. On the Tuesday I started off with my rucksack, intending to follow the line of the cliff, but the easterly gale was too much for me, and I struck inland on to the moors. I walked the whole of the day, a good thirty-five miles, and towards dusk got a lift in a farmer's cart. He was going to Chedsholme, and there I spent the night at the Ship Inn, a stone's-throw from the abbey church. I felt disinclined for a long tramp on Wednesday, so I walked on into Rapmoor in the morning, left my things with old Mr Robinson at the Crown, borrowed a rod and tackle from him, and spent the afternoon fishing the Lansdale beck. I found a splendid camping-ground, but no barn or building, and saw the farmer, a churchwarden, who readily gave permission for the setting up of our tents, if ever we brought the boys that way. Wednesday night I spent at Rapmoor, Thursday at Frankstone Edge, where I dined with the vicar, a college friend of Legge's, and Friday at Gorton. The landlady of the inn at Gorton kept a green parrot in a cage in the parlour. It was remarkably tame, and though I am not usually fond of such birds, I remember spending quite a long time talking to it in the evening.

I set out on the morning of Saturday prepared for a long walk and a probable soaking. Not that the rain was falling, but there was a mist sweeping inland over the moors from the sea, which I was obliged to face, since my track lay eastwards. I followed up the road to the end of the dale, and then took a rough path that skirted a plantation of firs past a disused quarry on to the moor. By noon I was right on the top of the tableland. I ate my sandwiches in the shelter of a peat shooting-butt, while I tried to find my exact position on the map. It was not altogether easy, but I made a rough approximation, and then looked to see which was the nearest village where I could find lodging for the night. Chedsholme, where I had slept on Tuesday, seemed to be the easiest of access, and though they had charged me just double what was reasonable for supper, bed, and breakfast, the fare was good and the house quiet, no small consideration on a Saturday night.

It was after two when I left the shelter of the butt. I had at first some difficulty in finding my way. There were no landmarks on the moor to guide me; the flat expanse was only broken by mound after mound of unclothed shale, running in parallel lines from north to south, which marked the places where men had searched for iron-stone many years before. Gradually the mounds grew less and less frequent, and I was beginning to think that I had left them all behind, when one larger than the rest loomed up out of the mist.

Every man has experienced at some period of his life that strange intuition of danger which compels us, if only it be strong enough, to alter some course of action, substituting for a reasonable motive the blind force of fear. I was walking straight towards the mound, when I came to a standstill. Something seemed to repel me from the spot, while at the same time I became conscious of my intense isolation, alone on the moor miles away from any fellow creature. I stopped for half a minute, half in doubt as to whether to proceed. Then I told myself that fear is always strongest when in pursuit and, smiling at my folly, I went on.

At the farther side of the mound was the body of a dead man. He was a foreigner, with dark skin and long oily locks of hair. A scarlet handkerchief was tied loosely round his throat. There were earrings in his ears. He lay on his back, with his eyes wide open and glazed.

My first feeling was one, not of surprise or pity, but of intense, overpowering nausea. Then with an effort I pulled myself together and examined the body more closely. I could see at once that he had been dead several days. The hands were white and cold, and the limbs strangely limp. His clothes were little more than rags. The shirt was torn open, and tattooed on the chest – even in my horror

I could not help but marvel at the skill with which the thing was done – was a great green parrot with wings outstretched.

At first I could see no sign of how the man had met his death. It was not until I turned the body over that I noticed an ugly wound at the back of the skull, that might have been made by some blunt instrument or a stone. There was nothing for me to do except report the matter to the police as quickly as possible. The nearest constable would be stationed at Chedsholme, ten miles away; and I decided that the best way of getting there in the mist would be to walk eastwards until I struck the mineral line that runs from the Bleadale ironstone quarries. This I did; and I shall not easily forget the joyful feeling of companionship in a living world that I experienced on hearing the distant whistle of an engine, and seeing five minutes later through a break in the clouds the long train of trucks crawling along the skyline.

Once on the permanent way my progress became less slow. Freed from the necessity of maintaining a sense of direction, I began to think more of my horrible discovery. Who could the man be, and why had he been killed? He seemed to have nothing in common with this wild, cold country – a mariner, whom one might have seen without surprise in the days of the Spanish Main, marooned with empty treasure-chests on some spit of dazzling, shadeless sand. And then, the man being killed, why had the murderer done nothing to hide the traces of his crime? What could have been easier than to have covered the body with the loose shale from the mound? 'I could have done the thing in five minutes,' I said to myself, 'if only I had a trowel.' But it was useless for me to wonder what might be the meaning of this illustration to a story I could never hope to read. I left the line at the point where it crossed the road, and then followed the latter down the ridge to Chedsholme. I must have been a mile or more from the village, when the silence of the late afternoon was suddenly broken by the tolling of a bell.

I remember once on Bob's ketch being overtaken by a sea fog. The current was running strong, and Bob was a stranger to the coast. 'It's all right; we shall worry through!' he said, and had hardly finished speaking when we heard the wild, mad clanging of the bell-buoy. I did not soon forget the look of utter surprise on Bob's face. 'There's some mistake,' he said, with all his old lack of logic; 'it's no earthly business to be there.'

That was how I felt on that September evening two years ago. What right had the church bell to be ringing? There would be no evening service on Saturday in a place the size of Chedsholme. It was too late in the day for a funeral. And yet what else could it be? For, as I passed down the village street, I noticed that the windows of the shops were shuttered. There were men, too, hanging about the green, dressed in their Sunday black.

I found the police-station without difficulty, or rather the cottage where the constable lived. He was away, so his wife told me, but would be back in the morning, and as there seemed to be no way of communicating with the authorities, I was obliged for the time being to keep my secret to myself.

The door of the Ship Inn was shut, and I had to knock twice before the landlady appeared. She recognised me at once. 'Yes,' she said, 'we can put you up, to be sure. You can have the same room as before, number three, to the right at the top of the stair. The girl's out, so I'm afraid I can only give you a cold supper.'

Ten minutes later I was standing before a cheerful fire in the parlour, while Mrs Shaftoe spread the cloth, dealing out to me in the meantime the gossip of the week. There were few visitors now; the season was too late, but she expected to have a houseful in a fortnight's time, when Mr Somerset from Steelborough was coming back with a party for another week's shooting. 'It's a pity we only get people in the spring and summer,' she said. 'A village like this is terrible poor, and every visitor makes a difference. I suppose they find it too lonely; but, bless my life, there's nothing to be afraid of on these moors. You could walk all day without meeting anybody. There's no one to harm you. Well, sir, there's your supper ready. If you want anything, you've only got to touch the bell.'

'How is it,' I asked, as I sat down, 'that the place is so quiet tonight? I always thought that Saturday evenings were your busiest times.'

'So they are,' said Mrs Shaftoe; 'we do very little business on a Sunday. It's only a six days' licence, you see. If you'll excuse me, sir, I think that's one of the children calling; I'm only single-handed just at present, for the girl's away at church.'

She left the room, seeing nothing of the effect that her words had on me. 'Sunday!' I thought. 'What can she mean? Surely she must be mistaken!' Yet there in front of me was the calendar; Sunday, the 28th. Less than an hour before I had heard the church bell calling to evening prayer. The men whom I had seen lounging about the street were only the ordinary Sunday idlers. Somewhere in the last week I must have missed a day.

But where? I pulled out my pocket diary. The space allotted to each day was filled with brief notes. 'First,' I said to myself, 'let me make certain of a date from which to reckon.' I was positive that I had started on my holiday on Monday, the 22nd. For further information there was the return half of my ticket stamped with the date. On Monday I slept at Dunsley; Tuesday at this same inn at Chedsholme, Wednesday at Rapmoor, Thursday at Frankstone Edge, and Friday at Gorton. Each day, as I looked back, seemed well filled; my recollection of each was clearly defined. And yet somewhere there was a gap of twenty-four hours about which I knew nothing.

I have always been absentminded – ludicrously so, my friends might say – it is, in fact, a trait in my character that has on more than one occasion put me into an embarrassing situation; but here was something of a nature completely different. In vain I groped about in my memory in search for even the shadow of an explanation. The week came back to me as no sequence of indistinguishable grey days, but the clearest of well-ordered processions. But was it really Sunday? Could the whole thing be a hoax, explicable as the result of some absurd wager? In default of a better the hypothesis was worth testing. I made a pretence of finishing the meal and, taking my hat from the stand, hurried out of the house. I walked in the direction of the church, but as I approached the building my heart sank within me. I passed half a dozen young fellows hanging about the church-yard gate, waiting to walk back home with their girls. 'It's been a dreary Sunday,' I said, and one stopped in the act of lighting a cigarette to agree. I stood in the porch to listen. They were singing Bishop Ken's evening hymn. Then came the thin piping voice of the priest, asking for defence against the perils and dangers of the night.

Under a feeling of almost unbearable depression, I made my way back to the inn and its empty parlour.

'After all,' I said to myself, 'there's nothing that I can do. Other men before now have lost their memory. I should be thankful for regaining it so quickly, and that no harm has been done. No good, at any rate, can result from my pondering over the thing.' But in spite of my resolution I found it impossible to control my thoughts. Again and again I found myself returning to the subject, fascinated by this sudden break in the past and the possibilities that sprang from it. Where had I been? What had I done?

I believe that it was the sight of an ordinary cottage hospital collecting-box on the mantelpiece that suggested to me a new way of approaching the problem. I have always kept accurate accounts, jotting down the expenses of each day, not in my diary, but in a separate pocket cash-book. This, I thought, might throw new light on the matter. I took it out and hastily turned over the pages. At first sight it told me nothing. There was the same list of villages and their inns; no new names appeared. Then I read it through again. This time I made a discovery. The amounts I had paid in bills for a night's lodging, for supper, bed and breakfast, were much the same at all the inns, with the exception of the 'Ship' at Chedsholme. The bill there seemed to be just twice as much as what it should have been. I only remembered to have spent one night there, Tuesday. It might be that I had spent Wednesday night as well.

I rang the bell and ordered what I wanted for breakfast; then, as Mrs Shaftoe was leaving the room, I asked when it was that I had slept at the inn.

'Tuesday and Wednesday,' she said. 'You left us on Thursday morning for Rapmoor. Good night, sir! I'll see that you are called at half-past seven.'

So my supposition was right. The day had been lost at Chedsholme. I wished, as soon as she had gone, that I had asked the woman more. She might have told me something of what I had done. And yet how could I have asked such questions except in the most general terms, without arousing the suspicion that I was mad? From her behaviour it was evident that I had conducted myself in a normal fashion. Very likely I had been out all day walking, only to return to the inn at night dead tired. Why should I worry about this thing, so small compared to the tragedy that centred in my discovery of the afternoon?

It was clear, however, that I should not find peace sitting by the fire in the parlour. The clock had struck half-past nine; I took my candle from the sideboard and went upstairs to bed.

My room was much the same as other rooms in country inns, but there was a hanging bookshelf in the corner, holding half a dozen books: Dr Meiklejohn's *Sermons in Advent*, *Gulliver's Travels*, *Yorkshire Anecdotes*, *The House by the Sea*, and two bound volumes, one of the *Boy's Own Paper*, and the other of some American magazine. The latter I took down and, turning over the pages, saw that the type was good and that the stories were illustrated by some fine half-tone engravings. I got into bed and, placing the candle on the chair by my side, began to read. The story dealt with a young Methodist minister in a New England town. The girl he loved had promised herself in marriage to a sailor, who had been washed ashore from a stranded

brig, bound for Baltimore from Smyrna. Maddened by the girl's love
for the foreigner, he forged a letter arranging for a rendezvous on
the sand dunes, met his rival there, and shot him through the heart.
There was nothing remarkable about the story. I read it to the end
unmoved. But on turning the last page over, I came across a full-page
illustration, that held me fascinated.

It showed the scene on the dunes; the minister in his suit of black
gazing down on the dead body of the Syrian sailor, just as I had stood
that afternoon, and underneath were the words, taken from the
letterpress of the story:

> What would he not have given to blot out the sight
> from his memory?

I suppose that up to the time of which I am writing, my life had
been a very ordinary one, filled with ordinary weekday pleasures
and cares, regulated by ordinary routine. Within the space of a few
hours I had experienced two great emotional shocks, the sudden
discovery of the body of the moor, and this inexplicable loss of
memory. Each by itself had proved sufficiently disturbing, but I had
at least looked upon them as unconnected. A mere chance had
shown me that I might be mistaken. I had stood, as it were, on the
watershed at the source of two rivers. I had assumed that they
flowed into two oceans. The clouds lifted, and I saw that they
joined each other to form a torrent of irresistible force that would
inevitably overwhelm me.

The whole thing seemed impossible; but I had a sickening feeling
that the impossible was true, that I was the instrument, the unwilling
tool, in this ghastly tragedy.

It was useless to lie in bed. I got up and paced the room. Again and
again I tried to shut in the horrible thought behind a high wall of
argument, built so carefully that there seemed to be no loophole for
its escape. My best efforts were of no avail. I was seized with an
overmastering fear of myself and the deed I might have done. I could
think of only one thing to do, to report the whole matter to the
police, to inform them of my inability to account for my doings on
the Wednesday, and to welcome every investigation. 'Anything,' I
told myself, 'is better than this intolerable uncertainty.'

And yet it seemed a momentous step to take. Supposing that I had
nothing to do with this man's death, but at the same time had been
the last person seen with him, I might run the risk of being punished
for another's crime. I owed something to the position I held, to my

future career; and so at last, dazed and weary, I lay down to wait for sleep. I did so with the firm determination that on the morrow I would retrace the path I had followed that afternoon. I might discover some fresh clue to the tragedy. I might find that the whole thing was but the fancy of an overwrought brain.

Slowly I became aware of a narrowing of the field of consciousness. A warm soft mist surrounded me and enfolded me. I heard the church clock strike the hour, but was too weary to count the strokes. The bell seemed to be tolling, tolling; every note grew fainter and I fell asleep.

When I awoke it was nine o'clock. The sun was shining in through the window, and pulling up the blind, I saw a sky of cloudless blue. Sleep had brought hope. I dressed quickly, laughing at the night's fears. In certain moods nothing is so strong as the force of unexpected coincidence. I told myself that I had been in a morbidly sensitive mood on the preceding evening; and in the clear light of day I took up the bound volume which had been the source of so much uneasiness. Really there was nothing in the story of the Methodist minister and the sailor, and as to the illustration, I turned the last page over and found that the illustration did not exist. Evidently I had imagined the whole thing.

'Another lovely day!' said Mrs Shaftoe, as she brought in the breakfast. 'Will you be out walking again, sir? If you like, I could put up some sandwiches for you.' I thought the idea a good one, and telling her I should not be back until four or five, set out soon after eleven.

For the first few miles I had no difficulty in retracing my steps, but after I crossed the mineral line there were no landmarks to guide me. More than once I asked myself why I went on. I could give no satisfactory reply. I think now it must have been the desire to be brought face to face with facts that impelled me. I had had enough of the unbridled fancies of the preceding evening, and longed to discover some clue to the mystery, however faint.

At last I found myself among the old ironstone workings. There was the long line of mounds, thrown up like ramparts, and there was the one standing alone in advance of the rest, beside which the body lay. Slowly I walked towards it. It seemed smaller in the light of a cloudless noon than in Sunday's mists. What was I to find? With beating heart I scrambled up the slope of shale. I stood on the top and looked around. There was nothing, only the wide expanse of moor and sky.

My first thought was that I had mistaken the place. Eagerly I scanned the ground for footprints. I found them almost immediately. They corresponded exactly to my nailed walking-boots. Evidently the place was the same.

Then what had happened? There was but one explanation possible – that I had imagined the whole thing.

And strange as it may seem, I accepted the explanation gladly, for it was the cold reality that I dreaded, linked as it had been with the awful idea that I had done the deed myself in a fit of unconscious frenzy; and in my thankfulness I knelt down on the heather and praised the God of the blue sky and sunlight for having saved me from the terrors of the night.

With a mind at peace with itself I walked back across the moor. I determined to end my holiday on the morrow, to consult some nerve specialist and, if need be, to go abroad for a month or two. I dined that night at the Ship Inn with a talkative old gentleman, who succeeded in keeping me from thinking of my own affairs, and, feeling sure of sleep, went early to bed.

My story does not end there. I wish that it did; but, Canon Eldred said in yesterday's sermon, it is often our duty to accept things as they are, not to waste the limited amount of energy that is given for the day's work in vain regret or morbid anticipation.

For, as I was sitting at breakfast on the morrow, I heard a man in the bar ask Mrs Shaftoe for the morning's paper. She told him that the gentleman in the parlour was reading it, but that Tuesday's was in the kitchen.

'Tuesday's?' I said to myself. 'Monday's, she means. Today is Tuesday'; and I looked at the calendar on the mantelpiece. The calendar said Wednesday. I looked at the newspaper and saw on every page, 'Wednesday, 1st October'. I got up half-dazed and walked into the bar. I suppose Mrs Shaftoe must have seen that there was something wrong, for, before I spoke, she offered me a glass of brandy.

'I'm losing my memory,' I said. 'I think I can't be quite well. I can't remember anything I did yesterday.'

'Why, bless you, sir!' she said, 'you were out on the moors all day. I made you some sandwiches, and in the evening you were talking to the old gentleman who left this morning on Free Trade and Protection.'

'Then what did I do on Monday? I thought that was Monday.'

'Oh! Monday!' said Mrs Shaftoe. 'You were out on the moors all that day too. Don't you recollect borrowing my trowel? There was something you wanted to bury, a green parrot, I think you said it was.

I remember, because it seemed so strange. You came in quite late in the evening, and looked regular knocked up, just the same as last week. It's my belief, sir, that you've been walking too far.'

I asked for my account and, while she was making it out, I went upstairs to my bedroom. I took down the bound volume from the shelf and turned to the story of the Methodist minister. The illustration at the end was certainly not there, but on close inspection I found that a page was missing. For some reason it had been carefully removed. I turned to the index of illustrations, and saw that the picture, with the words beneath that had so strangely affected me, should have been found on the missing page.

I walked to the nearest station and took the train to Steelborough, where I told my story to an inspector of police, who evidently disbelieved it. But in the course of a day or two they made discoveries. The body of an unknown sailor, a foreigner, with curiously distinctive tattooings on the breast, was found in the place I described. For some time there was nothing to connect me with the crime. Then a gamekeeper came forward, who said that on Wednesday, the 24th, he had seen two men, one of whom seemed to be a clergyman, the other a tramp, walking across the moor. He had called to them, but they had not stopped. I stood my trial. I was examined, of course, by alienists, and here I am. No, Canon Eldred, the world is a little more complicated than you think. I agree with you as to the necessity for cheerfulness, but I want better reasons than yours. These are mine – they may be only a poor lunatic's, but they are none the worse for that.

The world, I consider, is governed by God through a hierarchy of spirits. Little Charlie Lovel, by the way, says that he saw the Archangel Gabriel yesterday evening, as he was coming from the bathroom, and for all I know he may be right. It is governed by a hierarchy of spirits, some greater and more wise than others, and to each is given its appointed task. I suppose that for some reason, which I may never know, it was necessary for his salvation that he should die in a certain way, that his soul at the last might be purged by sudden terror. I cannot say, for I was only the tool. The great and powerful (but not all-powerful) spirit did his work as far as concerned the sailor, and then, with a workman's love for his tool, he thought of me. It was not needful that I should remember what I had done – I had been lent by God, as Gog was lent to Satan – but, my work finished, this spirit in his pity took from me all memory of my deed. But, as I said before, he was not omnipotent, and I suppose the longing of the brute in me to see again his handiwork guided me unconsciously to the bank of shale on the moor, though even at the last minute I had felt something urging me not to go on. That and the chance reading of an idle magazine story had been my undoing; and, when for the second time I lost my memory, and some power outside myself took control in order to cover up the traces before I revisited the scene, the issue of events had passed into other hands.

Sometimes I find myself wondering who that sailor was and what his life had been.

Nobody knows.

The Heart of the Fire

The Moorcock Inn stands on the loneliest of moorland roads, ten miles away from Daneswick station, five hundred feet above Brockleton church spire. From the top of the sugar-loaf hill that protects it from the south-west you can see the steely glimmer of the North Sea; on a foggy night when the wind blows in gently from the east you can hear the distant boom of sirens, for the colliers from Newcastle and the tramps from Steelborough, heavy-laden with rails, hug the coast charily until they can make a straight line for Flamborough Light.

One long, low building is the Moorcock Inn, two-thirds built of gritstone, the rest of brick, with a window jutting out on the southern side on to the moor. It carries a coat of whitewash, and white it stands in springtime against the heather, white and ghostly in the summer nights, when it rises up of a sudden through the mist.

Three sycamores and a larch tree, gnarled and bent like the old seafaring men who pass that way, overhang the back of the house, witnesses, if need were, to the strength of the winter gales.

To the July motorists, the inn seems no better than a dreary house of call in fit keeping with the surrounding wastes. But they are no true judges who pass the door at thirty miles an hour, for the glory of the Moorcock is its kitchen. In autumn, winter or spring, little else matters to the tired foot-traveller sitting on the settle with his beer beside him. Stone-flagged, oak-beamed, with sides of bacon getting ripeness and flavour in the sweet peat smoke, the room would be little different from a score of others in the parish, if it were not for the huge fireplace, as old as the road itself. On the stone mantel is carved a doggerel couplet:

> While on this hearthe of stone a fire you see,
> Kinde Fortune smiles upone ye house of Aislabie.

Mrs Bradley, who keeps the Moorcock, will not have time to tell you the story of the fire if you have but called for tea and turf cakes.

If you were staying at the inn it might be different; but few people care to stay there now.

The great days of the Moorcock were long ago, before the railway between Dunsley and Maltwick was opened, when four times a week the coaches stopped to change horses, and wagoners drew up daily with smoking teams. In the short summer months many a post-chaise from the Crown at Maltwick went by with venturesome gentlefolk from the south.

In the year 1841 the landlord of the Moorcock was one Thomas Aislaby, a big silent man twelve months married to a slip of a girl, who came with a spirit no greater than her wedding portion out of the East Riding.

He was seated one wild February evening by the fire listening to the chatter of the doctor – only a week before he had presented Aislaby with a fine healthy boy – when both men were roused by the unexpected sound of a horse's hoofs on the road outside. Taking the horn lantern from its hook by the door, Aislaby, followed by his dog, went out to meet the traveller. The doctor, left to himself, threw another peat sod on to the fire and stretched himself before the blaze. He was nearly dry after the soaking he had received on his way back from Black Fox Farm. In another half-hour he would have to be on his way again.

'An exceedingly stormy night, sir,' he said to the stranger who had entered the room; 'have you come far?'

'From Dunsley,' the man replied. He was slight of build, with a nervous manner and shifty eyes. He carried a small valise which never left his hand, even after he had sat down in the chair Aislaby had just vacated.

'We're both of us lucky in finding a fire like this on such a night,' the doctor went on, trying his best to put the little man at his ease.

The stranger did not seem to hear the remark. He began to ask a string of questions about the road. How far was it to Maltwick? Would he be likely to lose the track in the dark? He had passed one or two doubtful-looking characters on the way; was there any chance of the doctor's company on the road? The doctor regretted that he was going in the opposite direction. He advised the traveller, if a stranger to the district, to stop the night at the Moorcock. 'This fire alone,' he said, 'would make it worth your while.'

But the man was gazing into the embers with an absent expression of face, as if what he saw there only confirmed his fears.

'No,' he said at last, 'I must get on; I have no time to waste. You, sir, will perhaps join me with a bottle of wine. It is wonderful what heart it puts into a man on nights like these.'

Aislaby, coming in from giving the horse a feed of oats, fetched wine and glasses. (There was good wine in those days in the cellars of the Moorcock.) 'You had better stay here the night,' he said; 'you can start at dawn. The road's lonely enough for a townsman, and your horse seems ridden hard.'

But he would have none of it. He drank the wine, gulping it down as if it had been water, his eyes fixed all the while on the fire. Then, with a hurried 'Good night' to the doctor, he paid his reckoning and was gone.

'Thank the Lord,' said Aislaby, 'they're not all as surly as him'; and he drank what remained in the bottle. 'It's little company we see here, as it is; a curse on his coffin-face.'

'Will you join me with a second bottle, Aislaby?' the doctor asked. 'This is rare wine of yours. Yes; these moors are no place for lily-livered citizens like our friend. Between you and me that valise of his looked uncommonly heavy. If he feared robbery he would have been wiser to have slept here and gone on with the coach tomorrow afternoon. Well, well, I envy you your fire, Aislaby. If I were you, I should never leave it; but old men will die, and babies must be born, and time and tide wait for no man, not even for us doctors. Good night, Aislaby; your wife's doing famously. In ten years' time you won't be sitting here alone by the hearth, I'll wager.'

The doctor was gone. Outside the wind howled through the sycamores; the rain beat viciously against the uncurtained pane. Aislaby drew his chair up into the chimney corner and, like the stranger, gazed thoughtfully into the embers. He was an ambitious man, and in the fire he saw the things he wanted to do. There were patches of moorland he wished to reclaim; good land, water-sodden, that needed but draining to bear heavy crops; there was ironstone to quarry, easily workable, if once you had the capital, and easily got to the railhead when the Maltwick line was finished. He knew that the days of the Moorcock were passing with the coaches, and wished to have more than one iron in the fire as well as to raise again the name of Aislaby. What he saw in the heart of the flame were golden, glittering sovereigns; the clock in the corner ticked money, money, money.

He was aroused from his dreaming by a sharp double knock at the door. There was no sound of hoofs this time, but the traveller was the same. As he came into the fire-light, clutching tightly his valise, Aislaby saw that the man's head was bound with a blood-stained handkerchief. His tired horse had stumbled where the Cowgill beck crossed the road, and the rider – who was no rider – had been thrown. He had trudged back the five long miles on foot, leaving his beast to fare as best it might. Aislaby offered to show him his room. 'It's not what it should be,' he said, 'my wife being but poorly.' The stranger, however, declared that he would prefer to spend the night on the couch by the fire.

'I'll get you blankets then,' said the landlord, and stole upstairs on tiptoe, for he was a fond husband then. He found his wife sleeping soundly in the great four-poster bed, the baby by her side. Returning as quietly as he had come, he paused on the little landing half-way down the stairs. The door of the kitchen had been left ajar. The stranger, seated with his back towards him, had opened the valise. Aislaby caught the glint of golden sovereigns and heard them clink as the man counted them over in his hand. By the time the landlord entered the room, the valise had been closed. The stranger was standing before the fire, his sodden clothes smoking in the heat.

'This is a curious inscription,' he said, as his fingers traced the letters carved in the stone:

> While on this hearthe of stone a fire you see,
> Kinde Fortune smiles upone ye house of Aislabie.

'It's been there since my great-grandfather's time,' said Aislaby. 'For a hundred years and more the fire's never been out. I put on a few sods of peat last thing of a night, and it's always burning in the morning. Gentlefolk have come from Dunsley on purpose to see that fire. There's not another like it in the whole countryside.'

'I can well believe that,' said the stranger. 'There's a strange fascination about a fire. I remember as boys we used to read our future in the embers.'

They sat before the fire in silence. Presently the stranger closed his eyes, but Aislaby did not see him; he was slipping down a glowing cavern that seemed to lead to the warm heart of the world. The stranger fell asleep, his bloody head resting on his arm. And then the fire as it died began to speak to Aislaby. At the first whisper of what it said he threw on another peat, and the flame sprang up again, and the fire's voice was still. Again it sank and, as the shadow crept across the floor, the whisper came again louder and more insistent. Aislaby cast a frightened glance over his shoulder and saw the stranger huddled in his chair, his hand still clasping the valise. Then he knew what the fire was saying. He rose on tiptoe, took one of the empty glasses from the table, filled it with brandy, and drank. Quietly he closed the door. With one long-drawn-out creak, that caused the stranger to turn restlessly in his chair, he drew to the shutters.

Then, throwing a cloth across the man's face, he held his throat in a grip of iron, until a sudden limpness told him that the deed was done.

The work of the night lay ahead of him. Very carefully he removed the fire on to the stone flags that formed the kitchen floor. Then with a crowbar he began to raise the hearthstone. The task was one to tax the strength of two ordinary men, but Aislaby worked with a devil's fury. Next with a pickaxe and shovel he began his assault upon the hard baked earth beneath, stopping from time to time to feed the embers on the floor, lest the fire should go out. Again and again he filled the milking-pail with light yellow soil, creeping out with it into the garden. At last, as the first streaks of dawn came through the chinks between the shutters, he placed the stranger's body, covered with sacking, in the hole he had dug, threw back the rest of the soil, and stamped it down hard and even. When the business of the night was finished, the hearthstone stood again in its accustomed place, the hearth was swept, and the fire, piled high with peat and gorse-root, burned more brightly than it had done for twelve months past.

Out in the garden, walled with stone, Aislaby was busy digging. His wife, as she looked out of her window an hour before sunrise, noticed that he had come upon a patch of light yellow earth in the peaty soil.

Years passed by and Aislaby prospered. Nothing was discovered about the stranger's death; he was identified as a west country ship-owner, a man with few friends, of eccentric habits, who carried on a considerable trade in buying up rotten vessels and sailing them undermanned. He was supposed by many to have been murdered; others believed that his horse had wandered from the road and that, some day, when the bogs were all drained, the body would be found.

'If he had taken our advice,' the doctor would say, when called on for his opinion, 'and slept the night at the Moorcock, the man would have been going about his business now. The underwriters are content at all events, if half of what I hear is true.'

Aislaby took land from the moor, built walls, and cut dikes. He got hold of his ironstone quarry and sold the mining rights to a Steel-borough syndicate. He bought a cottage in this parish, an odd acre in that, and was known at Feversham market, and even as far away as Yokesly, where the great autumn horse fair was held, as a man with a comfortable balance at the bank, with enough of the true Yorkshire-man's knowledge of men and money to do well in the world.

If there were fewer travellers now in the kitchen of the Moor-cock, there were more children. Their first alphabet was the letters carved on the stone mantel. One and all were brought up with a fear in later years they regarded as superstitious lest the fire on the hearth should die.

And what of the man himself? Slow of speech, taciturn, hard as his own ironstone, he was esteemed by all who knew him. Men pointed him out as one whom prosperity had not spoiled; in spite of his money, he seemed fonder than ever of his own fireside. That, indeed, was his favourite spot. In the niche in the corner, where the shadow was deepest, he would sit for hours, watching the flickering flames, the peats stacked ready at his elbow. Last thing at night he raked out the white ash and added fresh fuel. In the early hours of the morning, when all the rest of the house was abed, he would be kneeling on the cold flags, blowing on the embers, or fetching kindling from the stables to tempt the dying flame.

Time passed. The eldest boy, tiring of the gloom that hung about the house and moors the long year round, ran off to sea. They had one letter from him, written in America. He spoke of joining the Federal army. A second, many months later, brought the news of his death in hospital from wounds. The daughters married: one, a farmer in the East Riding village Mrs Aislaby came from, the other, a trooper in the dragoon regiment stationed at Yorborough. Steven, the youngest, an idle ne'er-do-well, brought his wife to live at the Moorcock.

Little by little a change came over Aislaby that soured his nature. Where before he was taciturn, he was now morose. He accepted the narrow tenets of a sect whose zeal was fired by the fear of hell. He even stood up in the market-place at Feversham and proclaimed himself the chief of sinners.

'He makes himself gloomy,' his wife would say, 'by brooding in that dark corner by the fire,' and she tried to get him to like the parlour, with its bay window that looked down southward across the moor. Steven and his wife did not care for the kitchen; the stone floor, they said, was too cold for the children in the evening, and the room only got the afternoon sun. They talked of building out another window, but the old man would not hear of it.

'You waste the peat so,' said Steven's wife one day, 'with the big fires you keep up in the kitchen.'

'And who pays for the peat?' the old man snarled. 'The only thing you have ever brought to the house was your reputation, and we could have spared that.'

Another generation came into being. His wife was dead, buried, according to her wish, in her East Riding churchyard on the wolds. Steven was dead, after living to see his grandchild born, and the house seemed full of womenfolk and children. Aislaby was over ninety. For the last five years he had been unable to get upstairs, and his bed had been moved into the kitchen. They did the cooking now in a smaller room at the back. Visitors from Dunsley, who drove over in the summer to take tea and turf cakes at the Moorcock, would try to get the old man talking.

'He doesn't talk much,' his stout-armed granddaughter would say. 'The only thing he takes an interest in is the fire. He always looks after that, and brings in the peat from the stack outside. And the fires he makes, too! Sometimes of an evening the room gets too hot to live in.'

He was no longer wealthy; his children and grandchildren between them had squandered his earnings; he alone knew with what difficulty they had been won. The hard theology which had held him up ten years before had slipped away, leaving nothing in its place. The only person who seemed able to rouse the old dotard out of his lethargy was his great-grandchild, a girl of nineteen. Mary Aislaby seemed built of a different clay from the rest. Light-hearted and vivacious – too highly strung a close observer might have thought – the last of the old man's savings had been spent in giving the girl an education little suited for her station in life. For the past year she had been living at Stourton Hall as governess to Lady Louthwaite's children.

Little by little it had become the custom to leave Aislaby alone in the kitchen in the evening. He seemed to like gazing in silence into the heart of the fire, and would often drop off to sleep in his chair if left undisturbed. For the young folk the parlour was more cheerful; there was a piano there now and, as Mary said, the larger room rather gave one the creeps at night.

He was sitting propped up in his cushioned chair one August evening; the western window still showed a faint bar of chrome that marked the sunset. The fire on the hearth burnt low, for the day had been sultry. The womenfolk, with the exception of Steven's wife, were spending the night at Dunsley. There were to be great rejoicings at the little port next day; the swing-bridge that spanned the harbour mouth had been lengthened, and it was hoped that once again the slips up the river might send ships to the sea.

The tangled skein of events that had gone to make up his life slipped slowly through the fingers of his memory as the evening deepened into night. He scarcely thought of himself as the same man as the chief actor in the ghastly tragedy that had taken place in the room nearly seventy years before, any more than the fire on the hearth was the same. He had felt the gnawings of remorse, but remorse, too, had grown old along with him. The ill use his family had made of the money was as much a cause of grief as the ill means by which it had come.

Down the road came the soft whirr of cycles; a man and girl passed by; he watched the soft glow of the lamps as they breasted the opposite rise. The sound of the girl's laughter put him in mind of Mary; she at least would raise the fortunes of his house. The voice of Steven's wife, hard and coarse, could be heard in the bar. She was talking about him.

'He can't last much longer,' she said. 'It's not to be hoped that he will. The old man's seen over many days to be happy. It's a wonder that he's still got his wits; he never babbles like my old father would.'

Aislaby smiled to himself. He had certainly never babbled. They were talking again. Steven's wife was speaking. 'So you've heard about Mary?' she said. 'We only knew a couple of days ago. Yes, she's going to marry a lawyer from Yorborough, though I have my doubts whether it will ever come off. His mother and family are all against it.'

'I don't see why they should be,' said the woman she was talking to. 'You're as well known as any in these parts. They've only to go to yonder fire if they want a character,' and she laughed.

'It's easy to laugh,' said Steven's wife, 'but folk like that don't care to have a lot of new relations they know naught about. It's my belief at the least excuse they'd get him to break it off.'

And still Aislaby in his chair by the dying fire smiled the same foolish smile. They were talking again.

'And we shall put out another window in the kitchen,' said Steven's wife. 'It's a good room, and we could let it of a summer to strangers. There's a deal that wants altering about the place, I can tell you. Why, only the other day we found that what we took to be a stone at the back of the kitchen chimney was a great beam, crumbling with the dry rot; if it had been winter, the house would have been on fire before now. Once the old man is gone, it will have to come down, and the hearthstone be pulled up into the bargain. – What was that?'

'Only a sheep coughing on the moor,' said the woman. 'They're terribly human at times.'

In the dark of the kitchen Thomas Aislaby had sunk helplessly to the floor. He tried to call out, but the cry never reached his throat. He tried to move; the whole of his right side was helpless. His brain tingled as if lanced by a hundred needles, yet his thoughts were marvellously clear, clearer than they had been for years. They were only waiting for the fire to die. Up danced the flames. Again he read the old familiar words on the mantel. 'I remember as boys,' someone seemed to whisper in the shadow, 'we used to read our future in the embers.' Whatever happened the fire must not go out; better the house were burnt than that. With his left arm he tried to draw his body along the floor to where the peat stood stacked in the corner. He could not move. Up darted the flame again, but fitfully. Then it sank and all once more was darkness. Were those steps outside? If only he could speak.

'Good night, father,' said Steven's wife. She had scarcely opened the door. Each step of hers on the creaking stair seemed another mile between her and him; when he heard her footfall on the floor above, he knew that she had already gone out of his world. For his world had narrowed down to one twinkling point of light. It changed each moment of the long hours that he lay there on the stone; now it was the face of the stranger of seventy years ago, with the shifty eyes and miserly mouth; now the face of his dead wife, as he had first seen her in the East Riding village. Each picture faded away to be succeeded by another, smaller and fainter. The fire was dying. The moon had risen, and in its clear white light the floor seemed colder. Gradually a numbness crept up from his ankles to his knees, from his knees to his thighs. He made one last effort to reach the fuel, but the fire on the hearth was dead.

There came a double knock at the door that he remembered as well as if it had been yesterday. A window up above was thrown open.

'Who is there?' said Steven's wife, and her voice sounded loud and shrill in the silence of the August night.

Aislaby knew who it was; with a cry of mortal terror he half-raised himself on his arm, and then fell heavily with his head on the cold hearthstone.

The Clock

I liked your description of the people at the *pension*. I can just picture that rather sinister Miss Cornelius, with her toupee and clinking bangles. I don't wonder you felt frightened that night when you found her sleep-walking in the corridor. But after all, why shouldn't she sleep-walk? As to the movements of the furniture in the lounge on the Sunday, you are, I suppose, in an earthquake zone, though an earthquake seems too big an explanation for the ringing of that little handbell on the mantel-piece. It's rather as if our parlourmaid – another new one! – were to call a stray elephant to account for the teapot we found broken yesterday. You have at least escaped the eternal problem of maids in Italy.

Yes, my dear, I most certainly believe you. I have never had experiences quite like yours, but your mention of Miss Cornelius has reminded me of something rather similar that happened nearly twenty years ago, soon after I left school. I was staying with my aunt in Hampstead. You remember her, I expect; or, if not her, the poodle, Monsieur, that she used to make perform such pathetic tricks. There was another guest, whom I had never met before, a Mrs Caleb. She lived in Lewes and had been staying with my aunt for about a fortnight, recuperating after a series of domestic up-heavals, which had culminated in her two servants leaving her at an hour's notice, without any reason, according to Mrs Caleb; but I wondered. I had never seen the maids; I had seen Mrs Caleb and, frankly, I disliked her. She left the same sort of impression on me as I gather your Miss Cornelius leaves on you – something queer and secretive; underground, if you can use the expression, rather than underhand. And I could feel in my body that she did not like me.

It was summer. Joan Denton – you remember her; her husband was killed in Gallipoli – had suggested that I should go down to spend the day with her. Her people had rented a little cottage some three miles out of Lewes. We arranged a day. It was gloriously fine for a wonder, and I had planned to leave that stuffy old Hampstead house before the old ladies were astir. But Mrs Caleb waylaid me in the hall, just as I was going out.

'I wonder,' she said, 'I wonder if you could do me a small favour. If you do have any time to spare in Lewes – only if you do – would you be so kind as to call at my house? I left a little travelling-clock there in the hurry of parting. If it's not in the drawing-room, it will be in my bedroom or in one of the maids' bedrooms. I know I lent it to the cook, who was a poor riser, but I can't remember if she returned it. Would it be too much to ask? The house has been locked up for twelve days, but everything is in order. I have the keys here; the large one is for the garden gate, the small one for the front door.'

I could only accept, and she proceeded to tell me how I could find Ash Grove House.

'You will feel quite like a burglar,' she said. 'But mind, it's only if you have time to spare.'

As a matter of fact I found myself glad of any excuse to kill time. Poor old Joan had been taken suddenly ill in the night – they feared appendicitis – and though her people were very kind and asked me to stay to lunch, I could see that I should only be in the way, and made Mrs Caleb's commission an excuse for an early departure.

I found Ash Grove without difficulty. It was a medium-sized red-brick house, standing by itself in a high-walled garden that bounded a narrow lane. A flagged path led from the gate to the front door, in front of which grew, not an ash, but a monkey-puzzle, that must have made the rooms unnecessarily gloomy. The side door, as I expected, was locked. The dining-room and drawing-room lay on either side of the hall and, as the windows of both were shuttered, I left the hall door open, and in the dim light looked round hurriedly for the clock, which, from what Mrs Caleb had said, I hardly expected to find in either of the downstairs rooms. It was neither on table nor mantelpiece. The rest of the furniture was carefully covered over with white dust-sheets. Then I went upstairs. But, before doing so, I closed the front door. I did in fact feel rather like a burglar, and I thought that if anyone did happen to see the front door open, I might have difficulty in explaining things. Happily the upstairs windows were not shuttered. I made a hurried search of the principal bedrooms. They had been left in apple-pie order; nothing was out of place; but there was no sign of Mrs Caleb's clock. The impression that the house gave me – you know the sense of person-ality that a house conveys – was neither pleasing nor displeasing, but it was stuffy, stuffy from the absence of fresh air, with an additional stuffiness added, that seemed to come out from the hangings and quilts and antimacassars. The corridor, on to which the bedrooms I had examined opened, communicated with a smaller wing, an older part of the house, I imagined, which contained a box-room and the maids' sleeping quarters. The last door that I unlocked – (I should say that the doors of all the rooms were locked, and relocked by me after I had glanced inside them) – contained the object of my search. Mrs Caleb's travelling-clock was on the mantelpiece, ticking away merrily.

That was how I thought of it at first. And then for the first time I realised that there was something wrong. The clock had no business to be ticking. The house had been shut up for twelve days. No one had come in to air it or to light fires. I remembered how Mrs Caleb had told my aunt that if she left the keys with a neighbour, she was never sure who might get hold of them. And yet the clock was going. I wondered if some vibration had set the mechanism in motion, and pulled out my watch to see the time. It was five minutes to one. The clock on the mantelpiece said four minutes to the hour. Then, without quite knowing why, I shut the door on to the landing, locked myself in, and again looked round the room. Nothing was out of place. The only thing that might have called for remark was that there appeared to be a slight indentation on the pillow and the bed; but the mattress was a feather mattress, and you know how difficult it is to make them perfectly smooth. You won't need to be told that I gave a hurried glance under the bed – do you remember your supposed burglar in Number Six at St Ursula's? – and then, and much more reluctantly, opened the doors of two horribly capacious cupboards, both happily empty, except for a framed text with its face to the wall. By this time I really was frightened. The clock went ticking on. I had a horrible feeling that an alarm might go off at any moment, and the thought of being in that empty house was almost too much for me. However, I made an attempt to pull myself together. It might after all be a fourteen-day clock. If it were, then it would be almost run down. I could roughly find out how long the clock had been going by winding it up. I hesitated to put the matter to the test; but the uncertainty was too much for me. I took it out of its case and began to wind. I had scarcely turned the winding-screw twice when it stopped. The clock clearly was not running down; the hands had been set in motion probably only an hour or two before. I felt cold and faint and, going to the window, threw up the sash, letting in the sweet, live air of the garden. I knew now that the house was queer, horribly queer. Could someone be living in the house? Was someone else in the house now? I thought that I had been in all the rooms, but had I? I had only just opened the bath-room door, and I had certainly not opened any cupboards, except those in the room in which I was. Then, as I stood by the open window, wondering what I should do next and feeling that I just couldn't go down that corridor into the darkened hall to fumble at the latch of the front door with I don't know what behind me, I heard a noise. It was very faint at first, and seemed to be coming from the stairs. It was a curious noise – not the noise of anyone climbing up the stairs, but – you will laugh if this letter reaches you by a morning post – of something hopping up the stairs, like a very big bird would hop. I heard it on the landing; it stopped. Then there was a curious scratching noise against one of the bedroom doors, the sort of noise you can make with the nail of your little finger scratching polished wood. Whatever it was, was coming slowly down the corridor, scratching at the doors as it went. I could stand it no longer. Nightmare pictures of locked doors opening filled my brain. I took up the clock, wrapped it in my mackintosh, and dropped it out of the window on to a flower-bed. Then I managed to crawl out of the window and, getting a grip of the sill, 'successfully negotiated', as the journalists would say, 'a twelve-foot drop'. So much for our much abused gym at St Ursula's. Picking up the mackintosh, I ran round to the front door and locked it. Then I felt I could breathe, but not until I was on the far side of the gate in the garden wall did I feel safe.

Then I remembered that the bedroom window was open. What was I to do? Wild horses wouldn't have dragged me into that house again unaccompanied. I made up my mind to go to the police-station and tell them everything. I should be laughed at, of course, and they might easily refuse to believe my story of Mrs Caleb's commission. I had actually begun to walk down the lane in the direction of the town, when I chanced to look back at the house. The window that I had left open was shut.

No, my dear, I didn't see any face or anything dreadful like that . . . and, of course, it may have shut by itself. It was an ordinary sash-window, and you know they are often difficult to keep open.

And the rest? Why, there's really nothing more to tell. I didn't even see Mrs Caleb again. She had had some sort of fainting fit just before lunch-time, my aunt informed me on my return, and had had to go to bed. Next morning I travelled down to Cornwall to join mother and the children. I thought I had forgotten all about it, but when three years later Uncle Charles suggested giving me a travelling-clock for a twenty-first birthday present, I was foolish enough to prefer the alternative that he offered, a collected edition of the works of Thomas Carlyle.

Peter Levisham

I have just finished reading Sinclair's book on Peter Levisham. It is a thoroughly competent monograph, written primarily from the legal point of view, and is a worthy addition to the series in which it appears. It is a pity that no mention is made of the three years Levisham spent in the States, as it has been suggested that it was there that he acquired his knowledge of anatomy and pharmacology. And there is no real evidence to show that he was connected with the Dumbarton Case, cited on page 280. The bibliography at the end of the volume is an admirable bit of work. I see that there are at least half a dozen books and articles that are new to me and that curiosity will impel me to read.

I suppose it is only natural that I should be interested in Levisham. As a young man I was once briefed for his defence, and to this day believe that he was innocent of the crime with which he was on that occasion charged. But the real source of the interest that I have in everything appertaining to his life and career centres around the story which Daniel Crockett told me. Crockett's name is, of course, familiar to all students of the trial. He is referred to in Sinclair's book as a chance acquaintance. Crockett himself would never have used the phrase.

Prior to his appearance in the witness-box I had never seen Crockett, but I met him shortly afterwards, when I attended my first board meeting of the Crippled Children's Holiday Homes, and again later when he was Northcote's guest at one of the quarterly dinners of the Addison Club. It is from that evening that I date our friendship.

Crockett was a remarkable man. His business was connected with the Baltic trade. He was a liveryman of more than one City company, a man of high integrity, reserved in manner, and with a stiff, old-fashioned courtesy. He lived with an invalid sister in a large house at Dulwich, one of the most peaceful homes I have ever entered, and in perfect keeping with his character. If a fairy were to turn Daniel

Crockett into a chair or table, you felt that it would be just such chairs and tables as you found at Ventnor Place.

But why was he remarkable? I have often tried to find an answer to the question. There were three distinct sides to the man's life, Mark Lane and the City, his library and the Johnson Club, his pocket Greek Testament and the corner seat he occupied in the ministers' gallery in the Friends' Meeting House. Yet the three, with all their activities, though distinct, were congruous.

We were seated one evening in the library at Ventnor Place, when the conversation turned on Peter Levisham. I spoke of my first meeting with him, and I remember expressing regret that my advocacy had been the means of his acquittal. A verdict of 'Guilty' might have spared so many innocent lives, might, indeed, have kept him innocent and spared his own. Crockett was silent for some minutes; I could see that he was deeply moved.

'I should like to tell you the story of my relations with Levisham,' he said at last. 'My sister knows the facts, and at times we speak of them together; but she is the only person to whom I have confided them. Thirty years ago, on the evening of the first Friday in November, I was walking down Bishopsgate after attending a committee meeting. I had occasion to cross the road, and had almost reached the opposite pavement, when I was nearly run down by a rapidly moving dray. I had just time to jump aside and to clutch hold of a man who was closely following me.

' "If you don't look where you're going, you'll lose your life one of these days."

'Before I knew what I was saying, the words had come from my mouth. The man looked at me with a puzzled expression, laughed, thanked me, and was gone. It was the most trivial incident, and yet one which disturbed me. I am, as you know, somewhat slow of speech, and though the occasion called for haste and agility, comment was unnecessary. There was something contentious about the remark. It was not perhaps impertinent but it was unnecessary, and I felt that I should have resented it had I been in the stranger's place.

'Eleven years later, two days before Christmas, I was driving in a gig over a lonely road in the East Riding of Yorkshire, a district I knew from boyhood. The night was still and frosty and an unclouded moon showed every detail of the landscape. At the top of a low rise I overtook a man who was carrying a heavy burden on his shoulder. I asked him if he would like a lift. He accepted my offer and climbed up beside me. He told me that he was an American and that he had been visiting some relations. He was bound for Driffield, where he hoped to pick up an early morning train for York. I told him that he had far to go, but that I would gladly put him five or six miles on his way. The time passed quickly. He was an excellent talker, a shrewd observer of men and things. I stopped at the Driffield crossroads and explained to him how, by taking a certain short cut, he could lessen his journey. He thanked me and bade me good night. I touched the mare with the whip and shouted one final instruction: "Remember to take the stile through the wood and, whatever you do, leave the Gallow-tree Oak behind you." I had hardly spoken, when I realised how meaningless my words would appear. Gallow-tree Oak was familiar to me since boyhood, but I had made no mention of the spot in the directions I had given to the stranger. I had told him to avoid a place he did not know. And why had I spoken so emphatically? Even if he took the wrong turning by the Oak, it would only mean that he would join the high road again and lose little more than half an hour. I was both annoyed and perplexed, but the incident was for the time being forgotten.

'I pass on to the summer of 1891, when I was staying with friends at Porlock. It was the last Saturday in September. I had been for a long walk, and had sat down to eat my sandwiches by the roadside at a point where a footpath led into a plantation of larches. A notice-board, recently painted, called attention to the fact that the woods were private property, and that trespassers would be prosecuted with the utmost rigour of the law. I sat with my back against the post, and did not see the man who came down the path from the wood until he was climbing the stile. He was of middle height, bearded, aged perhaps fifty. From his dress I took him to be a Nonconformist minister. He wished me good day and then, as he read the notice, burst out laughing.

'"How typically British," he said. "Here have I been walking for an hour through the wood with no one to say me nay, only to find on gaining the high road that the path is private and that I am subject to the utmost rigour of the law! Why could not they have put a notice-board at both ends of the path? Isn't it just as reasonable to approach the road from the wood as the wood from the road? The warning, like most warnings, has come too late." As he spoke, a curious sensation of fear seemed to come over me; I felt cold; my limbs began to tremble.

'"You are not well," he said. "What is the matter?"

'While he was speaking, I knew that he was the same man whom I had met on the two occasions I have described to you. I rose to my feet. The bull-terrier, the companion of my walk, had been investigating a rabbit-burrow, but seeing that at last I was moving, he trotted up to me; round the bend of the road came a wagon loaded high with corn.

' "I don't know your name," I said, "but I have met you twice before, once in the traffic of Bishopsgate, and once on a winter night when I spoke to you at the Driffield crossroads. I beseech you to listen to this warning before it is too late and see to your ways."

'He turned round on me in a flash with a dark scowl on his face, and burst into a torrent of vile abuse. I believe he would have laid hands on me but for the dog, and the fact that the wagoner was within fifty yards of us. It was in the company of the wagoner that I walked back to Porlock. The stranger followed us in the distance for about a quarter of a mile, and then turned off down a lane that led to Minehead. I still remember how I hesitated that night before leaving my bedroom door unlocked.

'Those were the three occasions on which I met Peter Levisham prior to the trial. The 12th of November of that year was a Saturday. It is our custom at breakfast to read a portion of Scripture. I had closed the book and we were sitting for a few moments in silent meditation, when I felt it borne in upon me that my presence was required in London. Three or four times in my life I have had similar leadings. I have felt the presence of an impelling power, bidding me go I knew not whither to do I knew not what. It is a terrible experience, and I believe a very dangerous experience, one that no one should seek and which should be wrestled with in prayer to see whether it is of God. I retired to my own chamber, and then saw my sister and cancelled the engagements I had made for the morning. I travelled by train to Charing Cross, where I got out. Standing on the pavement in the Strand, I watched the stream of buses pass. I did not know which one to take. I did not know where I was going. While waiting, my attention was called to a blind man, who stood quite alone, and who seemed unaccustomed to the London traffic. I asked him if I could be of any assistance, and he handed me a slip of paper on which was written an address in the City. I told him that I would go with him, and we got on to a bus together. After seeing him to his destination, I walked a little way farther up the street, until I was accosted by a flower-woman, who stood immediately opposite a large block of offices. She was a cheery, importunate soul, and eventually she persuaded me into buying one of her roses. It was while I was speaking to the woman that I felt for the first time a strong conviction that I had rightly followed the leadings of my guide. I entered the block of offices, read the list of names in the lobby and, disregarding the lift, began to climb the stairs. I climbed to the very top of the building. On my right hand was a door marked "Mivart, Dixon & Co," on the left a door marked "P. W. Foster." I knocked at the latter and, as I did so, I heard the clocks strike the hour of eleven. There was no reply, and I knocked again. After waiting for a moment I opened the door and walked in. The room was empty.

'I confess that I was surprised. I sat down on one of the two chairs that the office contained, and looked about me. The room was sparsely furnished: an old roll-top desk, a table, a tear-off calendar, two or three directories, a safe, two large iron boxes with the name "P. W. Foster" painted in white letters, and over the mantelpiece a large framed photograph of the International Congress of Philatelists, taken at Berne in 1889.

'I sat in that room for an hour and no one came. Twice I rose to go, but on each occasion I was prevented by the strong conviction that I was doing what I was sent to do, that my presence was required there. I spent as little time as I could in speculation, trying to keep my mind quiet and passive. When the bells chimed twelve, the luminous cloud that seemed to have been present with me all morning lifted, and I left the room. As I walked down the stairs, I remembered that the tear-off calendar in the office showed the date as the 12th of November, and so would presumably point to the occupier having called there that morning. The flower-woman was still standing opposite the door of the building. "Well now, sir," she said, "if you haven't gone and left your rose behind you. And, as luck would have it, I've just another one left, a lovely rose, gentleman. It's just gone twelve and you're in a hurry to get home to dinner, but buy one for the lady!" I gave her a shilling and left the flower with her. I am not used to flowers, and I suppose that was the reason I mislaid the other in Foster's office.

'Most people, in considering my conduct that morning, would say that I acted foolishly on a foolish impulse. I had been of some slight service to a blind man and a flower-woman. That was all that could be set off against the hour I had wasted sitting in an empty room.

'It seems strange, on looking back, that until the time of the trial I never thought of connecting what I did on that Saturday with Peter Levisham. I do not as a rule read the criminal news in the papers, and so knew nothing of the murder of Mendelsohn, the Jew, in Blooms-bury, and the subsequent hue and cry that led to Levisham's arrest. The trial had actually begun before I was aware of it. I saw a repro-duction of a photograph of the accused man and recognised him at once. There remained the awful problem of what I was to do. You will remember the strong circumstantial evidence that pointed to the crime being committed between the hours of eleven and twelve. I read how the defence was an alibi, that Levisham, who was then passing under the name of Foster, declared that he was in his office in the city. I learned how the porter had seen him enter the building between ten and eleven; how he was prepared to swear that he had not passed out until half-past twelve, when Levisham had made some remark about a horse which both had backed for a certain race. All this is, of course, familiar to you, with the fact that the man was a past master in the art of disguise. There was, too, some other piece of corroborative evidence, that slips my memory.'

Crockett passed his hand wearily across his brow. I reminded him of how a clerk in the firm whose office was immediately opposite had seen Levisham some time about the hour in question, when he, Levisham, had looked in to borrow a copy of Bradshaw's Rail-way Guide.

'Yes, that was it,' said Crockett. 'Everything really turned on the alibi. I lay awake all night, torn by perplexity. In the morning I got in touch with the Public Prosecutor, and told him that I had waited for an hour alone in that office for the occupier to appear. I said very little about my previous meetings with Levisham. He gathered, I think, that he was a chance acquaintance, whom I had tried unsuccessfully to help and who had refused to profit by my counsel. The flower-woman was found without difficulty, and corroborated what I had said. The rose that I had bought from her was found, too, lying withered on the mantelpiece.'

I asked Crockett if he had any doubt as to Levisham's guilt.

'None,' he said. 'If I had, I believe I should have kept silence. But when I looked into his face that day at Porlock, I knew.'

I asked him, too, if he had ever compared the dates of his meeting Levisham with the dates of the murders to which Levisham ultim-ately confessed.

He told me that he had. A month after the Bishopsgate meeting, the rich widow, Mrs Jones, was poisoned at Highbury. A week after the encounter at the Driffield crossroads the body of the man McKenzie was found stabbed through the heart in an outhouse at Purworth

Hall, near Darlington. On the very day that Levisham met Crockett near Porlock he must have left for Bath, where he murdered old Mr Bengrove on the following morning.

'In the three cases between the warning and the commission of the crime,' he said, 'there was a decreasing interval. It had become more and more easy for him to kill pity; it had become more and more easy for him to kill.'

And Daniel Crockett, his story finished, bowed his head in prayer.

Yes, I suppose in a sense Sinclair's book is clever and competent, and it will, of course, meet with a large sale. He would not understand me, if I were to call it superficial.

Miss Cornelius

Andrew Saxon was senior science master at Cornford School. Cornford is a new school, remodelled on an old foundation. H.M.I.s, when they can afford it, and that is not often, send their boys there, especially if they have a bent for science. Many parents thought that Andrew should have been headmaster, but he himself was aware of his limitations. That he was more of a teacher than an administrator, more of a stimulus than a teacher, one might guess after reading that brilliantly disturbing book, Saxon and Butler's *Introduction to the Principles of Organic Chemistry*.

He was known to the boys as 'Anglo-Saxon', or 'Old Alfred', and was treated by them with an affectionate respect, which was increased by the knowledge that he was a first-rate rifle shot, and had once been runner-up for the King's Prize at Bisley.

Saxon had never shown any special interest in psychical research, but when his friend Clinton, the manager of the Eastern Counties Bank, asked him to take part in a joint investigation into what was going on in Meadowfield Terrace, he did not like to refuse. The house was occupied by Parke, a cashier in the bank, Mrs Parke and two children, a cook, who had been with Parke for five years, a rather slow-witted girl of sixteen who acted as nurse-parlourmaid, and Miss Cornelius. Saxon knew Miss Cornelius by sight as the elderly lady who lived in that rather delightful house by the vicarage. He understood from Clinton that it was undergoing extensive renovations, and that while the plumbers and painters were about the place she had suggested lodging with the Parkes, who were always glad to receive paying guests.

The manifestations had been going on over a period of three weeks. They consisted apparently of rappings, noises like those made by the dropping of very heavy weights, unaccountable movements of tables and articles of furniture, the mysterious locking and unlocking of doors, and, perhaps strangest of all, the throwing about, apart from any observed human agency, of all sorts of miscellaneous objects, ranging from chessmen and gramophone needles to lumps of coal and metal candlesticks.

'With a little luck it looks as if I should be in for an interesting evening,' said Saxon to his wife. 'If I were to hazard a guess, I should say that the servant-girl is somehow connected with it.'

Certainly the evening was interesting. In the drawing-room at Meadowfield Terrace Saxon was introduced by Clinton to Parke and Mrs Parke and Miss Cornelius. At his suggestion Parke recapitulated the happenings of the last three weeks, his wife and Miss Cornelius from time to time adding or correcting details. The account was given in a straightforward manner that impressed Saxon, nor could he see in any of the three traces of hysteria. All were obviously disturbed at what they had witnessed; Mrs Parke indeed looked worn and harassed; but neither she nor Miss Cornelius had lost their sense of humour.

'Let us agree on one thing,' he said, 'before we go any further. I know very little about poltergeist manifestations – I have an open mind on the subject – but we must not presume an abnormal (I use the word in preference to supernatural) explanation, until we have excluded conscious or unconscious fraud. Apart, too, from the question of fraud, what has been seen may be connected in some way with human agency. We must all watch each other; we must even be suspicious of each other. Anything for a peaceful life. That's right, isn't it, Mrs Parke?'

They all agreed.

'What about the maids?' said Clinton.

There was no difficulty there. It was the girl's night out, and the cook had been given leave to spend the evening with a friend.

Miss Cornelius suggested that they should lock both doors, and that two of the party should make a careful search in all the rooms, to make certain that there was no one hiding to play tricks.

'You had better go with Mr Clinton,' said Mrs Parke, laughing nervously. 'I'd almost rather anything happened than find a man under my bed.'

They sat in the drawing-room while Clinton and Miss Cornelius made the round of the house. Saxon looked at his watch. 'It's just half-past eight,' he said. 'And that's about the time that things begin to look lively,' said Parke. 'Listen! The rappings have begun already.'

There could be no doubt about the noises, low and muffled, as if someone were striking a rubber pad with a hammer; but it was impossible to locate them, to say whether they came from beyond the walls or the ceiling. They were quite distinct from the footsteps of Clinton and Miss Cornelius, who could be heard moving about in one of the rooms above. A minute or two later the voices of the two were heard in conversation, as they came down the stairs. Then there was a crash, and Miss Cornelius called out: 'What was that?' Parke and Saxon ran out into the hall. A wooden horse, belonging to the children, which Clinton declared that he had seen on the landing outside the nursery door, was lying with its head broken at the foot of the stairs. The evening's programme had commenced.

It was a full and varied programme, and the intervals between the items were short, filled with a tense, almost exhilarating, feeling of excitement as to what in the world would happen next. Saxon and Clinton, who had both previously agreed to take notes of what they saw, were kept busy writing. A little before half-past nine there was a lull in the proceedings.

'They usually close down about now,' said Parke with a rather forced laugh. 'What about some coffee, Maisie?'

'I wonder if you would mind Mr Clinton and me running over our notes together in the dining-room?' Saxon asked. 'I don't think we shall detain you very long.'

They went into the adjoining room, and Clinton noticed with surprise that his companion turned the key in the lock.

'Well, what about it?' said the bank manager. 'I confess the whole thing baffles me.'

Saxon was silent for a moment, and then broke out petulantly: 'I wish to goodness you had never brought me here, Clinton. We have got landed in the very deuce of a mess, and that is why you and I have got to come to some decision.'

'I'm afraid I don't quite follow.'

'I'll put a question to you. From what you have seen this evening do you suspect anyone?'

Clinton looked troubled and was silent.

'Parke?' went on Saxon. 'Do you suspect him?'

'No, oh, no!'

'Mrs Parke?'

'No, certainly not.'

'Miss Cornelius, then?'

'I don't think so. No.'

'You don't think so. Well, I do. Mind you, three quarters of what I have seen I can't account for at present. Why the rocking-chair should go on moving as it did, for example. I searched in vain for a thread of black cotton – I even looked for a hair. On the other hand, when that lump of coal flew across the room, I am almost positive that it came from the hand of Miss Cornelius. She had been standing by the coal-box only a minute before. If you noticed, she was constantly fidgeting with different articles on the table and mantelpiece. Her hands were never still. It seemed almost that she had to hold her itching fingers down. I did see – and that I am prepared to swear to – her throw the pen that stuck in the ceiling. The whole thing was suspicious. It's unusual, to say the least of it, to find pens lying about on the mantelpiece. There is one in this room, you will notice; put there, I suggest, by Miss Cornelius to await the opportune moment. In the case I'm speaking of she held it in her hand behind her back, and gave it a curious little flick with her thumb. I believe with practice I could do the same myself.'

He took the pen from the mantelpiece and repeated the action he had described.

'There!' he cried triumphantly, 'I told you it could be done. It's stuck in the sofa cushion instead of the ceiling, for which I was aiming; but you must admit that my hand was behind my back for not more than a fraction of a second. Why did you hesitate when I mentioned Miss Cornelius's name, when you were emphatic in denying that you suspected the Parkes?'

'A good many of the objects certainly seemed to come from her direction,' said Clinton slowly, 'and it struck me that once or twice she called attention to them almost too soon. You know the quick, startled way she had of exclaiming: "What's that?" so that all of us looked in the direction she was looking in. Well, it struck me as a bit fishy – that was all.'

'Look at your notes a minute,' Saxon went on. 'Things have happened this evening on the stairs, in this room, and in the drawing-room; while we have been sitting all together, and while some of us have been here and some in the drawing-room; but you will notice that the manifestations other than the noises and rappings only took place in the presence of Miss Cornelius.'

'And you suggest – ?'

'That the sole invariable antecedent is probably the cause.'

'Then what the deuce are we to do about it?'

'The only thing we can do,' said Saxon – 'I say we, but I mean I, because I don't see why you need be dragged into it – is to go into that other room and be perfectly frank with them. These things have got to stop. Apart altogether from the strain on Mrs Parke, there are the children to be considered. There will be an unholy row, possibly sleepless nights for some of us, but we've got to take the bull by the horns. Let's go in and get it over. It's like striking an old woman,' he added, after a pause. 'My God! Clinton, I wish you had never brought me here.'

'And what do you make of it all?' asked Miss Cornelius with a smile, when they were all assembled in the drawing-room. 'I do so hope you are going to set our fears at rest.'

Saxon looked her straight in the face. He saw the false fringe, the wrinkles, and the eyes, dark and challenging, in which cruelty lurked.

'Mrs Parke,' he began, 'I am more sorry than I can say, and I hate what I am going to say, but I believe that Miss Cornelius is closely concerned with what we have witnessed tonight. Miss Cornelius, won't you be frank with us? What is said now need go no farther than this room.'

They were all looking at her. Her face was the colour of old ivory.

'Maisie,' she said, 'this is an outrage! What right has this man, who has been talking to me this evening as if he were my friend, to turn suddenly round and try to blacken my character in the presence of people whom I have known intimately for years? I know nothing of what he has been saying. I am as guiltless of fraud or trickery as those two little children asleep upstairs.'

'Excuse me,' Saxon interrupted, 'it is only fair to remind you all that we did agree to see this matter through and to disregard the personal factor. I said I was going to be suspicious of everyone, and I have been.'

'That's right,' said Parke reluctantly. 'But what is it you accuse Miss Cornelius of?'

'I don't accuse her of anything. But I do say that I saw her throw a pen; on several occasions I almost saw objects leaving her hand; and that the phenomena we have witnessed this evening – I should be the first to admit that I cannot at present explain them all – have always occurred in her presence. One word more and I have done. I want to be charitable in what I say and think. I do not say that Miss Cornelius has consciously deceived us. I think that probably unknown to her-self she has developed unusual powers of legerdemain, and that she has used it to foster that extraordinary, exhilarating feeling of excite-ment and suspense which we have been conscious of this evening. And now I think I will go.'

'He thinks he will go!' said Miss Cornelius, speaking with pent-up fury. 'He sprinkles me with pitch and then he thinks he can clear off.

But let me tell you, Mr Saxon, an old woman speaking to a comparatively young man, that you will live to be sorry for this day. You will know what it is to pray that your tongue might have withered at its roots rather than it should have said the things it has said tonight.'

*   *   *

'I may have been too abrupt,' said Saxon, as he walked back home with Clinton. 'My wife tells me that I have no tact; but it struck me that the only thing to do was to cut quickly and deeply, and not waste time over the anaesthetic.'

'The fault is mine,' the other replied, 'in having dragged you into it. Though I'm sorry for the Parkes, I'm almost more sorry for you. I think you did the right thing, and I don't mind telling you that it's more than I could have done.'

Saxon found his wife sitting up for him. 'Were the spooks genuine after all?' she said. 'I'm longing to hear all about it.'

'I think I'd rather leave it over until tomorrow. It's not been exactly a pleasant evening, and I am afraid I have made one enemy for life – Miss Cornelius.'

*   *   *

He told her all about it next morning at breakfast.

'I don't know whom to pity most,' she said, 'you or the poor old lady. I've always thought of her as one of those quiet, inoffensive old dears, that give the atmosphere to the drawing-rooms of South Coast boarding-establishments. Anyhow, I'm not going to have you worried about it. Why not get off to Flinton for a long weekend of golf? You were going to some time during the holidays, you know.'

Saxon hummed and hawed, and raked about half-heartedly for excuses, but she could see that the idea appealed to him, and by noon she had seen him off.

That was on a Friday afternoon. It was certainly very jolly down at Flinton. They were an usually congenial little party at the Dormy House. MacAllister of Trinity was there with a young biochemist from King's, with whom he crossed swords to good purpose in the evenings. And he was on top of his form as well. Monday morning brought a long letter from his wife.

Dear Old Alfred [she wrote], I'm quite sure you did the right thing in getting away. The clouds – metaphorical – are blowing over. You'll hardly believe me when I tell you what I've done. I've bearded the lion and taken the bull by the horns. In other words, I've seen and spoken with Miss Cornelius. Now don't call me rash or foolish, until you hear how it all came about. Somehow I didn't feel like going to church this morning – the new half-warmed fish curate was preaching – and went for a walk instead down by the river. I saw Miss Cornelius in the distance, sitting on a seat, and looking lonely and withered, and to cut a long story short, I went up to her and told her how sorry I was that all this should have happened. At first I could see that she did not quite know what to make of me, but she soon began, if not to blossom out, at least to burgeon, and was really very kind. She admitted that she was inexcusably rude to you, and thought you would understand that the provocation was great. She says that she is entirely innocent of any attempt at deceit, and if she did throw the pen, that she knew nothing about it. She still believes that the manifestations are the work of some Poltergeist – I don't know if that's the way you spell it – and the utmost she will admit is that there is an element of infection about these things and that, unknown to herself, she may have got infected. I gather that the Parkes were very nice about it all, and that, as her house was practically finished apart from the outside painting, they mutually agreed – is that a right use of the word mutual, you old pedant? – that she should go back there. And there she is: and that's that.

There was a postscript too.

Don't come back until Wednesday, and get all the golf and exercise you can. In fact, you can't very well come back before then, because I have decided to spring-clean the study. It ought to have been done at Easter. I'll take care of your papers.

'Molly at her best,' thought Saxon, with affectionate pride, 'clearing up her husband's messes without his leave and making no fuss about it.'

When, after enjoying his days of grace to the full, he returned home on the Wednesday, the events of the previous week appeared strangely remote. It seemed indeed that, whatever his relations with Miss Cornelius were to be in the future, his wife had gained from his encounter a new acquaintance.

'Not only did I beard the lion, as I told you in my letter,' said Molly, 'but since then I have braved the lion, or rather lioness, in her den. And it really is the most charming old house, Andrew. I'd no idea Cornford could boast such a place. I've got some photographs somewhere that Miss Cornelius gave me. They make you quite covetous and uncharitable, like the illustrated advertisements of houses for sale in *Country Life*.'

The week that followed passed without incident. Miss Cornelius called one afternoon when he was out, and brought with her a new stereoscopic camera to show his wife. The old lady, curiously enough, was an ardent photographer – Saxon already had revised Molly's South Coast boarding-house picture of her – and offered to take some views of the house. Mrs Saxon jumped at the proposal. They would be just the thing to send to her sister in New Zealand, with the vivacious Molly in the foreground.

The prints were excellent.

'Now, if only you had married an actress, Old Alfred,' she said, 'we could turn an honest penny by making this into an illustrated article. Me in the garden – yes, I adore flowers; me in the study – I don't know what I should do without my books; me in the kitchen – I always make my own omelettes; me in my boudoir – yes, I picked up that old mirror in Spain.'

'My dear,' said Saxon, 'it's really wonderful the amount of unmitigated nonsense you can talk.'

Miss Cornelius sent, too, a few photographs of the interior of her own house. No one would have taken them for the work of an amateur, and when seen through the stereoscope an impression of solidity and depth was obtained, 'as if,' Mrs Saxon said, 'you were really inside the rooms.'

Then, as August drew to a close in a week of sultry heat and thunder, things began to happen, strange and purposeless things, that brought into the little house an atmosphere of tension that was completely foreign to it. At first they laughed when they found the toast-rack lying at the top of the stairs. Then one evening Molly's bedroom slippers moved across the room and landed neatly together in the empty fire-grate. On another occasion Saxon's pyjamas disappeared from underneath his pillow and, after a long search, were found tightly knotted together on the top of the wardrobe. The papers in his study were disarranged. One morning a jumper Molly had been knitting lay in the coal-box, unravelled, the wool wound in inextricable tangles around the legs of the tables and chairs. They could make nothing of it.

'It almost looks,' said Molly, with a forced laugh, 'as if spooks were trying to convince us that we had been too hasty in our judgment of Miss Cornelius.'

'Don't be foolish, my dear,' replied Saxon, testily. 'It's far more likely that that woman has been getting at the maids. My advice for the moment is to keep our eyes open and to say nothing to anyone about it.'

But he himself was deeply disturbed. Though professing an open mind on matters supernatural, he was hardly prepared for this cold and most unpleasant draught of doubt. He found himself thinking, more often than he liked to acknowledge, of Miss Cornelius and that venomous outburst of hate. What if she – ? But of course, there must be some natural explanation. And so the week dragged by.

It was Sunday morning. They had finished their breakfast and Saxon, rising from the table, stood looking out of the window, when, turning round suddenly, he saw his wife fingering the handle of the bread-knife. Next moment it flashed through the air and knocked over a vase on the mantelpiece.

'Andrew!' she cried. 'Where ever did that come from? Oh, I can't bear it. Andrew, don't you realise it might have hit me? Don't. Don't!'

He ran to her and put his arms round her. 'Molly, darling, it's all right. You mustn't be alarmed. We must pull ourselves together and not allow our nerves to get on edge. Let's go into the garden. We can talk better there.'

He hardly knew what he was saying, for his heart was torn with pity. He had longed for a natural explanation, never guessing that it would be one so terrible as this. He could see it all now. He had been far too graphic in his description of what had happened that evening at the Parkes. She had evidently been fascinated by the story – fascinated by the abnormal in Miss Cornelius – until, unconsciously, she herself had been infected by this vile lust of deception and trickery, that turned folly into terror. These were the thoughts that jostled each other on the threshold of consciousness while he tried to comfort his wife.

'We have both of us been brooding on this too much,' he said. 'My suggestion is that we get out of the groove of the last week and adopt a new routine. We'll go in for picnic lunches.'

'Things are pretty serious when Old Alfred suggests that,' said Molly, with a wintry smile.

'But not if we can laugh about it. You shall have all the picnic lunches that you want, and we'll sit in a cold wood on damp stones and eat sardine sandwiches. And then each day we'll have some people in for tea or supper. And I'll go to the cinema.'

Molly kissed him. 'I think your suggestions are very sensible. And now for mine. I believe we were wrong in not speaking of this to anyone. We've been too bottled up. I think we should each confide in someone. And, because you are a secretive old scientist, I want you to let me choose who your father confessor shall be.'

'I draw the line at Miss Cornelius and parsons.'

'No, it's Dr Luttrell. I'll ask him to tea tomorrow. You know you like him, and though we haven't seen much of him lately, I can never forget how good he was to us that winter two years ago.'

'All right,' said Saxon, after a pause. 'I agree. And now for your confidante. Not the vicar, and certainly not Mrs Saunderson. I've got it! The very thing; and we shall kill two birds with one stone. Your cousin Alice. Write and get her to stay a few days with us. She herself suggested a visit.'

Molly's face brightened.

'I believe she would come,' she said. 'I know you don't like missionaries; but she is a medical missionary, and I think you would get on very well together. I'll write to her today.'

As he listened to her talking, as he heard the old note of eager gaiety echoing again in her voice, Saxon found himself asking if he could not have been mistaken in what he had seen. If only he could believe that his senses had deceived him! If only he could persuade himself that there was something wrong with his eyes! If Luttrell came, he would get him to test his sight.

Molly went round with a note to the doctor that afternoon. He came next day a little later than they had expected. Saxon was working over in the laboratory, and when he got back to the house, he found Luttrell talking with Molly in the drawing-room. As soon as tea was over – he remembered afterwards the rather forced vivacity of his wife's conversation – Andrew suggested that they should stroll over to his room in the science block, where they could talk and smoke undisturbed.

'I shall come for you in half an hour then,' said Molly, 'because Dr Luttrell has promised to advise me on the rock garden before he goes.'

Andrew got a great deal into those thirty minutes. Luttrell made a good listener, and only interrupted him now and then with a question. He examined his eyes too.

'And if you find my vision wholly defective, if you tell me that I can't trust my sense of sight, God knows, doctor, that you will have taken an unbearable weight off my mind.'

'As a matter of fact,' said Luttrell, when he had finished his examination, 'your vision isn't exactly normal.'

'Then what do you make of the whole confounded business? You've heard the plain, unvarnished facts, and remember that I'm not imaginative or given to overstatement. I'm a trained scientific observer.'

Luttrell rubbed a long forefinger thoughtfully over his gaunt cheek.

'There are two things that arise out of what you have told me. The first is, what do I think of it? I'm not prepared at present to say. I should like myself to witness the phenomena you have described. The second and more important point relates to the immediate present and to Mrs Saxon. You are rightly anxious about her. I think you ought to have someone in the house whom you can trust. Not a nurse, I don't suggest that for a moment, but a cheerful companion.'

Saxon told him of the invitation that had been sent to Miss Hordern, the medical missionary, who was a cousin of his wife.

'Excellent!' he said; 'an admirable person to have with you at this juncture. When she comes, I should very much like to have a talk with her.'

Their conversation was brought to an end by the entrance of Mrs Saxon, who reminded Luttrell that he must not go without seeing her garden.

'And what about the new addition to my lab?' said Andrew. 'We'll go back that way. It won't take us more than a few minutes.'

The minutes, however, lengthened out, as Andrew dilated on the beauties of his new equipment, half-forgetful in his enthusiasm of the dark cloud which hung over him. He was busy explaining a rather complicated piece of apparatus to Luttrell, when they were startled by the noise of something falling and the sound of broken glass.

'I'm awfully sorry, my dear fellow,' said Luttrell. 'It was inexcusably clumsy of me. I knocked it off the bench in turning.'

'Richard,' shouted Saxon, and there was something curiously hard in his voice, 'leave that job you are doing at once, and come and clear up this mess. A bottle of sulphuric acid has broken on the floor. Molly dear, you go on. We'll be with you in a minute. I just want to see that the boy knows what to do.'

'Luttrell,' he said, when they were alone, 'you lied like a gentleman. But she threw that vitriol. You couldn't see her from where you were, but I could. The bottle came from there,' and he pointed to an empty place in the shelf at the farther end of the bench where they were standing. 'We must get her out of this, Luttrell; you must get her out of it, or I shall go mad myself.'

'It's more serious than I had thought,' said the doctor. 'Has she a mother she could go to for a few days?'

'Yes, but she lives up in town – a kind, fussy woman, not the sort of person who would be much help in an emergency.'

'Never mind! She's her mother. Your wife must go off tonight. I give you my most solemn assurance that away from this place she will be all right. I can't explain now, but I'm absolutely sure of it. She can pack her bag at once, and I'll see her to the station and into the 6.20. No, I wouldn't come with her, if I were you. It might only disturb her. You can write out a telegram to her mother and I'll send it off on my way back, because I'm coming back to see you. I shall bring you a stiff sleeping-draught. You've had about as much as a man can stand. Leave me to settle things with Mrs Saxon. And mind, she shall come back as soon as that missionary friend of hers can come and stay with you.'

'Luttrell, you're a true friend,' said Saxon with emotion. 'I don't know what – '

'Pooh! my dear fellow, you would do the same for me, if I were in your place. It's all in the day's work. Just leave it all to Mrs Saxon and me.'

Saxon went to bed that night with a feeling of relief. Decisions, and wise decisions too, had been made for him, and in the making of them he was conscious of events being controlled by one in whom he could put implicit trust. He drank his sleeping-draught, nor had he long to wait before the kindly mists of oblivion blotted out the memories of that eventful day.

Mrs Saxon was away for nearly a week. She wrote nearly every day, long and cheerful letters, which Andrew only half succeeded in answering in the same spirit. He spent the hours of daylight in the laboratory, trying to forget himself in the completion of a long-delayed piece of research work. But at night he found it impossible to concentrate, and paced the garden for hours together, hoping that the tired body would lull to rest the tired mind. He looked back on that fatal evening with horror. If only he had never met Miss Cornelius, had never crossed her path! He had not seen her since his visit to the Parkes; but one afternoon when he was out she called and left a card. The idea of anything approaching intimacy between her and Molly filled him with loathing, but, unwilling to risk an open rupture, he contented himself by writing a formal note, explaining that his wife was away from home and that the date of her return was uncertain.

One step he took in Molly's absence after long consideration, and that was to write to Bestwick, whom he had known at Oxford, and who was now second in command at the Raddlebarn Asylum, asking him if in his opinion Molly should undergo psychoanalysis. The reply he received – he locked the letter in a drawer in his desk – asked for further particulars, and suggested that Bestwick should be put in touch with their private practitioner.

Molly came on the same day that Alice Hordern arrived. His first impression of Molly's cousin was of a sad-faced woman of about fifty, with an attractive smile. She was silent and reserved, but the two felt in her presence the spirit of peace that had for so long eluded them.

There had been no outward cause of alarm since the happenings which Luttrell had witnessed in the laboratory, and Saxon had almost begun to hope that they were waking from a ghastly dream, when Miss Cornelius again called at the house and spent an hour or more alone with Molly.

'I didn't invite her, and I didn't want her,' she said, when Saxon asked her about it, 'but I couldn't tell her so. I had to be civil.'

'There's no need to go stroking vipers,' he broke out excitedly. 'All our troubles are due to that woman. You had better write to her and tell her that her acquaintance is not desired.'

'I shall do no such thing, Andrew. How can you be so foolish? She's more to be pitied than anything else. But for heaven's sake don't let's wrangle about it. It's not worth it.'

No, they were too tired to quarrel; too tired, rather, to go through all the emotion-wearying processes of reconciliation that would be bound to follow. Saxon, however, had made his decision. On the following afternoon, without saying anything to Molly about it, he called on Miss Cornelius.

'I rather expected that you would be coming to see me, Mr Saxon,' she said, when he was shown into the drawing-room. 'Pray sit down.'

'I am afraid – ' he began.

Miss Cornelius laughed.

'That's quite obvious; you are horribly afraid of me. But I interrupt.'

'What I came to say,' Andrew went on, 'was to – '

'Was to ask me not to call and to drop your wife's acquaintance. That was the sum and substance of it, wasn't it? And why, may I ask, should a request from you carry any weight?'

He hesitated for a moment, not knowing what to reply.

'Your difficulty,' she went on, 'and part of your fear too, is that you don't know what to make of me. A fortnight ago I was a poor old lady of the boarding-house type, with itching fingers and a passion for creating interesting situations. Now you are not quite so sure. But cheer up, Mr Saxon. We live in a rational world. There is not the slightest need for you to suppose that I am a witch. Telepathy will explain most things, and I don't see why the things that have been troubling you recently should not be explained on those lines. I can well understand what a relief it would be to have those troubles explained away. But if I were you, I should write to some psychoanalyst and suggest that he should treat your wife. There is a man at the Raddlebarn Asylum, I think, who goes in for that sort of thing.'

Saxon sat staring at her with horror-struck eyes.

'Yes, it must be fearfully confusing to you,' she went on. 'I know just what you must feel like, and the dilemma is awful. Either I have an altogether uncanny power of reading your thoughts, Mr Saxon, and of knowing what passes in your house, or else your good little wife has played false to you and has rifled the drawer of your desk, read that letter, and betrayed its contents to your enemy. No wonder you hardly know what to think.

'And the dilemma is even worse than I supposed it to be,' she went on, 'because, granted you have the courage to ask Mrs Saxon if she broke into that locked drawer, and granted that she indignantly declares that she has done no such thing, in view of what has happened in the last fortnight, you will never absolutely be certain that she is not lying.'

Miss Cornelius burst into a fit of laughter.

'What the devil do you mean by all this?' he cried, in a transport of fury.

She rang the bell.

'Chalmers,' she said to the maid, 'show Mr Saxon out, and please remember that when he calls again I am not at home.'

Saxon said nothing to his wife about that visit. He was haunted by the weary look in her eyes and the forced gaiety of her smile. She had more than she could bear already. But on the following evening, when Molly had gone early to bed, he had a long talk with Alice Hordern. The evening was chilly and the fire which had been lighted in the study invited confidence. Miss Hordern, who neither knitted nor sewed embroidery, echoed the invitation by asking Saxon if he had such a thing as a cigarette.

'I beg pardon,' he said with a smile, 'I am afraid I never associated women medical missionaries with tobacco.'

'You do quite right, Andrew, but I'm a woman first, doctor second, and missionary third; and number three, you must remember, is on furlough. You look worried. It's not Molly, is it? Because I don't think you have any immediate cause to be worried about her. Tell me about it.'

And so he told her everything, while his wife's cousin looked at him through the blue cigarette-smoke with wise and kindly eyes.

'And so, you see, it's no use your telling me not to mind,' he said, when he finished. 'Black hate like this, that strikes at you through the one you love, is devilish. You've got to mind.'

'Granted, though, that Miss Cornelius is all that you think she is – '

'I daren't think what she is,' he groaned; but Alice Hordern took no notice of the interruption.

'Surely you only play her game by reciprocating her black hatred.'

'It's the missionary who is speaking now, I suppose,' he said bitterly.

'No, it's just me. You can't hate a person without always thinking of them. Hatred is like love in that. People use the expression to forget and forgive; but they put the cart before the horse. Until you have forgiven, you cannot forget. It is necessary for your peace of mind to forget Miss Cornelius. And so you must forgive her.'

'It could only be juggling with words. How can I, when I know what she has done and is doing? And what right have I to forgive, when it is not me she is injuring so much as Molly?'

'I am not sure of that,' said Miss Hordern. 'You can but try. Remember this, though. If you ask Molly whether she opened that drawer and read that letter and she says no, believe her. Not even Miss Cornelius can break the truth in Molly. She cannot touch you there.'

The clock had struck eleven when they rose to go to bed. They went upstairs together, but on the landing Saxon stopped for a minute to close the window.

'Good God!' he exclaimed. 'She's there in the garden, standing in the shadow of the yew-tree, looking up at the house.'

Miss Hordern hurried to his side.

'Where?' she said. 'I don't see anyone.'

'She's gone now, but she was there a moment ago. I saw her face.'

'Come with me,' said Miss Hordern. 'We'll go into the garden. If Miss Cornelius is indeed there, it is a matter for the police.'

But they searched the garden in vain.

'My fancy, I suppose,' said Saxon wearily, 'my cursed fancy. Unless,' he added as an afterthought, 'it was an example of the attractive power of hate.'

Once more and once only was he to see Miss Cornelius before that fatal motor accident liberated him by her death from a life of daily torture and nightly despair.

Dr Luttrell, at Saxon's request, had written to Bestwick, who in his reply fixed a date for an interview with Molly. Luttrell himself was unable to go with the Saxons, but he arranged for his car to take them over, and Miss Hordern came with them for the sake of the ride. He was grateful for the consideration which made her choose the seat by the driver, for he could see that Molly was depressed and in no mood to introduce the countryside to her guest. He did his best to comfort her, explaining how a frank talk with Bestwick might help them both to see things in proper perspective, and assuring her that she would find him an easy man to get on with.

As they drew near their destination, he saw that she was crying.

'Andrew,' she said, 'dear Old Alfred, you do trust me, don't you? You'll never believe that I ever plotted against you or did anything to hurt or injure you? Promise me that.'

'Of course I trust you, my darling. I trust you implicitly and always will do.'

'And I'd like Alice to be with me when I talk to Dr Bestwick. You don't mind, do you? You see, she's been my father confessor and knows all about it.'

'I think it is an excellent idea,' he said. 'I have a very high opinion of your cousin.'

And so, when they had met and shaken hands with Bestwick, Saxon was left in a rather sombre reception-room, while the doctor took the two ladies off to his study for a preliminary talk. After ten minutes he returned alone.

'And now,' he said, 'I want to hear your statement of things from the beginning. Don't hurry. Take your time over it, but tell me everything, however trivial it may seem.'

'Saxon,' he said, when Andrew had finished, 'I am afraid what I am going to say to you will come as a great shock. But you can set your mind at rest over one thing, and I believe that for you it is the most important thing. There is nothing the matter with your wife. There is no need to examine her.'

The slight emphasis that he placed on the last word startled Saxon. 'What do you mean?' he said.

'You've passed through a most upsetting experience, that came on the top of a hard term's work when you were completely tired out. That first meeting with Miss Cornelius, and all that you went through then, threw you temporarily off your balance. Your natural anxiety for your wife's safety made matters worse.'

'You mean – you mean,' said Saxon slowly, 'that I'm mad.'

'The word means so many things. But you were not your normal self when you threw the bread-knife, or when Luttrell saw you throw the vitriol. You were not your normal self when you thought you saw the figure of Miss Cornelius from the landing window. And remember this, Saxon, your friends may have deceived you for your own good, but I speak now in absolute sincerity. I see no reason why you should not recover. You may only be here for a comparatively short time. But until you have recovered – you see I am speaking to you as if you were your old self, and that surely should give you hope – we must think of the safety of your wife. She has done what many a woman could never do; she has faced danger and misunderstanding with courage and devotion. It was I who persuaded her that it was best for her and for you not to say goodbye. She will be seeing you again in a few weeks' time, I expect.'

'But Miss Cornelius,' Saxon gasped. 'Miss Cornelius! What about her?'

'Miss Cornelius,' said the other, 'is a vicious and cruel woman. I think that your original judgment of her was correct. She has probably dabbled in Spiritualism, and together with abnormal powers she has very likely developed a habit of unconscious trickery and legerdemain. Many genuine mediums are wholly untrustworthy. But Miss Cornelius is the occasion, not the cause, of your trouble.'

'Then what is she doing there?' cried Saxon suddenly. He had sprung to his feet, and was pointing wildly out of the window. 'That closed car that is passing down the road now! Quick! She has lowered the window and is waving her hand to me.'

Bestwick caught a glimpse of a car and a hand waving.

'It may or may not be Miss Cornelius,' he said, 'but come with me and I will show you your room.'

The Man Who Hated Aspidistras

The earliest memories of Ferdinand Ashley Wilton were green memories – of aspidistras.

The aunt with whom he lived at Cheltenham was fond of the plants. As you entered the hall of Claremont Villa there was on the right an upturned drain-pipe painted a sage green and decorated with arum lilies. This contained Miss Wilton's umbrellas and her father's walking-stick. Projecting into the hall on the left a fretful erection of mahogany supported a mirror, hooks for cloaks, and two shelves. On the upper shelf was a porcelain bowl that contained the cards of callers; on the lower, in a sea-green earthenware pot, precariously rested the first of the aspidistras. The second stood in the dining-room – in summer in the fireplace, in winter on the ledge of the window that faced south. In the drawing-room was the third, raised high above the ground on a fluted wooden pedestal. The fourth and last aspidistra stood on the round table by the couch in Miss Wilton's bedroom. At night it was carried out on to the landing, for Miss Wilton, remembering something that her doctor had once said about sick-rooms and flowers, thought it on the whole wisest that she should sleep alone.

The aspidistras dominated Ferdinand's life. They were always liable to be upset, so that he was not allowed to run about in the hall or dining-room. When he was very small he had a fancy that they repeated to Miss Wilton the many things that he had done amiss, and especially did he distrust that fourth plant, which stood at night, a sleepless sentinel, on the landing close to his bedroom door. As he grew older he learnt, reluctantly, how to sponge their leaves with soapy water. When a gentle rain was falling he would carry them into the garden in order that they might enjoy what Miss Wilton called a thorough soaking. But if Ben, the poodle, were in the garden he had to be brought in straight away and dried. The laws governing the vegetable and animal worlds seemed to Ferdinand strangely different.

In very dry weather the bath would be half filled and the four aspidistras would stand in a row for hours partially submerged. Ferdinand was not allowed to sail his boat among the gloomy islands of this archipelago, but if his conduct had been satisfactory he was permitted to pull the plug before going to bed.

Ferdinand was still a very little boy when he was sent away to school. He was constantly ailing and even when he was well he received more than his due share of kicks and bruises. In the matron's room he felt as if he were back again in Cheltenham, the pot of aspidistras reminded him so much of his aunt. On it he vented the hatred of his schoolboy world. When the matron was called out of the room he would share with the aspidistras vegetable laxatives and iron tonics, or impart to their leaves an unnatural glow of health by polishing them with Scott's emulsion or liquid paraffin. A vertical section of the pot illustrating Ferdinand's activities would have shown a thimble, three hairpins, a number of needles, the case of a clinical thermometer and, an inch below the surface, an almost complete tessellated pavement of sugar-coated pills.

When, however, in a rash moment, Ferdinand, in applying the contents of a bottle of tincture of iodine to the leaves, found to his alarm that the black stains were irremovable, the fat was in the fire. The matron made a formal complaint, but nobody owned up. The ten more or less ailing boys who had visited the room on that fatal morning were indiscriminately punished. To them it was known that Ferdinand was the delinquent. He did not escape. Like the aspidistra he was poked and prodded and shaken to the roots.

Boyhood passed. At the university Ferdinand achieved a certain success. He published a volume of verse and was founder and secretary of the Mid-Victorians. He only met two aspidistras during the whole of the time he was up, one in the porter's lodge whose leaves he would absent-mindedly trim with pocket scissors, and the other in a dentist's waiting-room.

Miss Wilton died. She left to her nephew the villa at Cheltenham and four hundred pounds a year. Ferdinand was able to devote himself to literature, and from Bloomsbury lodging-houses wrote his first series of Antimacassar Papers. It was at this period of his life that he found himself once again under the influence of aspidistras. He began by nagging them, treating them as ash-trays, pen-wipers, and cemeteries for safety razor blades. He ended by torturing them. One, he slowly did to death with weedkiller; into another, following the example of the Good Samaritan, he would pour in oil and wine. A third he garrotted with rubber bands; a fourth, slowly succumbing to a solution of bath salts, filled his room for weeks with the faint perfume of lavender. A horticultural detective would, of course, have quickly got on the track of the Bloomsbury murders, but no suspicion ever fell upon Ferdinand. He was so inoffensive, so subtle, so respectable, and in his own way so quietly ornamental. His requirements were so few and he needed little looking after. His landladies were always sorry when he went. The aspidistras never got over his departure.

Ferdinand, of course, should have realised that it is dangerous to indulge in hatred. The man who hates open spaces as likely as not will be killed when crossing a square. It isn't the motor car but the square that kills him. Ferdinand had his warnings. Once on a wet morning a pot of aspidistras fell from a third-storey window ledge on to the pavement at his feet. On another occasion when travelling by train a sudden stop brought down from the rack a heavy and bulky package that indubitably involved risk of injury to passengers. If Ferdinand had not been sitting with his back to the engine he would have been struck on the head by the most monstrous aspidistra he had ever seen.

He was smoking one day in a despondent mood when his friend Basset Tankerville chanced to call. The *Blue Review* had noticed his latest volume of essays with less than its usual appreciation. 'Listen to this,' said Ferdinand to Basset. ' "We begin to be conscious of the limitations of his point of view – the interstices of a venetian blind. He is the embodiment of the aspidistra." And then,' said Ferdinand, 'they have the impertinence to give half a column to a review of Gertrude Stein.'

'Glorious jingles,' said Basset. 'You should really try your hand at them yourself. "Ferdinand Ashley Wilton with his dashed aspidistras that wilt unless fertilised with black tobacco ash. *Ad astra Aspidistra*." But seriously, you do remind me of the plants. You are becoming more and more green with envy, more and more pot-bound. And, by the way, have you ever thought of how applicable to aspidistras is St Paul's description of charity? That specimen which I see before me suffereth long and is kind. It vaunteth not itself, doth not behave itself unseemly, seeketh not her own, is not easily provoked. Beareth all things, believeth all things, hopeth all things, endureth all things. And the same, Ferdinand, in a large measure is true of you. You and the aspidistra are one.'

Those light words of Basset Tankerville, spoken as they were in jest, marked an epoch in Wilton's life. They stirred the vegetable fibres of his being. His conversation became more and more torpid. The wit that had enlivened the Antimacassar Papers vanished and though from time to time he still wrote, his style – polished and stately as it was – became dull. He left London to live once again in Cheltenham, but it was as an invalid that he lived. Though he took the waters regularly his skin acquired an unmistakable greenish tinge which the dark green cloak he always wore made all the more noticeable. A little odd, his housekeeper thought him, and very old-fashioned, but Mr Wilton gave next to no trouble. On sunny days she would pull up the venetian blinds and place his chair in the window, where he would sit quietly for hours occasionally sponging his long leaf-like hands with soap and water. He was happiest, however, when the faintest of drizzles was falling. Then the man who hated aspidistras would be wheeled out into the rain to enjoy a thorough soaking.

Sambo

One thing is certain: Arthur ought never to have sent Janey the doll.

It came about like this.

He wrote us one of his absurd letters from a place in Africa, where he had been helping to put down a native rising. It was embellished as usual with lively pen-and-ink sketches of his black soldiers (who seemed to bear an extraordinary likeness to Christy Minstrels), and in a postscript contained the information that he was sending Janey a little black doll he had discovered in a deserted hut.

The doll appeared a fortnight later, wrapped up in a year-old engineering supplement of *The Times*, tied together with three knotted pieces of string. The stamps I put by for my three-year-old nephew, until the time arrived when he would be able to appreciate their value.

Janey was disappointed, and I do not wonder at it. She had been looking forward to the arrival of this new member of her family, all the more eagerly because Cicely White had been unbearably conceited about a doll her godmother had sent from Paris. The little African, instead of having a neatly painted trunk containing an elaborate wardrobe, appeared on the removal of his paper covering in a state of absolute nudity. I think Janey could have forgiven his lack of clothes if he had been less ugly. Without doubt he was hideous. His nose was a shapeless, protruding lump; his lips were thick, and his hair was represented by a collection of knobs. The one redeeming feature was his size; he measured just two feet and a half, and could stand unsupported in the bath of Condy's fluid to which he was subjected. But I thought my sister wrong in punishing Janey for her tears; the contrast between Sambo and Cicely White's gay Parisienne was too great.

For three whole days Sambo remained unnoticed and uncared for, in the engineering supplement. During that period Mary in her leisure moments made a few alterations in a scarlet petticoat she had originally intended for a youthful inhabitant of Uganda.

Clothed in this garment, Sambo looked uglier than before. Janey would not come near him. She hated him. He was not a nice doll. She even asked Mary to take him away. But my sister has never spoiled her nephews and nieces. She drew a graphic if inaccurate picture of Arthur's surprise and resentment if he knew the manner in which his gift had been received.

Her authority, but not her arguments, prevailed. After an altogether unreasonable amount of crying, even in so sensitive a child as Janey, Sambo's rights were acknowledged.

Sambo was a name for which Janey was not responsible. If she had been left to herself she would have called the doll IT, and nothing more. But Mary is one of those people who believe that all dogs should be called Rover and all canaries Dick. When Sambo arrived there was never any doubt in her mind as to the name; my diffident suggestion of Lobengula was contemptuously dismissed on the ground that that individual came from an altogether different part of Africa.

The doll, at the period of his adoption, had fourteen brothers and sisters of different nationalities. As was natural, he took his place at the bottom of the class, was the last to be washed, the first to be put to bed, and if the plates and cups gave out at tea time, he was the one to suffer.

Sambo arrived at the beginning of October; by the end of the month a change had set in. One day I surprised Janey at tea. Sambo was sitting in the fourteenth place with the last cup and saucer before him, and Gulielma Maria, a plain but well-meaning doll, was going supperless to bed.

Needless to say, I accused my niece of injustice and favouritism. She was very pale, and tears were in her eyes. She told me that she was sorry for Guly, but she could not help it. It was Sambo's fault, and she hated him for it.

I thought the explanation a trifle lame, and offered to take Guly to tea downstairs; my proposal was promptly and joyfully accepted.

A week later Sambo was ninth on the list, Nelson, Tweedledum and Tweedledee, a golliwog, and Gulielma Maria being below him, and on his plate, in the manner of Benjamin of old, was a double portion.

In vain I remonstrated. It seemed that Sambo had insisted. Janey was exceedingly sorry for the others, but she could not help it.

On 1st November, Sambo had risen to the fourth place. He wore, in addition to his scarlet petticoat, a pair of stockings which belonged to the Salvation Army lass sitting next to him, and whose feet seemed to have suffered from the exposure that the absence of their usual covering involved. I asked Janey if she had offered the stockings to him of her own free will. No, the Salvation Army lass had almost broken her heart. It was Sambo's fault. He wanted them, and Janey had pulled them off when Susan was asleep.

On the eve of Guy Fawkes Day, I had my annual debate with Mary as to the feasibility of a small bonfire. One by one I abolished the same old objections, the danger to the house, the waste of good fuel when there were millions in London alone with no fires to warm them, the perpetuation of religious animosity, and the danger of contracting colds in the head. I went to bed, weary but triumphant. Next morning at breakfast I propounded my plans, and Mary gave official sanction for Janey and four dolls to watch the performance from the bath-room window. The greater part of the day was spent by my niece in settling the claims of rival dolls.

My surprise was great when, in the red glare of the bonfire, I recognised, propped up against the glass of the bath-room window, the expressionless faces of Rose, Eric (how I disliked that boy who, in his Eton jacket, was the very essence of priggishness), Alathea, and Sambo.

When I got to the stage of green Bengal lights I noticed that he was clad in a Japanese kimono he had certainly never had before, and wore a cocked hat, which I had a shrewd suspicion belonged to Nelson.

The next fortnight saw deliberate war between Sambo and Eric. The immediate object was the possession of the Eton jacket, the ulterior the privilege of sitting between Rose and Alathea, and dominating the rest of the family.

Janey's sympathies were all for Eric, who was for her the embodiment of English manhood; mine were on the side of his opponent, who came out as usual successful.

Eric, jacketless, was left to face the rigour of our English winter in his shirt-sleeves.

Now that all his male rivals had been defeated, I expected that we should see an end to Sambo's ambition.

No such thing occurred. In an altogether unchivalrous manner, he began to wage war on Rose, the oldest and most beautiful of Janey's dolls, who was the only possessor of that much prized accomplishment of falling into a trance-like sleep whenever she lay down.

When Christmas came, Sambo was the first to be served, the first to be dressed, and the last to be put to bed.

And Janey hated him.

For the next three months nothing noteworthy took place with regard to Janey and her dolls. For a large part of the time I was away from home and saw little of my niece.

On my return, Mary called my attention to a new development.

'I really believe that Janey is growing out of her childishness at last,' she said. 'She is putting away some of her dolls: she really ought to be content with fewer.'

Six weeks later, the numbers were reduced to one.

It was Sambo who remained.

Though Janey had carried out the change on her own initiative, she became low-spirited, and I have no doubt shed many tears in private. So much I had expected. What surprised me was the fact that she showed no signs of transferring her affection to the one remaining member of her family.

It was true that Sambo was always with her, in the house and out of doors. He had meals by her side and slept at the bottom of her bed at night. But it was not because she cared for him; I began to think she was actuated by fear.

One afternoon I wanted Janey, and she was not to be found in nursery or garden; I searched the house in vain and was beginning to despair, when I remembered the attics. The attics were out of bounds owing to an unrailed stair that led up to them, but I was none the less successful.

There, in a stockade composed of trunks and portmanteaux, sat Janey surrounded by her dolls.

Her face was wreathed in smiles. On her lap sat Eric, at her feet lay Rose in the well-known state of trance.

'So this is the way you spend your afternoons!' I said. 'I wonder what your aunt would say if she knew.'

'Oh, please don't tell her, uncle!' Janey replied. 'And whatever happens, don't tell Sambo!'

Until she spoke, I had not noticed the absence of that individual. On inquiry it seemed that Sambo had been left fast asleep in the garden. I raised the heavy attic window and looked out. Yes, there he was sitting propped up on the garden seat looking up at us with eyes that seemed to me very wide awake.

'I'm afraid he knows where we are!' said Janey, 'he is so very clever.'

Of course I said nothing to Mary of what went on upstairs. There was less need to, as Janey's visits to her banished family very soon ceased. It was my belief that Sambo had put a stop to them. Of what happened behind the raspberry canes I very seldom speak. I never told Mary, who being entirely without imagination would have believed that either I was lying or Janey mad.

The afternoon had been more than usually close. Mary was cross, Janey was listless, and I sleepy. I had as usual ensconced myself in the shady corner of the kitchen garden where the maid never thinks of looking when she comes to announce callers, and where I not infrequently surprise school children in search of our blackbirds' nests. I was awakened from my nap by the accustomed sound of someone in the raspberry canes.

In among the brown sticks, I caught sight of a white dress. I bent low and followed. Janey was some fifteen yards ahead of me. In her arms she was clasping a doll. She was sobbing bitterly.

Through the raspberry canes I followed her – along a little track that had not been there a fortnight before, over an open space which in autumn was trenched for celery, past the deserted graveyard where generations of cats and dogs had been laid to rest, to the very end of the long garden.

It was a deserted place given over to rubbish, broken flower-pots, piles of old pea-sticks, and mounds of yellow rotting grass cut from the lawns last summer. I hid myself behind a turf stack and watched.

On a chair that Arthur had given Janey three birthdays ago, sat Sambo, wearing his usual expression of utter vacuity. About a yard in front of him was a pile of straw and dried twigs; within reach was the silver matchbox I had spent hours in hunting for the previous two days. There was also a little saw from my tool chest.

I ground my teeth as I noticed the rusty blade. Janey placed her doll on the ground, cried over it and kissed it. Then before I realised what she was doing she had sawn off its legs and arms, and placed its dismembered trunk upon the wooden pyre. From the tennis lawn came Mary's voice calling 'Janey! Janey!'

It is no easy matter to strike matches on an old silver matchbox from which the roughness has long since departed. She was successful at last, and in a moment there was a blaze. The dried wood crackled with the heat. Then again came Mary's voice louder and more persistent, and Janey was gone.

I lit a cigarette, and watched the fire die down, controlling with difficulty an impulse to add more fuel to it in the person of Sambo. Before I left the place, I found the charred remains of eight dolls. One which I took to be Eric was hideous to behold, his head was featureless, one glass eye protruding from a lump of wax.

I made my way back to the house as stealthily as I had come. Under my coat I carried Sambo.

I had to go up to town that evening on business, and I wrapped up the doll in a paper parcel (my kit bag was already full), with the intention of consulting a friend at the British Museum as to its nature and origin.

Mary had apparently taken Janey with her to call on the vicar's wife. I saw neither of them before I left.

I did not carry out my plan; for as I was walking down Paternoster Row the following day, with my parcel under my arm, Sambo was stolen.

I had stopped opposite a stationer's shop in whose window was exhibited a large map of Africa, flanked by bibles. I was wondering why such an immense area had been covered black instead of the more customary scarlet, and had come to the conclusion that it probably referred to unexploited coal, when I received a push in the back. After apologising to the clergyman with whom I came into somewhat violent contact, I became aware that my parcel had disappeared. Of the thief there was no sign. Yards away I saw the imposing dark blue mass of a constable. I took two steps towards him with the intention of notifying my loss. Then I turned and walked in the opposite direction. Sambo after all had been no friend of ours.

*   *   *

Ten months later I went with Mary to the Agricultural Hall to see the 'Orient in London'. She had promised after my visit to spend a day with me at the Franco-British Exhibition, a bargain which to my mind was never fully ratified, as she resolutely declined free seats in the Scenic Railway and Flip-Flap.

I was glad I had gone as I met two acquaintances I should not otherwise have seen, Captain Carter, of my old regiment, who had taken orders and was going out to China as a missionary, and Sambo. The latter seemed to be superintending operations in an African village, and was very much at home. There was a label tied to his arm. On it I read:

This undoubtedly genuine African idol was found in a compartment in the Bakerloo tube. Nothing is known as to the circumstances in which it was placed there, but it was probably stolen from some museum. This idol affords an interesting example of the gods that were worshipped in the childhood of our race.

The childhood of our race appeared to me a particularly appropriate phrase as I thought of Janey.

The Star

The night outside was clear and frosty, not a cloud in the sky. There had perhaps been five such nights in the year, and the opportunity was too good to lose.

Jackson put his wife's cloak around her shoulders with more than his usual tenderness.

He even agreed with her that it was scandalous that he had not yet attended a single Lenten sermon; but he pleaded his cold in excuse.

He saw her into the carriage, and then walked across bareheaded, in his evening shoes, to the observatory.

He wanted to confirm one or two facts about the star on which Mortimer had reported in the *Review*. It would be a splendid thing if he could explode yet another of his rival's theories; and he chuckled as he remembered the comet of last June.

'It's a curious thing,' said Jackson to himself as he gazed at the speck of light in the eyepiece of the telescope. 'The betting's a hundred to one that Mortimer's looking at the star this very moment, and a thousand to one that we two are the only people who have the slightest interest in it. Confound the man's ugly face! I can see it now.'

How he disliked the fellow! He disliked his voice, his manner, the way he dressed.

And Mrs Mortimer! What a woman!

He wished that she and Eliza were not quite so intimate.

And what an absurd paper the man had read before the society the other evening: based on the wildest hypothesis, of course, and yet Linton and one or two others seemed to think there was something in it.

Jackson looked through the telescope again at the star, but found it hard to concentrate his attention. All the time he was thinking how ridiculous Mortimer looked now that he had shaved his beard. He had always told Eliza that he had a weak chin.

He remembered overhearing that the man had applied for some professor's post in Australia. Well, he hoped he would get it, there would be a few thousand miles between them; though the people out there would not consent to be gulled for long.

Jackson got up and stretched himself. It was a glorious night, but he felt strangely disinclined for work.

'I think I'll write to the *Review*,' he said to himself. 'There are one or two discrepancies in Mortimer's paper that ought to remain unanswered no longer.'

When Mrs Jackson came in, an hour later, she found her husband sitting with his feet on the library mantelpiece, dressed in his oldest Norfolk, and smoking his oldest briar. He was aware that his attitude probably annoyed his wife.

'You had better take your feet down, unless you wish the servants to see you in that ridiculous posture,' she said. 'I am about to ring for some hot milk. It's a pity you did not hear the sermon, George, I am sure you would have appreciated it; though I do wish the church-wardens or someone would see that place does not get so appallingly stuffy. Poor Father Trewhit looked quite pale when he pronounced the benediction.'

'So Father Peewhit occupied the pulpit,' began Jackson.

'Father Peewhit! I tell you once again that there is nothing funny in that inane appellation. The man comes from one of the oldest Cornish families. He works like a slave for the poor of East London, and hasn't had a holiday for five years, excepting alternate Tuesdays, when he plays golf at Mudbury with the vicar.'

'Yes, yes, I grant it all, Eliza. To oblige you I will refer to him in future as Father Lapwing.'

Mrs Jackson ground a predigested biscuit between her teeth, gulped down half a tumbler of milk and water, and went on.

'It's no use, George, I see perfectly well what you're aiming at. You're trying to irritate me. But I won't be irritated!

'It's too bad that you should try to spoil the good the service does one by these childish attacks on religion.'

'My dear Elizabeth,' her husband replied, 'I have not mentioned the word religion this evening. Because I call your spiritual instructor by the name of a pretty, inoffensive bird, that struts about in a ridiculous attitude, and only utters one note which it repeats over and over again, there is no reason to suppose that the foundations of Christianity are in danger. Well, well! What was the sermon about?'

Mrs Jackson had begun her second predigested biscuit. 'It was the fourth Lenten sermon on the "Witness of Nature".'

'An unsatisfactory witness,' said Jackson, 'but never mind.'

'He preached this evening on the "Witness of the Stars". He took as his text "For we have seen His star", somewhere in St Matthew, I think, but I am not sure. It was just the sermon you would have liked, George, with your scientific tastes and things.'

George was fully aware that by scientific tastes and things his wife meant his predilection for Sunday golf, a general distrust of missionaries, and an emphatic refusal to contribute to the choir of St Jude's when they came round at Christmas.

'He began,' went on Mrs Jackson, 'by describing the feelings of the first man who ever saw a star, how frightened he would be, and with what wonder he would look up to it. Then he told us of a woman he knew who always put a light in her window to guide her son home at night; and he said that the stars were the shining lamps of the windows of heaven.'

'How pleased the good man must have been when he thought of that! I suppose he'll print these sermons. Any more anecdotes?'

'He never tells anecdotes, you know, George! But he told us of a boy whose crippled sister, when she died, told him that whenever he looked at a particular star he was to think of her and do good. And when the little boy was in trouble ('Trials or perplexities is the correct phrase,' her husband interrupted), he used to stay awake for hours looking at the star through a crack in the attic roof above his bed.'

'Good heavens, Eliza! That's enough for the present. In the first place, the star would move, and he could not watch it for hours through a crack. In the second place, if a healthy English boy, who has never known the degrading influence of the Sunday school, finds out that there is a hole in the roof above his head, he plugs it up with something to keep the rain out. In the third place, what happened to the boy when he had his little trials and perplexities on a cloudy night? In the fourth place, why should the sister be crippled? It is nothing else than an unprincipled appeal to feminine sentiment.'

'I knew you'd scoff, George. You always do scoff at religion. Thank goodness, Roger is in bed and asleep hours ago.'

'As a matter of fact from the noise immediately above my head, I believe him to be in the process of having a hot bath. But do go on with your account of the sermon.'

'I'll proceed with pleasure if you promise to take me seriously. By the by, I must remind cook tomorrow about putting these biscuits in the oven before she sends them up. Well, Father Trewhit finished by describing to us the feelings of a man who was gazing at a star millions of miles away, a nameless, flashing pinprick of eternity, he called it. He described how the man would lose all sense of self, how he would cast aside all his little everyday petty squabblings and jealousies, losing all thoughts of time and space as he sees the fringe of new worlds, new universes, until, shielding his eyes, he would exclaim with the psalmist: What is man?'

There Mrs Jackson stopped, leaving her quotation unfinished. George was sitting in his chair convulsed with laughter.

She drew herself up, and in her most frigid manner left the room without speaking.

'Don't slam the door, for pity's sake!' said her husband, and then began to laugh again.

Across the Moors

It really was most unfortunate.

Peggy had a temperature of nearly a hundred, and a pain in her side, and Mrs Workington Bancroft knew that it was appendicitis. But there was no one whom she could send for the doctor.

James had gone with the jaunting-car to meet her husband who had at last managed to get away for a week's shooting.

Adolph she had sent to the Evershams, only half an hour before, with a note for Lady Eva.

The cook could not manage to walk, even if dinner could be served without her.

Kate, as usual, was not to be trusted.

There remained Miss Craig.

'Of course, you must see that Peggy is really ill,' said she, as the governess came into the room, in answer to her summons. 'The difficulty is, that there is absolutely no one whom I can send for the doctor.' Mrs Workington Bancroft paused; she was always willing that those beneath her should have the privilege of offering the services which it was her right to command.

'So, perhaps, Miss Craig,' she went on, 'you would not mind walking over to Tebbit's Farm. I hear there is a Liverpool doctor staying there. Of course I know nothing about him, but we must take the risk, and I expect he'll be only too glad to be earning something during his holiday. It's nearly four miles, I know, and I'd never dream of asking you if it was not that I dread appendicitis so.'

'Very well,' said Miss Craig, 'I suppose I must go; but I don't know the way.'

'Oh, you can't miss it,' said Mrs Workington Bancroft, in her anxiety temporarily forgiving the obvious unwillingness of her governess's consent.

'You follow the road across the moor for two miles, until you come to Redman's Cross. You turn to the left there, and follow a rough path that leads through a larch plantation. And Tebbit's farm lies just below you in the valley.

'And take Pontiff with you,' she added, as the girl left the room. 'There's absolutely nothing to be afraid of, but I expect you'll feel happier with the dog.'

'Well, miss,' said the cook, when Miss Craig went into the kitchen to get her boots, which had been drying by the fire; 'of course she knows best, but I don't think it's right after all that's happened for the mistress to send you across the moors on a night like this. It's not as if the doctor could do anything for Miss Margaret if you do bring him. Every child is like that once in a while. He'll only say put her to bed, and she's there already.'

'I don't see what there is to be afraid of, cook,' said Miss Craig as she laced her boots, 'unless you believe in ghosts.'

'I'm not so sure about that. Anyhow I don't like sleeping in a bed where the sheets are too short for you to pull them over your head. But don't you be frightened, miss. It's my belief that their bark is worse than their bite.'

But though Miss Craig amused herself for some minutes by trying to imagine the bark of a ghost (a thing altogether different from the classical ghostly bark), she did not feel entirely at her ease.

She was naturally nervous, and living as she did in the hinterland of the servants' hall, she had heard vague details of true stories that were only myths in the drawing-room.

The very name of Redman's Cross sent a shiver through her; it must have been the place where that horrid murder was committed. She had forgotten the tale, though she remembered the name.

Her first disaster came soon enough.

Pontiff, who was naturally slow-witted, took more than five minutes to find out that it was only the governess he was escorting, but once the discovery had been made, he promptly turned tail, paying not the slightest heed to Miss Craig's feeble whistle. And then, to add to her discomfort, the rain came, not in heavy drops, but driving in sheets of thin spray that blotted out what few landmarks there were upon the moor.

They were very kind at Tebbit's farm. The doctor had gone back to Liverpool the day before, but Mrs Tebbit gave her hot milk and turf cakes, and offered her reluctant son to show Miss Craig a shorter path on to the moor, that avoided the larch wood.

He was a monosyllabic youth, but his presence was cheering, and she felt the night doubly black when he left her at the last gate.

She trudged on wearily. Her thoughts had already gone back to the almost exhausted theme of the bark of ghosts, when she heard steps on the road behind her that were at least material. Next minute the figure of a man appeared: Miss Craig was relieved to see that the stranger was a clergyman. He raised his hat. 'I believe we are both going in the same direction,' he said. 'Perhaps I may have the pleasure of escorting you.' She thanked him. 'It is rather weird at night,' she went on, 'and what with all the tales of ghosts and bogies that one hears from the country people, I've ended by being half afraid myself.'

'I can understand your nervousness,' he said, 'especially on a night like this. I used at one time to feel the same, for my work often meant lonely walks across the moor to farms which were only reached by rough tracks difficult enough to find even in the daytime.'

'And you never saw anything to frighten you – nothing immaterial I mean?'

'I can't really say that I did, but I had an experience eleven years ago which served as the turning-point in my life, and since you seem to be now in much the same state of mind as I was then in, I will tell it you.

'The time of year was late September. I had been over to Weston-dale to see an old woman who was dying, and then, just as I was about to start on my way home, word came to me of another of my parishioners who had been suddenly taken ill only that morning. It was after seven when at last I started. A farmer saw me on my way, turning back when I reached the moor road.

'The sunset the previous evening had been one of the most lovely I ever remember to have seen. The whole vault of heaven had been scattered with flakes of white cloud, tipped with rosy pink like the strewn petals of a full-blown rose.

'But that night all was changed. The sky was an absolutely dull slate colour, except in one corner of the west where a thin rift showed the last saffron tint of the sullen sunset. As I walked, stiff and footsore, my spirits sank. It must have been the marked contrast between the two evenings, the one so lovely, so full of promise (the corn was still out in the fields spoiling for fine weather), the other so gloomy, so sad with all the dead weight of autumn and winter days to come. And then added to this sense of heavy depression came another different feeling which I surprised myself by recognising as fear.

'I did not know why I was afraid.

'The moors lay on either side of me, unbroken except for a straggling line of turf shooting-butts, that stood within a stone's throw of the road.

'The only sound I had heard for the last half hour was the cry of the startled grouse – Go back, go back, go back. But yet the feeling of fear was there, affecting a low centre of my brain through some little-used physical channel.

'I buttoned my coat closer, and tried to divert my thoughts by thinking of next Sunday's sermon.

'I had chosen to preach on Job. There is much in the old-fashioned notion of the book, apart from all the subtleties of the higher criticism, that appeals to country people; the loss of herds and crops, the break up of the family. I would not have dared to speak, had not I too been a farmer; my own glebe land had been flooded three weeks before, and I suppose I stood to lose as much as any man in the parish. As I walked along the road repeating to myself the first chapter of the book, I stopped at the twelfth verse.

' "And the Lord said unto Satan: Behold, all that he hath is in thy power . . . "

'The thought of the bad harvest (and that is an awful thought in these valleys) vanished. I seemed to gaze into an ocean of infinite darkness.

'I had often used, with the Sunday glibness of the tired priest, whose duty it is to preach three sermons in one day, the old simile of the chessboard. God and the devil were the players: and we were helping one side or the other. But until that night I had not thought of the possibility of my being only a pawn in the game, that God might throw away that the game might be won.

'I had reached the place where we are now, I remember it by that rough stone water-trough, when a man suddenly jumped up from the roadside. He had been seated on a heap of broken road metal.

' "Which way are you going, guv'ner?' he said.

'I knew from the way he spoke that the man was a stranger. There are many at this time of the year who come up from the south, tramping northwards with the ripening corn. I told him my destination.

' "We'll go along together," he replied.

'It was too dark to see much of the man's face, but what little I made out was coarse and brutal.

'Then he began the half-menacing whine I knew so well – he had tramped miles that day, he had had no food since breakfast, and that was only a crust.

' "Give us a copper," he said, "it's only for a night's lodging." '

'He was whittling away with a big clasp knife at an ash stake he had taken from some hedge.'

The clergyman broke off.

'Are those the lights of your house?' he said. 'We are nearer than I expected, but I shall have time to finish my story. I think I will, for you can run home in a couple of minutes, and I don't want you to be frightened when you are out on the moors again.

'As the man talked he seemed to have stepped out of the very background of my thoughts, his sordid tale, with the sad lies that hid a far sadder truth.

'He asked me the time.

'It was five minutes to nine. As I replaced my watch I glanced at his face. His teeth were clenched, and there was something in the gleam of his eyes that told me at once his purpose.

'Have you ever known how long a second is? For a third of a second I stood there facing him, filled with an overwhelming pity for myself and him; and then without a word of warning he was upon me. I felt nothing. A flash of lightning ran down my spine, I heard the dull crash of the ash stake, and then a very gentle patter like the sound of a far distant stream. For a minute I lay in perfect happiness watching the lights of the house as they increased in number until the whole heaven shone with twinkling lamps.

'I could not have had a more painless death.'

Miss Craig looked up. The man was gone; she was alone on the moor.

She ran to the house, her teeth chattering, ran to the solid shadow that crossed and recrossed the kitchen blind.

As she entered the hall, the clock on the stairs struck the hour.

It was nine o'clock.

The Follower

'They say miracles are past; and we have our philosophical persons to make modern and familiar things supernatural and causeless. Hence it is we make trifles of terrors; ensconcing ourselves into seeming knowledge, when we should submit ourselves to an unknown fear.'

Lyn Stanton had found at last the quotation he wanted in *All's Well that Ends Well*, and he had spent the best part of an hour in looking for it. He drew up his chair to the fire and filled his pipe. If only he could hit on the idea for the story, something uncanny, something sinister. It was not yet ten o'clock on an April morning, but he was just in the mood to submit himself to an unknown fear. The story was in him or around him, in the air. He knew the effect he wanted to get, but what was the story itself? Why wouldn't it take shape, come out into the open so that he could see at least the dim outline, the skeleton rather, which later he could clothe at will?

What was it, he asked himself, that was to account for this half pleasurable feeling of tingling apprehension? He had had, it was true, a disturbed night, for he had awakened from a bad dream about two, to lie for an hour gazing through the uncurtained window at a light burning in the Old Vicarage of Winton Parbeloe half a mile away across the valley. Canon Rathbone, the oriental scholar, was living there, he had heard, with a German friend, Dr Curtius. The light which would not go out had kept him awake. Canon Rathbone and Dr Curtius had kept him awake, though they were half a mile away across the valley.

'We have our philosophical persons to make modern and familiar,' he repeated, and then stopped. The idea for his story was coming. He began to see the vague, shadowy outline. The skeleton became clear.

At the end of half an hour Stanton took a new exercise book from his desk and wrote on the back of it 'The Follower', with the date. Then slowly but without erasures, he began the summary.

'An old scholar searching for manuscripts in the monasteries of Asia Minor comes across some palimpsests of an unusual character. The collector's fever overpowers him – usually the mildest and most honest of men – and with the help of a monk he acquires the documents by means which others would have undoubtedly described as shady. The monk persuades the scholar to take him back to England, since his help will be invaluable in deciphering the manuscripts. They live together in a remote country village. With extraordinary difficulty they make out the meaning of the palimpsests, which appear to be not fragments of a lost gospel but something very different. The scholar is held fascinated and pursues. The monk, who passes in the district as a Doctor of Divinity, is his constant companion and follower.'

Stanton was pleased with himself. The idea was a good one. It might even be worked up into a long story, but on the whole he felt inclined to keep it short, three or four thousand words perhaps. He didn't see how it would end, but he wasn't worried about that. Very likely it would end itself. The main thing was to get the atmosphere right – the seeming knowledge and the unknown fear.

Canon Rathbone, of course, and Dr Curtius had given him the germ of the idea. If he hadn't woken at two in the morning and seen the light burning in the Old Vicarage, half a mile away across the valley, there would have been no story. 'And Shakespeare too,' he said to himself. 'If I hadn't found that passage I was looking for, I shouldn't have got into the right mood.'

Lyn Stanton sat down to lunch with the feeling of a morning lazily and not unsatisfactorily spent. He would do some strenuous digging in the garden in the afternoon, he told himself, and then put in a couple of hours' work on his novel between tea and supper. The short story could simmer. After a day or two he would have another look at it and see how it was getting on.

But his equanimity was upset by his sister announcing that Mrs Bramley and Miss Newton were coming to tea. He had no particular fault to find with the vicar's outspoken wife. She was quite in keeping with Winton Parbeloe. But Miss Newton always got on his nerves. It was hard luck having as a neighbour a freelance journalist with a malicious pen. He disliked her literary gossip, chiefly because he knew that she would not scruple to work up some chance remark of his into a paragraph in some Book-Lovers' Causerie. Probably she wanted to pump him about his new novel. A dangerous woman who would have to be humoured.

So Stanton took his spade and in his shirtsleeves worked out his resentment on the stony patch of ground that he was double-trenching. He saw the visitors arrive soon after half-past three, gave them a quarter of an hour for garnering the first light crop of parochial scandal, and then with a reluctance adequately concealed joined them in the drawing-room. After all Mrs Bramley was quite an authority on roses. Tea had just been served and Stanton was trying to give Miss Newton a noncommittal reply to a question about the significance of a modern poet whose work he particularly disliked, when he heard the garden gate click and saw two figures approaching up the long gravel path.

The first was an old clergyman, clean-shaven, rather down at heel, who walked with a rapid and yet shuffling gait. He was followed by a tall man with a long black beard dressed in an old-fashioned frock-coat.

The bell rang, and a minute later the maid announced Canon Rathbone and Dr Curtius.

'I'm afraid, Miss Stanton,' said the canon, when the introductions had been made, 'that our call is a little irregular. We are strangers to your delightful village, and I have spent so much of my life in out-of-the-way places that I am all too apt to ignore the ordinary rules of etiquette. We keep very much to ourselves at the Old Vicarage, and quite unconsciously I am afraid we frighten our visitors away. But we want to be neighbourly – I assure you we want to be neighbourly.'

The old gentleman was obviously nervous, but Miss Stanton had the gift of putting people at their ease, and distinguished strangers were not too common at Winton Parbeloe.

Mrs Bramley, however, had a grievance to air.

'I am sorry, Canon Rathbone,' she said, 'that we have not had the pleasure of seeing you at church.'

The old man looked up with a start, but it was Dr Curtius who spoke. 'Asthma,' he said, 'de asthma.'

'Yes, yes,' Canon Rathbone went on hurriedly. 'It is a curious thing, a very real misfortune, but I find, I find that the use of incense invariably brings on an attack. I have to be most careful.'

'And Dr Curtius,' said the undaunted Mrs Bramley, 'he suffers from asthma too?'

'Dr Curtius,' replied Canon Rathbone, 'is not a member of the Church of England.'

It was at this point that Hilda Newton changed the conversation. 'I wish,' she said, 'you would tell us something about your discoveries,

Canon Rathbone. I know you must have had the most thrilling adventures in the East. We in Winton Parbeloe lead such humdrum lives – foxes are the only things we hunt, you know – that it's hard for us to imagine the excitement of tracking down some priceless old manuscript.'

Canon Rathbone put down his cup. 'You are quite right, my dear young lady,' he said; 'the fascination is extreme, the fascination is quite remarkable. And then to Stanton's surprise he began to talk. He was no longer the nervous little clergyman, but the enthusiast carried away by his subject. He spoke of the monasteries of Greece and Asia Minor and Sinai, of libraries ransacked again and again by scholars, of piles of rubbish where even yet documents of extraordinary value could be found, of monks who seemed simple and ignorant but were often scholarly and astute, knowing quite well the worth of what they kept in secret hiding-places. 'Dr Curtius could tell you more about that,' he said. 'His first-hand experience is far greater than mine, but unfortunately he speaks little English.'

'Dat ees so,' said Dr Curtius, breaking silence for the second time. 'Greek, yes, Latin, yes, Armenian, yes, Syriac and Aramaic, but Engleesh hardly no.'

'The secret languages of dead mysteries,' said Miss Newton, 'with words for things and experiences that mean nothing to us poor humdrum mortals. How I envy you!'

'What's that? What's that?' asked Canon Rathbone nervously. 'As I was saying, the task of deciphering these palimpsests is extraordinarily difficult. You must remember that – '

But Stanton's eyes were fixed on Dr Curtius. He had eaten nothing and was now slowly stirring his tea. Why was it that the motion looked so clumsy? Because he was stirring it from left to right, of course, and because all the time he was watching like a great black cat the birdlike little figure of his friend on the sofa. What a horribly luxuriant beard the man has, thought Stanton, and then he found himself trying to see if he had a tonsure, only to avert his eyes hurriedly when Dr Curtius looked up into his face with an enigmatic smile.

Canon Rathbone was still talking.

' . . . they were of course difficult to procure, extremely difficult to procure, and to tell you the truth we had considerable trouble in getting them out of the country. The task of deciphering them is laborious. We burn the midnight oil, Miss Stanton, we burn the midnight oil, and my eyesight is, unfortunately, not as good as it was, but Dr Curtius is always ready to act as my spectacles.'

'It all sounds perfectly thrilling,' said Miss Newton. 'And when are the results to be published?'

'I am afraid,' said Canon Rathbone, 'I am afraid it may be rather difficult to find a publisher.'

'But the whole story, canon! It's a shame that it should be wasted. You should get Mr Stanton here to write it for you.' Dr Curtius and Canon Rathbone looked up at the same moment. Their eyes met, and it seemed to Stanton that Curtius nodded his head.

'Do I understand,' said Canon Rathbone, 'that Mr Stanton is an author? I am afraid I did not know. I am afraid I may have been rather indiscreet, a little precipitate. You will, of course, Mr Stanton, regard what I have said as strictly confidential. I mean, I mean – '

'We know exactly what you mean,' said Miss Newton with a laugh. 'You don't want fact turned into delightful fiction.'

'I am sure Mr Stanton knows what I mean. I like to think of myself, Miss Stanton, as a philosophical person who makes modern and familiar, things . . . things that are rather difficult to understand. I fear, I distrust – you will forgive me I know, Mr Stanton, quite probably I am quite mistaken – the imagination of the writer of fiction. Such a dangerous gift it always seems to me, so disturbingly dangerous. Dr Curtius, we must be going. Such a very pleasant visit, Miss Stanton, my . . . my asthma, you know, Mrs Bramley, impossible almost for me to get to church. You must all come and visit us at the Old Vicarage. So very kind of you, such a very enjoyable afternoon. Don't trouble to see us to the door, Mr Stanton. I assure you we can find our own way out.'

'Goodbye,' said Miss Stanton, 'I am afraid we have done little to entertain Dr Curtius.'

'I am happy,' he said as he bowed low over her hand, 'to be Canon Rathbone's – what do you say? Disciple? No, follower.'

Stanton went with his visitors to the door. He put his hand for a moment into the hot, moist hand of Canon Rathbone, into the cold, dry hand of Dr Curtius. Without a smile he said goodbye and watched them depart down the narrow gravel path, the old man leading with that curious shuffling gait that yet was almost half a run, the other, black-bearded, black-coated, following in his shadow with long inexorable strides.

He didn't feel like facing the chatter of the drawing-room. Something queer had happened, and he didn't know what it was. Of course he couldn't write that story now. Even if Hilda Newton hadn't been there he couldn't have written it. But it didn't matter. It would only have been a trifle anyway.

But why had they spiked his guns? How did they know that he had guns to spike? Why had he been so unmistakably warned off? Unless . . . unless he had got too near the truth? What was the truth?

With a feeling almost of relief he opened the drawing-room door. The chatter at least was reassuring. He feared to submit himself to an unknown fear.

August Heat

Penistone Road, Clapham
20th August, 190—

I have had what I believe to be the most remarkable day in my life, and while the events are still fresh in my mind, I wish to put them down on paper as clearly as possible.

Let me say at the outset that my name is James Clarence Withencroft.

I am forty years old, in perfect health, never having known a day's illness.

By profession I am an artist, not a very successful one, but I earn enough money by my black-and-white work to satisfy my necessary wants.

My only near relative, a sister, died five years ago, so that I am independent.

I breakfasted this morning at nine, and after glancing through the morning paper I lighted my pipe and proceeded to let my mind wander in the hope that I might chance upon some subject for my pencil.

The room, though door and windows were open, was oppressively hot, and I had just made up my mind that the coolest and most comfortable place in the neighbourhood would be the deep end of the public swimming-bath, when the idea came.

I began to draw. So intent was I on my work that I left my lunch untouched, only stopping work when the clock of St Jude's struck four.

The final result, for a hurried sketch, was, I felt sure, the best thing I had done.

It showed a criminal in the dock immediately after the judge had pronounced sentence. The man was fat – enormously fat. The flesh hung in rolls about his chin; it creased his huge, stumpy neck. He was clean-shaven (perhaps I should say a few days before he must have been clean shaven) and almost bald. He stood in the dock, his short, clumsy fingers clasping the rail, looking straight in front of him. The feeling that his expression conveyed was not so much one of horror as of utter, absolute collapse.

There seemed nothing in the man strong enough to sustain that mountain of flesh.

I rolled up the sketch, and without quite knowing why, placed it in my pocket. Then with the rare sense of happiness which the knowledge of a good thing well done gives, I left the house.

I believe that I set out with the idea of calling upon Trenton, for I remember walking along Lytton Street and turning to the right along Gilchrist Road at the bottom of the hill where the men were at work on the new tram lines.

From there onwards I have only the vaguest recollection of where I went. The one thing of which I was fully conscious was the awful heat, that came up from the dusty asphalt pavement as an almost palpable wave. I longed for the thunder promised by the great banks of copper-coloured cloud that hung low over the western sky.

I must have walked five or six miles, when a small boy roused me from my reverie by asking the time.

It was twenty minutes to seven.

When he left me I began to take stock of my bearings. I found myself standing before a gate that led into a yard bordered by a strip of thirsty earth, where there were flowers, purple stock and scarlet geranium. Above the entrance was a board with the inscription:

CHS. ATKINSON   MONUMENTAL MASON
WORKER IN ENGLISH AND ITALIAN MARBLES

From the yard itself came a cheery whistle, the noise of hammer blows, and the cold sound of steel meeting stone.

A sudden impulse made me enter.

A man was sitting with his back towards me, busy at work on a slab of curiously veined marble. He turned round as he heard my steps and I stopped short.

It was the man I had been drawing, whose portrait lay in my pocket.

He sat there, huge and elephantine, the sweat pouring from his scalp, which he wiped with a red silk handkerchief. But though the face was the same, the expression was absolutely different.

He greeted me smiling, as if we were old friends, and shook my hand.

I apologised for my intrusion.

'Everything is hot and glary outside,' I said. 'This seems an oasis in the wilderness.'

'I don't know about the oasis,' he replied, 'but it certainly is hot, as hot as hell. Take a seat, sir!'

He pointed to the end of the gravestone on which he was at work, and I sat down.

'That's a beautiful piece of stone you've got hold of,' I said.

He shook his head. 'In a way it is,' he answered; 'the surface here is as fine as anything you could wish, but there's a big flaw at the back, though I don't expect you'd ever notice it. I could never make a really good job of a bit of marble like that. It would be all right in a summer like this; it wouldn't mind the blasted heat. But wait till the winter comes. There's nothing quite like frost to find out the weak points in stone.'

'Then what's it for?' I asked.

The man burst out laughing.

'You'd hardly believe me if I was to tell you it's for an exhibition, but it's the truth. Artists have exhibitions: so do grocers and butchers; we have them too. All the latest little things in headstones, you know.'

He went on to talk of marbles, which sort best withstood wind and rain, and which were easiest to work; then of his garden and a new sort of carnation he had bought. At the end of every other minute he would drop his tools, wipe his shining head, and curse the heat.

I said little, for I felt uneasy. There was something unnatural, uncanny, in meeting this man.

I tried at first to persuade myself that I had seen him before, that his face, unknown to me, had found a place in some out-of-the-way corner of my memory, but I knew that I was practising little more than a plausible piece of self-deception.

Mr Atkinson finished his work, spat on the ground, and got up with a sigh of relief.

'There! what do you think of that?' he said, with an air of evident pride.

The inscription which I read for the first time was this:

SACRED TO THE MEMORY

OF

JAMES CLARENCE WITHENCROFT

BORN JAN. 18TH, 1860

HE PASSED AWAY VERY SUDDENLY

ON AUGUST 20TH, 190—

'*In the midst of life we are in death*'

For some time I sat in silence. Then a cold shudder ran down my spine. I asked him where he had seen the name.

'Oh, I didn't see it anywhere,' replied Mr Atkinson. 'I wanted some name, and I put down the first that came into my head. Why do you want to know?'

'It's a strange coincidence, but it happens to be mine.'

He gave a long, low whistle.

'And the dates?'

'I can only answer for one of them, and that's correct.'

'It's a rum go!' he said.

But he knew less than I did. I told him of my morning's work. I took the sketch from my pocket and showed it to him. As he looked, the expression of his face altered until it became more and more like that of the man I had drawn.

'And it was only the day before yesterday,' he said, 'that I told Maria there were no such things as ghosts!'

Neither of us had seen a ghost, but I knew what he meant.

'You probably heard my name,' I said.

'And you must have seen me somewhere and have forgotten it! Were you at Clacton-on-Sea last July?'

I had never been to Clacton in my life. We were silent for some time. We were both looking at the same thing, the two dates on the gravestone, and one was right.

'Come inside and have some supper,' said Mr Atkinson.

His wife is a cheerful little woman, with the flaky red cheeks of the country-bred. Her husband introduced me as a friend of his who was an artist. The result was unfortunate, for after the sardines and watercress had been removed, she brought out a Doré Bible, and I had to sit and express my admiration for nearly half an hour.

I went outside, and found Atkinson sitting on the gravestone smoking.

We resumed the conversation at the point we had left off.

'You must excuse my asking,' I said, 'but do you know of anything you've done for which you could be put on trial?'

He shook his head.

'I'm not a bankrupt, the business is prosperous enough. Three years ago I gave turkeys to some of the guardians at Christmas, but that's all I can think of. And they were small ones, too,' he added as an afterthought.

He got up, fetched a can from the porch, and began to water the flowers. 'Twice a day regular in the hot weather,' he said, 'and then the heat sometimes gets the better of the delicate ones. And ferns, good Lord! they could never stand it. Where do you live?'

I told him my address. It would take an hour's quick walk to get back home.

'It's like this,' he said. 'We'll look at the matter straight. If you go back home tonight, you take your chance of accidents. A cart may run over you, and there's always banana skins and orange peel, to say nothing of falling ladders.'

He spoke of the improbable with an intense seriousness that would have been laughable six hours before. But I did not laugh.

'The best thing we can do,' he continued, 'is for you to stay here till twelve o'clock. We'll go upstairs and smoke; it may be cooler inside.'

To my surprise I agreed.

* * *

We are sitting now in a long, low room beneath the eaves. Atkinson has sent his wife to bed. He himself is busy sharpening some tools at a little oilstone, smoking one of my cigars the while.

The air seems charged with thunder. I am writing this at a shaky table before the open window. The leg is cracked, and Atkinson, who seems a handy man with his tools, is going to mend it as soon as he has finished putting an edge on his chisel.

It is after eleven now. I shall be gone in less than an hour.

But the heat is stifling.

It is enough to send a man mad.

Sarah Bennet's Possession

The man looked into the old cracked mirror,
    For years he had ceased to polish it;
He saw the nature of his error,
    And vowed he would abolish it.
He cleansed his house of all sign of revel,
    He shuttered his windows to the night;
And never saw the laughing devil
    In the shadow cast by the candle light!

Through the long dark night, his fears allaying,
    His eyes were closed and he could not see,
He knelt in abject terror praying
    To the image nailed on the wooden tree.
And he has done with wine and revels –
    Was that the gnawing of a mouse?
Or was it the laughter of the devils
    As they enter again into his house?

They laugh to themselves, the devils seven,
    As they think of the women and wine of old,
For the gulf still lies between Hell and Heaven,
    And there's none to hear in the shrine of gold.
He'll tread for ever the easy levels –
    Someone tapped on the window pane;
And as he knelt, the seven devils
    Laughing came to their own again.

Risingham Farm stands on the skyline of one of the great whale-backed Berkshire downs. Its roof of tile, red once, but weathered now by rain and softened by lichen, seems ever in keeping with the soft browns and greys of the short, sheep-trimmed grass.

Half a mile along the Roman road stands Risingham Castle, from which the farm had taken its name; a great square piece of land, surrounded by ditch and rampart, with a view of hill and valley, ploughland and pastureland for close on fifty miles.

I first learned to know the farm because it was the home of Frank Dicey. Here he came to spend the week or fortnight's leave that was given him, before his ship set out once again for the other side of the world, and from the farm, only two years ago, he married the youngest of the three princesses.

The three princesses were his cousins. It was he who gave them their names, in the days before Grimm had been buried with the last of the school books in the lumber-room at the back of the barn. In accordance with the unwritten law of Fairyland, they were known in age order as the Wicked, the Ugly, and the Beautiful.

They, like Frank, were orphans; and their parents dying almost before their children could remember, they had been brought to Risingham by their great-aunt, Mrs Bennet (Sarah Bennet she would have called herself, in the plain Quaker fashion), who had ever since been a fairy godmother to her nieces and nephew.

I remember the old lady best as first I saw her, dressed in the delicate lilac-coloured silk of a bygone age, with a large Quaker bonnet, a purple aureole, enclosing her face.

Her delicate hands, on which the veins showed so clearly, seemed wonderfully frail; but she was a woman of unlooked-for strength and unabating energy, with a voice clear and distinct, that changed when she spoke in meeting to a musical treble.

This woman, a saint in true communion with those of old, was closely associated with, was indeed the centre of, a series of unusual occurrences that spread over a period of five years, and which, for all I know, may have been going on for a much longer time. In themselves they seem disjointed, perhaps insignificant. Taken together they form a tragedy.

* * *

It was a late September evening, dark, for the harvest moon had not yet risen behind the down, and with the faint scent of the cornfields in the air. I had met Frank Dicey in Southampton that afternoon, and now at nine we were climbing the last hill that separated us from the lights of Risingham Farm.

We stopped on the ridge, and as we waited we felt something of the wonderful peace which dwells on the downs, where the sky seems more open and the earth more remote than among the mountains or in the plains.

Then as I looked, I suddenly saw a lantern flash half a mile to our right, by the dew-pond.

When Frank was a boy, he and the youngest princess had saved their pocket-money all summer to buy a little signalling lamp, and when autumn came they went about in the evenings flashing their badly spelled messages from hillside to hillside.

'I expect she wants to speak to you now,' I said. 'You needn't mind me; it's a language I can't understand.'

'Take down the letters,' he answered, 'as I tell you them.'

It was certainly an unexpected message; part of it was undecipherable, but what Frank made out read as follows. I omit a preliminary string of oaths.

'This is . . . trying to get into communication. Why the devil won't you answer? I want to say – '

The point of light had ceased to move. It remained steady for a minute, and then went out.

I looked at Frank curiously.

'Some joke,' I suggested.

'I suppose so,' he answered. It was evidently a joke he did not appreciate. It was not until we had been welcomed and fed, that Frank remembered.

'Who was it signalling down by the dew-pond an hour ago?' he asked.

No one had been signalling. They had all been busy in the kitchen, except Aunt Sarah, who had been down with the lantern to see that the paddock gate was closed.

Frank said he must have been mistaken.

'But I'm blest if I am,' he added, when the others had left the room.

* * *

I was at Risingham Farm in the September of the following year. It was Sunday, and the others had gone to meeting, leaving me to profit by their absence by indulging in the luxury of a pipe. I am afraid Mrs Bennet believed that I never smoked.

From the steep down-side, where I lay, I watched them leave the meeting-house, the old lady leading the way with the Wicked and Ugly Princesses on either side, and Frank and the Beautiful Princess bringing up the rear.

They had had a quiet meeting, Frank said; no one had spoken, with the exception of aunt. She had preached about heaven, had in fact given a general description of it, from which it seemed that it was just the place for a friend of his, a Bond Street jeweller who had designed his own house on not dissimilar lines.

I asked leave to accompany them to the evening meeting.

'Aunt generally makes her biggest score in the second innings,' said Frank, but he was reproved for levity.

There are times when nothing is so impressive as a Quakers' meeting. That September evening was certainly one.

The lamps had not been lit – there was no need for them. The silence was unbroken. Now and then across the open door, for the day had been warm, a bat flitted.

Sarah Bennet sat alone in the ministers' gallery; the outline of her bonnet was almost lost against the dark oak of the wainscot.

At the end of half an hour, just as Frank had produced a pencil and paper to begin a sketch of his cousin's profile, she spoke.

She took as her text those terrible words of the Gospel: 'And beside all this, between us and you there is a great gulf fixed: so that they which would pass from hence to you cannot, neither can they pass to us that would come from thence.'

She described to us a battlefield, not beneath an English sky, but a battlefield burnt and scorched by a tropical sun. She pictured the agonies of the wounded, their unslaked thirst, the unmasking of the beast in those who conquered, the terror of the defeated. She told how all the while up in the blue dome of heaven above the carnage, birds were singing, oblivious of all.

And with this as a picture, she spoke of hell, of its awful reality, until I shuddered.

Yet from beginning to end her voice never changed from the sweet, monotonous treble chant. She never raised her eyes from the gallery rail on which she leant, which her thin blue-veined hand clasped so tightly.

When we left the meeting-house, the red disc of the moon was just showing over the treetops. Neither Frank nor I spoke till we were in sight of home. Then he said: 'I remember talking with a fellow once, about those accidents in coal mines. He was an insignificant little chap with spectacles and a stutter, but he knew how to talk. I told him afterwards that he had a morbid imagination. "Oh, no, I haven't," he said, "I was shut in the pit once for four days. I'm talking about what I've seen." That's what I felt when I heard Aunt Sarah.' Then after a pause, he added: 'It's curious, you know. On the face of it her description of heaven ought to have been the best.'

* * *

The night outside was dark and gusty, a night that made the small room with its large fire more than usually comfortable.

The blinds had not been drawn, for unlike most ladies, Sarah Bennet had no objection to see the shadowy branches of the laurels as they tapped against the pane; and the country people liked her the better, for the light of the lamp as it stood on the table by the window served as a beacon for travellers who otherwise might have fancied themselves alone on the broad back of the downs.

We had been seated around the fire, talking; Frank and the youngest princess in the corner where the shadows were longest, while I held a skein of soft grey wool for the old lady to wind.

It was the Wicked Sister who, having finished her book, suggested a game. I forget what we played, but I remember Frank did not win. I think he was busy drawing the Beautiful Princess. She did not admire the likeness, though he was certainly clever with his pencil.

'I could do better with my eyes shut,' she said.

'Very well,' he replied. 'Let us see who can make the best portrait of anyone in the room without looking.'

'Turn out the lamp,' said Margaret, 'and we'll begin.'

The flickering light of the fire had for the time being died down; the flames curling under a huge log of wood were too intent on searching for a hold to show themselves, except in sudden darts and flashes.

Mrs Bennet sat in her high-backed chair slightly turned from us, looking into the garden beyond. A pencil and paper lay on her lap, but her hands were folded.

'Well, is it to be anyone in the room?' asked the youngest princess. 'That rules out Frank, he being nobody. I think we might be allowed a little more light.'

For three minutes no one spoke.

'Time!' said Frank. 'Light the lamp and let's see the results. Give me the papers, and we'll guess who they are. So you've been drawing, auntie?' he said as he took her sheet, 'I thought you had gone to sleep.'

Frank's was the first portrait we saw – a most spirited sketch of a goose. 'You see,' he explained, 'if I am to be snubbed by being called nobody, I must have my revenge.'

Then the rest followed, amusing caricatures, for the most part unrecognisable.

Suddenly Frank started up.

'Who in the world is that?' he said.

He held in his hand the piece of paper that had been in Mrs Bennet's lap. On it was a drawing, as cleverly executed a sketch as I have ever seen of a man, a young man, dressed in an officer's uniform of half a century ago. He was kneeling with his hands clasped in the attitude of supplication. His features, coarse and ugly as they were, were cast into an expression that seemed to demand pity. It was not entirely a black-and-white drawing; for on the side of his coat was a little patch of red, put in with coloured chalk. There was a little pool of red on the ground on which he knelt.

Frank looked puzzled. 'I never dreamed you could draw as well as that, auntie. But it was to be someone present in the room!'

Mrs Bennet was still gazing out into the night.

'Well, children,' she said, 'what have you been playing at? Francis, what is that thou hast in thy hand? Bring the lamp a little nearer.'

We stood watching her impatiently. She had placed the spectacles on her nose, and had taken up the paper in her hand, when suddenly her face blanched and she let drop with a cry.

'Henry!' she said, in a deep voice that we hardly recognised, and then again: 'Henry!' She stood up trembling, and walking to the fire, thrust the paper into the flame.

Then she turned round.

'Francis,' she said, 'I must ask thee never to draw that man again.'

*   *   *

A year afterwards we were seated once again in the little parlour. The girls had been singing, and Frank had taken their place at the piano. He sat down with a sailor's confidence and began to play; he said he had forgotten the name of the piece, but I think I recognised it as coming from an opera.

Mrs Bennet had a strong affection for Frank. She had paid little attention to his cousins while they sang, but as soon as her boy began to strum, she left her work and stood behind him at the piano, while her foot beat time to the music.

I should say while she tried to beat time to the music. For she had no ear for either time or harmony.

I noticed that as he went on, Frank looked perplexed, nor was he playing as well as he was able. He stopped abruptly. 'Come outside,' he said, 'the room is stifling.'

'You don't happen to know the Morse code?' he asked. 'If you did I think you would be more surprised than you are at present. I wonder how long it took her to learn it?'

'What on earth are you talking about?' I said.

'I'm not quite sure,' Frank replied, 'but when you thought Aunt Sarah was marking time to the music, she may have been doing so; but at the same time she was spelling out a message to someone in the Morse code.'

'What was it?' I asked.

'Oh, utter nonsense,' he replied: "Present arms! Fire! No, damn it. Why won't you hear me? I shall be done for unless you – "

'I don't know how it ended, for I couldn't play any more.'

We went inside again. Mrs Bennet was reading her Bible in the high-backed chair by the fireside.

'I am afraid thou hast caught cold, Frank,' she said. 'I will go into the kitchen and make thee some camomile tea.'

*   *   *

The last link in this chain of strange occurrences was given me the following September, the year of Frank's wedding.

We were at the breakfast-table, and I had just finished narrating an absurd dream in which I encircled the island of Corsica in a flying machine.

'Thy dream seems to have been very curious,' said Mrs Bennet, 'but I had one last night, that I believe I may say was even more so. In my dream I was present at a large ball, I think it must have been a ball, though I never attended one in my life. Everyone wore beautiful white dresses, and we all drank soup out of large china bowls. I had begun to drink mine, when someone pushed me violently from behind, with the result that I spilt the whole of the contents of the basin over my dress, and I am sure must have ruined it. At the same time, I heard an odd voice behind me say: "Yes, Sarah, it was I who did it, and for the last fifty years I have been trying to apologise." I looked round to see who it was speaking in so unusual a manner, and thou canst picture my surprise when I saw a monkey, I think it must have been a monkey, dressed in men's clothes and standing at my elbow. There was something so human in the pathos of its look, that I burst out laughing. The poor animal seemed quite offended, and slunk away to the sideboard where the waiters were serving soup. It turned round once, and with a snarl that showed all its teeth, muttered "Too late!" and then was gone.' And Mrs Bennet laughed heartily. The old lady had a great gift of humour.

Each of the occurrences that I have narrated impressed me more or less forcibly at the time, but I should probably soon have forgotten them if I had not heard the story which to my mind links them together in a very definite way.

When Sarah Bennet was a girl, she had loved and married a captain in the Engineers.

He was clever, with a love of poetry and literature unusual in one of his profession, but his nature was wild and dissolute. He was cruel too. I heard only yesterday a story told of him, that dealt with the sacking of a Burmese village; it was only part of a story too, for a peppery Indian colonel stopped the teller before he was half-way through.

This captain, I learned, had married his wife for a bet. He had gone with a friend of his out of curiosity to a Friends' meeting, and there they had seen Sarah Cruikshank. I suppose the difference between the quietly dressed Quaker girl and the disreputable scoundrel at his side seemed so immense to the man who proposed the wager, that he staked his guineas recklessly. But he lost his bet, and the captain married his bride against the wish of her parents, taking her from her quiet country home to a life of squalor and misery in a garrison town. At the end of six months the regiment was to move, but he deceived her as to its destination. She awoke one morning to find that her husband had left with his company for India, while she, with hardly a shilling to pay for the next meal, was saddled with his bad debts. Through the kindness of the members of her society, Sarah Bennet was able to return home, and there she lived with her parents, trying to forget that she had ever left them.

No tidings ever came to her from her husband. She had thought of him as dead long before she read in the paper the brief notice of the action in which he was killed. And so as time went on the tragedy of her past was forgotten by others; even for herself it lost its sting.

The evil which befalls us is often forgotten. It is harder to forget the evil that we do.

When the little that remained of Captain Bennet that was not carnal passed into the great unknown, he realised, as his wife had never realised, the extent of the evil that he had done. He tried with all his power to let her know his sorrow, tried perhaps with all the more success, because his soul was not far removed from earth. But, as of old, there was the great gulf fixed, the unbridgeable abyss between good and evil. There was the tragedy of it, his repentance had come too late.

I sometimes think that if she had been less holy, he might have succeeded in letting her know of his repentance; but as it was, his greatest strivings appeared to her nothing more than the ludicrous images of a dream.

In the past, he scarcely lingered in her memory; in the present there was no channel left, there was nothing in common between her and him.

Mrs Bennet, laughing over her dream, is an epitome of the cruelty of perfect justice.

After her death when I was looking through the old lady's papers, I came across two sets of verses written in her exquisite hand. I do not think she could have copied them. As a conscientious minister of the Society of Friends, she would have disapproved of the sentiments. These verses I have placed at the beginning and end of my story, for they seem to afford final proof of the fact of Sarah Bennet's possession.

> Plenty followed after Peace,
>   And bought her men with gold,
> Who spoke of the time when wars should cease,
>   Forgetting the days of old.
> But men for ever will arise
>   Who hate with holy rage
> The easy cant of compromise,
>   Who know their heritage!
>
> It's not for the sound of fife and drum;
> But they like the life and so they come,
>   As their fathers came before –
> English boys from the playing fields –
> To taste the joys that slaying yields,
>   To play the game of war!
>
> Give us war in our time, O Lord!
>   For peace let women pray,
> A hardened heart and a two-edged sword
>   And a lust to kill and slay!
> Fire and famine in our wake,
>   The cities lie before,
> Nerve your arm for the plunder's sake,
>   Follow the dogs of war!
>
> They'll come to the call of the drum and fife,
> And laughing leave their home and wife,
>   As before their fathers came.
> The tattered flag has cleft the wind,
> And it's only the wounded are left behind,
>   For war, red war's the game!

The Ankardyne Pew

The following narrative of the occurrences that took place at Ankardyne House in February 1890, is made up chiefly of extracts from letters written by my friend, the Rev. Thomas Prendergast, to his wife, immediately before taking up residence at the vicarage, together with transcripts from the diary which I kept at the time. The names throughout are, of course, fictitious.

February 9th. I am sorry that I had no opportunity yesterday of getting over to the vicarage, so your questions – I have not lost the list – must remain unanswered. It is almost a quarter of a mile away from the church, in the village. You see, the church, unfortunately, is in the grounds of the park, and there is a flagged passage, cold and horribly draughty, that leads from Ankardyne House to the great loose box of the Ankardyne pew. The squires in the old days could come in late and go out early, or even stay away altogether, without anyone being the wiser. The whole situation of the church is bad and typically English – the House of God in the squire's pocket. Why should he have right of secret access? I haven't had time to examine the interior – early eighteenth-century, I should guess – but as we drove up last evening in the dusk, the tall gloomy façade of Ankardyne House, with the elegant little church – a Wren's nest – adjoining it, made me think of a wicked uncle, setting off for a walk in the woods with one of the babes. The picture is really rather apt, as you will agree, when you see the place. It's partly a question of the height of the two buildings, partly a question of the shape of the windows, those of the one square, deep-set, and grim; of the other round – the raised eyebrows of startled innocence.

We were quite wrong about Miss Ankardyne. She is a charming little lady, not a trace of Lady Catherine de Burgh, and is really looking forward to having you as her nearest neighbour. I will write more of her tomorrow, but the stable clock has struck eleven and my candle is burning low.

February 10th. I measured the rooms as you asked me to. They
are, of course, larger than ours at Garvington, and will swallow all
our furniture and carpets. But you will like the vicarage. It, at least, is
a cheerful house; faces south, and isn't, like this place, surrounded by
woods. I suppose familiarity with the skies and wide horizons of the
fens accounts for the shut-in feeling one gets here. But I have never
seen such cedars!

And now to describe Miss Ankardyne. She is perhaps seventy-five,
petite and birdlike, with the graceful, alert poise of a bird. I should
say that sight and hearing are abnormally acute and have helped to
keep her young. She is a good talker, well read, and interested in
affairs, and a still better listener. Parson's pride! you will exclaim;
since we are only two, and if she listens, I must talk. But I mean what
I say. All that the archdeacon told us is true; you are conscious in her
presence of a living spirit of peace. By the way, she is an interesting
example of your theory that there are some people for whom animals
have an instinctive dislike – indeed, the best example I have met.
For Miss Ankardyne tells me that, though since childhood she has
had a fondness for all living creatures, especially for birds, it is one
which is not at first reciprocated. She can, after assiduous, continuous persevering, win their affection; her spaniel, her parrot, and
Karkar, the tortoiseshell cat, are obviously attached to her. But
strange dogs snarl, if she attempts to fondle them; and she tells me
that, when she goes to the farm to feed the fowls, the birds seem to
sense her coming and run from the scattered corn. I have heard of
cows showing this antipathy to individuals, but never before of
birds. There is an excellent library here, that badly needs cataloguing. The old vicar, had, I believe, begun the task at the time of
his fatal seizure.

I have been inside the church. Anything less like dear old Garbing-
ton it would be impossible to find. Architecturally, it has its points,
but the unity of design, on which everything here depends, is broken
by the Ankardyne pew. Its privacy is an abomination. Even from the
pulpit it is impossible to see inside, and I can well believe the stories
of the dicing squires and their Sunday play. Miss Ankardyne refuses
to use it. The glass is crude and uninteresting; but there is an uncommon chancel screen of Spanish workmanship, which somehow
seems in keeping with the place. I wish it didn't.

We shall miss the old familiar monuments. There is no snubnosed
crusader here, no worthy Elizabethan knight, like our Sir John Park-
ington, kneeling in supplication, with those nicely balanced families

on right and left. The tombs are nearly all Ankardyne tombs – urns, weeping charities, disconsolate relicts, and all the cold Christian virtues. You know the sort. The Ten Commandments are painted on oak panels on either side of the altar. From the Ankardyne pew I doubt if you can see them.

February 11th. You ask about my neuritis. It is better, despite the fact that I have been sleeping badly. I wake up in the morning, sometimes during the night, with a burning headache and a curious tingling feeling about the tongue, which I can only attribute to indigestion. I am trying the effect of a glass of hot water before retiring. When we move into the vicarage, we shall at least be spared the attention of the owls, which make the nights so dismal here. The place is far too shut in by trees, and I suppose, too, that the disused outbuildings give them shelter. Cats are bad enough, but I prefer the sound of night-walkers to night-fliers. It won't be long now before we meet. They are getting on splendidly with the vicarage. The painters have already started work; the new kitchen range has come, and is only waiting for the plumbers to put it in. Miss Ankardyne is leaving for a visit to friends in a few days' time. It seems that she always goes away about this season of the year – wise woman! – so I shall be alone next week. She said Dr Hulse would be glad to put me up, if I find the solitude oppressive, but I shan't trouble him. You would like the old butler. His name is Mason, and his wife – a Scotchwoman – acts as housekeeper. The three maids are sisters. They have been with Miss Ankardyne for thirty years, and are everything that maids should be. They belong to the Peculiar People. I cannot desire that they should be orthodox. If I could be sure that Dr Hulse was as well served . . .

February 13th. I had an experience last night which moved me strangely. I hardly know what to make of it. I went to bed at half-past ten after a quiet evening with Miss Ankardyne. I thought she seemed in rather poor spirits, and tried to cheer her by reading aloud. She chose a chapter from *The Vicar of Wakefield*. I awoke soon after one with an intolerable feeling of oppression, almost of dread. I was conscious, too – and in some way my alarm was associated with this – of a burning, tingling, piercing pain in my tongue. I got up from bed and was about to pour myself out a glass of water, when I heard the sound of someone speaking. The voice was low and continuous, and seemed to come from an adjoining room. I slipped on my dressing-gown and, candle in hand, went out into the corridor. For a moment I stood in silence. Frankly, I was afraid. The voice proceeded from a room two doors away from mine. As I listened, I recognised it as Miss Ankardyne's. She was repeating the Benedicite.

There were such depths of sadness, so much of the weariness of defeat in this song of triumph of the Three Children saved from the furnace of fire, that I felt I could not leave her. I should have spoken before knocking, for I could almost feel that gasp of fear. 'Oh, no!' she said, 'Oh, no! Not now!' and then, as if bracing herself for a great effort: 'Who is it?'

I told her and she bade me enter. The poor little woman had risen from her knees and was trembling from head to foot. I spent about an hour with her and left her sleeping peacefully. I did not wish to rouse the house, but I managed to find the Masons' room and arranged for Mrs Mason to sit by the old lady.

I can't say what happened in that hour we spent together in talk and in prayer. There is something very horrible about this house, that Miss Ankardyne is dimly aware of. Something connected with pain and fire and a bird, and something that was human too. I was shaken to the very depths of my being. I don't think I ever felt the need for prayer and the power of prayer as I did last night. The stable clock has just struck five.

February 14th. I have arranged for Miss Ankardyne to go away tomorrow. She is fit to travel, and is hardly fit to stay. I had a long talk with her this morning. I think she is the most courageous woman I know. All her life she has felt that the house is haunted, and all her life she has felt pity for that which haunts it. She says that she is sure that she is living it down; that the house is better than it was; but that at this season of the year it is almost too much for her. She is anxious that I should stay with Dr Hulse. I feel, however, that I must see this business through. She then suggested that I should invite a friend to stay with me. I thought of Pellow. You remember how we were obliged to postpone his visit last September. I had a letter from him only last Friday. He is living in this part of the world and could probably run over for a day or two.

* * *

The extracts from Mr Prendergast's letters end here. The following are excerpts from my diary.

February 16th. Arrived at Ankardyne House at midday. Prendergast had meant to meet me at the station, but had been suddenly called away to visit a dying parishioner. I had in consequence a couple of hours by myself in which to form an impression of the place. The house dates from the early eighteenth century. It is dignified though sombre, and is closely surrounded on three sides by shrubberies of rhododendrons and laurel, that merge into thick woods. The cedars in the park must be older than any of the buildings. Miss Ankardyne, I gather, has lived here all her life, and the house gives you the impression of having been lived in, a slightly sinister mansion, well aired by a kindly soul. There is a library that should be well worth exploring. The family portraits are in the dining-room. None are of outstanding interest. The most unusual feature of the house is its connection with the church, which has many of the characteristics of a private chapel. It does not actually abut on the building, but is joined to it by a low, curved façade, unpierced by windows A corridor, lighted from above, runs behind the façade and gives a private entry from the house to the church. The door into this corridor opens into the spacious hall of Ankardyne House; but there is a second mode of access (of which Prendergast seemed unaware) from Miss Ankardyne's bed-chamber down a narrow stair. This door is kept locked and has never been opened, as far as Mason, the butler, can recollect. The church, with the curved façade connecting it to the house, is balanced on the other side by the coach-house and stables, which can be approached in a similar manner from the kitchens. The architect has certainly succeeded in conveying the idea that religion and horseflesh can be made elegant adjuncts to the life of a country gentleman. Prendergast came in just before luncheon. He does not look well, and was obviously glad to see me and to unburden himself. In the afternoon I had a long talk with Mason, the butler, a very level-headed man.

From what Prendergast tells me I gather that Miss Ankardyne's experiences have been both auditory and visual. They are certainly vague.

Auditory. The cry of a bird – sometimes she thinks it is an owl, sometimes a cock – sometimes a human cry with something birdlike in it. This she has heard almost as long as she can remember, both outside the house and inside her room, but most frequently in the direction of the corridor that leads to the church. The cry is chiefly heard at night, hardly ever before dusk. (This would point to an owl.) It has become less frequent of recent years, but at this particular season is most persistent. Mason confirms this. He doesn't like the sound, and doesn't know what to make of it. The maids believe that it is an evil spirit; but, as it can have no power over them – they belong to the Peculiar People – they take no notice of it.

Visual and Sensory. From time to time – less frequently, again, of recent years – Miss Ankardyne wakes up 'with her eyes balls of fire'. She can distinguish nothing clearly for several minutes. Then the red spheres slowly contract to pinpricks; there is a moment of sharp pain; and normal vision is restored. At other times she is aroused from sleep by a sharp, piercing pain in her tongue. She has consulted several oculists, who find that her sight is perfectly normal. I believe she has never known a day's illness. Prendergast seems to have had a similar, though less vivid, experience; he used the term 'burning' headache.

I have elicited from Mason the statement that animals dislike the house, with the exception of Karkar, Miss Ankardyne's cat, who seems entirely unaffected. The spaniel refuses to sleep in Miss Ankardyne's bedroom; and on one occasion, when the parrot's cage was brought up there, the bird 'fell into such a screaming fit, that it nearly brought the house down.' This I believe, for I tried the experiment myself with the reluctant consent of Mrs Mason. The feathers of the bird lay back flat on its head and neck with rage, and then it began to shriek in a really horrible way.

All this, of course, is very vague. We have no real evidence of anything supernatural. What impresses me most is the influence of the house on a woman of Miss Ankardyne's high character and courage.

February 18th. Certainly an interesting night. After a long walk with Prendergast in the afternoon I went to bed early with a volume of Trollope and a long candle. I did what I have never done before – fell asleep with the candle burning. When I awoke, it was within an inch of the socket; the fire had settled into a dull glow. Close to the candlestick on the table by my bedside stood a carafe of water. As I lay in bed, too sleepy to move, I was conscious of the hypnotic effect induced by gazing into a crystal. Slowly the surface of the glass grew dim and then gradually cleared from the centre. I was looking into the interior of a building, which I at once recognised as Ankardyne church. I could make out the screen and the Ankardyne pew. It seemed to be night, though I could see more clearly than if it had been night – the monuments in the aisle, for example. There were not as many as there are now. Presently the door of the Ankardyne pew opened and a man stepped out. He was dressed in black coat and knee-breeches, such as a clergyman might have worn a century or more ago. In one hand he held a lighted candle, the flame of which he sheltered with the other. I judged him to be of middle age. His face wore an expression of extreme apprehension. He crossed the church, casting backward glances as he went, and stopped before one of the mural monuments in the south aisle. Then, placing his candle on the ground, he drew from his pocket a hammer and some tools and, kneeling on the ground, began to work feverishly at the base of the inscription. When he had finished – and the task was not long – he seemed to moisten a finger and, running it along the floor, rubbed the dust into the newly cut stone. He then picked up his tools and began to retrace his steps. But the wind seemed to have risen; he had difficulty in shielding the flame of the candle, and just before he regained the door of the Ankardyne pew, it went out.

That was all that I saw in the crystal. I was now wide awake. I got out of bed, put fresh fuel on the fire, and wrote this account in my diary, while the picture was still vivid.

February 19th. Slept splendidly, despite the fact that I was pre- pared to spend a wakeful night. After a late breakfast I went with Prendergast into the church and had no difficulty in identifying the monument. It is in the east end of the south aisle, immediately opposite the Ankardyne pew and partly hidden by the American organ. The inscription reads:

IN MEMORY OF
FRANCIS ANKARDYNE, ESQUIRE
of Ankardyne Hall, in the County of Worcester,
late Captain in His Majesty's 42nd Regiment
of Foot
He departed this life 27th February 1781
Rev. xiv. 12, 13

I brought the Bible from the lectern. 'Here are lives,' said Prender- gast, 'which can fitly be commemorated by such verses: "Here is the patience of the saints; here are they that keep the commandments of God." Miss Ankardyne's is one. And I suppose,' he added, 'that there may be some of whom the eleventh verse is true.' He read it out to me: 'And the smoke of their torment ascendeth for ever and ever; and they have no rest day nor night, who worship the beast and his image, and whosoever receiveth the mark of his name.'

I thought at first that he was right; that the 12 might originally have been engraved as 11. But closer scrutiny showed that, though some of the figures had certainly been tampered with, it was not either the 2 or the 3. Prendergast hit on what I believe is the right solution. 'The R,' he said, 'has been superimposed on an L, and the 1 was originally 5. The reference is to Leviticus xiv. 52, 53.' If he is correct, we have still far to go. I have read and re-read those verses so often during the day, that I can write them down from memory.

> And he shall cleanse the house with the blood of the bird, and with the running water, and with the living bird, and with the cedar wood, and with the hyssop, and with the scarlet:
> But he shall let go the living bird out of the city into the open fields, and make an atonement for the house; and it shall be clean.

Miss Ankardyne told Prendergast that she was dimly aware of something connected with pain and fire and a bird. It is at least a curious coincidence.

Mason knows nothing about Francis Ankardyne except his name. He tells me that the Ankardyne squires of a hundred years ago had a reputation for evil living; in that, of course, they were not peculiar.

Spent the afternoon in the library in a rather fruitless search for clues. I found two books with the name 'Francis Ankardyne' written on the flyleaf. It was perhaps just as well that they should be tucked away on one of the upper shelves. One was inscribed as the gift of his cousin, Cotter Crawley. Query: Who is Crawley, and can he be identified with my man in black?

I tried to reproduce the crystal-gazing under conditions similar to those of the other night, but without success. I have twice heard the bird. It might be either an owl or a cock. The sound seemed to come from outside the house, and was not pleasant.

February 19th. Tomorrow Prendergast moves into the vicarage and I return home. Miss Ankardyne prolongs her stay at Malvern for another fortnight, and is then to visit friends on the south coast. I should like to have seen and questioned her, and so have discovered something more of the family history. Both Prendergast and I are disappointed. It seemed as if we were on the point of solving the mystery, and now it is as dark as ever. This new society in which Myers is interested should investigate the place.

So ends my diary, but not the story. Some four months after the events narrated I managed to secure through a second-hand book dealer four bound volumes of the *Gentleman's Magazine*. They had belonged to a Rev. Charles Phipson, once Fellow of Brasenose College and incumbent of Norton-on-the-Wolds. One evening, as I was glancing through them at my leisure, I came upon the following passage, under the date April 1789.

At Tottenham, John Ardenoif, Esq., a young man of large fortune and in the splendour of his carriages and horses rivalled by few country gentlemen. His table was that of hospitality, where, it may be said, he sacrificed too much to conviviality; but, if he had his foibles, he had his merits also, that far outweighed them. Mr A. was very fond of cock-fighting and had a favourite cock upon which he won many profitable matches. The last bet he laid upon this cock he lost, which so enraged him that he had the bird tied to a spit and roasted alive before a large fire. The screams of the miserable bird were so affecting, that some gentlemen who were present attempted to interfere, which so enraged Mr A. that he seized a poker and with the most furious vehemence declared that he would kill the first man who interposed; but, in the midst of his passionate asseverations, he fell down dead upon the spot. Such, we are assured, were the circumstances which attended the death of this great pillar of humanity.

Beneath was written:
See also the narrative of Mr C— at the end of this volume.

I give the story as I found it, inscribed in minute handwriting on the terminal flyleaves:

During his last illness the Rev. Mr C— gave me the following account of a similar instance of Divine Judgment. Mr A— of A— House, in the county of W—, was notorious for his open practice of infidelity. He was an ardent votary of the chase, a reckless gamester, and was an enthusiast in his love of cock-fighting. After carousing one evening with a boon companion, he proposed that they should then and there match the birds which they had entered for a contest on the morrow. His friend declaring that his bird should fight only in a cockpit, Mr A— announced that he had one adjoining the very room in which they were. The birds were brought, lights called for, and Mr A—, opening the door, led his guest down a flight of stairs and along a corridor to what he at first supposed were the stables. It was only after the match had begun, that he realised to his horror that they were in the family pew of A— church, to which A— House had private access. His expostulations only enraged his host, who commenced to blaspheme, wagering his very soul on the success of his bird, the victor of fifty fights. On this occasion the cock was defeated. Beside himself with frenzy, Mr A— rushed back to his bedchamber and, declaring that the Judgment Day had come and that the bird should never crow again, thrust a wire into the embers, burned out its eyes, and bored through its tongue. He then fell down in some form of apoplectic fit. He recovered and continued his frenzied course of living for some years. It was noticed, however, that he had an impediment in his speech, especially remarkable when he was enraged, the effect of which was to make him utter a sound like the crowing of a cock. It became a cant phrase in the neighbourhood: 'When A— crows, honest men must move.' Two years after this awful occurrence, his sight began to fail. He was killed in the hunting field. His horse took fright and, bolting, carried him for over a mile across bad country to break his neck in an attempt to leap a ten-foot wall. At each obstacle they encountered, Mr A— called out, but the noise that came from his throat only seemed to terrify his horse the more. Mr C— vouches for the truth of the story, having had personal acquaintance with both the parties.

The supposition that the Rev. Mr C— was none other than the boon companion of Francis Ankardyne did not seem to occur to the mind of the worthy Mr Phipson. That such was the case, I have no doubt. I saw him once in a glass darkly; and I saw later at Ankardyne House a silhouette of Cotter Crawley in an old album, and recognised the weak, foolish profile.

Who it was who drew up the wording of the monument in Ankardyne church, I do not know. Probably the trustees of the heir, a distant kinsman and a mere boy. Perhaps the mason mistook the R for an L, the 1 for a 5. Perhaps he was a grim jester; perhaps the dead man guided the chisel. But I can picture the horror of Cotter Crawley in being confronted with those suggestive verses. I see him stealing from the house, which after years of absence he has brought himself to revisit, at night. I see him at work, cold, yet feverish, on the telltale stone. I see him stricken by remorse and praying, as the publican prayed, without in the shadow.

Part of this story Prendergast and I told to Miss Ankardyne. The family pew is pulled down, and of the passage that connected the church with the house, only the façade is left. The house itself is quieter than it has been for years. A nephew of Miss Ankardyne from India is coming to live there soon. He has children, but I do not think there is anything of which they need be afraid. As I wrote before, it has been well aired by a kindly soul.

Miss Avenal

My friends could never understand why I went in for mental nursing. I could have stayed on at the Yorborough Infirmary, as ward-sister, but I disliked the matron and knew few people in the place. Then I had heard, too, that mental nursing was less poorly paid, and I had a certain amount of influence behind me, since my uncle had been for many years the chief medical officer of the Raddlebarn Asylum.

I went from the Yorborough Infirmary to The Haven. It was a large place, one of the best semi-private asylums in the north, and certainly the oldest. I liked the work. I was strong and happy. I did not worry, and the other girls were lively. We had dancing and music and private theatricals, and a really good hockey team. But after a time the routine became too monotonous, and I took up private nursing. The home, which adjoined the asylum, was in charge of the same committee that managed The Haven, and, since most of the nurses had been trained at The Haven, I was among friends.

One Monday in August three years ago – I remember it was the first Monday in the month – the matron after breakfast called me into her room. I can picture the scene quite clearly: Miss Simpson, with her cheerful face and white cap, seated at her desk, with a tea-tray at her elbow and her old grey parrot in the bow window pecking impatiently at the husks in his seed-tin.

'I want you,' she said, 'to go to this case, a Miss Avenal; some sort of nervous breakdown, I gather; but you had better read the doctor's letter for yourself. It should be light work, more of a companion than anything else, and since you've had some rather unfortunate experiences lately, I felt it only fair to offer it to you. It will mean leaving first thing tomorrow morning. I understand Miss Avenal has taken rooms somewhere on the moors. If you can go, I will wire to her at once.'

As Miss Simpson had said, I had had a run of disagreeable cases, and, as this promised to be quiet and uninteresting, I was only too glad to go. I met Miss Avenal next afternoon at the Station Hotel at

Yorborough. I could not say how old she was. Her hair was dark, and, though untouched with grey, was strangely lustreless. Her eyes were dark, but with no spark of fire in them. She would have been beautiful, for her features were good, but her face lacked expression. There were no telltale wrinkles; the skin was stretched smoothly, somewhat tightly, over her forehead.

She shook hands with me, letting her limp, cold fingers lie in mine, while she told me that her doctor, who should have been there to give me my instructions, had at the last moment been unable to come.

'He told me that he would write to you in a day or two,' she said. 'What I want most of all is the companionship and sympathy of some cheerful young person like yourself. That, I am sure, you can give me. We shall be very quiet at Kildale, alone together on the moors.'

'I hope you have plenty of books with you,' she said again as we stood on the platform. 'We shall be very lonely at Kildale in the evenings.'

There is only one other thing I remember in connection with that afternoon at Yorborough. Just before the train started, I had got up from my seat in order to take out a novel from the handbag which the porter had placed in the rack, when, looking round, I saw that a gentleman had walked up to the carriage door and was speaking to Miss Avenal.

I don't think I have ever met anyone who filled me with so strong a dislike. His face and figure were those of a young man who would never grow old because he was old already in the experience of all that life could bring.

'Fancy meeting you here!' he said, in a voice smooth and expressionless. 'And so you are off for your cure again? To the same place? It's years since I've been there. Well, I hope it will be as successful as the last. You certainly look as if you could do with another lease of life. Goodbye! So glad to have met you once again. You change at Maltley for the local line.'

The train started.

'You'll be alone,' he said, hurrying along the platform.

'Oh, yes,' Miss Avenal replied, 'quite alone; it's part of the cure, you know.'

We stayed at Kildale Mill. I had been to Kildale Church before, the oldest Saxon church in the Riding and close to Kildale Cave. Kildale Church had seemed far enough from the string of villages that fringe the great plain, but Kildale Mill was two miles farther up the valley.

It was a very quiet valley, steep slopes, thickly wooded, rising from green meadows. The Kildale Beck ran down past the mill and there was swallowed, so that the course of the stream, except in flood-time, was only marked by dry boulders. Below the mill the dale was strangely silent, for though the stream was there, the stream was dumb.

Kildale Mill was very old. I believe it is mentioned in Domesday. It was more of a farm than a mill, though the water-race is kept open and the water-wheel in repair for the sawing of timber. I think it was the quietest place I had ever seen. Above the valley were the moors, and many miles beyond the moors the sea.

Three rooms at the end of the house were reserved for Miss Avenal. A large room downstairs, which we used as a sitting- and dining-room, faced on to sombre woods of larch and pine. Above were two bedrooms, reached from the room below by a separate stair and communicating with one another. Indeed these three rooms were quite cut off from the rest of the house, and except for the rare occasions when Miss Avenal came to Kildale they were not used. The lord of the manor had strict rules prohibiting his tenants from taking in summer visitors, so that there were only occasional cyclists on the valley roads, and no strangers on the moor.

I found Kildale intensely lonely. The house was reached by a rough track through the woods that went no farther than the mill. The people of the house seemed as silent as the dumb Kildale Beck that was swallowed in the limestone meadow below the weir; they were as hard as the dry rocks of its bed.

Naturally I saw a great deal of Miss Avenal. I was with her the whole day long, except for two hours in the afternoon, when I was free to go walks. I am not fond of solitary country rambles. I do not know the names of birds and flowers, for all my life has been lived in towns.

Kildale was so far from any village, that I never had time to escape from the solitude of the empty valley. The walk I took more often than any other was by a path through the fields that followed the side of the dried-up riverbed to Kildale Church. There were no houses by the church. It stood alone, two miles from the nearest village, and the door was always locked. The locked, ever-empty church, silent and solitary, the valley with its waterless riverbed, shut in by woods too thick for birds to sing in, made a deep impression on my mind. For the stream seemed to be the soul of the valley, and when it disappeared it was as if it took with it all the valley's life that mattered.

Kildale evidently suited Miss Avenal. For a week or two after our arrival she would lie all day long on a couch I made for her among the fern in the woods. She did not talk much, but she could not bear to be left alone. Hour after hour she would spend looking up at the little patches of sky that pricked through the pine branches, as if she were gazing into blue pools hidden in the crevices of dark rocks.

'You must not leave me, nurse,' she would say. 'I am so weak and feeble, and you are so young and so strong. Talk to me, nurse. Make me forget myself.'

As I sat beside her in the fern, I did not mean to speak more intimately than I should have done to any other chance acquaintance; but the world seemed very small, and everything in these hot August days was so remote, that when a week had passed there must have been little about me that Miss Avenal did not know. She was a wonderful listener.

Then, as the days stole by in monotonous procession, her strength gradually came back to her; her cheeks, which before had had something of the horrible bloodless pallor of old ivory, were tinged with colour, and there shone on her long, dark hair a new lustre.

'I am already feeling so much stronger, nurse,' she said once, as leaning on my arm she walked by the waterless stream. 'If you only knew what it is to have been without sympathy for as long as I have been; what it is to have been cut off from the strong currents of life, you would realise how thankful I am for all that you have given me.'

And yet what had I given her beyond my confidence? She had said that I sympathised with her. How could I sympathise with her, when I knew so little about her?

The letter which Miss Avenal told me that the doctor would send never came. 'I cannot conceive how it has miscarried,' she said; 'but after all the matter is of no importance, since you can now judge of me for yourself. Doctors claim too much and nurses far too little for themselves. It costs more to give sympathy hour after hour through tedious days and wakeful nights than to label with a learned name some case they can never even remotely understand.' It seemed that Miss Avenal shared that belief, so common among nervous hysterical women, that hers was no ordinary illness to be cured by ordinary means.

She had spoken of wakeful nights, and for the first few days after our arrival at Kildale she must have had but little sleep, though the heavy air of the valley, or perhaps the unaccustomed fragrance of the pine-trees, had on me an exactly opposite effect. Yet whenever I got up in the night to see if my patient in the next room was in need of anything, I always found her lying wide-eyed and awake on her bed by the open window.

'Go back to bed and to sleep, nurse,' she would say. 'I rest more easily when I know that you are sleeping.'

As she grew stronger, our walks took us farther afield. Sometimes we followed the stream up the valley, and these walks I liked the best, for the woods no longer clung to the steep hillsides, and the dale, broadening with its farms and green pastures, brought us back into the world of men. In the meadows by the river there were in spring-time, so Miss Avenal said, millions of daffodils. They were flowerless now in August; it was the moors that held the colour. From Miss Avenal I learned to recognise the birds, the white-throated dipper, that darted out from the alder-roots, and the ponderous heavy-eyed owls, that sulkily flapped from their resting-places in the hollow oaks. But more often our walks took us below the mill, where the vale was waterless, towards the church at Kildale, built by men of pagan England for the worship of their new God.

'I think of the church,' said Miss Avenal, 'as the last outpost of the new religion, standing sentinel over the passes that lead to the hills. And the stream I picture as the friend of the old spirits that were driven by the priests into the fastnesses of the moor. It carries their secrets still; but lest the old sentry should discover them, it has made for itself a way underground.'

I had been at Kildale for a fortnight, when something went wrong. A feeling of lassitude such as I had never felt before stole over me. The longer walks made me weary. I slept as we lay in the fern in the daytime, slept even when Miss Avenal was talking to me; and in my dreams I heard her voice going before me, as it seemed, down long echoing corridors of black marble, or calling after me down gloomy avenues of tall clipped yews. But at night I could not sleep. It was I now who lay awake, gazing through the open window into the fir woods, listening to the cries of the nightjars or to the perpetual alarm of the corncrakes in the sun-warmed meadows up the dale. It was Miss Avenal who stole into my room on tiptoe with lighted candle, who held my hand, who smoothed my pillow. She seemed to grow stronger, to regain her hold on life with every day that passed. The sunlight sparkled in her eyes and shone back reflected from her hair. All day long she never left my side. She talked to me, telling me strange tales of her past life, that seemed, as I lay half-waking, half-sleeping in the heather or in the fern, to take me back to the very beginnings of the world.

I remember how on one brooding afternoon of thunder she led me through the fields towards Kildale Church. We stopped before we reached it, and, as we sat on a grass-covered knoll, looking towards the weather-stained tower that rose graceless and strong like the bastion of some border fortress, she sang to me a song whose words I still remember.

> The valley has lost its memory;
> The stream flows silent underground.
> It has left the wind and the sun and the rain
> To creep into the dark world again
> With the secret of life that it has found.
>
> For the stream has found the secret of life;
> It has gathered its knowledge from the hills:
> Of darkness and evil from the owls,
> Of beauty and joy from the daffodils.
>
> Its waters hold the memory
> Of age and youth, of death and pleasure and pain.
> It is creeping down to the starless world,
> To the underworld of night again.

At last, when every day I felt that I was growing weaker, when every day I saw that she was growing stronger, I wrote to Miss Simpson at Yorborough asking to be allowed to come away. Then it was that I realised that I should have written before, for she misunderstood my letter. In her answer to me she said that she had heard already from Miss Avenal, and that she had offered to keep me as her guest at Kildale until I was strong enough to travel. Miss Simpson advised me to accept the invitation. Yorborough, she said, was like an oven, and she envied me the quiet and the bracing air of the moors. How poorly my letter must have expressed my thoughts! I could have said nothing of what I had meant to say.

'And why should you go back?' Miss Avenal asked, when I tried to speak to her about it. 'You shall stay here with me and I will nurse you. I will be with you all day long. How can I leave you when you have given me so much?'

I was too weak to resist. Indeed, had I not then known that resistance was hopeless, I must have realised it ten days after. It was afternoon, and Miss Avenal had left me alone in the meadow by the mill, when I saw two children, a boy and a girl, coming down the stream. They walked barefoot hand in hand, their boots slung across their shoulders. They laughed as they came towards me, clambering over the slippery stones, as they crossed and recrossed the stream.

'Hallo!' said the boy. 'There's the lady of the mill. Let's ask her the way to the cave.'

'Please, Mrs Miller,' said the little girl, coming up to me without a trace of shyness, 'will you show us the cave where they found the elephants' tusks?'

'And the hyena's skull,' said the boy.

'And the wolves' teeth,' said the girl. 'It was when the plain was a lake and they crept into the cave to die. Mother has been telling us all about it.'

They brought with them all the hope of laughter and sunlight. I said I would go with them to the Kildale Cave, and I told myself that I would escape from the valley with the children. For half a mile I went with them hand in hand through the meadows; then the girl stopped.

'There's auntie calling us, Roger,' she said. 'I wonder if we ought to go back.'

'I don't hear her,' the boy answered. 'Let's go on to the cave now that we've got as far as this. It may be wet tomorrow, and the holidays will be over in a week.'

'It's going to rain now,' said the girl. 'I felt a drop on my hand. And look at the big cloud that's come from nowhere. I really think, Mrs Miller, that we ought to be going, and there's auntie calling again.'

A voice came from high up in the valley woods. 'Come back, children; come back, come back!'

'I don't believe it is auntie,' Roger said gruffly, 'but it's going to rain. I expect we'd better be going home or we shan't get any tea. Perhaps father will show us the way to the cave tomorrow. I'll race you home, Peg!'

Away they ran across the grass, waving goodbye and saying that tomorrow they would be back.

Listlessly I retraced my steps. It was all I could do to reach the mill, and when I got there I was wet to the skin. Miss Avenal put me to bed; she herself lit the fire in my bedroom, but that night I was delirious.

I have no clear recollection of the week that followed. When I awoke on the morning of the eighth day, the first person I saw was Nurse Harrison. She used at one time to share my room at The

Haven; and, though perhaps we had often quarrelled, it was like meeting my oldest friend to see her at Kildale.

'When did you come?' I asked.

'I've been here nearly a week,' she said, 'and tomorrow I am going back with you to Yorborough.'

'And Miss Avenal?'

'Miss Avenal left this morning. You've been very ill, you know, and you mustn't talk.'

I went back to Yorborough next day. I expected to be glad to leave Kildale; but when the time came, I do not think I really cared, for I was dazed, only half responsive to the life of the outside world.

Nurse Harrison was very gentle with me, and this surprised me, as at one time I had thought her rough with her patients. I asked if we should be sharing our old room together, and then she told me that, since The Haven was quite full, Miss Simpson had made arrangements for me to have one of the rooms in the new wing. I did not altogether like the idea, but everyone was so kind to me that I could not well complain. I thought as the weeks went by that I was kept there apart from the other nurses in order that I might the better regain my strength; but that hope left me when I realised that my strength and beauty had been taken from me by Miss Avenal. I wondered at the strange thoughts that passed through my mind in the daytime. I thought at first that I should soon cease in the quiet and peace of Yorborough to be troubled by those stranger dreams at night. But now I understand. I know now that when Miss Avenal took away my strength, she left me with her memories.

Last of the Race

Little Billy Mungo, who kept the Accommodation House on Jackson's Sound, refused to believe in them. Flinders, who had prospected the whole country for coal, and was besides a naturalist, had seen them himself. He said that they were the footprints of a large apteryx.

But old Macnaughten, whisky-sodden and argumentative, still held to his original opinion, that somewhere between Te Anau and the sea there was a new bird – rather a bird so old that with its death the race would become extinct.

And though in Pembroke, where Macnaughten spent his money, the man's story was taken for what it was worth, there was something in it that rang true.

So at least thought Tradescant, as he sat listening to the fellow, watching his reserve thaw beneath the combined influence of the whisky and the naturalist's congenial company.

'I ought to know,' said Macnaughten; 'I've seen apteryx by the hundred in the North Island, and I've killed them too before the Government made their regulations. I've seen the mud by the lake shore covered with their footprints, and I'll bet my bottom dollar that not a single one was over three inches long. Why, those I saw in the bush that spring were twice as big. And Flinders says it's an apteryx! I measured them myself, and that'll tell you if I lie!'

He took out of his pocket a slip of brown paper with two marks in pencil about eight inches apart. To Tradescant the proof hardly seemed conclusive.

'I'll tell you how I first came across them,' he continued. 'I was working on my own, trying to find a new route to the West Coast Sounds from this side. It was just at this time of the year, and the weather was cold, and there was rain. I'd been out all day, and when at night I came to the place where I was camping, there were footprints everywhere. The bird had been looking for something to eat. I've seen them every year since, barring last year. This much I'll say. They're not so common as they were. Have you ever seen a feather like that before?' He took out of his leather purse a scrap of news-paper, and a little piece of down lay on the table.

Tradescant took it up, held it in his hand, and after carefully scrut-inising it with his lens, handed the feather back to Macnaughten.

'My dear fellow,' he said, 'I've seen hundreds of feathers like that. Open your pillow case when you go home, and you'll find a few more.'

'By God!' exclaimed Macnaughten, 'you mean I'm a liar?'

'Hardly that,' the other replied. 'I mean that I don't believe you. I should be glad to listen to anything more you have to say when I've seen your footprints.'

There was silence in the room, silence broken only by the ticking of the cheap alarum clock on the mantelpiece.

Then Macnaughten spoke.

'Look here,' he said; 'I'm a poor man, but I've got brains, and I know how to use them. When I left England, a thick-headed fool could always earn a shilling a day and his keep by standing outside the barrack doors. Give me what your blasted Tommy gets for a week, and I'll show you them. If I don't, I'll call Flinders a gentle-man to his face!'

'Very well,' said Tradescant, and he drank to the bargain.

He was standing alone in the heart of the New Zealand bush. Macnaughten had left him three hours ago. He had done what he had promised to do, and it was no business of his if the conceited English fool lost himself before he reached Mungo's Accommod-ation House.

As for the bird, Macnaughten had no fears of it ever being discov-ered by a man who took that feather for goose's down, by a naturalist who called a kea a hawk, and who asked if there had ever been kangaroos in the island.

Macnaughten could have laughed in his face; but then he never saw Tradescant as he knelt in the mud, scanning eagerly that faint impression on its surface, smelling it like a dog. He had only donned for a short week the unpopular but effective disguise of ignorance.

Tradescant had taken stock of his belongings. In his knapsack was food that might at a pinch last for three days. He had his maps and his compass.

'One cigarette,' he said, 'and then my last little bid for fame.'

His whole life was traversed, from the time between the lighting of the match to when, five minutes later, the glowing stump burned his fingers.

His whole life was traversed. Perhaps that was why the cigarette was not so pleasant as it might have been.

He had made so many mistakes.

There was the mistake of ever being born, that all the future honour of his family should have been left to him alone to augment or mar. There was the mistake of his marriage; though perhaps that was not a mistake, but only a tragedy. Then there was that awful failure of his scientific career. It was intolerable that, after spending the ten best years of his life in perfecting his discovery, an American, with all his nation's luck, should have proved and published the identical thing six months before his work was finished. He who should have been first, followed with the rest of the honourably mentioned.

It was a mistake Jack dying as he did at Eton, just the boy any man would have wished for an only son.

Perhaps the least of all his mistakes was this wild goose chase.

For Tradescant had sickened of the laboratory. The vibrations of the ether which had fascinated him of old, had become too intangible. And here he was in the heart of the primeval forest with the old ancestral passion for nature strong upon him.

A Maori carving had first put the idea into his head, and then he had seen a paragraph in an evening paper at Christchurch.

'My boy's dead,' he said to himself, as he gazed at the grey cigarette ash, 'but I'll hand my name down to posterity somehow, and this bird shall do it. "Apteryx Tradescantii, Number 999 in the catalogue. Unique." Yes, little bird, I'm afraid your days are numbered.'

He shouldered his knapsack and followed the footprints into the bush.

The evening of the third day found Tradescant wet through, sitting at the foot of a giant totara. He had lit a fire of the driest twigs he could find, and was warming himself before the spluttering flame.

It was a foolish thing to do, for the bird was not far away now; all day the footprints had been fresher, and he knew that the smoke might frighten it.

But he was chilled to the bone, and felt certain of his success.

His face, as he bent over the flame, glowed; he was beginning almost to enjoy the cleansing feel of the three days' rain. And all the time his hand never left the barrel of his gun. He fondled it, stroking the dull metal lovingly.

What days those had been! The midday gloom of the forest with its wealth of timber, the rippling of the streams, English streams where English trout would thrive far better than in limpid Hampshire waters or brown North Country becks.

Then the scarlet wonder of a late flowering rata, that giant parasite of the forest; the scramble up the slopes where the tree ferns no longer showed their shabby dressing of faded fronds, and nothing but shrub and thorn found root on the shelving screes.

Was it yesterday or the night before that he had camped high up on the hill, and had seen to the eastward the snow-clad range of the Southern Alps rise cold and ghostly against the blue night with its strange stars?

Then there was the moment when, kneeling to pick a gentian, he had found the feather, and the feelings of love and wonder which the flower had aroused in him, suddenly changed into one of strange lust and hate, as he held the grey little piece of fluff in his palm.

There was the wonder of the rain, too. The torrents that scoured the hillsides, the shrouding mist. And, best of all, three hours ago, when he had come to an impenetrable thicket of some dark-leaved thorny plant, to find more feathers, and, how his heart had exulted, a little patch of blood.

Tradescant was fondling his gun as twenty years before he had fondled his boy.

He arose in the morning stiff and with a fever. There was only half a round of bread in his wallet, and this he kept, breakfasting on the contents of his flask. From his sodden maps he calculated that he could not be more than twenty miles from civilisation, represented by ten tin roofs and a beer and spirit licence. This was to be the last day's hunt.

The rain had not ceased all night, the streams were rivers, but Tradescant did not heed. He could hear now and then a monotonous piping ahead, and now and then the cracking of twigs.

The bird was leading him into the valley, and by midday he had reached the spot where two streams joined, a narrow tongue of land jutting between. Here he stopped, uncertain what course to pursue. Then he felt a sudden throbbing in the arteries of his neck. A tree had fallen across the smaller of the two streams, forming a natural bridge, and in the centre stood his bird. Of this much he could be sure, that no bird like this had ever before been seen by a white man. It was perhaps four feet high, almost wingless, as Tradescant had surmised, and covered with a softly-dappled plumage.

The man waited till the bird had reached a point where its body would fall clear of the water, took steady aim, and fired. The shot rang through the bush sharp and clear; the bird gave a shrill pipe, and half-fluttered to the tongue of land.

'Missed!' said Tradescant, 'but I'll kill you yet.'

It was no easy thing to cross the river, swollen with the three days' rain. The only way was to follow the bird.

Creeping on hands and knees, clutching the slippery bark with bleeding fingers, he had almost reached the further side when there was a cracking underneath him.

The bridge had broken. A minute's frantic scramble, with the water rushing below his dangling legs, while branches struck him in the face, and he was on firm ground again.

Then a mighty log, carried down in mid-stream, crashed against the broken tree and bore it away.

Of a truth the floods were out.

The spit he was on was low and sandy. There was little to hinder the flight of the bird. Tradescant began to run.

He ran a hundred yards, and then he burst out laughing, for he was on an island. The bird had gone into a death-trap. There it stood by the waterside, flapping the useless wings, uttering its monotonous pipe. Tradescant had laughed, now he smiled, his old sarcastic smile, for he realised that if the bird had walked into its death-trap, it was to be his own too. Between the island and the further bank, there was a brown flood three hundred yards across, and he was no swimmer.

'But I've got the bird.'

It did not resist. The bird opened its long, thin beak and made a faint hissing sound, as Tradescant, after tying the legs together, swung it over his shoulder. At the end of the island stood the stump of a tree, hollowed, and affording shelter from the rain. The ground around it was higher than elsewhere.

There he sat and waited. After a time he felt in his pocket for a piece of cord. He was no fisherman, and had always been clumsy with his fingers, but he finally succeeded in making a running noose to his liking, and slipped it over the bird's neck.

It was not perhaps the simplest way of killing it, but the body would not be spoiled. He tightened it, and the bird opened its mouth and began to gape, beating its wings.

'Come,' said Tradescant, 'no fuss, and don't look at me in that pathetic way, as if you'd never deserved this. It's the way of the world! Confound it!' he said, 'the bird struggles too much. I shall have to postpone the operation,' and he loosened the knots. 'Cheer up, bird!' he said, addressing the beast. 'I have no wish to put you to unnecessary discomfort. Now no shamming! When my boy carried on as you are doing now, I used to call him Charles Edward, known to history as the Young Pretender. Pluck up courage, Charles Edward, the date of your execution for the time being is postponed.'

The south wind was bitterly cold; it might have come straight from the Antarctic icebergs, and the rain was turning to sleet.

Late in the afternoon, Tradescant awoke with a sense of warmth he had not felt all day. The bird had crept within his coat and now lay nestling close.

'A remarkably good idea, Charles Edward,' he said. 'I appreciate your returning good for evil in this way, and overlook the fact that your ulterior motive was probably selfish. If you'll excuse me one moment I'll ring for tea. I beg pardon, I was forgetting where I was. But I can still offer you refreshment. I have here,' he continued, 'brandy and bread. The brandy, I am informed, will cause a temporary dilation of the skin capillaries, accompanied by a feeling of warmth, which, however, is shortly followed by slight cardiac and nervous depression. As a stimulant it should only be used under exceptional circumstances and with moderation. I think we may call these circumstances exceptional. The state of the flask forbids excess. You decline the brandy? Let me call your attention to the bread, I believe a large part of its nutritious constituents has been removed in the process of manufacture, but it contains a percentage of carbohydrate varying from 55 per cent. in the best white bread, to 40 per cent. in the coarser varieties. The sample I hold in my hand would be classed among the coarse varieties. As a food, it far exceeds the value of the alcohol. Estimable bird! You choose the bread. It would have been my own choice, but you are my guest.'

The bird pecked greedily at the crumbs Tradescant offered it, and showed the whites of its eyes every time it swallowed.

As the brandy reached the brain, the man began to laugh.

'Charles Edward!' he said, 'has it ever struck you how grotesque it is, that I, the last of my family, should be sitting talking to you, the last of yours? We came over with the Conqueror. Tell me something about your ancestors!'

'My dear bird, if you must yawn in that shockingly rude manner, do put your flapper in front of your mouth. If you have no objection to make, I now intend to go for a short stroll.'

He had hardly walked a dozen yards when he came to the edge of the island. While he gazed, he saw the water rising inch by inch. Out in mid-stream the sodden body of a sheep was carried by. It was held for a minute entangled in the branches of a tree; then the eddy swept it clear, and bumping against logs and boulders, the yellow water washed it downwards. Far up the glen Tradescant heard the bleating of a solitary lamb.

After ten minutes, Tradescant walked back to the hollow trunk; the fever was still upon him. He was delirious now.

'There's no sign of the carriage yet,' he said, addressing the bird, 'so we must shelter here as best we can. You'll have to sit close. I'm afraid your feet will be simply sopping, and you'll catch your death of cold, but if you were such a goose to come out – ' He broke off laughing.

'Not goose,' he said, 'I'm forgetting myself, Apteryx. Apteryx Tradescantii. That's what I meant.

'And by the way, that reminds me I wanted to ask you about your wings. What's the use of having wings if you can't fly with them? I've often been told that I have wings myself, and my friends tell me that I ought to try and fly, and all I can do is to flop, flop, along the ground just like you. There's something wrong there, you know, Charles Edward.'

Tradescant laughed again, the high-pitched senseless laugh of delirium. He no longer saw the water rising inch by inch, making the ground at his feet a sponge-like mass. It was of the past he was thinking, of the other Charles Edward, his boy. And amid the rain thresh, his voice drowned by the turbulent cry of the stream, he talked to the phantasms he saw.

The bird crept nearer to its strange companion, it no longer seemed to fear him. And he putting out his hand, drew it towards him, wrapping it in his coat.

'Keep close, and don't gape, Charles Edward. One of us may weather it yet. Half a minute though; I was forgetting there are advantages in the appurtenances of civilisation, even in the bush!'

He searched in his pocket-book and took out a card.

MR MONTAGUE TRADESCANT
9 Ilsley Gardens, W.

On the back, his half-numbed fingers scribbled:

Apteryx Tradescantii

He tied the slip of pasteboard to the cord around the bird's throat.

'It's awfully cold,' he said. 'I'll tuck you up, and then we'll both go to sleep, and I think I owe you an apology for hustling you so, the last three days. Good-night!'

Deaf and Dumb

Mr Brownsmith walked through the park to the lodge, making vicious thrusts with his cane at the thistles as he went.

He had been on the bench for thirty years, and he was proud of the fact that for all that time he had been hated and feared by every poacher in the county. But no sooner had he come down to Collington Park than he learned that something like a definite compact existed between old Tom Longwood, his keeper, and every rascally miner who preferred ferret and pheasant net to pick and shovel.

For the first time that year he had rented the shooting from Colonel Barton. The price was a mere nothing for the estate, three thousand acres of fine woodland with a tumble-down Georgian mansion, but there was little chance of its being sold. It was too near the mining district. Once outside the ten-foot wall that surrounded the park you could count a dozen chimneys straggling southward in a thin, long line to where a grey smoke haze for ever hung over the horizon.

But the park had been well preserved, and, as Mr Brownsmith's own estates were within a few hours' motor ride, he had readily accepted the opportunity offered him. The only stipulation that Colonel Barton had made was that Tom Longwood should be retained as keeper.

There was one disadvantage about Tom Longwood: he was dumb. Mr Brownsmith, however, was not in the habit of conversing with his servants, and he made little of his keeper's infirmity; that a man could be dumb and dishonest had never entered his mind.

For now it seemed that Longwood was not to be trusted. Mr Brownsmith had been mistaken in his judgment, and he was in consequence intensely annoyed.

It was only through a chance encounter in the train that afternoon that he had become acquainted with the facts.

Ever since he had been adopted as Prospective Liberal Candidate for the division he had made a point of travelling third class.

In the compartment he had entered two local tradesmen were talking about the prospects of a purchaser for Collington.

'They'll want a big price,' said one, 'on account of the likelihood of coal.'

'But if there isn't coal,' the other replied, 'the place will be hard to sell. It's too near the collieries for people nowadays; but the park is as lonely a place as you can find for miles round. If it wasn't for the poachers, Tom Longwood would see no one from one week's end to another.'

'I shouldn't care to be in his shoes. One man against half a dozen, and the nearest police station five miles away; it's no laughing matter.'

'Oh, you bet Tom takes no risks. Why, when the boys are out for the night they go round to the lodge, smoke a pipe by his fireside, and let the old man know that it's a bit too chilly for him out of doors, and the best thing for him to do is to go to bed. He nods and shakes their hands as meek as any Methodist parson. I don't blame him either. They are all his own folk, and his niece is married to Tom Watson, the biggest poacher of the lot. It's not worth risking your life for the matter of a few pheasants.'

That was the conversation that had aroused Mr Brownsmith's anger, that had sent him in a straight line from the park gates to the keeper's lodge. He found Longwood seated by the kitchen fire cleaning his gun. He was a tall man with a long sandy beard, already turning a dirty yellow in places.

Mr Brownsmith wasted no time in preliminaries; he always pictured himself as the type of the bluff, hearty Englishman who never minced matters.

'It has come to my knowledge that you have been shirking your work,' he said. 'There has been too much poaching going on lately, and it must be stopped. If you want to draw your wage you must earn it.'

The old man looked round the room uneasily.

'Things have got to mend or else you have got to go. There are plenty of younger men who would be only too willing to take your place. If you have anything to say, speak up.'

The keeper touched his lips with his hand.

'Oh yes! dumb, I forgot; well, I suppose you have heard what I said and understand. It's a case of choosing between me and these poaching friends of yours. You're cleaning your gun, I see. Well, let them hear it bark once or twice, and the dogs will make off quick enough. Good-night! And remember what I've said.'

Mr Brownsmith felt the better for giving vent to his feelings; but one thing was obvious – his keeper was too old for his work. He had evidently lost his nerve, if he was not actually a coward.

When he reached the house it was already dusk. He had not seen a single person during his hour's walk; for the first time he began to realise the loneliness of the place.

Mr Brownsmith had come down that afternoon to see for himself what the prospects were for next month's shooting. He had arranged to stay at the house; in fact he had stipulated at the time of the agreement with Colonel Barton that a couple of rooms should be at his disposal for odd visits like the present.

The solitary caretaker seemed pleased to see him.

He dined that night in what had once been the smoking-room. The meal was dreary enough, the chop and potatoes were half cold, and the oil lamp, even after he had lowered the wick, sent a streak of smoke towards the ceiling.

The floor, covered with a shabby oilcloth, had only been hastily swept, for a cigar end was still visible in one corner.

He had intended to spend the evening in writing letters, but the ink which the caretaker had brought after he had pulled the bell-rope half a dozen times was of such a colour and consistency that he abandoned his pen in despair.

Instead he sat by the fireless hearth and began to read the morning's copy of *The Times*.

At nine o'clock he heard footsteps on the stairs: it was the old woman going to bed. He wished her a curt good-night, but she made no reply; she was too deaf to hear.

Mr Brownsmith looked through the curtainless windows. The night was dark, with the faintest of new moons. The wood came close to the house on this side, and he could distinctly hear the rustling of the firs like the gentle lapping of waves upon the seashore.

Mr Brownsmith shivered.

He was cold. He made up his mind that the best thing to do would be to take a sharp walk along the drive for ten minutes, and then go to bed. He went downstairs, through the billiard-room, and out by the adjoining conservatory. The white benches where the flower-pots had stood were empty now. Some of the panes in the roof had been broken; he trod on the fragments of glass in passing.

He did not walk far, for it was too dark to see. More than once he found himself stumbling in the thick grass by the side of the drive. And there were noises too which were new and strange to him, the hooting of an owl, the soft beating of some night-bird's wings as it flew past, and just before he re-entered the house, the sound of a gun repeated twice.

The fresh air had brought a warm glow to his whole body, and he was asleep five minutes after he had got into bed.

He awoke an hour later to see the moonlight resting on the white handles of his water-jug; the patch of light fascinated him. He got out of bed to draw down the blind. Then for the first time he saw the figure of a man crawling across the drive towards the house.

Mr Brownsmith's first feeling was one of surprise. It was so un-expected. He had never dreamed of the possibility of burglars. And then fear seized hold of him, and his knees began to tremble.

The man slowly crept nearer to the house; then standing up he began to try to unloose the shutters: they did not give. He crept on to the next window and tried again, then on to the next, until he disappeared behind the corner of the house.

Mr Brownsmith opened the door of his room and ran down the corridor to watch what happened from the window on the landing. The man below was still feeling at the shutters, crawling from window to window. Then quite suddenly he changed his plans and began to beat with his fist against the heavy woodwork regardless of the noise. Upstairs the watcher at the window held his breath; it seemed impossible that the rotten wood could stand the shower of blows, but just as it was about to give way the man stopped, and crawling on hands and feet, returned as he had come. Mr Brownsmith hurried back to his room. As he passed the door there was the sound of breaking glass, and a stone fell upon the floor. There was a second crash, and then another. It was more than he could stand.

Running across the bare floor he jumped into bed; his teeth chattered as he covered his head with the blankets. Now he remem-bered an article he had read only that evening which described an attack upon some Irish landlord by his ejected tenants. It was not a matter of burglars then. He was a fool not to have seen it before. There was nothing in the house worth stealing. Tom Long-wood must have met his rascally confederates at the Three Feathers that evening. He had managed to make them understand – perhaps the keeper's infirmity was in part assumed – and the poachers had come in force to teach him a lesson. True he had only seen one, but there were others probably hidden behind the trees waiting for some signal. Never before had he been so thankful for the security given by lock and key. Then he suddenly remembered that in returning from his evening's stroll he had forgotten to lock the conservatory door.

In a minute they would be in the house. He sprang out of bed, opened the door and listened, expecting every instant to hear the stairs creak. But all was still. There might yet be time.

Without waiting to light his candle, Mr Brownsmith ran along the corridor and down the stairs, little heeding the splinters which pierced his feet. Through the hall he went, bruising his shins against huge pieces of furniture that suddenly loomed up out of the darkness swathed in white sheetings, through the empty dining-room, until he was brought to a standstill before the billiard-room door. There he stopped and listened. Was it fancy, or was that in very truth a sound, soft and rasping, the sound of a man creeping along the ground, a sound half concealed by the sharp throbbings of his own heart?

Impulsively he opened the door and almost ran into the room. It was empty. He crossed it and stood before the glass-panelled door which led into the conservatory. That too he opened. But a minute later he rushed back with a hoarse cry. For the man was there, crawling on his stomach towards him with red, bloodshot eyes. Mr Brownsmith locked the door. He locked the door of the billiard-room and barred it. He could hear nothing now except the sound of someone scratching upon woodwork. Then with shaking hands he struck match after match and made the round of the house, feeling every bolt as he went.

Once back in his room he closed the shutters, swept aside the broken glass, and placed a heavy chest of drawers in front of the door. Then when he had set his lighted candle in the middle of his water basin, he got into bed.

Hour after hour he lay there tossing from side to side until the first streaks of dawn made the candle flame look a whiter yellow and the first birds began to answer the rising sun. It was not till then that he fell asleep.

It was not till then that a farmhand, passing across the park to the milking sheds, saw blood upon the grass. He followed the marks towards the house, he traced them across the drive, and round the cold stone building that rose silent and shuttered above the morning mists. Not until he reached the conservatory did he see the body of

Tom Longwood lying stiff and still. It seemed that the keeper had been shot by poachers; he had managed to reach the house, but no one had heard him.

He was dumb, and from his evidence at the inquest it appeared that Mr Brownsmith was at times very deaf.

A younger and more active man has taken Tom Longwood's place.

Mr Brownsmith never sleeps at Collington now; but he still keeps on the shooting. He tells his friends that it is wonderfully cheap.

A Middle-Class Tragedy

As was usually the case on Saturday mornings, Hickman was late for breakfast.

When he entered the room, his wife was already seated at the table reading the morning's paper, which she had propped up in front of her by means of a fork and the cream jug.

There was to his mind something disagreeably masculine in both her occupation and attitude. He kissed her on the brow, noticing as he did so that she was wearing a brooch he particularly disliked; it was of gold and unnecessarily massive, containing a lock of hair, neither white nor brown, that had once belonged to some distant relative.

Mrs Hickman handed over the paper to her husband and began to make coffee.

'Nothing very much seems to have happened,' she said, in a voice whose weariness Hickman failed to notice. 'Another collision in the Channel – thirty-five lives lost; there are more rumours about a rising in the Balkans, the Prime Minister does not seem to have had much to say at Manchester.'

So she went on, while Hickman, with his eyes glued to the paper, corroborated her statements. He was used to this habit of hers, but it was none the less irritating.

Previous to his entrance his wife had already removed the cover of the dish which stood opposite his place. He saw that it contained kidneys and bacon. The secret of the breakfast table was not his to discover.

In the same way she had abolished the mystery of the morning paper. The headlines were all hers; she knew what was on the other side of the page he was reading; she even directed his attention to articles that might interest him. Left to himself he would have read them, but after his wife's summaries, their piquancy had gone.

'Get on with your breakfast, Julia!' he said impatiently, 'it's half cold. Your letters won't spoil by being kept waiting a few minutes.

No wonder you haven't got an appetite, when the coffee's no warmer than the toast.'

'I fail to see why I should not eat my breakfast in my own way,' she replied. 'That clock's a quarter of an hour slow; you've no time to lose.'

'Confound it!' said Hickman. 'I asked you to put it right a week ago, but I suppose it's no good complaining.'

There was silence for five minutes; then, 'I'm going to Aunt Grace's today,' she said. 'You may have forgotten she asked me to stay there till Tuesday.'

'Of course. I remember. Well, goodbye, and take care of yourself, and mind you don't let your aunt drag you out to all her evening meetings.'

He kissed his wife and was gone, only to return a couple of minutes later with his hat and coat.

'Oh! by the bye,' he said, 'where are my skates? They told me yesterday there was skating on the mill dam at Bleadon. I may as well spend my afternoon there as anywhere.'

'They're either in the tool chest or in the cupboard under the stairs,' she answered.

He was in too great a hurry to wonder why she sat in that despondent attitude, her face buried in her hands, and, closing the door impatiently, he hurried into the hall.

The skates were neither in the cupboard nor in the tool chest, and when he found them after a search of five minutes, the blades were covered with the rust of last February's thaw.

'I asked her to clean them; she said she would; and here they are, exactly as I left them;' he muttered. 'That woman has no more idea of method and order than a girl of sixteen.'

Hickman was in a thoroughly bad temper.

As he hurried down the path to the road, he caught a glimpse of the kitchen maid scouring the steps of the back door; her hair was in curling pins.

'How many times have I told Julia to speak to the girl about that habit,' he said to himself, 'but, of course, nothing has ever come of it. This is a houseful of sluts. I wish I was rid of it all.'

He met Simpson at the corner of the road waiting for the car. He was as usual objectionably cheerful, having just made up a party of bachelor friends to spend the weekend with him at Silkstone. 'You'd better come too, Hickman,' he said. 'The bungalow's only a couple of minutes from the links, and I've just got a new billiard table. I'm quite sure your wife can spare you for once.' But Hickman was not to be persuaded. It was impossible for him to catch the 12.45 to Silkstone, and the ice, they said, on Bleadon Dam was better than it had been for years.

He took his skates to the ironmonger's to be ground. The man shook his head when he saw their condition. 'A duster and a little vaseline would have saved all this,' he said.

'Of course it would,' Hickman had replied: 'only I was fool enough to hand them over to my wife, instead of looking after them myself.'

Yes, there was skating on at Bleadon, but the man doubted whether the ice would be strong enough for a Saturday afternoon's crowd.

He promised to have the skates ready by half past one.

There was very little to be done at the office, a few letters to answer, and that was all. Business was unusually slack, and Hickman wished now that he had accepted Simpson's invitation.

The last letter he opened bore the New Zealand stamp. It was from his brother Bob, who ten years ago had settled in the North Island. For some time he had been doing well; but now it seemed that his many ventures had prospered beyond all expectation. He urged Hickman to come and join him. Their oil borings gave promise of a big future, if they only had a man on the spot capable of floating the concern. Bob had just obtained the agency for the new American Harvesting Combine, but he would give it up without a thought, if only they could make sure of the other.

Hickman lay back in his chair, gazing into the fire. The prospect was certainly attractive, for he knew his brother would not write as he had done unless he had the best of reasons for so doing. Bob was at least as shrewd as he was close in his business dealings.

After calling at the bank to cash a cheque, he lunched in town. He took the car to the terminus, and then walked briskly up the hill to the dam. There were hardly more than fifty people skating, while nearly half that number of ill-clad out-of-works stood on the bank, blowing their fingers, waiting for the opportunity of fixing skates. The ice was almost perfect, black and ringing, and Hickman, as he buttoned close his jacket, for the wind was in the east, no longer envied Bob, who was spending his New Year yachting with some Auckland friends.

Bob had been disappointed in love; that was why he left England; but he had soon managed to forget Eva Jamieson, and now, instead of envying his brother's successful marriage, he had begun, half banteringly, to pity him.

Hickman, however, pitied himself in deadly earnest. Nothing could be pleasanter than an afternoon like this, when he could indulge to the full in his favourite pastime. He did not quarrel with his business: he could do as he liked; he had no partner to consult. But at Virginia Villa everything was different. There, it was true, he was senior partner, but with only one room, his study, which he could call his own, where everything had its place. It was his wife who seemed to endow the house with her personality. If only he could have made his home a second office!

Hickman was a stout man, but a wonderfully graceful skater. The figure he cut on land was often commonplace; never those which he cut on ice.

By four o'clock the dam had become uncomfortably crowded, and Hickman, with the more proficient skaters made a movement towards the end by the weir, where the ice, spoiled in places by the dropped twigs of the overhanging willows, was still black and ringing.

'It's beginning to get too cold for me,' he said at last. 'I shall skate up to the other end and then go home. Are you coming, MacDougal?'

'Not for another hour or so. I must make the best of this wretched English winter. I can't go off to Davos, you know, like you and Robinson. But take care down at the far end. There are far too many on; they are wearing through the ice at an awful pace.'

Hickman indeed had never seen the dam more crowded. Already one or two officials were making an attempt to clear the ice, but with no apparent success. Good-humouredly the people refused to be driven in front of the rope that the men were drawing across the ice. It was the simplest thing in the world to duck beneath it. They had paid their money, and it was ridiculous to suppose that, after tramping for miles through the snow, they were to be deprived of their enjoyment on the one afternoon in the week that they were free.

To Hickman, skating enthusiast though he was, the folly of their obstinacy was evident. He had in fact turned toward the bank, when a stranger collided with him, knocking off his hat, which a sudden gust of wind caught and whirled before it. Then, as he started in pursuit, the catastrophe occurred. Suddenly, without a moment's warning, the ice gave way. There was a cry, at first of surprise rather than of horror, from the mad, struggling mass in the water; then Hickman turned and fled, conscious only of a picture, confused yet strangely vivid, of white, upturned faces, while his ears rang not with the ceaseless clamour, but with the lower crunching sound of the breaking ice, as it collapsed in ever-widening circles beneath the outstretched hands of the drowning.

Driven by terror, the water had appeared hardly a yard ahead of him, Hickman struck out for the opposite bank. He wrenched off his skates and started to run. Once he turned, but the utter immobility of the black crowd that lined the edge of the dam increased his horror. 'They are drowning,' he said to himself; 'if I had turned a second later, I should have been there too;' and he saw now in that picture, which seemed stamped for ever on his brain, his hat, half-filled with water, in the frantic clutch of the stranger.

At the foot of a hill he stopped to wipe his face: he was bareheaded and his skates were gone. In his confusion he must have left them on the bank, after taking them off.

Then he began gradually to realise what had happened. He had been present and had miraculously escaped from the most appalling skating accident of recent years. He saw the evening posters, the columns in the morrow's paper, the long list of drowned and missing.

What was it that he heard the other day about the missing? He remembered now it was Travers who was saying at the club how after every big battle or catastrophe the number of missing men was always greater than could be accounted for by any explanation other than the rational one, that everywhere there were people tired of life, only too willing to throw over their past with its old surroundings, when Fate allowed them the opportunity.

Once again Hickman wiped his face; but, as he replaced the handkerchief in his pocket, he felt Bob's letter. If he had put the letter in his pocket-book in his left breast pocket, I do not believe he would ever have acted as he did; but, as it was, the crinkly touch of the foreign envelope brought back to his mind the thoughts of the morning.

Five minutes later Hickman was walking in a direction exactly opposite to that of his home, with a step that seemed to lack something of its usual firmness.

At Iredale he found a draper's shop open. Here he purchased a hat; not a bowler, such as he was accustomed to wear, but a soft felt. As he stood in the door, a white-faced cyclist passed. He heard him speaking to a constable at the corner and caught the word 'doctor'. Then a second cyclist went by. He was besieged by quite a crowd of loafers, but they could get little from him. All he knew was that beds were wanted at the Red Lion. They had told him to send back the station bus at once.

At Lower Burton, Hickman took the tram into Burchester. He had plenty of time on the way to think over his plan. Luckily for him, he carried an unusually large sum in notes and gold; in London he could raise money on his diamond ring; there should be no difficulty in getting together a sum sufficient to buy a second-class ticket to Auckland. If the worst came to the worst, he could wire for money to Bob. As to Julia, she would of course have a few days of awful suspense. He knew that she would suffer. But, as time passed, and the certainty of his death became more apparent, she would find herself a widow, indeed, but comfortably situated, with an assured income of her own, and a nice little sum of money which she could claim at the bank.

At Burchester, Hickman caught the 7.12; the dining-car was crowded; but he finally installed himself comfortably in a corner seat with his back to the engine.

'Today I begin life anew,' he said, as he ordered a half-bottle of Burgundy.

Had he only realised it, a quarter-bottle would have been more than sufficient to do justice to the occasion.

'You like your beef underdone, sir, I think,' said the waiter, as he placed the plate before him; and Hickman acquiesced. Even if he was starting life afresh, there was no reason why old habits should be dropped, so he drank his usual liqueur and smoked his usual cigar, unconscious of the fact that his past self was laughing at his present self in a manner that was altogether fatherly.

I will not describe in detail the five days which Hickman spent in London. A large part of Sunday was occupied in reading the papers. Only one or two contained in the stop press column an account of the accident of the previous afternoon. The loss of life was not so great as had at first been feared, but thirty bodies had been recovered and there was reason to suppose that the complete list of casualties would be even greater. Then he looked out the sailings to New Zealand. No boat left before Friday, unless he chose to go by way of Australia, starting on the Thursday afternoon. He made up his mind to call at the shipping company's office in the morning.

Monday's papers were full of the catastrophe, which was of a magnitude unparalleled in recent years. Over forty names were printed of people dead or missing; but, to his surprise, his own did not appear in the list.

However, there was no turning back once the step had been taken, so at least he assured himself. Yet for some reason or other he made no attempt to secure a berth; instead he wandered about aimlessly in the South Kensington Museum, chilled by the soulless splendour of its corridors.

In the evening he went to the theatre. The play was a new one, dealing with the marriage problem in a lower-middle-class family; none of the characters wore evening dress. To Hickman the whole thing seemed peculiarly sordid.

Tuesday and Wednesday passed in the same uneventful fashion.

On Thursday, strolling aimlessly through the National Gallery, he saw the back of a woman that might well have been Julia. He turned away, half wishing that his wife were with him. It was useless to deny that he was bored.

On Friday he came across a paragraph in the morning paper, which stated that certain oil borings in New Zealand were not likely to fulfil the expectations originally held concerning them. It mattered little to Hickman that they were not the ones in which Bob was interested; the idea of possible failure had entered his mind. What a fool he had been to give up a well-established business with tangible profits for a wild-goose chase in the Antipodes. It was too late, though, to turn back. Was it? What stood in the way of his return? He had only to put his pride in his pocket, to confess all to Julia and be forgiven, and the old life, with all its petty annoyances, it is true, but with all its comforts and peculiarities made doubly dear by the unbroken habit of twenty years, would be his again.

Inclination having made clear her voice, Duty also began to whisper: he owed his return not only to his wife but to Society as a whole.

He packed up the few things he had bought in town in the state of mind of a schoolboy returning home from school rather than that of a prodigal son. From time to time he became aware of the incongruity, and made ineffectual attempts to lower his spirits.

It was no easy matter to decide whether it would be best to send a telegram, announcing his arrival; but he finally made up his mind, as he drove in his taxi to the station, that the safer plan would be to trust to a generous impulsiveness on the part of his wife rather than to her second thoughts.

He was fortunate in catching the luncheon car express, and in securing the same waiter who remembered his preference for under-done beef. But after the meal his spirits began to fall. Of all things, he disliked a scene, and yet a scene was inevitable. The occasion demanded one; he owed that much at least to his wife.

He began to wish that he had not caught the express; a slow train would have been better, one that stopped at every station. Then he might have had time to compose his mind, to think.

There was the usual bustle of porters at the station, the usual string of disreputable four-wheelers, drawn up on the cobbled yard outside. 'Drop me at the corner of Beechwood Avenue,' said Hickman to the driver. For some reason or other he did not wish to alight at his own gate.

The jobbing gardener was at work on the border at the back of the narrow lawn. He touched his cap as Hickman passed up the path. 'You said something last week, sir, about putting a couple of flower beds in the grass. Whereabouts was it you wanted them?'

How quickly the time had gone! The new experiences which had crowded the last eventful week seemed already to be slipping away from him by the touch of some magic wand.

He found on passing up the steps that the door of Virginia Villa was locked. His wife had evidently gone out, and Kate, as was usual in such circumstances, took fully five minutes to prepare herself for answering the door. She seemed surprised to see him, but not to the extent he had anticipated.

Hickman had given much thought to the manner he should adopt in dealing with the maid. 'I suppose your mistress is not yet back,' he said. 'Very well; bring me a cup of tea into the study. I shall be busy writing there.'

He gave a great sigh of relief, as he hung his coat up on the second peg in the hall, next to his mackintosh. What a fool he had been! To think of changing anything at his time of life! Why, only a fortnight ago he had objected to Julia purchasing a new hat and umbrella stand for the hall, because he had grown so accustomed to the old one. And the good familiar smell of the soap, as he washed his hands! There was something homely even in the slight scent of the clean towel, not too rough, but with that certain stiffness that is never found in the limp rags of the hotel; and the water came from the tap in no scalding stream, but exactly at the right temperature.

In the study he lit a cigar and sat down in the easiest chair, waiting for the tea to appear. The fire had not been lighted, but in a few minutes the chips were crackling cheerily. From the fact that every-thing appeared to be in its proper place, Hickman supposed that Julia had not been using the room. There was a great deal to think about. So far all had gone well. True, he had still to discover what was the opinion of the household as to his disappearance. From Kate's manner he judged that urgent business would serve as an excellent excuse. In any case it was obvious that they had entertained no suspicions of his being a victim in the tragedy of Bleadon Dam.

The worst, however, was still before him. A single lie is easy. Lies to explain lies are more difficult, and the longer he thought of facing Julia, the less he liked it.

She was a woman of eternal questions, and he a man of no imagination.

He had no excuse, absolutely none. For the office anything would suffice, a sudden summons to France – his wire explaining things must have miscarried.

But that would not do for Julia; her curiosity would be satisfied by nothing less than the truth.

His thoughts were interrupted by the coming of tea. The bread and butter was, as usual, thicker than he liked; but he was pleased to see that Kate had remembered to bring a breakfast cup; he detested the new crinkly edged service that Julia bought at the stores.

He drank three cups slowly, turning over in his mind the possible alternatives. Then with the fourth he suddenly determined to make a clean breast of it. He would tell her all, or rather he would write. A letter was, of course, the simpler way. The sooner he did it, the better.

Yet the simpler way was difficult enough.

'Dear Julia,' he began: then thinking the words prosaic, he tore up the sheet and started afresh.

'My own wife'. Then he remembered a letter he had written a month after their marriage when he had been hurried away on business. It was the first separation they had had; he had begun in exactly the same way. After the events of the last four days he could not now start off like that.

He compromised with 'My dear Julia', and then dashed blindly at the first page.

He approached the subject from the standpoint of nerves, and at the end of the fourth page had already begun to feel an intense pity for himself.

'I was becoming a complete wreck,' he wrote. 'Every little thing seemed to affect me; the way you dressed, the way you wrote your letters at table. When the accident came, I saw a way out of it all involving no more suffering to you than my death in any case would cause. I took with me a comparatively large sum which I had in cash, conscious of the fact that my balance at the bank would amply suffice for your needs.

'All these details of my absence I might, of course, have kept from you, but during those miserable days I spent alone, I became convinced of the necessity of candour.

'If you think, and I can forgive your so thinking, that some other affection has turned my heart from yours, you would be absolutely mistaken; it has been solely a question of temperament, and in that light I would have you view it, and to forgive an action which would otherwise be hard to forgive.'

Having finished the letter, Hickman placed it in an envelope by the clock on the mantelpiece; and then turned his chair to the fire to warm his feet before the blaze. He was awakened from his reverie, which was not altogether unpleasant, by the entry of the maid with the evening post. 'If you please, sir,' she said, 'I forgot to give you this note; the mistress left it on Saturday, but I did not forward anything, because you left no address.'

'No, I was called away at a moment's notice,' said Hickman, turning colour in spite of himself: 'when will Mrs Hickman be in?'

'Mrs Hickman, sir? She hasn't come back yet. We expected she'd be with you.'

'Well, well,' said Hickman, testily, 'it's my own fault for leaving no instructions for forwarding letters. I expect she had to alter her plans. Dinner at eight o'clock sharp; I shan't want much. A chop, or anything you have in the house.'

He was not surprised at his wife's absence. It was quite typical of Julia to forget that there were others besides herself whose convenience had to be thought of. 'I only hope she'll keep clear of those suffrage people,' he said to himself, as he opened the envelope with his paper knife. He read it through, then jumped to his feet with a cry. 'Good God! The woman's mad.'

For a mad woman the note was short.

DEAR JIM [he read]. By the time you have got this, I shall have gone away, not to Aunt Grace's as you supposed, but for good. It's no use mincing matters: I can't go on living with you any longer. I don't sympathise with you, and you have never felt for my ideals. I don't believe you ever allowed me any. One thing I can honestly say I am sorry for, and that is the position my action may put you in. You can say I've gone to stay with Sarah for six months. It's not true and I know you hate lies, but I believe you hate scandal worse. I don't think it's any use my saying more, because I have lived with you long enough to know how inconceivable my action will seem to you. We are made differently. I don't think you can ever have been tempted in the way I have been. Pray for me sometimes, and thank God we have had no children. I should never have gone then.

JULIA

P.S. – I need hardly say there is no man in the case.

James Hickman stood leaning against the fireplace, as if he had been stunned.

His first words were characteristic of the man. 'May she be forgiven,' he said.

Then, having satisfied the claims of conscience, he made no effort to stem the irresistible tide of his indignation.

He had erred himself, but he had given way to a temptation which had presented itself without the shadow of a warning, when his reason had been almost unhinged by being brought face to face with death. And if he had sinned, he had repented; he had returned; he had prepared himself to be forgiven.

But with Julia the case was absolutely different. In cold blood she had planned to leave him; for weeks she must have been inventing her scheme, calculating the value of her lies, plumbing the depths of his credulity.

For the first time in that memorable week Hickman realised in dim fashion the extent of his dependence upon his wife: for the first time he was conscious of the immense difference between running away from her and her running away from him.

His bitter reverie was at length broken by someone ringing at the door. He stopped the maid as she went to open it to tell her that he was not at home to callers. As he sat down again in the chair by the fire, he was dimly conscious of voices in the passage outside; before he had grasped the situation, the door opened and his wife stood before him.

She never for a moment lost her presence of mind. 'You had better lay the table for two, Kate,' she said. 'Show the cabman where to carry my box.'

As soon as the maid had left the room, she turned to her husband. 'Yes, I've come back, you see. I made an awful mistake, and I'm sorry for it. It is for you to say whether it's too late. We've been married for twenty years, James; I thought I could easily forget about that, but I can't. I am too old to change.' She stood at the window, her back half turned towards her husband, plucking at the curtains; she did not see his face; she had no opportunity of guessing what were the emotions that struggled there for mastery.

'I see now how selfish I was,' she went on, 'how for years I have been thinking of myself, judging everything from my own point of view. It was only after those days alone in London. Oh! James, say that you will forgive me, that you will try to forget.'

'Of course I forgive you,' said her husband stiffly. 'Come, don't cry. We will try and let bygones be bygones. You made a very grave mistake, which you have had the good sense to rectify.'

His words, halting and ungracious, were more than Julia had expected.

'If you would only blame me,' she cried, 'as I blame myself when I think of all the suffering I must have caused you.'

'There, there, say no more about that,' her husband answered; 'I suffered, indeed, more than I care to think of now; but go upstairs and take your things off. I ordered dinner for eight o'clock.'

She went, and in half an hour returned with hardly a sign of the emotion she had so recently experienced. She walked across the room and stood in her old masculine attitude with her back to the fire.

Just then the clock struck the half hour and Julia, turning, saw the note which Hickman had left upon the mantelpiece.

'A letter for me, and in your writing, James. I wonder what it says.'

Her husband had risen from his seat; his face was white, and his hand shook.

'Julia,' he said in a voice that sounded strangely hoarse, 'you must not read that letter. It refers only to the past, which we have agreed to bury. Hand it to me.'

She gave it to him, but her composure had vanished. 'I can see what it is,' she said. 'You have upbraided me and wish now to spare me the pain of seeing what suffering I caused you; but you ought not to destroy it. I must drink my own cup to the dregs.'

He threw the letter into the heart of the fire, and then, when the yellow flame died down, leaving only the thin grey ash, he answered her.

'You are quite wrong,' he said, 'in thinking that I wrote reproaching you. There has been wrong on both sides, that is all.'

'No, no, you are far too generous,' she cried. 'The fault has been all with me. But, James, I can't be altogether sorry for what I've done. I seem to have learned more of your true self, of your own noble self, this afternoon, than ever I did before. I seem to have begun life afresh today.'

And so, ten minutes later, they sat down to dinner, the first meal of the wonderful new life; they ate it in silence; to Julia it seemed a second wedding breakfast; but, try as he would, Hickman could not take his mind away from the fact that the chops were half-cold.

The Fern

Henry Porter was a very ordinary man For thirty years he had occupied the same desk at Fuller's Emporium in the Edgware Road, during which period his salary had been raised three times.

He had occupied the same desk, he had worn clothes of the same dark cloth, he had used the same pen nibs bought in purple cardboard boxes at a dingy shop in Bloomsbury.

For thirty years he had risen at seven. At breakfast he read the *Daily News* because his father had read it; and his father had read it because he had once exchanged a remark with Dickens on the top of an omnibus.

Every day he was carried to business by the same train; his ticket was punched by the same collector. Every day at one o'clock he made his way to the same restaurant, where the waiter for thirty years had addressed him as Mr Walker. He had not yet corrected the mistake. After all Walker and Porter are not unlike. Walker is an ordinary name, and he was a very ordinary man.

His grandfather was born and bred in the country, somewhere in Herefordshire, close to the Welsh border. For some reason he had come up to London after his marriage, and had set up a naturalist's shop.

But he was an ambitious man; he laughed at the idea of his son continuing the business, and so Henry's father had lived and died a clerk.

Yet there was one thing that distinguished Henry Porter from the thousands like him. He possessed a secret. He alone knew the one place in England where grew the Killarney Fern. It was true that the fern was found in Wales. But even there it was so rare that perhaps not fifty people knew of the place.

His grandfather had discovered the fern nearly a hundred years ago, and his father had visited the spot regularly every five years.

Henry Porter well remembered his first initiation into the secret, and the solemn oath he had sworn never to divulge it. Ever since that time, when he had stood dripping wet in the bed of the little stream, holding in his hand the glistening frond he had plucked from the mossy cave behind the waterfall, he had had a purpose in life.

Little by little a resolve formed itself in his brain, a resolve to purchase some day the barren acre on that far-away hillside. It would be an easy thing to do, he had no doubt. The field belonged to a farmer; it was not part of a great landowner's estate. There was nothing to prevent it if the money were found.

That was why he worked so cheerfully, this sombre, commonplace clerk of fifty, in November fog and on sunny April afternoons, when all the country folk that misfortune has placed in the towns long for the cool embrace of the wind as it sweeps across field and moor.

And every year when his hard-earned holiday came round he travelled down to Herefordshire, to spend a few perfect days beside the brook where grew his fern. This summer he was happier than ever.

He had made elaborate calculations, and had come to the conclusion that in five years' time he would be able to leave Fuller's Emporium, when he received news of the death of a cousin in Australia.

The forgotten fact of a common grandfather was the cause of Henry Porter being richer by four hundred pounds. With that and his savings he could retire when he wished. Then he would look out for some shrewd lawyer and open negotiations with the farmer; and as for cottages, there were half a dozen within a mile of the spot that were empty and which he could take for a few shillings a week.

He travelled down to the Welsh border that year, filled with the pride of future ownership.

The morning after his arrival saw him pacing up and down the platform of the west-country station waiting for the local train. He had come there early, for though he had only fifteen miles to go, it was market day, and he feared the trains might be crowded.

But there were only three other people in the carriage he entered, a couple who sat in a corner laughing over a yellow-backed journal, and an elderly man with spectacles and sandy whiskers, dressed in a rather shabby suit of grey tweeds.

Henry Porter sat down opposite him and began to study his map, a new one, of a scale larger than he had ever had before.

When he looked up, the stranger was regarding him intently. Henry quickly folded up his map and replaced it in his pocket.

'I can't be too careful,' he said to himself. Then he noticed two things which confirmed his worst suspicions.

The man in grey was reading the *Naturalist*, and in the rack above his head was a much-battered botanical tin.

'Do you think it is going to rain?' asked the stranger.

'No!' said Henry almost rudely.

'I only asked,' the other replied, 'because I see that you have brought your mackintosh. With the wind in this quarter and a rising barometer, I was hoping that we were to be favoured with a few days of finer weather.' Long experience had taught Henry Porter that in groping in the dark behind the waterfall in search of his fern it was as well to be provided with some sort of protection. He did not like this observant traveller.

In the corner at the other end of the compartment the couple were still giggling over their yellow-backed paper. He could just manage to make out the title of the article they were reading: 'Is life worth living after fifty?'

Where could they find the men to write such trash?

The train stopped at the station, bright with flowers, and Henry Porter got out.

To his surprise he was followed by all the occupants of the carriage. Unwilling to be noticed, he gave up his ticket and sat down on a seat outside the waiting-room.

The couple, still reading their yellow-backed paper, strolled arm in arm down the dusty road, scarcely glancing at the hills which surrounded them.

The man in grey went up to the station-master and asked him some question about an alpine plant that was growing on his rockery, and finally walked off at a quick pace with a spray in his button-hole.

Henry Porter waited half an hour in the sun, tracing patterns in the pebbles with his stick.

Then he followed the others down the road. At the third gate on the left he entered a footpath, bordered on either side by rough, moss-covered walls that led to a farm. He went through the yard, across a meadow of bright green grass (the hay had been stacked five weeks past), into a second lane, and then on to the hillside.

There was his stream, tumbling over the glistening brown boulders, with its ever-circling eddies scooping out deep pools beneath the overhanging banks.

Henry Porter looked round to see that no one followed him, and then clambered up the bed of the stream. Battered by the alder branches, slipping on the water-worn rock, tearing his mackintosh in the briar thickets, he came at last to the little waterfall, where the water, never frozen in the coldest winters, fell from the height of four or five feet into a sandy basin. Through the swaying boughs of the trees he could see far away to the south-west range after range of hills, and beyond them lay the sea across which years ago the spores of the fern had been carried by the wind.

He put on his coat, and armed against the showers of spray, scrambled round to the little cave. His fingers followed the niches in the rock until they were stopped by something smooth and moist. Deftly he felt the stems of the fronds; there were twelve at least – no, thirteen. He counted them again; yes, thirteen, three more than last year. Then with thumb and forefinger he detached one, and shielding it with his hand, passed out through the thin veil of falling water that shone in the sunlight with all the colours of the rainbow.

Then he sat down by the pool and examined his prize. It was only as large as his hand, but it was a thing of perfect loveliness, at any rate in his eyes. He looked at it in silence for five minutes, and then taking a book out of his pocket, placed the fern in the middle of the volume between two sheets of blotting-paper. With a pointed stake he removed all signs of his footprints, scrambled up the sides of the little gully, and was once again on the hillside.

The only people in sight were the couple who read the yellow journal. They were lying in the grass half a mile away; the man was smoking; the woman sleeping, with the paper spread over her face.

There was no sign of the botanist in grey.

Henry Porter took out his watch. It was just two o'clock, and his train left at a quarter-past three. It was time to be going.

He was very happy as he walked back to the station. He was not a naturalist; he did not know the names of a quarter of the flowers he saw, he saw not a quarter of the flowers he passed. He was London born and bred. He was not a poet; he had no poetic feeling. He only felt in a vague, uncertain way that the air was fresher and sweeter here than in the Edgware Road, and that the intense blue of the sky was almost too dazzling. He had been a clerk for thirty years. And the source of his happiness was the fern, whose frond he carried in his pocket pressed between the leaves of *Bradshaw's Railway Guide*. Suddenly he stopped. He remembered that it was market day. There would be a slow train at seven. He would go back to the hillside and spend another couple of hours with his fern.

He turned round and once again climbed the hill.

As he walked a sudden idea took hold of him. Why should he wait another month before leaving the emporium? Why should he not leave it now, and take a room in one of the farmhouses that provided for visitors? He might begin to negotiate for his plot of land. He sat down on a fallen tree trunk and wrote the rough draught of a letter to his employers.

When he reached the waterfall it was nearly five o'clock.

For the second time that day he put on his mackintosh, for the second time he felt with his fingers in the slippery crevices.

There was nothing there! The fern had gone. He searched again; he must have made a mistake. He tried to light a match, and after many unsuccessful attempts produced a spluttering flame by whose light he saw that the little cave was indeed empty.

Gradually the fact penetrated his numbed brain. The fern had been taken; the old gentleman in grey must have followed him unseen. He would be miles away by now; he could not overtake him, and if he did, the fern was not his.

A feeling of impotent rage seized him. The fool! Why should he take the plant? He could have forgiven him discovering the place, he could have forgiven him for taking one frond – no, two, three, four. But to have taken the fern itself, to have torn away the roots from the soft, black soil which they had clasped for so many years! He would never be able to make it grow. He would water it, five times a day perhaps with the softest rain water, but it would die in a week or two.

Slowly, with dragging footsteps, Henry Porter made his way back to the station, heavy of heart and limb. At the place where he had stopped to write his letter only an hour before he stood still, and taking the paper from his pocket, tore it to pieces. Through the fields, across the farm, and down the lane he went. All his grand projects were shattered now; they formed a vast, as yet unexplored, background of misery to the thought which now filled his mind. He was still thinking of the fern. For perhaps it would live after all. This stranger might be wealthy, he might have streams of his own, and planted in a south-west aspect in the right soil and with the right amount of moisture, it might survive. He would find out the name of the little man in grey; he would write to him. Very likely he would give him permission to come and see it. Perhaps in a year or two he might be willing to divide the root.

He was once again in the dusty road that led up to the station. He had missed his train; all that he could see of it was a long horizontal line of smoke in the woods at the head of the valley. And then when he was only a hundred yards from the station-master's house, close to the seat on which he had sat that morning, he noticed a yellow piece of paper lying in the gutter. It was the cover of the magazine he had seen so often that day. Without knowing why he picked it up. Something dead and faded fell from its folds into the soft dust. It was the fern.

Yes, the botanist had had nothing to do with Henry Porter's tragedy.

By some chance the man and girl had found their way to the little waterfall. Something had prompted him to look behind the watery curtain, and then he had seen and taken the fern. It was nothing to him, something a little less important than watercress because it did not look good to eat.

They had carried it with them on their way back to the station, and had left it here. It was not worth the trouble of taking any further; it was only a faded fern.

Mechanically Henry Porter's eyes followed the thick black letters printed on the journal's cover: 'Is life worth living after fifty?'

Far away in the village the church clock struck the hour.

And then he saw that the shadows had begun to lengthen.

The Angel of Stone

For many years it had been the custom of the Senior Fellow to spend part of the Long Vacation in travelling through Normandy on his tricycle. Each time that he returned he always made the remark to one or other of his many friends, that the Church was still a living power among the peasants, and that the fact promised well for the future of the French people, whom otherwise he despaired of. It should be added that the Senior Fellow was shortsighted, and had for many years worn spectacles.

He made his annual excursions with his younger brother, an old man of seventy, who still practised as a solicitor in a cathedral town. Besides their parents they had little in common. But they rode the same pace, they had a distrust of the free-wheel, and a secret unacknowledged inclination for inns which had not yet discontinued the use of the old-fashioned feather bed.

The Junior Bursar, who had passed them once near Beauvais, pedalling westward, had applied to the brothers one of his usual happy quotations –

Two old toads, totally tired, trying to trot to Tetbury.

The Senior Fellow had left his brother Charles in the courtyard of the hotel of the 'Three Crowns' mending a punctured tyre and talking to a crowd of little children. Children were a weakness of Charles, and so was his French. But this he never knew; for he always acted on the belief that deafness was the reason of his being misunderstood by his listeners.

That morning the Senior Fellow had examined the outside of the great church which long ago had been the seat of a bishopric. He was in a good humour, for on the masonry he had found the marks of the workmen who had built the cathedral church of Dol. But when, hot and perspiring, he had climbed the steps that led up to the great south door, he was annoyed to find three small boys busy playing marbles in the shadow of the porch. 'This is

no place for games,' he said to them in stilted French; but they
did not understand him.

Inside it was wonderfully quiet. There was no glare; only a flickering light that played upon the cold stone. The Senior Fellow knelt
down and prayed. He thanked God for the beauty of the building
that had stood there for centuries through rain and sun, the undying
symbol of an enduring Faith. Then he got up, brushed the dust from
his knees, and began to take notes.

The church was far more interesting than he had been led to
believe. Blake, in his *History of Ecclesiastical Architecture in Normandy*,
had failed to do it justice. For nearly two hours he wandered round
the building, now making a hurried sketch of capital or piscina, now
intent on deciphering the subject matter of a window that had been
carelessly filled with fragments of priceless glass. He was not disturbed; only now and then a peasant woman entered to pray before
one of the many shrines.

The Senior Fellow had nearly filled his notebook, when his eye
rested on a stone figure half hidden by the black iron piping of the
heating apparatus; it had evidently been taken from the ruins of some
church or abbey and built into the wall. The figure was that of an
angel, clothed in heavy drapery, and blowing with inflated cheeks
upon a horn. There was nothing remarkable about it; the execution
was clumsy – it might have been carved in the early years of the
sixteenth century.

He took out his handkerchief to wipe away a cobweb that spread
between the wings. Suddenly his hand disappeared. There was a hole
in the middle of the angel's back. He stood on tiptoe and groped
round with his fingers; he felt a piece of paper and pulled it out.
It was black with dust and smeared with raindrops which must
have fallen from the window ledge above. After some minutes he
deciphered the writing which was scrawled upon it –

O holy St Anthony [he read], hear my prayers and intercede with
the Blessed Virgin for my child, for the pains in his back and
belly he can no longer bear; and at Easter day thou shalt have five
candles at five sous the piece.

The Senior Fellow looked towards the little side chapel where
stood the brightly coloured image of St Anthony of Padua, holding
the Child in his arms. 'Whatever made the woman think this angel
was the saint?' he said to himself. 'Perhaps the wings seemed to
promise her speed. She and her child must have died two hundred

years before ever I was born.' Again he stood up on tiptoe and felt in the hole. Yes, there was another piece of paper, not so old as the first, but yellow and stained by the passage of many years –

I waited all the afternoon by the fountain, but you did not come, and again I waited at evening until the moon had risen. What you had promised before, wherefore cannot you now fulfil? For the days are long and my heart is heavy. When I asked at the house they said you had gone, and I dared not ask more. But when you read this, come quickly or answer, for Mary answers not.

The Senior Fellow stood silent for many minutes. 'Poor girl!' he said. 'Poor girl!' There was nothing else to be found in the stone angel. Yes, wedged into a crack close to the opening was a wad of paper. He unfolded it, and read in a boy's clumsy hand: –

I wish mamma had not caught me to bring me to Mass. For I can hear the rain, and the fish will all be rising in the pool below the bridge. I wish I could swing the censer like little Jacques. He got the key on Thursday from the Curé when he was asleep after dinner and he showed me how to do it in the vestry. There's a caterpillar crawling up Monsieur Ferier's neck, but he can't scratch it because he's wedged in so tight between Lucille and Adeline. And Aunt Henriette's wig is slipping all on one side. That's why she can't bow her head any lower. (Signed) Henri Ferdinand Golay, son of Henri Golay, Bootmaker, 5 Rue St Pierre. But we move into the Grand' Rue tomorrow, April 18th, 1789. When this you see, Remember me.

It had remained there unnoticed, unread, since the year of the French Revolution; that is, if he remembered rightly; for the Senior Fellow's interest in modern history ended with the Reformation.

Without knowing the reason he passed out of the church sad at heart. His brother Charles was waiting for him in the porch. He was seated on the warm stone playing marbles with the boys. 'You must be cold after being in there all the afternoon,' he said. 'It's far pleasanter out in the sunshine. I've mended my puncture, and we can start in an hour. But I've promised this little chap to go and fish with him in the pool below the bridge. He says the fish are all rising.'

'I think I'll come, too,' said the Senior Fellow.

The Tortoise

One word as to the documentary part of my story.

The letter was written by Tollerton, the butler, five weeks before his death. Sandys, to whom he addressed it, was, I believe, his brother; in any case the man was not known at Revelstoke Mansions, and the letter came back to Baldby Manor unopened.

I read it twice before it dawned on me that the man was writing of himself. I then remembered the diary which, with the rest of his belongings, had never been claimed. Each partly explains the other. Nothing to my mind will ever explain the tortoise.

Here is the letter –

Baldby Manor

MY DEAR TOM – You asked in your last for particulars. I suppose, as the originator of the story, I am the only person able to supply them, but the task is rather hard. First as to the safety of the hero. You need not be alarmed about that; my stories have always ended happily.

You wonder how it all came about so successfully. Let me give you the general hang of the plot. To begin with, the man was old, a miser, and consequently eccentric. The villain of the piece (the same in this case as the hero, you know) wanted money badly, and moreover knew where the money was kept.

Do you remember Oppenheim's *Forensic Medicine*, and how we used to laugh over the way they always bungled these jobs? There was no bungling here, and consequently no use for the luck that attended the hero. (I still think of him as the hero, you see; each man is a hero to himself.)

The victim occasionally saw the doctor, and the doctor knew that the old fellow was suffering from a disease which might end suddenly. The hero knew what the graver symptoms of the disease were, and with diabolical cunning told the doctor's coachman how his master had begun to complain, but refused to see any medical man. Three days later that 'intelligent old butler – I rather think he must have come down in the world, poor fellow' is stopped in the street by Aesculapius.

'How is your master, John?' 'Very bad, sir.' Then follows an accurate account of signs and symptoms, carefully cribbed up from old Banks's handbook. Aesculapius is alarmed at the gravity of the case, but delighted at the accuracy of the observations. The butler suggests that an unofficial visit should be paid on the morrow; he complains of the responsibility. Aesculapius replies that he was about to suggest the very same thing himself. 'I fear I can do little,' he adds as he drives away.

The old man sleeps soundly at night. The butler goes his usual round at twelve, and enters his master's room to make up the fire, and then – well, after all, the rest can be imagined. De Quincey himself would have approved of the tooling, cotton-wool wrapped in a silk handkerchief. There was no subsequent bleeding, no fracture of the hyoid or thyroid, and this because the operator remembered that aphorism in Oppenheim, that murderers use unnecessary violence. Only gold is taken, and only a relatively small quantity. I have invented another aphorism: the temperate man is never caught.

Next day the butler enters the bedroom with his master's breakfast. The tray drops to the floor with a crash, he tugs frantically at the bell-rope, and the servants rush into the room. The groom is sent off poste haste for help. The doctor comes, shakes his head, and says, 'I told you so; I always feared the end would be this!'

Even if there had been an inquest, nothing would have been discovered. The only thing at all suspicious was a slight haemorrhage into the right conjunctiva, and that would be at best a very doubtful sign.

The butler stays on; he is re-engaged by the new owner, a half-pay captain, who has the sincerity not to bemoan his cousin's death.

And here comes a little touch of tragedy. When the will is read, a sum of two hundred pounds is left to John the butler, as 'some slight reward for faithful service rendered'. Question for debate: 'Would a knowledge of the will have induced a different course of action?' It is difficult to decide. The man was seventy-seven and almost in his dotage, and, as you say, the option of taking up those copper shares is not a thing to be lightly laid aside.

It's not a bad story, is it? But I am surprised at your wanting to hear more about it than I told you at first. One of the captain's friends – I have forgotten his name – met you last winter in Nice; he described you as 'respectability embalmed'. We hear all these things in the servants' hall. That I got from the parlourmaid, who was uncertain of the meaning of the phrase. Well, so long. I shall probably chuck this job at the end of the year.

P.S. – Invest anything that is over in Arbutos Rubbers. They are somewhere about 67 at present, but from a straight tip I over-heard in the smoke-room, they are bound to rise.

That is the letter. What follows are extracts from Tollerton's diary.

*   *   *   *   *

Kingsett came in this morning with a large tortoise they had found in the kitchen-garden. I suppose it is one of the half-dozen Sir James let loose a few years ago. The gardeners are always turning them out, like the ploughshares did the skulls in that rotten poem we used to learn at school about the battle of Blenheim. This one I haven't seen before. He's much bigger than the others, a magnificent specimen of Chelonia what's-its-name.

They brought it into the conservatory and gave it some milk, but the beast was not thirsty. It crawled to the back of the hot-water pipes, and there it will remain until the children come back from their aunt's. They are rather jolly little specimens, and like me are fond of animals.

*   *   *   *   *

The warmth must have aroused the tortoise from its lethargy, for this morning I found it waddling across the floor of the hall. I took it with me into my pantry; it can sleep very well with the cockroaches in the bottom cupboard. I rather think tortoises are vegetable feeders, but I must look the matter up.

*   *   *   *   *

There is something fascinating in a tortoise. This one reminds me of a cat in a kennel. Its neck muscles are wonderfully active, especially the ones that withdraw the head. There is something quite feline in the eyes – wise eyes, unlike a dog's in never for a moment betraying the purpose of the brain behind them.

*   *   *   *   *

The temperature of the pantry is exactly suited to the tortoise. He keeps awake and entertains me vastly, but has apparently no wish to try the draughty passages again. A cat in a kennel is a bad simile; he is

more like a god in a shrine. The shrine is old, roofed with a great
ivory dome. Only occasionally do the faithful see the dweller in the
shrine, and then nothing but two eyes, all-seeing and all-knowing.
The tortoise should have been worshipped by the Egyptians.

     *   *   *   *   *

I still hear nothing from Tom; he ought to have replied by now. But
he is one of those rare men whom one can trust implicitly. I often
think of the events of the last two months, not at night, for I let
nothing interfere with that excellent habit of sleeping within ten
minutes from the time my head has touched the pillow, but in the
daytime when my hands are busy over their work.

I do not regret what I have done, though the two hundred would
weigh on my mind if I allowed it to do so. I am thankful to say I bore
my late master no ill-will. I never annoyed him; he always treated
me civilly. If there had been spite or malice on my side I should
never have acted as I did, for death would only have removed him
beyond my reach. I have found out by bitter experience that by
fostering malice one forfeits that peaceable equanimity which to
my mind is the crown of life, besides dwarfing one's nature. As it is,
I can look back with content to the years we have spent together,
and if in some future existence we should meet again, I, for my part,
shall bear no grudge.

Tortoises do not eat cockroaches. Mine has been shut up in a box
for the last half-hour with three of the largest I can find. They are
still undevoured.

     *   *   *   *   *

Some day I shall write an essay upon tortoises, or has the thing
already been botched by someone else? I should lead off with that
excellent anecdote of Sydney Smith's. A child, if I remember, was
found by that true-hearted divine stroking the back of a tortoise.
'My dear,' he said, 'you might as well stroke the dome of St Paul's
in order to propitiate the Dean and Chapter.' Tortoises are not
animals to be fondled. They have too much dignity, they are far
too aloof to be turned aside from their purpose by any of our
passing whims.

     *   *   *   *   *

The pantry has grown too warm, and the tortoise has taken to
perambulating the passages, returning always at night to the cupboard. He seems to have been tacitly adopted as an indoor fixture, and
what is more, he has been named. I named him. The subject cropped
up at lunch-time. The captain suggested 'Percy' because he was so

'Shelley', a poor sort of joke with which to honour the illustrious dead, but one which of course found favour with a table full of limerick-makers. There followed a host of inappropriate suggestions. I am the last person to deny the right of an animal to a name, but there is invariably one name, and one name only, that is suitable. The guests seemed to think as I did, for all agreed that there was someone of whom the beast was the very image: not the vicar, not Dr Baddely, not even Mrs Gilchrist of the Crown. As they talked, I happened to notice an enlargement of an old portrait of Sir James which had just come back from being framed. It showed him seated in his bath-chair, the hood of which was drawn down. He was wrapped up in his great sealskin cape; his sealskin cap was on his head, with the flaps drawn close over his ears. His long, scraggy neck, covered with shrivelled skin, was bent forward, and his eyes shone dark and penetrating. He had not a vestige of eyebrow to shade their brilliance. The captain laughingly turned to me to end their dispute. The old man's name was on my lips. As it was, I stuttered out 'Jim', and so Jim he is in the dining-room. He will never be anything else than Sir James in the butler's pantry.

Tortoises do not drink milk, or, to avoid arguing from the particular to the general, Sir James does not drink milk, or indeed anything at all. If it were not so irreverent I should like to try him with some of our old port.

* * * * *

The children have come back. The house is full of their laughter. Sir James, of course, was a favourite at once. They take him with them everywhere, in spite of his appalling weight. If I would let them they would be only too glad to keep him upstairs in the dolls'-house: as it is, the tortoise is in the nursery half the day, unless he is being induced to beat his own record from the night-nursery door to the end of the passage.

I still have no news of Tom. I have made up my mind to give notice next month; I well deserve a holiday.

Oh, I must not forget. Sir James does, as I thought, take port. One of the gentlemen drank too deep last night; I think it must have been the Admiral. Anyhow there was quite a pool of dark liquid on the floor that exactly suited my purpose. I brought Sir James in. He lapped it up in a manner that seemed to me uncanny. It is the first time I ever used that word, which, till now, has never conveyed any meaning to my mind. I must try him some day with hot rum and water.

* * * * *

I was almost forgetting the fable of the hare and the tortoise. That must certainly figure in my essay; for the steady plod plod of Sir James as he follows one (I have taught him to do that) would be almost pathetic if one did not remember that perseverance can never be pathetic, since perseverance means ultimate success. He reminds me of those old lines, I forget whose they are, but I think they must be Elizabethan –

> Some think to lose him
> By having him confined;
> And some do suppose him,
> Poor heart, to be blind;
> But if ne'er so close ye wall him,
> Do the best that ye may,
> Blind love, if so ye call him,
> He will find out his way.
>
> There is no striving
> To cross his intent;
> There is no contriving
> His plots to prevent;
> But if once the message greet him
> That his True Love doth stay,
> If Death should come and meet him
> Love will find out the way.

I have given notice. The captain was exceedingly kind. Kindness and considerate treatment to servants seem to belong to the family. He said that he was more than sorry to lose me, but quite understood my wish to settle down. He asked me if there was any favour he could do me. I told him yes, I should like to take 'Jim' with me. He seemed amused, but raised no objection, but I can imagine the stormy scenes in the nursery.

Mem. important. – There is a broken rail in the balustrade on the top landing overlooking the hall. The captain has twice asked me to see to it, as he is afraid one of the children might slip through. Only the bottom part of the rail is broken, and there should be no fear of any accidents. I cannot think how with a good memory like mine I should have forgotten to see to this.

These are the only extracts from Tollerton's diary that have a bearing on what followed. They are sufficient to show his extraordinary character, his strong imagination, and his stronger self-control.

I, the negligible half-pay captain of his story, little dreamed what sort of man had served me so well as butler; but strange as his life had been, his death was stranger.

The hall at Baldby Manor is exceedingly lofty, extending the full height of the three-storeyed house. It is surrounded by three landings; from the uppermost a passage leads to the nursery. The day after the last entry in the diary I was crossing the hall on my way to the study, when I noticed the gap in the banisters. I could hear distinctly the children's voices as they played in the corridor. Doubly annoyed at Tollerton's carelessness (he was usually the promptest and most methodical of servants), I rang the bell. I could see at once that he was vexed at his own forgetfulness. 'I made a note of it only last night,' he said. Then as we looked upward a curious smile stole across his lips. 'Do you see that?' he said, and pointed to the gap above. His sight was keener than mine, but I saw at last the thing that attracted his gaze – the two black eyes of the tortoise, the withered head, the long, protruded neck stretched out from the gap in the rail. 'You'll excuse a liberty, sir, I hope, from an old servant, but don't you see the extraordinary resemblance between the tortoise and the old master? He's the very image of Sir James. Look at the portrait behind you.' Half instinctively I turned. I must have passed the picture scores of times in the course of a day, I must have seen it in sunlight and lamplight, from every point of view; it was a clever picture, well painted, if the subject was not exactly a pleasing one, but that was all.

Yes, I knew at once what the butler meant. It was the eyes – no, the neck – that caused the resemblance, or was it both? together with the half-open mouth with its absence of teeth.

I had been used to think of the smile as having something akin to benevolence about it; time had seemed to be sweetening a nature once sour. Now I saw my mistake – the expression was wholly cynical. The eyes held me by their discerning power, the lips with their subtle mockery.

Suddenly the silence was broken by a cry of terror, followed by an awful crash.

I turned round in amazement.

The body of Tollerton lay stretched on the floor, strangely limp; in falling he had struck the corner of a heavy oak table.

His head lay in a little pool of blood, which the tortoise – I shudder as I think of it – was lapping greedily.

After the Flower Show

I know Wentley people well, for I have doctored Wentley people for over half a century.

On the whole I like and respect them: my opinion, too, is anything but prejudiced, for each year one patient after another deserts me in favour of young Lambert. I don't blame them. I used to have more work than I wanted, and a change of doctor is the very next best thing to a change of air. My bedside manner, too, is not what it was. I know old Martha Goodwin far too well to treat her as an expiring saint; but it pays, and Lambert should have a fine future before him.

I said that on the whole I like Wentley people. But I was annoyed with Mrs Travers, the vicar's wife, when she said exactly the same thing to me at the Wentley Show last week. For Mrs Travers has been just a month in the place. She has seen the best of the summer, the shadows sweeping across the fells, the fern-grown lanes, the deep emerald of the water-meadows after the hay harvest. She has seen the vicarage front, it faces the sunrise, one mass of clematis: 'the Purple East' she calls it.

But she has yet to call on the Squire when the gout is making his own and everyone else's life unbearable, and she has still to find that the vicarage cellars and wash-house are flooded as regularly as clockwork every November, when the water pours from the hills like rain from an umbrella. Why, only the day before yesterday she asked me what a cockroach looked like!

I rather think Mrs Travers is not so domesticated as she makes out. When Roper and I used to smoke in the vicarage kitchen at night, the very floor crawled around us. They are, I admit, at the best of times unpleasant; but I disliked the way the old man shovelled them into the fire. He used to say the crackling made him think he was burning wood, a luxury he could never afford.

But to return to Mrs Travers. We were walking round the show tent together.

'You have no idea of the unspeakable relief,' she said, 'in getting away from suburbia, with all its petty jealousies and unworthy subterfuges. You live on a different scale here; there is something of the mountains about you, something of the hard ruggedness of the fells.'

I was gazing as she spoke at the section devoted to sponge cakes, and thought her words singularly appropriate. 'Come and look at the flowers,' I said.

We sauntered down the long trestles to where the children's exhibits stood. It was a Miss Morton (she's dead now, poor lady!) who, ten years ago, thought of the excellent idea of getting the youngsters to show bunches of flowers they themselves had picked and arranged. I consider the plan to have worked well for Wentley. It is true that three summers ago the bunches in every case but one were definitely proved to have been plucked and arranged by mothers, aunts, and even fathers. To err is human: the fault was corrected, and the following year the schoolmistress was told off to take the children to Wychley Common, and there to watch in person the gathering in of the spoil.

But I am afraid it is also true that, as the crocodile came home through the village (this sounds unwittingly like an extract from a missionary's lecture) the mothers were at the doors, and successfully substituted bunches of their own gathering. They did it so barefacedly, and with such pride in the prospects of their children, and they all did it, and they knew they all did it, and they knew that the teacher was so shortsighted, poor thing! that I, for one, can readily forgive them.

So I admired with all my heart the jam-pots filled with foxgloves, meadowsweet, a late dog-daisy or two, golden tansies, and brazen monkey-flowers; but something jarred when Mrs Travers buried her face in the blossoms and said that flowers and children were all alike, and that flowers ought never to be picked except by their innocent little hands; which was indeed Rule 14, paragraph a, put into poetical language.

I hurried past the section devoted to embroidery. I find it difficult to distinguish between table centres and patchwork quilts. Drawn-thread work has always been, and will ever remain, a profound enigma to my mind. A woman sends her best tablecloth to the new laundry where they do things so well. It returns with a hole, not in the centre or at one end, but in some out-of-the-way corner which can never be covered by a bowl of flowers or the soup-tureen. She proceeds to darn it or patch it, and the operation is successful; but she refuses to be comforted, and the new laundry which Evelyn recommended so strongly knows her no more. Next day she purchases a square of sound linen, which she informs you is to be made into an afternoon teacloth. With a pair of scissors she proceeds deliberately to make a series of holes far more extensive than the one which spoiled her temper so short a time before. She spends hours in making those holes, she wrecks the cloth, and it is good for nothing but the next bazaar, where, in all likelihood, she will buy her own fancy work back at a fancy price.

Give them the vote by all means – anything to stop drawn-thread work!

Mrs Travers was, of course, interested in embroidery. She expressed some astonishment that the first prize had been given to Amy Stoddart.

'Poor girl! she is lame,' I said.

'Oh! that explains it, then. You country folk, in spite of your rough exterior, are always so chivalrous at bottom.'

'She is lame,' I went on. 'Mrs Toogood and Miss Butler are the judges in this section.'

I did not add that both these ladies are Amelia's aunts. It is the world's business, not mine, to disillusion people. After all, the girl is lame, and undoubtedly handicapped in her walk in life. Besides, the peacock embroidered on the cushion, reposing on a basket amid the bulrushes, was an entirely novel design, inspired doubtless by some old Sunday-school lesson on the finding of the infant Moses.

We passed on to the eleventh trestle-table, on which were spread specimens of childish calligraphy.

Thirty sheets of foolscap paper brought before our admiring gaze the statement, still widely accepted even in Wentley, that 'Honesty is the best policy.'

Albert Smallbones, for the third year in succession, had succeeded in carrying off the prize, though his mother had been obliged to change his birthday to the 3rd of August from the 31st of July in order that he might not be debarred by the age limit.

Lucy Pinfold was commended, but she had forgotten to dot the 'i' in 'Policy'; and Bertha Webster, whose up-strokes and down-strokes were as thin and plump as could be desired, was disqualified by spelling Honesty without a capital. She told me afterwards she thought it was an improper noun. I gave her sixpence, for the iron of the world must have entered into her soul.

The flowers are, of course, the main feature of Wentley Show. For purposes of competition, we are divided into three classes – Gentlemen, Professionals, and Cottage Gardeners. The Squire is in a class by himself. Year after year he sends down his governess-cart filled with begonias, which eventually stand on a table alone, entirely hidden by a label bearing the words, 'Not for competition. Exhibited by Mr Thomas Robinson, Gardener to Sir James Allen, of Riddersome Hall.'

The Committee has always had difficulty in defining each of the three classes mentioned above. A Cottage Gardener was originally anyone who lived in a cottage. But what is a cottage? Mr Jones, for instance, the retired draper from Seaton-on-Sea, lives in Laburnum Cottage, and for two years took all the prizes for roses. Then a rule was passed enacting that a cottage with a name to it became a villa, and Mr Jones became in consequence a Gentleman.

There was the case, too, of Jerry Porter, of the Goat and Compasses. He took a prize in Cactus dahlias (six blooms to be shown, all different). The Committee subsequently met to consider his status. It was unanimously agreed that he was not in any sense a cottager, and he was handed over to the Gentlemen. The Gentlemen, already smarting after the inclusion of Jones, wrote letters threatening to withdraw their patronage, and one or two of them began to open accounts with the Felstone butcher and grocer. A Special Committee was summoned and a rule drawn up, nominally in the interests of temperance and sobriety, which excluded all publicans and licensed victuallers from exhibiting. The Goat and Compasses being the only inn in the village, Jerry Porter, in cricketer's parlance, retired hurt. He now breeds bantam hens, where once the stately dahlia raised its head.

But Mrs Travers knows nothing of this. Hers is no sordid soul. She was not even interested in the vast material bulk of Joe Perry's vegetable-marrow. She told me that she had never seen a watermelon of that size except in Spain, and then catching sight of her husband left me to my thoughts.

They were interesting thoughts. Last week I attended the show in Croptondale, and saw there an exactly similar marrow exhibited by one Smith. With the idea of seeing whether the vast vegetable would explode I had thrust a pin into one end, and then, thinking in my guilty conscience that I had been detected, left it there, not having the moral courage to extract it. The same pin was gazing at me now. Oh, happy vegetable! So you, too, like our excellent

Conservative member, tour the constituency, attending show after show, speaking little, but enlivening everyone by your massively cheerful appearance.

Shall we meet again next fortnight at Little Wolfington, or will the tedious round of engagements have made a rest imperative?

On the Sunday after the show, Mr Travers, full of suburban energy, inaugurated the first flower service the village has ever seen.

He chose the time well. The aisles received the Squire's pink begonias; the children's bunches of wild flowers (to which he referred in the course of his sermon in connection with the raiment of Solomon) hung in faded festoons about the pillars, effectively hiding the glories of our Early English capitals. Jerry Porter, to the vicar's embarrassment, had sent a basket of beautiful bronze bantam eggs, which lay embowered among roses on the top of the font, for that day idle.

As sidesman I saw it all. And as the organ gave out the opening chords of 'We plough the fields and scatter' – a hymn that is not really long enough when the church is full and the collection is for the Universities' Mission to Central Africa – I saw my old friend, the vegetable marrow, seated in state on the highest step of the pulpit, and a passing gleam of sunshine from the new window in the aisle lighted exactly on the pin until he seemed to wink.

The Desecrator

The proposal was first made in the dining-room at the vicarage.

The cloth had been removed, and the vicar and his brother-in-law, the genial fellow of Trinity, sat on either side of the polished mahogany with the wine between them. Mrs Merivale had drawn her chair to the window in order to get sufficient light to pick up a stitch she had dropped in the stocking she was knitting.

On the lawn outside a thrush was busy initiating two fledglings into the mysteries of the great worm problem; a task the magnitude of which can be realised by imagining the difficulties an ordinary human would encounter in the endeavour to dispose gracefully of live asparagus.

Dr Simeon was the first to speak. 'I am thinking,' he said, 'of erecting a small mausoleum or temple upon the summit of Jerry Nab.'

In the silence which followed you could almost hear Mrs Merivale drop her second stitch. As it was, the four needles fell to the ground with a clatter. She looked towards her husband, who was gazing through his gold-rimmed spectacles at his brother-in-law with eyes that were filled with blank astonishment. If Dr Simeon had suddenly prostrated himself upon the prayer rug on which his chair was standing, the sensation could not have been more profound.

'My dear Charles,' said Mrs Merivale at last, 'I can only hope that you will do nothing rash.'

'My purpose in erecting this temple or mausoleum on Jerry Nab – the exact form the memorial will take is still uncertain – is primarily to draw the attention of the public to one of the loveliest view-points in the whole county. Arkengarth is putting up the land for sale next month, and there is more than a likelihood of its being bought by some speculative builder. I could never forgive myself if the Diceys got hold of it and prevented our right of access.'

'If you build a mausoleum,' said Mrs Merivale in her quiet, matter-of-fact tone of voice, 'I suppose you will have to be buried there. It would be very chilly, and I cannot imagine how a hearse could get up that hill. Only last evening when the Gunters were leading their hay, the waggon stuck half-way up, and they had three of their strongest horses harnessed to it. The white mare was in the shafts, James; the one we thought of buying last October. I believe eventually they had to unload at the corner and make two journeys. Of course, if you had not so strong an objection to cremation, there would be no difficulty with the ashes, but – '

'Mausoleum was perhaps an ill-chosen word,' said Dr Simeon gloomily. 'My final resting-place is, after all, of little account: though I confess the idea of entering upon my long sleep at a spot where I have indulged in so many shorter ones is not unattractive.'

The vicar's face suddenly became very grave.

'But in any case, Caroline,' Dr Simeon went on, 'I can safely leave the matter to you. You are a born manager, and if extra horses are really necessary, you will of course see to it. I am afraid, though, that in my case it will be impossible to lighten the load when they get to the corner.'

'You mentioned a temple,' said the vicar, endeavouring to lead the conversation into safer paths. 'What exactly would be the purport of a temple upon the top of Jerry Nab?'

'I called it a temple,' Dr Simeon replied, 'but it would be little more than a simple building of stone, with four windows command-ing the landscape on each side, and perhaps a flat roof from which to view the panorama. If you would prefer me to build a chapel there, I have no objection.'

'I hardly think the site suitable for a place of worship,' said the vicar. 'Of course we should have to keep it locked, and it would be exceedingly annoying for Parker to be constantly bothered by people coming for the key when he was busy cleaning the harness. The place, too, would be sure to get damp, and the hassocks and prayer-books would constantly have to be renewed.'

'Why is it necessary to build either a temple or a mausoleum?' asked his wife. 'I, for one, am strongly in favour of a well or drinking fountain. It would be far more unusual in such a situation, and I am quite sure it would be appreciated.'

'The disadvantage of a well,' said Dr Simeon, 'is that it would be far more difficult to get the water to the top of the hill than my hearse. As it is, the Gunters have to bring theirs in carts for nearly three miles.'

'A well is obviously out of the question,' the vicar after a pause remarked, 'but I see no reason why a seat should not be sufficient;

either one of the iron sort, such as we have in the garden, or a teak seat, which some firms deal in. They are made, I believe, from the wood of old battleships. On second thoughts, you might very appropriately link your gift with the name of some local naval celebrity. It would certainly not involve you in any extra expense.'

'There is a good deal in what you say,' said Dr Simeon, 'but I still hanker after my temple, built four square to all the winds of heaven. Do you know of any local builder capable of doing the work?'

Mrs Merivale paused for a minute. 'There is a man at Winterton,' she said, 'who is an excellent builder, and he has the additional advantage of being able to do his own plumbing. He was the man we employed for the new coach-house. Don't you remember him, James?'

'Do you really mean to tell me,' said Dr Simeon, getting up from his chair to pace the room, 'that a temple requires plumbing? I never in my wildest dreams imagined such a thing!'

'I don't think it would be necessary for a temple, but if you decided subsequently to use the place as a mausoleum, a good deal of lead work would be probably necessary.'

'What a fund of useful information your wife possesses, James!' Dr Simeon exclaimed.

'It's all very well for you to laugh, Charles, but I know for a fact that when the Diceys built their billiard-room, the man strongly advised them to cover the wooden roof with lead sheeting. Of course they refused, and the result was that after the first autumn gale the water began to come through and absolutely ruined the cloth. They had to get it recovered eventually.'

'Why is a parson like a billiard-table?' asked the doctor under his breath. 'I suppose the answer would be that with both we are bound to respect the cloth.'

'A thing you never do, Charles. To judge by your flippant talk one would scarcely suppose that you yourself were in orders.'

'Ah well!' said Dr Simeon, with a smile, 'you must put it down, Caroline, to the sadly cynical outlook of the young men among whom I live. They grow old so quickly nowadays; the age of doubt is younger every year. But I have often thought that they make a great mistake in trying to solve the riddle of the universe at the universities. Well, what do you say to a stroll in the garden, James? It seems a pity to miss this glorious July moon.'

'By all means,' said the vicar; 'and I can show you the iron seat I was speaking of. This particular one has some special springs, which makes it rather expensive; but you could doubtless get a cheaper sort for Jerry Nab.'

The site was bought and the temple began to be built. Dr Simeon insisted upon calling it a temple, though his sister always referred to the place as the shelter.

'I don't like the idea,' she said, 'of the village people talking of a temple. It hardly seems right, when the Bishop has taken such trouble in organising this splendid missionary campaign, to do anything which might, however remotely, serve as a stumbling-block to the parish. I know what you are going to say, Charles; but when the Peabodys were staying with us the month you were away – they are home on furlough from China, and are such kind, well-meaning people – I noticed that Mrs Peabody looked quite grieved when James incidentally mentioned the fact that you were building a temple. Of course she said nothing. She is far too good a woman ever to dream of raising an objection to anything of which she does not approve; but I could see that she felt it deeply.'

'Never mind the Peabodys,' Dr Simeon had in effect said.

'I don't know how you can use so wicked an expression,' his sister had replied. 'Try and imagine how you would feel if, after spending years in heathen countries, you returned to England to see what in name, at least, is nothing less than a symbol of idolatry in process of erection on Jerry Nab.'

The vicar personally had no objection to calling the place a temple, though he fully saw the force of his wife's remarks. He rather quarrelled with his brother-in-law over the question of expense.

'There are a number of societies,' he said, 'which make it their business to secure these beauty spots for public use.' – Dr Simeon shuddered involuntarily at the word 'beauty spot' – 'The easiest course to adopt, in my opinion, would be to write to a paper like the *Spectator*, making an appeal for funds; and, if you cared, you could offer to give, say, a hundred pounds on condition that the other nine hundred was forthcoming by the end of the year. People are always very slow in giving.'

'It would not be quite the same thing,' Dr Simeon had answered; 'and besides, the place has for me peculiar associations. In the hazel copse up there I found my first chaffinch's nest. Don't you remember, Caroline, with what delight we watched the eggs hatch out, and how tame the young birds were? And it was down the slopes that we used to test our home-made toboggans, which were never for some reason or other a success. I remember, too, that it was to the top of Jerry

Nab that my old father toddled the day before his last illness. For years he must have walked up there whenever the evening was fine to see the sunset.'

Under the capable hands of the man from Winterton who did his own plumbing, the building progressed, and Dr Simeon spent many happy hours up on the hillside, now lending a hand with the spade, now chatting with the old mason as he dressed the great blocks of stone. He tried the experiment once of reading to him Collins's 'Ode to Evening'.

'Yes,' he said at the close. 'It's beautiful language that. There's a deal of poetry like that in Mrs Fiddler's visitors' book down at the Stutteville Arms. I often read it of an evening; but it's more comic like than that. Not but that what you've said hasn't its points.'

As the building neared completion, Dr Simeon conceived the idea of inscribing something on the stone below the windows. The recollection of Mrs Fiddler's visitors' book turned his mind from the quotations from the English poets he had originally planned. He had no intention to waste money in casting pearls before swine. Latin would be the only possible medium.

At last the temple was finished.

On a perfect July afternoon, just a year from the day on which Dr Simeon had first broached his scheme in the vicarage garden, the elect of the neighbouring parishes assembled together on the top of Jerry Nab to witness the dedication of the hillside to the public. To the relief of everyone the claims of the hay harvest prevented the public being present in person; but they were ably represented by the vicar, who contributed a lengthy description of the ceremony to the local paper, where it appeared under the heading, 'Another Beauty Spot Preserved'.

The villagers as a whole were not as grateful as they might have been. From time immemorial they had trespassed on Jerry Nab, and though the legality of their presence was now no longer questioned, it was still in an attitude of stealth that they approached the place.

In spite of the fact that his gift was taken as a matter of course, Dr Simeon saw no reason to repent of his munificence. He had actually begun to hope that the temple might have a definite educational value by attracting attention to the beautiful, when an incident befell which for many months unsettled his sane belief in human nature.

He was returning to Wenderby after an absence of nearly a year. His luggage he had left at the station to be called for by the carrier in the morning, and since towards evening a breeze had arisen to temper the noonday heat, Dr Simeon declined the offer of old Thompson's shaky waggonette, and stepped out briskly in the direction of Jerry Nab and home.

Anyone who judges of the broad vale between Lexborough and Rivington by the little he sees through the windows of the train which crawls along the single line half a dozen times a day, has an altogether inadequate idea of the grandeur of the country that surrounds him. For the lanes which creep up slowly from the dale would seem only to pass by easy gradients into a valley as wide and fertile as the one they have left. Instead they come to an end on the bare summits of headlands that, separated from each other by deep and wooded valleys, jut out into a vast expanse of rolling moor.

After walking for an hour along the narrow lanes, Dr Simeon found himself at last on the top of Jerry Nab, the highest of these inland promontories, and with a sigh of complete satisfaction sank down on the closely cropped turf. In front of him the hillside sloped precipitately to the narrow valley below, which ran right up into the heart of the moors. Wenderby lay there in the hollow, the red-roofed cottages straggling on either side of the village green; at the further end, almost under the shadow of the church, stood the vicarage, an ugly, square house of stone, that ivy and creeper were ever struggling to efface. To the right, where the Whinstone Beck joined the river, the squat chimney of the old saw-mill was just visible; the straight line of smoke that rose above the trees around which the rooks were circling marked the site of Thornton House. Dr Simeon remembered his sister telling him that the Diceys had been staying there since the twelfth.

When he turned to the south, the prospect was no less lovely; the great plain stretched out before him, a constant reiteration of greens and golds, broken in the distance by the long white streak of steam that marked the last northbound train.

The sounds, too, were all in perfect accord; the monotonous cawing of the rooks, the happy shouts of children in the village below, the faraway whirr of a reaping machine in some patch of late-standing corn. From the church came the notes of the old cracked bell as it struck the hour. It was seven.

'One glance inside the temple,' said Dr Simeon, 'and then I must hurry down to dinner.'

He was pleased to see that the place was clean and tidy. No matches littered the floor; the receptacle he had placed for orange peel was obviously empty. It was only after a more careful examination that he became aware of the awful desecration done. Beneath the western window, through which the sun now shone, he had had carved a line from his favourite Georgics –

> O fortunatos nimium, sua si bona norint,
> Agricolas!

Immediately below this, ineffaceably graven in the stone, were the words –

ALBERT HERBERT HOGSON,
8 CLARISSA CRESCENT, SHUNTER'S ROAD,
STEELBOROUGH

Dr Simeon was silent for a full minute: then for the first time for many months he swore.

He might have guessed that this sort of thing would happen. His forty years' experience as an archaeologist was more than sufficient to have uprooted any belief that he once possessed in the British public's innate sense of reverence. Desecrated tombstones, broken-nosed effigies of templars, priceless woodwork hacked about to test the blades of the yokel's newest pocket-knife – all these were matters of everyday occurrence. He ought, doubtless, to congratulate himself on the fact that his temple had so long escaped the vandals. Yet Dr Simeon wished from the bottom of his heart that the thing had been done with less energy. Those letters were so huge and staring; from their depth the man must have spent hours in this attempt to leave a lasting memorial to his hideous personality. Gloomily he closed the door and locked it. 'It is incidents such as these,' he said, 'that make one despair of Liberalism. I have half a mind to vote for Carew at the next election.'

'Only think,' he said to his sister that evening, 'of the state of mind that such an act exhibits. The man who does a thing like that should really not be allowed at large. Of course he agitates for shorter hours of work, for longer holidays, and this is the disgusting result of his leisure. I have not the slightest doubt that the time he spent in the train in his journey from Steelborough was occupied by a similar mutilation of the various notices in the railway compartment. Men of this stamp are of a singularly low order of intelligence. Hogson, for instance, seems to have forgotten that by leaving his address I have it in my power to prosecute him.'

'After all, Charles,' his sister answered, 'I do not see that you have any real cause for complaint. He saw that there were inscriptions in the shelter already, in a language he could not read. He probably saw, too, your name over the door; and, since you refused to adopt my suggestion of a visitors' book, it is only to be expected that this sort of thing should occur.'

Miss Dicey, who chanced to be dining at the vicarage that evening, regarded the question from an altogether different aspect.

'I have often thought,' she said, 'of the annoyance caused to the gentleman who rented the sporting rights of the Forest of Arden by the vulgar way in which Orlando ruined his choicest trees. His feelings must have been the same as yours, Dr Simeon, though the provocation was far greater. He and his friends would, of course, litter the place with discarded lunch-packets and empty flagons of canary. But what was the result? We remember nothing about the querulous individual who rented the shooting; we have not the slightest interest in the steps he took to prevent picnickers, and the duke's party, at least, must have made a horrible mess of the place. All our interest goes out to Orlando, the young vandal, the immortal counterpart of Albert Herbert Hogson. As for the latter, I am confident his name will be famous long after the time when Simeon's edition of Theocritus lies dust-covered and forgotten in the college libraries.'

'My dear lady,' said Dr Simeon, 'what you say has ever my best attention; but you have, I believe, been prejudiced against me ever since I was rash enough to publish that insignificant volume, which, by the way, is about to reappear in a third edition. However, I for one am convinced that Hogson is a man whose whole endeavour has been to live in accordance with his name. I have to go to Steelborough on business next week, when I shall certainly make a point of visiting 8 Clarissa Crescent, Shunter's Road.'

The object of his search was by no means easy to find, and Dr Simeon had spent a long half-hour in following advice that was as often as not contradictory before he met with the ragged urchin who informed him that he was actually standing in Shunter's Road. Clarissa Crescent was the second turn to the right, and it came as no surprise to find that the road was no crescent at all, but a straight street of red-brick houses, only differing from each other in the extent of their squalor.

It was Monday afternoon, and across the street hung the ragged banners of poverty in the shape of the week's washing. Opposite No. 6 a tall, bony woman, slatternly in her attire, but with a face that was not unkind, was endeavouring to close-haul a sheet that a gusty wind bellied out before it. Dr Simeon waited until her task was finished before accosting her. 'I believe that Albert Herbert Hogson lives here?' To his amazement the woman burst into a flood of tears. 'He's dead, sir!' she sobbed. 'He died only ten days ago. Them's his breeches hanging up there.' She pointed, as she spoke, to a very diminutive though extensively patched article of apparel that hung from the further end of the line. 'You're from the Sunday School, I suppose, sir?' she continued. 'Will you kindly step inside?'

'I had not the pleasure of knowing your son,' Dr Simeon said, as soon as he had sat down. 'The fact is, I come from Wenderby. I happened to see his name carved in the temple on the top of the hill. It was so well done that I thought I would make further inquiries as I passed through Steelborough.' Mrs Hogson was not unwilling to pour out her story into the ears of a listener so seemingly sympathetic. In the ten days that had intervened since her loss, Clarissa Crescent had had other troubles.

'It was last Bank Holiday,' she went on, 'and me and Jim – that's my husband – took Albert 'Erbert out for the day. We got to the top of the hill where they've built the shelter in memoriam of the vicar's brother what fell in South Africa, and Jim being tired, he went down to the public, in the village, to rest himself before going home. Me and Albert stayed up at the shelter, and then the little feller gets out a chisel and hammer what belonged to his dad, he being a stonemason when in work, which it's little enough he's had of late. He sets to work and cuts out his name right proper. "Won't dad be pleased?" he kept on saying. And his father was pleased and all, when he saw it, and promised him that he'd have him apprenticed to a monumental mason, where he could cut out real texs on the gravestones. It was a grand day was that. And when we went back to the station, what should the boy see but a throstle's nest up in a tree. He was right tired, but he would climb it to get the eggs for Annie, that's his little sister. And then, if you'll believe me, there weren't no eggs, but young throstles just about fledged. My word! the lad was vexed. The language he used nigh broke my sides with laughing. But he got them young birds, and he carried them in his handkerchief all squeaking to a pond that was near, the old birds raising a din fair fit to deafen one. And when he got to the pond, he drowned them one by one, he was that disappointed that they weren't eggs. Albert 'Erbert was like his dad, always fond of a bit of sport when he could get it.' Dr Simeon moved about uneasily in his chair; he was getting more than he had bargained for. Mrs Hogson went on. 'The doctor said he died of gallopin' consumption, but it's my belief he caught a chill in that damp shelter what the vicar erected in memory of his son as got shot on Spion Kop. He was a smart boy was our Albert. He was top but one in his class, and went to Sunday School as regular as could be, until they began giving away prizes for early attendance as were not up to standard, the curate being a young man and new to the job. My husband tried to get him a place at Dawson's, the monumental mason's, since 'Erbert seemed to take to carving so, and we thought some of the texs as he learned at Sunday School might come in useful. But it was no good; so we arranged with the butcher to take him on, it being a likely trade, and 'Erbert was to have gone there today. If ever a boy had a future before him, it was him.'

'Well,' said Dr Simeon, as he rose to go, 'you have interested me exceedingly in what you have said about your son. His was evidently one of those lives from which a great deal can be learnt. I shall always think of him when I see his name in the shelter. It was erected, I think you said, in memory of the vicar's nephew?'

'It was either his nephew or his grandson, I can't quite remember which, but I know that he was killed in South Africa. Good-day, sir, and mind the step. I am much obliged, I am sure, for your comforting words.'

'The complexity of this world seems to increase as we grow older,' said Dr Simeon to himself, as he retraced his way down the now deserted street. At Shunter's Road he turned to look back. Mrs Hogson was busy at work again, bending over her clothes-basket. The only thing that occupied the clothes-line were the diminutive breeches of Albert Herbert. The signs of mending were even more obvious than before.

'What patched-up things we are,' he said; then he chuckled to himself.

'I wonder what mischief the boy is up to now.'

The Educationalist

There is a certain seat in a northern cathedral city that is remarkable for the fact that it is always occupied by old men. It stands in the shade of an elm tree, half a mile beyond the battered gateway that once commanded the London road. The seat is not a comfortable one; I have tried it myself. There is no back to lean against, and in summer it is well within the dust-producing area of the slowest automobile. But it is placed at the summit of a gentle rise, that is just steep enough to cause an old man to pause and wipe his brow, and it is so low that, when once the old man has been tempted to sit down, he finds himself obliged to get out his pipe and tobacco, that he may give greater consideration to the problem of how to get up again.

The occupiers of this seat are well-known to the passers-by; usually they are pensioners of the railway company, as fine-looking figures as any to be found in the old guard of the army of labour. A loose sleeve, a well-worn crutch, show that they have not all come out of the fight unscathed.

Once a week, on Thursday afternoons, the seat is occupied by a different set of men; they too are old, but instead of passing the time in a conversation that, if not sprightly, is at least intelligent, they sit with wooden, apathetic faces in an attitude of resigned hopelessness. They are poorly, if neatly, dressed. Occasionally one of them is called by a passing acquaintance to share a drink at the Crossed Keys, where for a happy quarter of an hour he has an opportunity of forgetting that he is an inmate of that House, whose old, grey walls he knows so well.

Thomas Birkenshaw, when I first met him, must have been nearly eighty years old. He was far the most distinguished occupier of the veterans' seat, where he was to be found on nearly every sunny day, when the wind was not in the east, a straight stove-pipe hat on his head, a wonderful black cravat tied in a bow beneath his chin, and a tail coat that by its very survival, testified to the pathetic economies of the bachelor.

His face, tanned a deep-brown by tropical suns, was as striking as his dress. The varied emotions of a life that had been lived to the full had left their indelible mark in the fissures that furrowed his forehead. The eyes that shone out black and piercing beneath the shaggy eyebrows seemed to show much the same aspect of his character as the thin and mobile lips around which a smile, slightly cynical, was often playing. For an old man he wore his white hair unusually short, and this, with the half-military cut of his whiskers and the straightness of his carriage, served to emphasise an appearance already sufficiently distinguished.

He had at one time served in the ranks, but then there was little that he had not done, from teaching children in a National School to sub-editing an atheistic review. 'Tinker, tailor, soldier, sailor,' he would say, 'but never a rich man, and so never a thief.' Even in ordinary conversation it was impossible for him to keep away from his prejudice against wealth; since boyhood the happiness of the few had ever been associated with the misery of the many. Though in the conclave of old men Birkenshaw seldom spoke, he was always welcomed; if he came late, and he usually did not appear until eleven, they sat closer together, and in summer the corner beneath the elm was always vacated as soon as he arrived. As soon as the cathedral bell chimed the quarter before twelve, there would generally be a movement in the company. Pipes would be knocked out, and then someone would get up and, after carefully scratching his head, declare that it was time to be going home.

It was on these occasions, when everyone else had returned to the city for dinner (I found later that the old man had hardly ever more than two meals a day), that Birkenshaw would begin to talk. Then it was that I heard him first propound his views on the subject of Education.

'No one,' he said, 'who has lived for nearly eighty years can fail to value a good education. I remember the days when there were hardly a score of people in the parish who could read, and even then the squire said there were nineteen too many. But I have never believed in the type of education the modern child receives. The money is only wasted. Look at the boys who year after year win scholarships, until they find themselves at last at Oxford or Cambridge. Are they the men of the future? Of course not! They come back with any spark of enthusiasm they once possessed carefully extinguished; with nothing to show for their years of idleness but a drawl that is as long as their tailor's bill, and socks as glaring as their ignorance. And the boys who count, the boys who can teach a whole class of meek little Sunday School children to swear and to rob orchards, end their school-days by being expelled because they have "influence". Expel the others, if you like, but keep the boys with character, no matter whether it be good or bad. The results would be far more substantial than any obtained in the senseless attempt to make great men and women out of ordinary little boys and girls.

'You said just now that you dislike children. Shake hands over it!' and here the old fellow gripped me with a grasp that made me wince. 'In these days of sentimental twaddle it is a pleasure to meet men who dislike children and have sufficient courage to admit as much. I have taught children for five years, acting from what I took to be a sense of duty. Before that time I knew comparatively little of idleness, folly, and cruelty.

'On three afternoons a week I walk up to this seat. I always see the children as they come out from St Margaret's just up the road, and they, little spitfires, always laugh and mock at me and my hat. There is one boy, and one boy only, who will come to anything in that school. If it were not a contradiction in terms, I should say he was a good boy.'

The old man was silent for some minutes, while he made ineffectual thrusts at a thistle in the grass in front of him. Then he went on: 'I sometimes think that I am happy, but more often unhappy, in that I have survived all my relations. If I have claims on no one, no one has certainly claims on me; and since I have no better use for my small savings, I intend to leave them to some boy or girl as the means of procuring an education they would not otherwise receive. I have at present three children in my mind; the task of deciding between their respective claims is as interesting as it is difficult. This boy at St Margaret's is one. Every ordinary educationalist would pass him over. He is bottom but one in his class, and his master has long given him up as hopeless, which, of course, is all to the boy's credit.

'I don't know whether you are interested in the spinning of tops. I judge that you are not. You make a great mistake; there is a great deal to be learnt from tops. In the first place boys do not spin them all the year round. There is a definite close season, unfixed by Act of Parliament, when anyone found spinning a top is knocked down and kicked. I often wondered what determined the beginning of the season; it was certainly no Saint's Day, nor any date mentioned in the almanacks. For a long time I thought that the whole thing was controlled by the shopkeepers; but then I found that the shop windows were filled with tops and whips long before the boys had begun to play with them. I once ventured to ask a shopkeeper about it. He was quite unintelligent. The only answer he gave me was, that about that time of the year boys came in and asked for tops. I put it to him that what he really meant was that a boy came in, followed after a very appreciable interval by other boys. He did not seem to see the difference; and, as he regarded me somewhat coldly, I bought a half-penny box of matches and went away. That spring I watched the shops carefully; at last, about ten days after the tops had been placed in the window, one Saturday afternoon I saw Jim Reffit, the boy of whom I am speaking, go in and purchase a whip. By the following Monday all the boys in his school had either bought new tops or produced their old ones. By the Wednesday the children of every school in the city were busy making the life of passers-by unbearable. Of course, if Jim Reffit had not started the craze, someone else would have done – the same might be said of the maker of every new invention – but the fact remains, that it was due to his initiative. A boy who can so influence others is surely worth educating.

'His leadership in the matter of tops was only one instance out of many. It was the same tale over again with the Boy Scouts. One afternoon I saw a little chap come to school dressed in their usual toggery, a complete novelty to St Margaret's. Reffit saw him too. For a brief space of time the future of the Boy Scouts in that parish hung in the balance. It was a question of either twisting his wrist or taking the paraphernalia from him and appropriating it for his own use. In less than a minute the boy had weighed the two alternatives and made his choice. Both the curates of St Margaret's have been obliged to become Scout Masters, and I hear that since last month they have been joined by the curate of St James'. Reffit's attitude to Boy Scouts shows, however, a weak point in his character, and makes me doubt whether money invested in his education would be really well spent. I fear that, carried away by a love of authority and lacking the patience to discover what sort of authority is really worth possessing, the boy will end by becoming a sergeant in the army, absolutely content with the existing order of Society, and lending all the weight of his influence towards its support. He is never discontented for long, and has that vilest of all habits, for ever making the best of things which are intrinsically bad.

'So much for Reffit,' said the old man, as he raised himself from the seat. 'It is getting rather chilly here since the sun went in. Some day I will tell you about the other two children I have in view.'

I lost sight of Birkenshaw for some weeks, and when I saw him again, it was not in his usual place. He told me that the wind was too cold up on the hill; he had taken to sitting on a far more comfortable seat he had discovered in a garden recently opened to the public in the heart of the city, almost under the shadow of the cathedral. 'They have spoiled the place by the new war memorial,' he said, 'but the Valentine Lane Schools are just round the corner, so that I have ample opportunity for studying the children. Last week, when I was ill, I made a little calculation; I find that if I die within the next two years, I shall be able to leave quite a considerable sum of money, so that I am more anxious than ever to choose the recipient with every care.

'That is the boy I am thinking of at present,' he said, pointing to a ragged urchin, who was busy counting out what seemed to be an unlimited store of marbles. I confessed that I was not attracted by his appearance. He had none of the robust self-confidence of the English schoolboy, so strikingly emphasised in Reffit, but seemed, on the other hand, undersized, with pinched features that had a certain suspicion of shrewd slyness.

'I thought you would probably dislike him,' said Birkenshaw. 'I detest the boy; at the same time his abilities are extraordinary. You see him at present balancing up his books after one of the smartest deals in Valentine Street. When the electric cars were introduced, I expect you noticed, no matter where you alighted, the extraordinary way in which the children pestered you for your ticket. I believe the reason was that certain tradesmen used the tickets for advertising purposes, promising free samples, and all the other tricks of the trade, whenever the ticket was produced. The magistrates, acting from an altogether exaggerated idea of the value of child life, eventually put a stop to the thing, but not before Metcalfe had been caught in the snare of accumulating wealth. It was then he conceived the brilliant notion of giving to tram tickets a value that was entirely fictitious. He entered into a conspiracy with two other boys, and for a fortnight they surreptitiously collected all the tickets they could lay hands on. At the end of that time he let it be understood that he was a purchaser of tram tickets at the rate of one marble for twenty. Other boys laughed at him, telling him that he was behind the times, that the shopkeepers no longer held to their agreement. Metcalfe smiled and said nothing. Then a small boy, with charming innocence, presented him with twenty tickets he had collected from the gutter; he received in exchange a marble which, to everyone's surprise, was not only without crack or flaw, but was of a mottled colour as rare as it was fascinating. When other boys had found that Metcalfe was actually in earnest, the whole school took to collecting tickets again. Something approaching a sensation was caused by the announcement that he was prepared to give a marble for eighteen tickets instead of twenty. A wild rumour spread that Metcalfe was buying up tickets for the Corporation; others held a saner hypothesis based on the fact that he had been observed in deep confabulation with a rag and bone merchant. The inevitable result was that those boys who prided themselves on their shrewdness became purchasers of tickets on their own account and watched carefully for developments.

'It was then that Metcalfe was taken seriously ill. He still, however, managed to control his business affairs, and, acting through his two agents, gradually sold out his vast supply of tickets at prices which at one time actually reached the high-water mark of ten per marble.

'On a certain black Friday he reappeared. For some time previous the Valentine Street schools had been bordering upon a state of panic. His arrival was greeted with the frank demand that he should at once declare what was the actual value of certain sack loads of tickets, and how that value could be realised. His plea of ignorance was, of course, taken as a piece of impudent bluff. Pressure was then brought to bear, a phrase that can be literally interpreted whenever boys are concerned. Metcalfe is built of very different stuff from Reffit. He howled for mercy, which was refused; he demanded time, and this, after long consideration, was given him. He seized the opportunity afforded by the dinner-hour to complain to the head-master. For the last ten days his life would have been unendurable had he not bribed or hired six of the strongest boys to escort him to and from school. He is counting out their wages now.

'It was only by chance that I learned all this from one of Metcalfe's two lieutenants, whose admiration for his chief was tempered only by the fact that he had twice been cheated out of the fruits of his industry. The general schoolboy public, however, still believe that on some memorable day Metcalfe will show them how to dispose of their tickets for their weight in copper, and I believe that the more innocent still half-heartedly collect them.

'Well, that is Metcalfe; and whenever I see the boy, I have a vision of the horrible future that awaits him. Rise he will by fair means or foul. He will begin by cheating his work-people when they are not looking; and then he will find it easier to employ work-people whom he can cheat even when they are looking. Some day he will have a nest to feather, and then he will become a Guardian of the Poor, and so he will climb the many-runged ladder, until the voice of the people bids him join the Army of Progress in Parliament. I despair of Reffit, because his temperament is such that he will never see that three quarters of the people of England are the blind slaves of the rest. If Metcalfe does not know that already, he very soon will, and the chief business of his life will be to prevent them regaining their sight and freedom. The question I cannot decide is this: Is it too late to inspire that boy with some sort of an ideal? I almost think it is. But even yet I might breed in him a savage hate that might go far to take its place.'

The tone in which the old man spoke surprised me. White hot passion is rare at eighty.

I saw Birkenshaw a week later. An article in the *Rationalist Review*, which he had expressed a wish to see, served as the excuse for my call. The clean little four-roomed cottage was empty. I had noticed with some uneasiness a half-filled medicine bottle on the kitchen dresser, but his voice, clear and firm as ever, that called to me from the back garden, quickly reassured me. I found him seated in his solitary armchair, wrapped in a heavy overcoat. 'Yes,' he said, 'I've not been as well as I could have wished, though I'm all right again now, and Mrs Muggleton next door has been very kind in looking after me. I'm much obliged to you for bringing the *Review*. I think I'll keep it until tonight to read in case I don't get any sleep. At present, I should like to introduce you to a friend of mine, Sally Muggleton, Mrs Muggleton's daughter. I believe she is busy pulling up radishes on the other side of the wall. You will find the broken half of a ladder over in the corner. You might hand it over to her. Of course she could come round through the house,' Birkenshaw remarked, as with difficulty I passed the ladder across the wall, 'but all women are alike in preferring the romantic to the practical.'

Sally Muggleton, having climbed to the top of the wall, refused my proffered assistance and jumped down neatly on to the path. Birkenshaw introduced me formally to the little girl, who made me a charming curtsy. 'She learnt that from me,' he said. 'Curtsies are very properly excluded from the democratic school curriculum of today.'

At first sight no one would have called Sally Muggleton a pretty child; her features were plain, and her hair, which she wore in a tightly-plaited pigtail, was of a bright carroty-red. But, as she stood before us, the colour of her cheek heightened by a natural shyness, she seemed the embodiment of health and happiness.

'I've brought you a relish for your tea, Mr Birkenshaw,' she said, as she produced with difficulty from a pocket that in itself was hard to find, a bunch of seven radishes, their tops neatly tied together with black thread. 'If you're not very hungry, you'd better leave the biggest one to the last, because a slug's inside it. I tried to get it out with a pin, but it wouldn't come. You can't see it now, because I've filled up the hole with salt to kill it; so that if you do swaller it by chance, it won't do you no harm, Mr Birkenshaw.'

'I'm really very much obliged, Sally. I shall eat my tea with twice as much enjoyment, especially since I know that the slug is dead.'

'Well, he's nearly dead, you know,' she answered. 'You can still see him squirming about, if you blow out the salt.'

'You left me last evening, Sally, without ever telling me about your dolls. Sit down on the arm of my chair and let me hear what they've been up to lately.'

'Well, Mr Birkenshaw,' she began, 'it's very kind of you to ask, I am sure. Matilda has got a cold in the head again and does snuffle fearful, and Percy has come out all over in spots, so that he can't go to school; and if I've got enough red paint left, Victoria is going to sicken for scarlet fever, the same as Mrs Jones's little baby. 'Scuse me, Mr Birkenshaw, but that's my mother calling. It's Mr Simpson from St James', him with the piping voice; he'll have come to know why I wasn't at Sunday School. My word! Shan't I catch it!'

'Very well, I suppose you must go. I see you have brought a medicine bottle with you; you can fill it up from the one on the dresser in the kitchen. I expect it will do your children as much good as it has done me.' The little girl gave the old fellow a resounding kiss, and then ran off.

'Very lovable,' said Mr Birkenshaw, 'very lovable indeed. She has, of course, certain weaknesses which go with the sex; as, for instance, this half-concealed delight in seeing people ill, which furnishes her with the excuse of pouring out an endless amount of sympathy and medicine.'

'I shall never forget my first meeting with Sally Muggleton,' he said after a moment's pause. 'Two years ago last November I was walking across the Stray about five o'clock in the evening, when I saw a middle-aged gentleman stop a hundred yards ahead of me and accost a little girl. He was a tall man with a long black beard; I remember that he wore a shade over his right eye. No sooner had he spoken to Sally than she burst into a flood of tears. The man was evidently perturbed, and being apparently unused to children, he put out a hand and began to pat her rhythmically on the small of the back. This was more than the girl could bear, and, diving between his legs, she started off running towards me. I purposely dropped my handkerchief as she approached, and as I bent to pick it up, we collided with some force. I asked her if I should take her home, and she sobbingly assented. We started off at a great speed, which I gradually slackened, until we reached a shop in Minstergate, where they sell hot meat-pies. I remember how Sally's eyes gaped with admiring awe as the young woman behind the counter poured in the gravy by means of a tin funnel inserted in a hole in the pastry. After our meal we became more confidential, until finally, with all the signs of returning tears, she whispered to me what the man had actually said to her.

' "He told me to come along with him and join his Band of Hope." For a second time the storm broke, and, as a pie shop was not in sight, I began to talk as rapidly as possible of the good done by these excellent institutions. I told her that thousands of little boys and girls joined the Band of Hope; that they were joining it at the rate of one a minute; that they were all good little boys and girls, who all went to heaven when they died. Even so lively a stretch of the imagination as this failed to reassure her, and when I parted with Sally at Mrs Muggleton's door – it was the first intimation I had had that we were neighbours – she still sobbed out in tones of utter despair, "He said I must join his Band of Hope."

'From that day to this I have been unable to find out the reason of her aversion; she still resolutely refuses to join the Band of Hope; but that, I imagine, is due to her love of consistent conduct. I have formed two hypotheses: the first does great credit to her intellect, but is, I am afraid, improbable. It explains everything by supposing that Sally had passed judgment on the Band of Hope movement and had found it wanting. Her tears were due to the bitterness of seeing results so small following after an expenditure of energy so great. The second hypothesis depends on the fact that a fortnight before her adventure a band of gypsies, who had been camping on the far side of the Stray, were brought up on an absolutely unfounded charge of attempted child-stealing. I have come to the conclusion that Sally disregarded the hallmark of orthodoxy stamped upon the face and figure of the man who had spoken to her, and, judging solely by the shade which covered his right eye, supposed that she was in the power of a band of desperate kidnappers. The incident, trivial in itself, has had one unlooked-for result; Sally has ever since had a deep-rooted dislike of black-coated benevolence. This prejudice extends, of course, to the clergy; I have not the slightest doubt that she will be more than a match for the unfortunate Mr Simpson, who is at present admonishing her. This independence of mind, combined with her loving heart and heavy hand, will help to make Sally an ideal mother of men; and any money spent in teaching her to play the piano, to walk with her toes turned out, and to intersperse her conversation with tags of French will certainly not be wasted, if it helps her to secure a good husband. But then there are Reffit and Metcalfe; I wish I had sufficient to provide for the three of them.'

Autumn came, and, as the short, sharp frosts of October gave place to the November fogs, it was all too evident that Thomas Birkenshaw would never have to face an English winter again. Not that he was confined to bed; he still took his walks abroad, but his figure was no longer erect, and his tread, once so firm, had changed into a weary shuffle.

'I've almost served my life sentence,' said the old pessimist. 'I have never had the chance of an appeal, and, though it's not been always hard labour or solitary confinement, I'm glad it's over.'

The end came more suddenly than we had expected, hastened by a slight accident that he met with on the Saturday before Christmas. He had managed to drag himself along the snow-covered pavements to watch the children as they came out of the Valentine Street schools. There was the usual snowball throwing, and the old fellow had stopped to watch, smiling to himself, as he noticed how the big boys always threw at the little boys, and the little boys at the girls, when a ball of icy hardness hit his stove-pipe hat and knocked it into the gutter. He made an attempt to clutch hold of it and fell. The tragedy of the thing was sufficient to suppress the laugh that had been raised. Half a dozen boys lent their help to get the old man on his feet again. 'It was Alf Metcalfe what throwed it,' said one. 'Let's catch him and pay him for it.' In a minute the excitement of the chase had sent them all off down the street, and Birkenshaw would have been left staggering in the narrow entry, had I not found him and helped him into a cab. Next day he sent for me to witness his will. He had left nearly two hundred pounds to Metcalfe, to be spent in a certain manner on the boy's education.

'If he goes on living like this,' he said, 'his harmful influence on the community will be far greater than any good that Reffit or Sally might do. I could have forgiven him for throwing that snowball,' added the old fellow with a smile, 'if I thought that he regarded my top-hat as a symbol of aristocracy; but I believe the fashion in top-hats has changed too much of late years.'

It was impossible to argue with him; he was too ill and tired. I hardly stayed more than half an hour, but before I left he asked me to see whether Sally Muggleton would come over and talk to him.

Ten days later Thomas Birkenshaw died. The first will, I found, he had destroyed. By a second he left his little property to the children of James Reffit and Sarah Muggleton in the event of their marriage. Should this not occur, the money is to be handed over to some obscure society for the free distribution of Rationalist Literature. The Secretary of this Society and myself he appointed as his trustees.

I dislike Rationalists now that Birkenshaw is dead, and so I have been writing two notes to Reffit and Sally, asking them to come to tea on Sunday next and stay the afternoon. Sally will not be able to go to Sunday School, it is true; but I remember that one of her many good points is the way in which she stands up to the clergy.

Dead of Night

Athelstan Digby lay reading in bed. It was after eleven; the servants had long since retired to rest. All was still except for the ticking of the grandfather's clock on the landing and the gentle slit, slit of Mr Digby's paper-knife as he cut the pages of his book: *Across Arabia on Foot*.

He was not a great reader, but he was fond of travel, and he held a theory that for reading in bed no books compared with travel books.

'Every night,' he would say, 'we set out on a journey in the dark, and though we are unable to choose the route, it lies in our power to suggest it; and I, for one, prefer to cross the frontier of dreams at Baghdad or Trebizond. I see enough of Bradborough during my waking hours.'

On the present occasion he found the adventures of the young American, whose steps he followed in the blazing heat across the desert, more than usually interesting. The watch on the chest of drawers by the bedside impatiently reminded him of the seconds of slumber wasted, but Mr Digby read on.

Suddenly the room was darkened. For half a minute he was conscious of a faintly glowing filament in the globe of his reading-lamp, and then all was blackness.

Mr Digby jumped out of bed, and putting aside the heavy curtain that hung in front of the window, he raised a corner of the Venetian blind. Somewhere an air-raid was in progress in the distance. Not a light was to be seen, except in the hollow to the south, where a faint glow – he supposed it must come from one of the Blackman Lane forges – showed carmine against the February sky. From the next house but one in the terrace came the sound of a window sash noisily lowered; then, as he looked, the lamps in the road went out, not suddenly, but one by one. It takes time for terror to extinguish hope.

Mr Digby's heart went pit-a-pat.

'Thou shalt not be afraid of the terror by night, nor for the arrow that flieth by day,' he said. 'I am glad the maids are in bed and asleep.'

Turning, he groped for the candlestick that stood on the chest of drawers, struck a light, and looked at his watch. It was nearly half past eleven. Then, putting on his dressing-gown, he placed the candle on the floor in a corner, where its light would not be directly visible from the road, and went over to the window. The glare was still present in the southern sky; but, as he gazed, an angry tongue of flame shot forth. Fire had chosen that night of nights to betray their sheltering darkness.

'It's not in Blackman Lane,' he said to himself. 'It's far more like the paper mills in Clancy Street. Ah! there's the engine!' as from the blackness there came the sound of a clanging bell and the clatter of wheels on the cobbles.

The night's keen edge of terror was blunted already for Mr Digby. He was familiar with fire. It was an old enemy. He was a shareholder too in the Clancy Street paper mills. 'I shall feel far happier,' he said to himself, 'if I see what's going on.'

He dressed hurriedly and not very carefully. For a collar he sub-stituted a thick woollen muffler, and his coat and overcoat were the oldest his wardrobe contained. Instead of the hard felt hat he usually wore, he put on a cap with flaps which pulled down over his ears. Then, after having pinned a note for Mrs Wilkinson, the cook, on his bedroom door, in case the servants should wake later and wonder where he had gone, he made his way silently out of the house. The time was twenty minutes to twelve.

To a man like Mr Digby, who had lived in Bradborough for sixty years, there was no difficulty in finding his way through the darkened streets. Few people were abroad, but something told him that the town was not asleep; there was nothing of the regular snoring rumble of night traffic. At the corner of George Street he came upon a long row of deserted trams, a huge dark clot in the city's main artery. Bradborough was not sleeping; it was paralysed.

*   *   *

The accident occurred at the corner of Signet Street and Spindle Lane. For some time Mr Digby had been following an elderly man, who carried a handbag and seemed a little uncertain in his walk. At the end of Spindle Lane he noticed that the man paused, seemingly uncertain as to his direction; then, leaving the pavement, he walked slowly into the centre of the road and dropped the bag, as if seized with sudden pain. Mr Digby hastened towards him at the same time as a taxi turned out of Signet Street without warning sound or light. For a moment he hesitated. He seemed to be held by the white face of the driver, by the noise of the brakes. He tried in vain to reach the old gentleman and push him into safety. Something caught him on the point of the jaw; he fell like a log.

Far away, as if from another world, came voices talking in a golden vortex of light.

'First door on the right,' said the night porter. 'Jack, tell Mr Walker that he's wanted in the receiving room – two ambulance cases. He's in Mr Simpson's room playing bridge. Any news of the Zepps?'

'They were over the east coast, Hull way, half an hour ago,' the policeman who had come with the ambulance answered. 'A nasty smash this; taxi bowled 'em clean over. I'll just look in their pockets, now that we've got a light, to see if I can find out who the parties are.'

'Right you are, constable. Just wait till we've got 'em off the trolley.'

Mr Digby felt a hand deftly searching him. 'Ah! here's a card,' said the policeman. ' "Riley, Gilder and Picture-frame Maker, 28a Redpole Street." And the other man – he doesn't look as if he'd last very long – no letter or card; linen marked "Jessop".'

Little particles of lilac light swam round in the golden vortex, and the voices died away. Someone lifted first Mr Digby's right eyelid and then his left.

'Pupils a bit dilated, but they react all right,' he heard; 'concussion and a fractured jaw. He seems to have got off lightly. Well, dad, how are you feeling? What's your name?'

'The constable's got his name, sir.'

'All right! Here, sister, just fix him, until he gets up to the ward. The other fellow's bad; fractured base. That's a nasty cut, too, under the chin. I'll put in a couple of stitches now. Hand me the iodine, Tom. No, I don't want a clip; the stitches will stop the bleeding. And so, sister, you don't like Zeppelins? They mean well, you know. Not failure but low aim is crime.'

'I've no time to listen to your nonsense, Mr Walker. I wonder how many more we shall have tonight.'

'I shall turn in anyhow. Send these two up to Ward 16, Tom. It's their take-in week.'

'There are no beds vacant, sir. That acute appendix we admitted at eleven took the last.'

Mr Walker swore. 'Shove them in A16 private ward then, till we find room.'

Again there came the golden vortex, but this time the colour was less vivid, and somewhere in the centre was pain, dull and gnawing. A cold draught struck Mr Digby's face. The trolley on which he lay was being wheeled along stone-flagged corridors. An iron gate clashed to; now he was in the lift. More stone-flagged corridors, and then a second bump into something which every bone in his bruised and shattered body welcomed as bed.

'You'll have to manage as best you can,' said Nurse Coates, the senior night nurse in A16 ward, to Nurse Farrell. Allison will help you to get his things off. It doesn't matter about washing; that will have to wait until the lights go on again. There's a case for the second bed on the way. Allison, don't be a little fool. The Zepps aren't here yet, and they're not likely to be. You can manage all right without a torch? I want mine for 27. I believe he's started to haemorrhage again; anyhow the dressing is all through.'

Nurse Coates moved away to the other end of the long ward, stopping on her way to bank up the fire with a shovelful of dusty coal. When she had finished, the darkness seemed complete. Though all was silence as she walked to the far end, where the movable dressing-table stood with its basins and bowls of lotions, the ward was not asleep. Men lay there on their backs, listening, looking up through the floor above, through the roof, to the starlight vault of the February sky, searching for those other men who hovered somewhere in the night.

Nurse Coates finished her dressing, straightened the draw-sheet, and wheeled back the dressing-table to the little alcove by the bath-room. Then she walked down the long length of the ward, stopping for a minute by the bed of a boy of fourteen. The old men on either side of him slept peacefully.

'Not asleep yet, Johnny?' she asked. 'Why, it's after one! Your leg is not hurting you now?'

'No,' said Johnny, 'I was only thinking how convenient it must be when they drop bombs on hospitals, having everything so handy, doctors and all.'

'You're an optimist,' she said.

'I don't know,' he answered with a weary smile, 'I never got into the sixth standard.'

When Nurse Coates reached the private ward, which stood just opposite the sisters' sitting-room at the end of the main ward, she saw the white-coated figure of the house surgeon.

'I'm late tonight,' he said. 'It must be pretty bad working up here without lights. They cut us down to practically nothing in the theatre while Mr Cavendish was doing that appendix. I don't think he'll last long,' he went on, with his hand on one of the two beds; 'fractured base. The other fellow must have had a nasty knock too. I expect Mr Darbyshire will want to wire that jaw. How are the others?'

'Fairly comfortable. Most of them are awake, of course. I've just re-dressed Number 27. Number 5 was complaining of pain an hour ago, but he seems quiet now.'

'Poor beggar! You can give him a quarter of a grain of morphia, if it comes on again. Have you his bed-board? Never mind, I'll write it up in the morning.'

'Do you want to be called in case the fractured base . . . ?'

'No, you needn't bother,' said the house surgeon. 'I can't do anything; he's bound to go. I wonder if the Zepps will come. I shan't wait up for them anyhow. Good night, nurse!'

At a quarter past two the man in the bed next to Mr Digby died. When Nurse Coates came into the room, she no longer heard the puffing, snoring breathing. She went to the telephone and rang up the night sister.

'He died ten minutes ago,' she said. 'Mr Simpson said it was not necessary to call him.'

'He wasn't in pain,' said the sister. 'He'd have been a long case to nurse, and you are short of beds. Tell Nurse Farrell to get a screen. I'm sending Nurse Allison off duty. She's done up, poor girl, and I find that she had a wire this evening to say that her brother has been killed at the front. She hasn't had a moment to herself since. I'll send down the probationer from 17 to give Nurse Farrell a hand. Without lights it makes things very awkward. They say Mr Cavendish in the theatre was simply awful because he couldn't have the big headlight on. I'd like to see him left in charge of a ward with only an electric torch and a probationer. He's still operating.'

* * *

'One, two, three' – Athelstan Digby listened to a man's voice that seemed to come from the other side of nowhere – 'now lift.' For the second time that night he felt pain, as his bruised body was seized none too gently and dropped into something that was harder than the bed. Where was he? In hospital, of course; in the Bradborough Infirmary, on whose weekly board of management he had sat for years. He had been knocked down; there were Zeppelins somewhere; his jaw had been broken. Hadn't one of those young doctors said something about an operation? Now he was in the lift; now they were once again in the region of cold, stone-flagged corridors.

'Mr Cavendish was in an awful temper tonight. He was throwing things all over the theatre. You should have heard him swearing at the sister.'

'He's all nerves, that's what he is,' said the second voice. 'I don't blame him. He's been operating since six o'clock, Mr Darbyshire's list as well as his own. This wouldn't be a bad place to be in if they started to drop bombs. What sort of a smash was he in?'

'Knocked down by a taxi; two of them. The old cove got his jaw broke, while she only had her bonnet knocked off. Reminds me of a Saturday night scrap with my missis. Steady on, George! Mind the swing-doors. Now, on that table there when I say "lift". Are you ready? Now! We're keeping poor old Simeon busy. You've never seen him operate? Very neat; large, clean incisions, and no anaesthetics. I wonder if they've got permission from the old gentleman's people. Do you remember that case six months ago and the row there was afterwards? You should have seen Simeon's sewing up.'

'I've never been in here before,' said the other voice.

'No? Well, there's nothing much to see. But wait till we've got the new buildings; marble-topped tables and tiled floors; beautifully cool in summer. I wonder if those Zepps are coming after all.'

Mr Digby heard the door swing to behind them and the footsteps die away down the echoing corridor. His brain had become clear; but how cold it was, and they had pulled the sheet over his face. He didn't dread the operation, but it was very lonely there in the dark without even a nurse. What was it the man said about no anaesthetic? He must have been joking, of course, pulling the other fellow's leg. Perhaps they would use local anaesthesia in a case like his. Anyhow, he hoped they would have enough light in the theatre to see properly. Oh! but it was dark and cold! He hoped they would not keep him long; they might at least have sent a nurse.

Mr Digby waited and waited, but no one came. The only sound he heard was the distant howling of a cat that cried like a baby in pain. He could not move; every bone in his body ached; never had he been so cold.

The cat ceased to howl. Half a minute later he heard a noise which he had only once heard in his life before, the dull, muffled boom of an exploding bomb.

When Mr Digby regained consciousness, he found himself back again in the little private ward at the end of Ward 16. The lights were turned on; the fire was burning brightly. His feet felt the grateful warmth of a hot-water bottle. There were hot bottles under the blankets at his side. He smiled faintly at the night sister, who was tucking in the blanket at the foot of the bed, and wondered why the nurse who was helping her had been crying.

'You're feeling better?' said the night-nurse, with a cheerfulness that somehow seemed to be assumed. 'Now I want you to drink a little hot milk.' She put the spout of the feeding-cup between his lips.

'And the operation? That's over all right?'

'Come, don't worry about operations, dad. It may not be necessary for you after all, and it's bad for you to talk. Drink the milk and go to sleep. Look, I've brought my knitting, and I'm going to sit beside you for a little while.'

'She's very kind to me,' thought Athelstan Digby as he closed his eyes, 'very kind; but I wonder why she looks at me in that curious way, as if she were afraid of me.'

When on the following day it became known that the occupant of A16 private ward was Mr Digby, one of the members of the weekly board of management, and not Mr Riley, of 28a Redpole Street, Gilder and Picture-frame Maker, the authorities of the Bradborough Infirmary were profuse in their apologies. The secretary brought a large bunch of early daffodils and sent them to Mr Digby with his compliments. The matron, white-capped and starched, arranged for a special nurse, and made a point of coming into the room herself to find fault with her for not having pulled down the blinds to shut out the sun. 'Pull them up again,' said Mr Digby as soon as she was gone, 'and never mind what she says. An old bachelor like myself knows how to deal with matrons.'

The house surgeon who had called him 'dad' tried to efface the impression he had made by referring to him as Mr Danby, while giving the nurse wrong instructions as to details of nursing which she had already rightly carried out. Mr Darbyshire found time to keep the whole of the theatre staff and his honorary anaesthetist waiting while he cheered Mr Digby up with an account of his play on the links the previous afternoon. Even Samuel Travers managed to look in and condole with him as a humble physician on having fallen into the hands of surgeons.

None of his visitors stayed very long; all would have liked to stay longer, but they declared that rest and quiet were absolutely essential. Mr Digby began to think that they were right.

In after years Mr Digby declared that he learned more about hospital management during those days of tedious convalescence than he had during the whole of his ten years' conscientious attendance on the weekly board. He watched the greater light that ruled by day and the lesser light that ruled by night. Names became personalities. He had known who got the credit; now he knew who did the work.

He saw comedy waiting impatiently behind the scenes until tragedy stepped off the boards. Sometimes he saw them together on the stage. Old men, white-haired and venerable, could go through life, he found, without having found the patience of a boy of sixteen. And he was quite certain that when the gramophone was turned on to *Pack up your troubles in your old kit-bag*, no one wanted to see the chaplain. He felt sorry for the chaplain. The priests of this temple all wore white coats. The outside of the cup and platter was always clean, and whenever they performed their rites, their hands, like the Pharisees', were never defiled and unwashen. He was shocked, of course, to find that nurses smoked when they were off duty; he was more than shocked when first he heard a probationer swear; but from the bottom of his heart he admired them. So callous were they, and so kind. He was almost reconciled to the prospect of their getting a vote.

He learned much during those ten days in hospital, but not nearly all that he wished to learn. A curtain was drawn over the happenings of that first night. There were times when he wished to draw it aside; but in the evening, when all was quiet in the great ward beyond, something, no stronger perhaps than fear of the unknown, held him back, cowering before his surmises.

It was his last day in hospital. The sister came in for the visit which she usually paid in the interval between Mr Digby's afternoon nap and her afternoon tea.

'You've treated me very well, sister,' he said. 'I shall never forget my time in the infirmary.'

'I'm glad you think so, Mr Digby,' she answered, smiling.

'Especially the first night,' he added. The smile vanished. Then there was something after all which they were concealing?

'Come,' he said, 'what was it that really happened then? I bear no malice. Old men tell no tales.'

'I'm afraid I can't say,' she answered. 'I don't quite know what you are referring to. You see . . . '

'There's the matron. Yes, I know all about matrons; but I'm a member of the weekly board, you know; and though perhaps you'll never forgive me if I say it, I helped to get the matron her job. However, I won't press you; but you can tell me this. Is there a house surgeon called Simeon?'

The sister smiled.

'Not that I've heard of,' she said.

'Then who is Simeon, who operates without anaesthetics and who – no, I won't finish the sentence.'

'I believe,' said the sister, 'that the porter who helps in the post-mortem room is called Simeon.'

'And if you wait,' said Mr Digby, 'I believe I can tell you how you get there. You take the lift to the basement, turn to the right and again to the right, and then through two swing-doors. No, I don't bear anyone a grudge. It's a mistake that might so easily happen. Only, sister, don't let's talk about it again; and if you were to invite me to share a cup of tea, I don't think I should refuse. And I think I could do with another blanket on the bed. You see, it was very cold, sister, very cold.'

Mishandled

'The fingerprints are there all right,' said Detective Inspector Crewdson, 'but somehow I doubt if the man will hang.'

Dr Bentall filled his pipe.

'I think you may be underestimating the value of your evidence, Crewdson. Let us have the facts of the case from the beginning. Remember that I have only seen the accounts in the papers.'

The two men were seated by the fire in Dr Bentall's study. The house stood little more than a stone's throw from the town hall and the hospital, for St Helen's Square was the doctors' quarter of the great city where surgeons, physicians, and radiologists had their consulting-rooms. Dr Bentall, senior consulting physician to the hospital and lecturer in medical jurisprudence, differed from his colleagues, however, in being content to live where he worked. That was why there was only one brass plate on the door of Number 16.

'Yes,' he went on, 'the facts from the beginning, not the fancy embroidery of the bright young men of the *News* and *Echo*. I won't offer you a cocktail – too old-fashioned to hold with them – but help yourself from the decanter.'

Crewdson, having acted on his host's advice, settled himself comfortably in the easy chair and took out his note-book.

'Here are the facts,' he said. 'At five o'clock on the evening of the 14th the police at Gadswick were rung up by Mr Thomas Boltby. He said that his uncle, Mr Simeon Boltby, had just been found stabbed in the library at Boltby Manor. Superintendent Jones went over right away, taking with him the local doctor. The body of Simeon Boltby was lying on the floor in a far corner of the room behind a large bureau with a dagger in the heart. Want to hear particulars of the wound?'

'Not at the moment.'

'The doctor gave it as his opinion that death was practically instantaneous and had occurred some time about an hour before. Boltby Manor is an isolated house of moderate size. On the 14th there were living there Simeon Boltby, his nephew Thomas, and three maids. The gardener, who throughout the afternoon was at work in the garden, lives in the lodge by the main entrance. Simeon Boltby was having a new rock garden constructed by a Harrowby firm of land-scape gardeners. Three of their men were employed on the job. I gather there had been difficulties with Boltby, who only that morn-ing had had a violent dispute with the foreman.'

'Yes, yes,' said Dr Bentall, 'but you are not going to tell me that the nature of the proper subsoil for gentians was the reason why a dagger was found in the body of Mr Simeon?'

'I am not,' replied Crewdson. 'I only mention it because it bears out what I've already heard about Simeon Boltby being a man of very uncertain temper.' The inspector turned over the leaf of his note-book. 'Some time after three, from 3.15 to 3.30 – I can't fix the time more exactly – Mr Conroy called on Boltby. He lives not far away from Boltby Manor and the two men appear to have been only slightly acquainted. They were both interested in old china and met occasionally to talk over their hobby. Conroy was shown by the maid into the library. She then went out through the french window into the garden where Mr Boltby was resting in the summerhouse. She told him about his visitor, and saw the old man go into the library through the french window. At a quarter to four Conroy was seen to leave the library by the same way. The witness was one of the men at work on the rock garden. He remembers the time because the stable clock was striking. Conroy walked across the garden, made some remark about the work the men were doing, and then took a field path that led him back home. His housekeeper brought him his tea at 4.15. He did not wash his hands before tea, and she noticed nothing unusual about his manner. Incidentally, if he went straight back home he would pass neither pond nor stream.

'Shortly after Conroy left Boltby Manor Mr Thomas Boltby was seen to enter the library by the french window. According to his evidence he passed straight through the room, across the hall, and into the morning-room where he wrote two letters. If what he said was true he would not see the body which was lying on the floor, screened by the bureau.

'At five minutes to five the parlourmaid came into the library to announce that tea was ready. It was she who discovered the body. She at once notified Mr Thomas, and he rang up the police.'

'And it was the same day, if I remember rightly,' said Dr Bentall, 'that Mr Thomas Boltby was unfortunate enough to meet his death.'

'Yes,' answered Crewdson. 'That messed up the whole case. He made a clear statement to the police and ended up by saying that his aunt, Miss Boltby, who lived three miles away, was expected that evening to dinner. He suggested that he should run over in his car to break the news to the old lady, as she had only recently recovered from a severe illness. Jones, though he had nothing against the man – he had known him ever since he was a boy – was taking no chances and he found some excuse for sending one of his men along with him. At the Maltby crossroads their car collided with a lorry – the fault was the lorry driver's – and Thomas Boltby was killed.'

'And was Miss Boltby expected to dinner that evening?'

'Yes. If you think that Boltby was trying to make a getaway there's nothing doing.'

'And what is the evidence against Conroy? I saw that he had been arrested.'

'His fingerprints were found on the polished handle of the dagger, and he was the last man but one seen to enter the library before the maid discovered the body at five o'clock. The last man, as I have said before, was Thomas Boltby. There is no means of telling whether the old man was alive or dead when his nephew entered the room.'

'Appearances certainly are against Conroy,' said Dr Bentall. 'Has he made any statement?'

'Yes; he said he had nothing to hold back. He admitted handling the dagger, which was kept on the table in the library. Mr Boltby used it as a paper-knife. Conroy says that while he was waiting for the old boy to come in from the garden he was cutting the pages of a book.'

'A little free and easy, I should have thought,' remarked the doctor.

'But Conroy is the free and easy sort, as casual a fellow as I've ever met. He doesn't deny the prints – he couldn't deny them. He even told me that I should probably find them on the handle, and suggests that the murderer got a lower grip of the dagger with a hand gloved or wrapped in a handkerchief. The murderer left no marks of his own, trusting to the fingerprints to put the police on the wrong track.'

'And how would the murderer know that they were there?'

'He wouldn't, unless he happened to see Conroy cutting the pages of the book. Conroy says young Boltby passed the window while he was waiting for the old man and might have noticed what he was doing.'

'And Thomas is dead,' grunted the doctor. 'He has undergone his last cross-examination, and what the recording angel says isn't evidence.'

'Thomas queers the pitch every time,' the inspector went on. 'Take the question of motive. He was the old man's heir, and though they seemed to have hit it off fairly well they were known to quarrel. Old Boltby wasn't an easy man to get on with and plenty of people disliked him. And yet Conroy, as far as we know, had no motive for doing the old man in. They were little more than acquaintances who had a common hobby in the collection of old china. Nothing appears to have been stolen. Conroy is a fairly wealthy man. Though he collects porcelain it's only in a small way. I'm told that he is more interested in gardening than in anything else.'

'I wonder if he reads detective stories,' said Dr Bentall. 'There are a certain number of people – I myself am one of them – who at times when they cannot sleep give their minds over to planning a perfect crime. It is nearly always an innocent form of mental exercise, though for a few I can imagine it to be a very dangerous one. The easiest crime to get away with is the apparently motiveless one. I might leave this room, go into the square (I wish, by the way, you could arrange for it to be better lighted) and sandbag the first person I met with that old-fashioned contrivance that effectually keeps the draught from the bottom of the door. There would of course actually be a motive, though I might be unconscious of it. Call it blood lust, call it the excitement of pitting my wits against the best brains of Scotland Yard, the liberation by death into a life of enforced action, the thrill of a terrific gamble for the greatest of all stakes. I should not put too much stress on the apparent absence of motive. There may have been some secret enmity between Conroy and Thomas Boltby; he may even have committed the murder in order that the other might hang for it – quite a favourite theme with writers of detective stories, but murders have actually been committed with that end in view. Again, Conroy might have been seized with some overwhelming dislike for some trick or habit of the old man which he wished to obliterate for ever. All this is really beside the point. Get back to the fingerprints, Crewdson. I want to hear more about them and the dagger.'

'I'll take the dagger first. It was really more a knife with a sharp point and one cutting edge. The blade was about eight inches long, and the handle as long again. The weapon was all of a piece, and, as I said before, highly polished. It would be quite possible to get two grips on the handle, as Conroy suggested. Conroy's fingerprints were on the upper part of the handle. They showed clearly the marks of the right thumb, and less clearly the tips of the first, second, and third fingers.'

'And the wound showed that the knife entered in a slightly downward direction?'

'Yes, it was a slightly downward thrust. The blunt edge of the knife was uppermost.'

Dr Bentall was silent for a moment.

'Let us adjourn to the pantry,' he said suddenly. 'No, not for a drink. I want to look at knives. Move silently, Crewdson. My housekeeper is a light sleeper and she has a wholesome fear of burglars and no faith at all in the police.'

In the pantry Dr Bentall drew from the silver basket an assortment of knives.

'Which,' he asked, 'is most like your dagger?'

Crewdson examined them carefully, and finally picked out a carving knife for game.

'It was not unlike that,' he said, 'but the handle was a little longer.'

'And the blunt edge was uppermost in the wound. We will go back to the study. I'm beginning to see light on your problem, Crewdson. And now,' he went on, when they were seated once again round the cheerful blaze, 'I want a most important piece of information. If you haven't got it there may still be a possibility of obtaining it. Conroy himself might even volunteer to give it to us. He said that he made use of the knife to cut the pages of a book. Do you know what that book was?'

'Yes,' said Crewdson, his face lighting up. 'I checked all Conroy's statements myself. There was a book lying on the table in the library. Half of the pages had been cut. It was an illustrated supplement to one of these high-class art magazines on old Bristol china.'

'You don't remember the exact title? Still, I don't think that matters. Now if you'll excuse me for a moment I'll telephone to my friend the curator of the Art Gallery. He keeps late hours, I know. He is somewhat of an authority on china, and it is just possible he may have the monograph.'

Five minutes later Dr Bentall was back in the study.

'Conroy is your man,' he said. 'Those fingerprints can't be explained away.'

He went to one of the book-cases and, after turning over the pages of several thin volumes, placed two on the table.

'These,' he said, 'are little books of modern verse. I am not interested in poetry. Nor, I suppose, are you.'

Crewdson smiled.

'I always switch off the wireless,' he said, 'when the highbrows get busy. I can't stand their voices. I'd rather listen to the fat-stock prices any day, but then my father was a butcher.'

'But unfortunately,' Dr Bentall went on, 'I have a niece who is always hoping that her bachelor uncle may cease to be a Philistine. She sends me little books of modern verse for Christmas presents. There are two. Now sit down at the table, Crewdson, and let me see you cut the pages of *Sparklings and Delights* by someone called Alison Montgomery. Here is the knife.'

Crewdson cut the page. He began at the right-hand top corner and cut downwards.

'That is interesting,' said Dr Bentall. 'The majority of people, I think, would cut the page upwards. You will note from the way in which you held the knife that your fingerprints would correspond with those of Conroy. You will note, too, that holding the knife as you did it would be possible to give a forward and downward thrust into a man's body. It's not perhaps the most natural grip, but it is certainly a possible one. Now lend me the knife. This is the way I should cut the page, beginning at the bottom. If you think a minute you will see that it would be exceedingly difficult for the fingerprints made with the hand in that position to correspond with those made in a forward and downward thrust into the body, which left the blunt edge of the knife uppermost. With the fingers like that the thrust would have to be forwards and upwards, and we know that this does not correspond to the position of the wound as you have described it.'

Crewdson's face fell.

'Then Conroy's story is borne out. Someone else with a gloved hand might have seized the handle low down, leaving Conroy's fingerprints intact.'

'Wrong, Crewdson, wrong! Take this other book. Its pages too are uncut, but there is a difference. It isn't only the sides that are uncut. The tops of the pages are uncut as well. To cut the pages you would have to begin at the bottom and continue along the top. This monograph – the curator had a copy – was like that. Conroy admits to cutting the pages. In that case he would be bound to hold the knife in such a way that it could not inflict the wound it did.'

'And all this means what?' asked the inspector.

'That Conroy used the knife for two purposes and that he held it in two different ways. He used it first for cutting the pages of the monograph upwards. He used it secondly for stabbing Simeon Boltby with a slightly downward thrust. It was a clever crime, a mad gambler's crime. As I said before, I see no motive. The defence will probably produce an imposing array of medical evidence which may be difficult to rebut. You will, I suppose, exclude the possibility of there being a woman in the case. I have nothing to do with that. It is outside the bounds of medical jurisprudence.'

'Well, doctor,' said the inspector as he rose to go, 'you've given me a lot to think about. You pulled me through that time I was in hospital ten years ago, and I've always said there was no one like Dr Bentall for getting to the bottom of things. I wish I were one of your students and could listen to your lectures.'

'You would follow them far better than they do, Crewdson. My lectures are supposed to be rather dry. They lack the light touch that characterises some of my younger colleagues. But I must not keep you. Let me know how things go on. The fingerprints, as you say, are there all right and I think the man will hang.'

From the tower of the town hall came the deep notes of the big bell slowly tolling the final passing of the day.

'It sounds like it,' said the inspector. 'Good night, doctor.'

'Good night, Crewdson.'

The Habeas Corpus Club

Peregrine Pocock is a prolific writer. His stories are sensational, but his characters – and usually they are bad characters – live. For they are his own children, plentifully endowed with Peregrine's vigorous vitality. Writing primarily for cave men of the low-browed Cro-Magnon type, he yet numbers among his readers prime ministers and archbishops.

But even the ordinary lay student of Pocock and those authors who laboriously follow his footsteps in the dark must have been struck by the fact that less than justice is done to the characters they murder at the end of the first or second chapter.

A corpse has to be discovered in startling circumstances – on the farther side of the bunker that guards the thirteenth green, in a reserved sleeping berth on the Orient express, in Sir Marmaduke's family pew at Widdecombe Basset, in a pantechnicon outside Number 10 Downing Street. The corpse is the important thing. It is the springboard that projects frail clues and dark suspicions.

But what of the man to whom it belongs? Cut off in the first few pages, he has no opportunities of displaying, to say nothing of developing, his character. His entry coincides with his exit; he dies that romance may live, a clothes-peg for the garrotter's scarf, a receptacle for the chemist's poison, a shooting target for the Baby Browning, a fleshy sheath for the assassin's knife.

Remembering that Peregrine Pocock's characters are alive, and that the fact is vouched for by all our younger clergy and the whole of the medical profession, there is nothing really surprising in their founding the Habeas Corpus Club. The suggestion of a permanent home where, in the words of the club's prospectus, 'men and women who have given their lives for the novel-reading public may have an opportunity of developing their characters in a more sheltered environment', was first mooted by the widow of a wealthy stockbroker who had been done to death in the opening sentence of a popular detective story. The idea caught on, and when she herself was stabbed in the sequel after a life of quiet unostentatious penal service, a few friends desirous of commemorating her career decided to extend the original scheme by admitting as associate members characters who were eligible for murder but who, for one reason or another, had been unable to meet their authors. The secretary, himself the victim of a Spanish vendetta, in showing me round the club summed up this side of its activities in the phrase, 'the self-determination of smaller personalities'.

The visitor is at once struck on entering the building by the spaciousness of the lounge for associate members. An arrangement of boxes, not unlike that of the old coffee taverns, gives ample opportunity for associates to meet with authors and to discuss with them in privacy the details of their deaths. On the occasion of my visit there must have been at least thirty people in the room. Wealthy businessmen in fur-lined overcoats chatted with collectors of eastern curios and eccentric numismatists. Old sea captains, remarkably hale and brown, seated on their iron-bound chests before the fire, discussed rude ciphers with miners from Australia and California and compared tattoo marks. An elderly Mormon, conspicuously bewigged, carried on a tender conversation with a beautiful German spy. From time to time an author would break into a little group and then withdraw with one of its members to a box. I was told by the secretary that booking up engagements is no easy matter, and with the comparatively low death-rate in many novels it is difficult to avoid cut-throat competition. One of their associate members, an old lady of over ninety, the morganatic wife of one of the crowned heads of Europe, had been on their books ever since the club was started. She had stipulated at first for a life extending over at least six chapters and for serial publication, but had been obliged to lower her terms. She was actually thinking of offering to be murdered in the foreword and had sketched out an effective dust-cover for her pall.

'Hers is a very difficult problem,' said the secretary, 'but there is just a chance that she might be used by Lady Julia Longbow in her *Memories of a Diplomat's Wife.*'

When terms have been satisfactorily discussed with an author, a contract is drawn up and signed, and the associate member's name is posted in the lobby on a board inscribed 'Forthcoming Deaths'. I myself had the privilege of witnessing a charming little ceremonial that arose out of such an announcement. A page boy entered the lounge, telegram in hand. I recognised him at once as Eddie Kershaw, one of Pocock's earliest creations, the boy, it will be remembered, whose body was found in such intriguing circumstances in the Vale of Health in Hampstead.

'Telegram for Sir Lazarus Money!' he cried.

A tall, florid gentleman, with a carnation in his buttonhole, sprang at once to his feet. 'It's my call, boys!' he said as he made his way to the bar. Instantly there was a buzz of conversation.

'Who's the author?'

'Old Rickaby; Rape and Carnage are to publish it at seven and six.'

'A first-class show.'

'And what about cinema rights?'

'Is he going to let you talk?'

'No, confound him! I only half whisper a woman's name.'

'Never mind, old boy. One crowded hour of glorious life; it's worth it, you know. They'll motor you down, of course?'

'Yes, in the usual Rolls Royce, to some out of the way shooting-box on the Yorkshire moors.'

They thronged around him, loud in their congratulations. Two men especially attracted my attention from their extraordinary likeness to one another.

'Who are they?' I asked the secretary.

'Twins,' he replied. 'They have recently joined as associates, but I don't expect we shall have them long on our books. They have hit on a really novel line in mixed identities – each is murdered by the other's wife, who mistakes him for her own husband. The public will get double value for its money, since everything will be duplicated. I have seldom met with a situation so lavish in false clues. Gore-Hemmeridge is meeting the twins tomorrow to talk over details. Goodbye, Sir Lazarus, and the best of good wishes.'

'And now,' said the secretary, 'I expect you would like to see something of the residential side of the club.'

We passed through swing-doors marked 'Members Only' into the reading-room, where conversation appeared to be general. I suppose I must have shown surprise, for the secretary quietly drew my attention to a printed notice over the mantelpiece:

IN LIFE YOU WERE SILENT; YOU MAY TALK NOW.

'The things that are said,' remarked the secretary, 'when death has at last unsealed their lips are remarkably interesting. This room is rich in reminiscence, and it is most encouraging to observe how members' characters unfold as they talk. Mr Luker, whom the world knew only as a miser (you will remember how he was found shot in the back in the fourth chapter of *The New Guinea Mystery*), has, through his friendship with Otto Schmid, the secret service agent, become intensely interested in the ethical basis of internationalism. Again, Mr Schmid has been led through his talks with Professor Maguire to make a special study of instinct and behaviour and their relation to each other in the Social Commonwealth. Occasionally, of course, we find members unresponsive. Colonel Woodcocke, of the Indian Army, and Janet Strong, the asylum nurse, could only be aroused from a morbid and taciturn brooding over the past by a common interest in the game of chess. They are now the life and soul of the Entertainments Committee.'

The members, I was told, follow events in the publishing world with the greatest interest. Many of them have personal friends among prospective victims in whose fate they are naturally concerned, and details of forthcoming novels are anxiously looked for. 'We don't in any way discourage it,' said the secretary, 'since it tends to take them out of themselves. Every day I become more and more convinced of the value of the work the club is doing. It is a necessary corollary to all imaginary and creative effort. There should be similar institutions in every city if only the charitable public gave with their heads as well as with their hearts. But millions now giving will never try.'

He shook hands with me warmly as I left.

'One question,' I said. 'Do members never leave the premises?'

'Never by day,' he answered, 'always by night. There is still a place in the scheme of things for retributive justice. What I am about to say does not, I am sure, apply to you. We have no quarrel with journalists. At night the club is closed. We go to haunt the authors who murdered us. Do you wonder that Peregrine Pocock hardly ever sleeps?'

The Long Road

Shenstone is the Carricksville doctor, an unmarried man of forty. If you ask Miss Winter, who deals in local gossip, wholesale and retail, she will tell you that he is in love with the younger of the two Miss Ashtons of Kiwa station, and that that lady has refused him chiefly because he dislikes golf and cannot dance. There may be some truth in the first of Miss Winter's statements, for the doctor, as if regardful of the even tenor of his days, sees no more of the Kiwa people than he can help; the second is based on spite and utter ignorance of her own sex.

Shenstone has means of his own, and this is fortunate, for his practice is small, births and deaths, with an occasional broken limb in between. For consolation – if he needed consoling – he has his garden and the knowledge that no other doctor would ever dream of setting up his plate in so unpromising a place as Carricksville.

It is the easiest matter in the world to analyse the reasons that make men enter the medical profession. Roughly speaking – so Shenstone will tell you – they are three. First there are the sons of doctors, boys who see little chance of any legacy more tangible than a few out-of-date text-books and a trusted name. The family skeleton reappears from the cupboard, including the round cardboard box with those puzzling little bones of the skull wrapped up carefully in cotton wool, and the boy with the light heart sets out on the long five years' pilgrimage to the promised land across deserts (the oases are few and far between) screened by the wonderful mirage of youth.

Then there are those who come to their decision by a process of elimination. They dislike lawyers' offices – stools are uncomfortable to sit on all day long – there are too many architects and Tom, lucky dog, is in the army, and the governor can't afford to keep a second son. After all, some very good fellows are doctors. You are your own master and you can have a rattling good time in a country practice with very little hard work once the examinations are passed. Anyone can get through if he only sticks to a good seven hours a day.

Shenstone would probably place himself with these, though he belongs in fact to the third class, the few and innocent who took up medicine with the idea that it is the finest profession on earth. They don't expect to be well paid in cash; but if they know their work they will be very well paid, whether they like it or not. They picture themselves as ending their life in some London slum beloved by all. These are they who are chiefly visited by disillusion. In medicine it matters little that you mean well. Kindly intentions can never make up for want of knowledge, or sympathy for a poor memory. All that the sick want is to be healed, and many a bad man makes a good doctor.

There are times in the life of every medical practitioner, and they are not always rare, when he is improperly flattered and rightly alarmed by receiving confidences that a priest or lawyer would never receive. Then it is that the successful consultant feels that he is something more than a mere money-making machine. He has been acknowledged in the best sense as a man of the world by one of the world's poor victims.

Shenstone in his quiet country practice has not had many such experiences. There are fewer tragedies in a New Zealand township than in an English village, for there are no picturesque two-roomed cottages and the wages – so Mrs Dobbert will tell you – are quite absurdly high.

The doctor had been out five years from England when he met Oakshot. It was an evening in May, a cold southerly blowing with rain behind it, and Shenstone driving back from Pipinui sat shivering beneath coat and rug. Three miles away from home, at the top of the hill where a patch of standing bush closed in upon the road shutting out the last of the twilight, his horse shied. A man was lying propped up against a fallen log, and, getting down from his seat, Shenstone saw that he was either ill or drunk; he went back for the buggy lamp and came to the conclusion that he was both. As house surgeon at his hospital he had very nearly made the fatal mistake of sending to the lock-up a case of basal fracture of the skull. Ever since, he had erred on the side of caution. With difficulty he managed to lift the man into the buggy, while the swag, far heavier than its owner, was bundled up behind.

Shenstone, who in those days was a faddist in the matter of food, lived by himself, Mrs Cardwell coming in from next door for a couple of hours every morning to disturb the dust that had settled in the course of the preceding twenty-four. He was in consequence solely his own master in the matter of visitors, and early determined – necessity was the motive – that the stranger should spend the night under his roof.

After all, there seemed little the matter with the man, excepting only that he was dead drunk and obviously a hopeless wreck. Less obviously – Shenstone judged by the cut of the coat and the shape of the nails – he had been a gentleman. As he watched his heavy breathing as he lay stretched full length on the sitting-room couch Shenstone could scarcely refrain from a smile, for the stranger reminded him subtly of a priggish cousin of his own whom he had always disliked, yet had never caught stumbling.

On the morrow the man told him that his name was Oakshot. He asked for a job and the doctor put him on to dig the garden. He did the work well, five times better than the ordinary swagman, so that Shenstone kept him a second day, paid him his ten shillings, and told him that if ever he happened to be passing that way he could always count on getting work.

As he watched him go down the road bent beneath the heavy swag, his felt hat pulled low over his eyes, Shenstone had an intuitive feeling that the lines of their destinies had crossed, and that not at right angles; he wondered when they would converge upon each other again.

It must have been in the middle of July, on an evening so cold that Shenstone ran the risk of burning his trousers as he sat, legs outstretched, before the fire of manuka with its big back log of willow. The man at the door was wet through but on this occasion he was sober, and in spite of the haggard look about his eyes things material seemed to have prospered with him.

'He may have had the luck to receive his last remittance at some place where there was no pub,' thought Shenstone.

'Look here, doctor,' said Oakshot nervously, 'I want to see you professionally, and, if you don't mind, to spend the night here again. It will make me more comfortable to pay your fee in advance. That's a five-pound note. I suppose it's more than enough, but I want to talk and I don't want to be interrupted.'

'Just nine times too much,' said Shenstone, 'but if you really want to see me I've got the evening before me and nothing to do. You'd better slip into my bedroom though and change some of your things. You'll find socks and an old pair of slippers in the bottom drawer in the wardrobe and a dressing-gown somewhere hanging about. I'll make some coffee.'

Oakshot smiled. 'Coffee's all very well,' he said, 'but I'm going to tell you a lot of drivel and you can't expect me to do that on slops. I shan't get drunk, not tonight, so if it's all the same to you, mine's a whisky.'

There is an electrical atmosphere about an approaching confession that to the healthy man is disturbingly unpleasant. Though Shenstone was interested in Oakshot, he would have much preferred to pass the evening with his catalogue of sweet peas.

'Would you mind turning down the lamp?' said Oakshot as he took the chair farthest from the fire. 'It's easier to talk in the firelight. I hope you don't mind my smoking this tobacco. It's beastly strong stuff, Wortley's, but I find I can't get on without it.'

'That's all right,' said Shenstone, 'I smoke it myself. It's good, but not so good as it used to be. I hear he married again.'

'Yes, a barmaid, I believe. What was the name of the pub just opposite his shop? The Queen's Arms? Poor little Wortley! And to think of your knowing him too! The world's very small.'

'Yes,' said Shenstone, as he lay back with his eyes half shut. 'Wortley's Medium Smoking Mixture, with his abominable signature in red ink on every label.'

'Well, never mind him now,' Oakshot went on, 'though it's something to come across a man who smokes the same tobacco. I came here, doctor, because I want to talk to you, to get your advice, and then to clear off and never see you again. I half thought of going to Father Kelly instead. I don't know why I didn't, unless it was that he's the sort of man, I fancy, that likes hearing confessions, and you, I can see, are not.'

'Don't mind me,' said Shenstone. 'Spout away. It often does a man good to let things out.'

'Well,' said Oakshot, 'you can pretty well guess the sort of man I am; you saw me a couple of months ago when I was tight, and I suppose you think I'm one of the fools that can't keep away from drink. But I'm not, and to show you that I'm not I'll leave that glass of whisky untasted until I've finished. What's wrong with me, what's spoiled the little that was worth spoiling, is that I've always been too confoundedly conscientious. I suppose you'll laugh there, but it's the honest truth. You see, I inherited the Puritan tradition from both my parents. Of course it's a great heritage, but I've a theory that to get the most out of Puritanism every alternate generation should lie fallow. One can't go on for ever without laughter and sunlight.

'I think the earliest time that the essential flaw in my character showed itself was when as a child I hated dirt. If I fell down in the garden and dirtied my pinafore I was never happy until my mother had changed it and given me a clean one. My nurse was different – she would only tell me not to fuss – that if I minded dirt like that I should never get through life, and then I'd go and roll in the gutter and get up plastered with mud from head to foot.

When I began to learn to write, things were much the same. I had a copy-book and I suppose I spent about ten times as long in writing the pot hooks as an ordinary child would have done. I remember the first smudge I made. I was miserable for hours afterwards, and though my mother said I had done very well for a little boy and would do better some day I was still unhappy, and when I found out where the clean copy-books were kept, I opened the cupboard door when no one was looking and tore the old one up. Next morning I started again with a new book, and wrote three pages without a mistake. I had never been so happy. Then came the smudge again. My mother said she could not always be buying books for me, and so for the rest of that page I made my letters anyhow. When I got to the top of the next, I imagined that it was a new book and began again.'

'I know the feeling,' said Shenstone thoughtfully. 'It was just the same with me.'

'And so that was how all my school books came to be, a mixture of the very best and the very worst. That was why later on I was always near the top of my class or away among the dunces at the bottom. It was the same thing over again when I went to the grammar school, a little fellow of twelve with everything to learn. I was told by my father to keep the rules of the school, and I kept them as long as I could and became in consequence an insufferable little prig, until one day I was given lines for talking in prep. All that night I lay awake because I had broken a rule of the school, and they, I knew, were never made to be broken. When I got my mother's letter that week, in which she said that she hoped I was good and obeyed the masters, I could not answer it, and from that Sunday to the following Saturday I laughed and played like other boys with a heavy heart, staying in in the afternoons to do my punishment. But when Sunday came and the headmaster said something about turning over new leaves, a feeling of joy suddenly came over me. I had never heard of new leaves before, but somehow the expression took hold of me, and with Monday morning I determined to begin afresh. Since then I suppose I have turned over as many leaves as a gale in autumn. Well, that sort of thing went on for years. Sometimes the good mood lasted a day, sometimes half a term, but it was sure to end sooner or later and then the reaction came. Little by little I discovered that the worse I was one week the better I became the next, and so I went to extremes to which I should not otherwise have gone, trusting to the strength of the moral recoil. What friends I had were of two distinct types that never knew each other; the bad ones laughed at me and thought me something of a hypocrite, the good ones thought me a still bigger hypocrite, and some of them prayed for me. But I was never a hypocrite. I have never been one. I used to think sometimes that my ideal was too high. I know now that my life has been shipwrecked because I never had a sense of proportion; I knew nothing of the sanity of compromise. I left school, making, of course, on the last day a resolution to start life afresh. The opportunity was a good one, fostered by that silly talk of schoolmasters about boys beginning life at sixteen or seventeen, instead of at the moment when they come howling into this miserable world. So for three whole months I stuck to the same leaf, longing all the time for the stimulus of the clean page. A year or so later an uncle died quite suddenly; I was left with means of my own, and my guardian decided that I should go up to Cambridge. In the humdrum of office routine I might have settled down into a normal existence, but the sudden prospect of a life of new possibilities was too much for me. The day before I went up I came to the conclusion that this event was to mark an epoch, that a new start was to be made. Oh, the joy of waking up in a new city, in new surroundings, with a future all rosy and a past forgotten! For I could forget my past with an easiness that was surprising; my conscious self could forget it, that is, for I suppose that some part of my brain was registering the whole sordid business just the same. And then to show you the triviality of the whole thing, I will tell you what began to trouble me. I had made up my mind that this latest leaf was to start with the commencement of my career at Cambridge. I went up on the Thursday night and Friday was the day I reckoned from, Friday morning when I awoke fresh from sleep. Then I discovered that the full term did not actually begin until the Sunday, and by Sunday I had done one or two things that I was ashamed of (nothing to be ashamed of to a normal healthy person), and so to Sunday I postponed that momentous starting-point.

'I tell you all this now, and of course I emphasise it, for though these morbid thoughts occupied but an insignificant fraction of my life they coloured the whole of it. I was a good enough fellow to my friends, but I don't think one of them understood me. For their sake it's certainly to be hoped that they did not. Later, when I went into business, things were just the same. I had one chance of escape and I believe I should have used it, but she died, and there was the end of the matter.

'Then I took to drink, more with the idea of disgusting myself with myself than anything else, and having more money than I knew how to use, I chucked the business over and tried to kill time by travel. My life hasn't been altogether as selfish as you might think. I have ideas as to some of the uses to which wealth can be put, and where it did not involve too great an amount of application, I have carried them out, but never with any pleasure, never with any satisfaction. I have seen a good many doctors from time to time. They start off by going into my family history – diseases, not ideas – and end up by talking of neurasthenia, with nothing better to suggest than a course of Weir-Mitchell treatment, massage, or golf. And the church is no better. If I've been converted once, I've been converted fifty times – each was the only genuine variety. I've hung round the outskirts of East End Salvation Army crowds longing for the stirring of the waters. I've made myself drunk, and gone up to the penitent form hoping that a fuddled brain might understand what a clear brain had never grasped, and all without avail. I spoke of one great chance I had early in life. A second of a totally different nature came in a big financial crash. I was left penniless, and for a time I thought that the mere working for a living would save me. I was in Australia at the time and I got a job as gardener; I've always been fond of flowers, especially carnations. But as luck would have it, a distant cousin died and left me a hundred or so a year, just sufficient pocket-money for one's vices. I came over here – as I've been to every new country – with the idea of beginning life afresh, and I had luck on my side too, for I landed in Auckland on the first of January. That was eighteen months ago. Last New Year's Day was the first I ever remember on which I made no good resolutions;

the struggle's beginning to be too much for me. Well, that's most of what I've got to say, and now that I've finished I'll take the whisky. I expect you think that I've been talking nothing but nonsense and drivel. It is nonsense, of course – that's just the tragedy of the thing.'

Oakshot got up and thrust viciously at the logs with the poker. 'A saturated solution of a salt that won't crystallise out – churned cream that won't make butter – those are the only two analogies that I can think of,' he said.

Shenstone was silent. Something in the stranger's narrative, perhaps a similar flaw in his own personality, hidden though long suspected, appealed to him with a strange force. He remembered later how it accentuated his senses; the china asters in the bowl on the table had a faint scent that he had never noticed before.

'What was your reason in telling me this tonight?' he said at last.

'Because tomorrow is my fortieth birthday, and if I'm ever to throw off this cloud of melancholy it seems as good an opportunity as any. I came into the world close upon the stroke of twelve on the night of the thirteenth of July, 1871.'

'Of course,' said Shenstone, 'though I'm not going to say anything about massage and Weir-Mitchell treatment, I believe they'd probably do you a lot of good, and I think before I'd do anything else I'd try them. But it may be simpler to get at the matter through some other way. Suggestion, for instance.'

'Hypnotism, you mean?'

'If you like to call it that. The way I look on it is this. I have always been a great believer in the value of sleep. Not only does it blot out the memory of our transgressions, but it seems to sensitise the mind or the soul in a wonderful way to new impressions. For instance, I know of at least two cases where patients after long operations, during which they had been under the influence of chloroform for two or three hours, have undergone a noticeable change in character. Of course the surgeon puts it down to the absence of the source of irritation. It may be so, though I can't help thinking otherwise.'

'Excuse my saying so,' said Oakshot, 'but I believe you're talking sense. Give the soul a complete holiday; I see what you mean.'

'Soul or mind, or whatever you like to call it, yes. Only in your case I think that probably the hypnotic sleep would be infinitely more beneficial; it allows of my influencing you by suggestion. Of course, I take it for granted that you have confidence in me.'

'Yes,' said Oakshot, 'and even if I hadn't, I've got to such a pitch of misery that I don't mind what happens.'

'Well,' Shenstone went on, 'I'll tell you what we'll do. Your own will, weak as it is, has already fixed on the time when this change is to take place, at twelve o'clock tonight, that is to say, on the anniversary of your fortieth birthday. A little before twelve, then, I'll put you into the hypnotic state, so that you'll have the advantage of both your own self-suggestion and mine. Meanwhile, I may as well explain things a little. All those paper-covered books on the top shelf are French works dealing with hypnotism. You see, I'm interested in the subject. There's nothing uncanny about it; it has been studied by scientists in the same manner that they would approach any other problem. The Trilbys and Svengalis only exist in fiction; there's no melodrama in real life.'

'No,' said Oakshot, 'real life is infinitely worse.'

Shenstone went on to speak of the possibilities of hypnotism with enthusiasm, explaining theories, enumerating results. And his enthusiasm was contagious, for as he spoke Oakshot's pale weak face lit up with new hope.

'I believe you're right,' he said. 'Anyhow, it's well worth trying. What's the time now?'

'Half past ten. I'll put you to sleep just before midnight. Until then I don't think it matters much what you do, only I wouldn't have anything more to drink.'

'No,' said Oakshot, 'I don't feel as if I wanted it. I take it that you won't cross-examine me when I'm under, or anything of that sort. What I've told you already is the truth; the rest's only sordid.'

'On my word of honour, no.'

Shenstone raised the wick of the lamp, and for some time the two sat in silence, the doctor turning over the pages of an illustrated weekly, Oakshot gazing into the glowing embers as if he could snatch from the fire the answer to the riddle of his wasted life. At twenty minutes to twelve Shenstone got up.

'It's rather hot in here,' he said. 'Suppose we go into the surgery. There's nothing of the surgery about the place, but there's a good couch and the light's better.'

Oakshot sat up with a start. 'I believe I was right away at the other side of the world,' he said, 'watching our old gardener budding roses.'

The surgery was cold. 'Here,' said the doctor, 'take this rug and wrap it round you. Now, tell me if the couch is uncomfortable.

That American cloth makes it too slippery. Put this cushion underneath your shoulders. That's better. Now lie as easily as you can and relax your muscles. Is the light too strong? I'll lower it a little. I want you to fix your eyes on the metal top of this pocket-book pencil. That's it,' and he drew a chair to the foot of the couch, sitting astride it. 'Now keep on breathing steadily. You are getting sleepy. It's been a hard day for you, and no mistake. There's heaviness in your limbs. You only see my face now and the top of the pencil. Keep on watching it. Your eyelids are growing heavy – you'd better close them, so. It's five minutes to twelve now; you can only hear my voice, but you'll be able to keep perfect count of the time, and when the clock strikes you'll hear it plainly. After that, you'll find that all those foolish nightmares of the past have slipped away from you and you'll wake from your sleep in the morning a new man.'

Through the thin wooden walls came the loud ticking of the clock in the room they had left, and then the sudden click that it gave a quarter of a minute before striking the hour.

Oakshot turned restlessly on his couch, and half raising himself gave a long low cry of joyful wonder, as if at the sight of some vista of marvellous beauty.

The hour struck. A man passed down the road whistling a merry tune. Shenstone, placing his fingers on his patient's pulse, found to his horror that he could feel nothing.

'Wake, Oakshot!' he said. 'For God's sake wake!'

The strychnine and the hypodermic were on the shelf at his elbow, but even while he fumbled with the screw of the needle he knew that it was too late. And still down the road he could hear the man whistling. He had finished the end of the verse and got to the swinging chorus.

Since Shenstone lived by himself, there were no witnesses to his experiment. The stranger had died in his sleep; that was all. Was the doctor to blame? For omitting all physical examination, most decidedly yes; though as he told himself again and again there might have been nothing to indicate, when living, the cause of Oakshot's death – embolism of the coronary artery. But whether to blame or not, Shenstone has more than earned the stranger's fee in the restless days and sleepless nights of that, to him, memorable July.

He is not a great reader of poetry – the volumes on his shelves were of his father's collecting – but, taking down the other day Hazlitt's

Miscellany, dog-eared and dusty, he opened the book at Rochester's 'Satire against Mankind'. Most of what he read he forgot, but one verse will live for ever in his memory, so associated is it with the events of that tragic night.

> Then Old Age and Experience, hand in hand,
> Lead him to Death and make him understand
> After a search so painful and so long
> That all his life he has been in the wrong.

TWELVE STRANGE CASES

The Lake

I hope this story will be published for three reasons: I should like to see myself in print – that's fame; I should like to see myself in satin (I would buy a lovely satin dress if I got what the story is worth) – that's vanity; but, above all, I should not like to be seen in my coffin for many years to come – that's common sense and prudence.

If this story isn't published there is just a chance that I may be murdered. If it is, my murderer wouldn't dare, and I shall cease to walk warily and dream at night.

My nephew, who is a journalist, describes it as a jolly good yarn and has offered to write it for me, but why shouldn't I try myself? After all, it's my affair and my life that is remotely, yes, very remotely, in danger.

I am a middle-aged nurse, not too young and not too old, and, like all nurses, I have had some rather curious experiences. Some of them make me quite anxious for the day to come when I can live outside other people's lives instead of being forced into intimacy with all sorts of conditions of men and women.

Last spring I went south, not far from my own home, to nurse an old lady, Mrs Carstairs, who was suffering from heart disease. It was as much old age as anything, but from time to time she had attacks that came on quite suddenly and left her mind confused. A good, capable companion would have served her purpose, but she was a little nervous about herself, fancied that her digestion was weak and that some of her food ought to be specially prepared, and since she was very wealthy and the people about her seemed rather incompetent, her doctor had suggested getting a nurse.

I seemed to give what is called general satisfaction, for at the end of the eight weeks, which is the longest time that the hospital allows us to stay with one case, she paid the additional fees which enabled her to retain my services for another month.

'General satisfaction.' 'Retaining my services!' I wonder they get girls to enter the profession, but if I had my choice again and I couldn't afford to be a doctor I'd still be a nurse, in spite of everything.

Mrs Carstairs lived in a large house in the country. She had no children, but two nieces and one nephew. The elder niece had married a Mr Waldron, who, I understood, was a great entomologist. They lived in a house that was far too big for them, but which they couldn't sell. The younger niece, Philippa Clarke, lived with her aunt. She was a colourless sort of girl, always bemoaning the fact that she was buried in the country. Personally, I would rather be buried in the country than cremated at Golders Green. In any case, that won't happen to me. I have left instructions that in no circumstances shall my body be cremated. Morbid, perhaps, but one has one's reasons.

The nephew, Dr Clarke, had a practice in Yarminster, ten miles away. He was married, with one child, a boy of nine. His wife was a thoroughly vulgar woman. I think he must have met her when he was a student. Dr Clarke didn't attend his aunt professionally, I was glad to find – not that he wasn't a pleasant man and an able doctor; I believe he was extraordinarily clever – but to my mind it is a mistake for a doctor to attend his relations. He is apt to lack authority and prestige, and then there is always trouble in one way or another with fees. He charges nothing, or too little, or too much. I thought Dr Clarke very wise in being content to leave his aunt in charge of Dr Rumbolt, the local man.

And now about Mrs Carstairs herself. She was seventy-six and young for her years. She enjoyed a little gardening (cutting off dead flowers and going through nurserymen's catalogues), she sketched a little, she did really beautiful needlework. She listened every night to the news on the wireless, and was far better informed politically than her niece. Indeed, while I was with her we listened to the whole of Professor MacElwey's weekly talks on *Relativity and the World of Today*, about which I remember relatively nothing.

I liked Mrs Carstairs – she really was an old dear. While I was with her at Stonegate she had two attacks, one of which was accompanied by alarming nose bleeding. Happily she didn't realise their serious nature; she became very confused, her memory went, and for a week or so she had to be kept very quiet. But in each case she made a good recovery, and though Dr Rumbolt, a fussy little man, impressed on me the necessity of restraining her activities, he saw no reason why she should not pay a visit to her niece that had long been planned.

Two days before we left, Dr Clarke came over from Yarminster with his little boy to say goodbye. Mrs Carstairs and I were in a far corner of the garden. She was finishing a pretty little sketch of the house against its background of elms – the wistaria was all in flower; I had never seen so lovely a wistaria – when they joined us.

'Don't get up,' said the doctor; 'we mustn't interrupt your work. We can wait – for tea if you invite us – but this afternoon light goes all too quickly. It will do Roger good to watch you. When he lays on the paints he is far too impatient.

'Don't go, nurse,' he said. 'I met an old friend of yours the other day,' and he mentioned one of the most trying patients I had ever had, who, it seemed, had now settled in Yarminster, and to Dr Clarke's disgust lived, so he informed us, on his doorstep.

Mrs Carstairs soon finished her sketch, we gave it the admiration it deserved, and I quickly picked up the cushions and painting paraphernalia, of which Dr Clarke as quickly relieved me, leaving me, as always happens when my hands are empty and I have nothing to do, exceedingly awkward and out of place. However, I had the laugh of him later when the sketch-book slipped out of his hands and the contents of the paint-box were scattered over a gorse bush. It was young Roger, I noticed then, that was put on to their retrieving.

We had tea on the terrace, where Miss Clarke joined us. Candidly I disliked that girl. She took no interest in her young nephew and less in her brother, though he had left that vulgar wife of his at home. I was glad that we were seeing the last of her.

Before he left I had a few words in private with Dr Clarke.

'There's no need to ask how your patient is,' he said. 'She's far better physically and mentally than when I saw her last. The great thing is to keep her contented with doing little. It's just as well that at Bradgate she will be away from her garden. Stooping down and stretching, it seems little enough for her, but it may be too much. I should encourage the sketching. You'll have to see that she doesn't spend too long by the lake – the whole place is far too damp and shut in – and I'm writing to my sister to get their doctor to keep an eye on her. I'm afraid that professionally this isn't a very interesting case for you, nurse, but it has meant a great deal to us to know that you are at hand in case of an emergency. Miss Clarke, as I expect you know, would only get flustered.

'Now you've no commissions in Yarminster?' he added, taking out a slip of paper from his pocket. 'Paints, folding-chair, *Has Russia a Plan?*, *Eminent Victorians*, *Crime at the Folly*, and any other books by the same writer – is that for you, nurse? No, I know the old lady has a weakness for thrillers; I was only teasing. Three skeins of wool to match this, and to remind Coltman to forward two additional bottles of the mixture as before direct to Bradgate Manor. That will keep my wife busy. Where's the boy? Come along, Roger, it's high time we got back.'

We managed the journey down, a long cross-country journey too, without what Mrs Carstairs called undue fatigue. From the first I didn't like Bradgate Manor. As Dr Clarke had said, it was far too much shut in with trees, and the lake was little more than two hundred yards from the house. The house itself was low and rambling and in bad repair. It would have been a drug on the market, and a noxious drug at that. It was altogether a depressing place, and to make matters worse, the rain fell almost continually for ten days after we got there.

The Waldrons were rather queer people. Mr Waldron was, as I have said, a great entomologist. He had cabinets full of insects neatly arranged and labelled that smelt of camphor and killing bottles. He was a botanist, too, and grew all sorts of outlandish plants in the garden and tumbledown vineries where no grapes ever ripened. I expect he would have been interesting when once launched on his favourite subjects, but he struck one as rather a curmudgeonly sort of a man who had been put on his best behaviour and was in consequence not quite at home. Mrs Waldron was a distinct improvement on her sister, a little colourless, a little harassed, but quite a friendly sort of person, obviously willing to be completely dominated by her husband.

The bad weather kept us more or less indoors for a fortnight Mrs Carstairs had what she called a slight digestive upset which provided us with the occasion for calling in the Waldrons' family doctor, Dr Bickerton, a physician of the old school, who gave her – again I quote from Mrs Carstairs – 'a thorough overhaul' and altered her medicine. She always had great faith in doctors who altered her medicine. Meanwhile she kept herself amused with knitting, needle-work, and detective stories and painted some rare but insignificant-looking moths to illustrate a paper Mr Waldron was writing for one of the learned societies. It was the sort of thing she could do really well, beautiful and delicate brushwork.

Mrs Carstairs was an indefatigable correspondent. I was always filling her fountain-pen. She wrote to Philippa, she wrote to Dr Clarke. She forwarded Dr Clarke's letters to her to Philippa, and

Philippa's letters to her to Dr Clarke, slipping in newspaper cut-
tings about the condition of affairs in China, the most successful
method of growing hyacinths in pots, and the teaching of English
in schools until the envelope weighed two ounces when it was
scaled. I am afraid she did not get as many letters in return but Dr
Clarke managed to find time to write weekly, and his second letter
enclosed one from Roger which Mrs Carstairs handed me to read
before sending it on to Philippa, who, she felt sure, would be
interested in seeing it.

It was quite an ordinary letter:

DEAR GRATE AUNT
I hope you are very well. I have now got eight rabbits and
I painted the do yesterday. She is black. Are you painting? I
wish you would paint me a picture of the Lake. Dad says the
red roadadendrums will be lovely, and I have never seen red
roadadendrums, so please paint them for me.

With lots of love from
ROGER

'A nice little boy,' said Mrs Carstairs. 'Not at all like his mother. I
think I must try and do a little sketch of the lake for him.'

When Dr Bickerton had come over to see Mrs Carstairs he had
told me that Nurse Orde, of St Christopher's, was looking after a
patient of his, Colonel Gibbons. We were old friends, and as we had
not met for some time I arranged to go over and see her on the first
fine Wednesday. I am not likely to forget that afternoon. I hadn't
been with Orde for more than half an hour when the telephone bell
rang.

'Please, Nurse Wilkie,' said the maid, 'you're wanted on the
phone; it's urgent.'

I should think it was urgent. Mr Waldron – I hardly recognised his
voice – informed me that Mrs Carstairs had had a sudden attack
while sketching by the lake. They had managed to get her to the
house and had sent for the doctor. Would I arrange with Colonel
Gibbons to be motored back immediately?

So that was that. Something of the sort was likely to happen some
day. That was why I was at Bradgate; but it was unfortunate, to say
the least of it, that it should have happened on my day out. Doctors
and matrons in charge of nursing staffs have a habit of not understanding these things. Poor old Mrs Carstairs. It must have happened
just when Orde had been telling me about the marvellous evening

frock she had fallen for at Jenkyns & Jones and which she would never have occasion to wear this side of kingdom come.

I was back in less than a quarter of an hour. They had placed Mrs Carstairs on a couch in the morning-room. Mrs Waldron was holding a bottle of smelling-salts to her nose and dabbing her forehead with eau-de-Cologne. Mr Waldron was anxiously pacing up and down the room.

I saw at once that Mrs Carstairs was desperately ill. Her face was flushed and I could barely feel her pulse.

'Get some hot-water bottles,' I said, 'and tell them to warm the bed.' She opened her eyes as I spoke and gave me a smile.

'So kind, nurse,' she said. 'Silly to faint like that. Something very wrong about the lake.'

Then she was still.

It was half past four when she died. Dr Bickerton arrived before five. He confirmed the fact of death and we all adjourned into the library. It seemed that soon after I had left to walk to Colonel Gibbons's Mrs Carstairs had expressed a wish to make a sketch of the lake. Mrs Waldron had accompanied her, carrying her painting things and the folding-chair, and after sitting with her aunt for a little while had at her suggestion returned to the house, intending to come back for her in an hour's time. She had no hesitation in leaving the old lady, for Mr Waldron was down by the lake well within earshot making observations on dragon-flies. It was Mr Waldron, indeed, who had first noticed that anything was wrong. Looking up, he chanced to see Mrs Carstairs fall from her chair; by the time he had reached her she was unconscious.

Dr Bickerton made a few inquiries about the previous attacks and promised to make the necessary arrangements about the death certificate.

We naturally were a subdued party at the dinner table that night. In the drawing-room, when Mrs Waldron and I were alone together she was really very kind and thanked me for what I had done, which was just nothing, and hoped I would stay on till after the funeral. As soon as Mr Waldron came in I made an excuse of letter writing and went upstairs. As I passed through the hall I noticed that poor Mrs Carstairs's sketch-book – why does one say poor as soon as a person is dead? – was lying on the table. I looked at the unfinished sketch. It showed the dark foliage of the pinewoods on the far side of the lake relieved by the great bank of rhododendrons, which were reflected in the water.

I did the things that still remained to be done in Mrs Carstairs's room and then went to my own to write my report to the matron.

Then I drew up the one easy-chair – nurses, of course, don't appreciate easy-chairs – to the window and lit a cigarette.

I was really sorry about Mrs Carstairs's death, not at the manner of it then – that was all that anyone could wish; she loved sunny afternoons, she loved her sketching – but because she had gone too soon. She easily might have lived for a few more years, the lady bountiful of her village, the efficient mistress of a very peaceful home. And now Stonegate Lodge would be sold. The old gardener would be out of a job, the young chauffeur who was thinking of getting married would go on just thinking; the cook and parlour-maid would be pensioned off and sink all their savings in running a lodging-house at Eastbourne (lodging-houses for cooks are as subtle a temptation as nursing homes for retired members of our profession), and Miss Clarke would have her little flat in London and find London a little flat, too.

As I sat there by the open window looking out over the garden I had not the faintest notion that all was not as it should be. I wondered, it is true, what was at the back of Mrs Carstairs's mind when she said that there was something wrong about the lake, but I had been with her in two attacks when she had been quite incoherent. This was like the first and the second except that it was the third and the last.

Mrs Carstairs was buried there. Dr Clarke and Miss Clarke came over for the funeral, and the solicitor read the will in the library. I understood that after a large number of legacies the residue of the estate was to be divided equally between her nephew and nieces. The old dear had actually left me a hundred pounds. It is the only legacy I have ever received, and I must say that Dr Clarke, Mrs Waldron, and Miss Clarke went out of their way to congratulate me.

We all dispersed on the following day. Miss Clarke went back to Stonegate Lodge, taking her aunt's belongings with her with the exception of the sketch-book and paint-box, which Dr Clarke wanted Roger to have as a little memento of his aunt. The child, it seemed, was fond of painting. The Waldrons went off to Bournemouth, and I returned to town to report to the hospital and then to take a fortnight's holiday, which I felt was only indifferently well earned.

I think it must have been a chance remark of a gossiping vicar's wife who called while I was staying with my mother that first put me on the track and caused me in consequence to alter my views on the celibacy of the clergy. She began as soon as she heard that I had been with Mrs Carstairs.

'I know all about Yarminster,' she said, 'though it's many years since I saw dear old Mrs Carstairs. That young nephew of hers has come into his fortune at the right time. His wife is on the point of divorcing him, you know, and it's one of those cases where if she is successful the Medical Council or whatever it calls itself will have to take action. That means he won't be allowed to practise, and a very good thing too. But George Clarke is a very clever man. They've got to prove their case, and I don't know anyone more capable of laying a false trail or concealing the issue. Why, when – '

'Emily,' said my mother, 'help yourself to some toast and don't talk scandal. You ought to be ashamed of yourself.'

Now I had liked Dr Clarke, I suppose because he had treated me with kindness and politeness, and it came as a surprise to hear him spoken of like that. It looked as if I might have to revise my judgment of him. There was no getting away from the fact that Mrs Carstairs's sudden death had been exceedingly opportune for four people at least, for Dr Clarke (if this piece of scandal could be believed), for the Waldrons, saddled with an estate they could neither keep up nor get rid of, and for Miss Clarke, who wanted to break away from her aunt's leading strings and to lead a life of her own. Just supposing, I said to myself, letting my imagination play.

Then I recalled the picture of Mrs Carstairs as I had last seen her alive, laid out on the couch in the morning-room at Bradgate Manor, her face a little flushed, her pulse almost imperceptible, her hands cold.

'So kind, nurse,' she had said. 'Silly to faint like that. Something very wrong about the lake.'

I had concluded that she was wandering, but on thinking over the matter it seemed to me that the first part of her statement was clear enough. It was the reference to the lake that had made us jump to the conclusion that her mind had again become confused. Could there be any sense in it? Dr Clarke had said something about not spending too much time by the lake. Mr Waldron had been pottering about there hunting for dragon-flies, but Mrs Carstairs was accustomed to his eccentricities. Had she seen anyone else, man or woman, whose presence might have alarmed her?

I tried to remember the unfinished sketch. Would that tell me anything? Dark trees, dark water, masses of rhododendrons in full flower, reflections in dark water – there was nothing else.

I have a weakness for detective stories, and for several nights before I went to sleep I used to let my mind play upon the Mystery of Bradgate Manor. The crime was murder, and the suspects were Dr Clarke, his sister, the two Waldrons, and a middle-aged nurse, who benefited by a legacy of a hundred pounds.

And then came the crossword puzzle to enlighten me.

I was held up by two clues, one vertical, the other horizontal. They intersected, so that if I guessed the one I should be more able to solve the other. 'Four down' was a light stamp; 'five across' a colour with fish inside. I concentrated on 'five across.' What fish was there of three letters? Cod? Dab? Could the word be daub? To daub was to colour, and it contained dab. That must be it. But the last letter should have been *e* if my solution of 'six down' were correct.

Then someone gave me the light stamp. Brand, of course – flaming brand, that was the light, and the iron you burn traitors with and packing-cases that was the stamp.

Colour with fish inside was –*a*–*e*. Lake – crimson lake, the colour of those rhododendrons.

'There was something wrong with the lake?'

I had an awful feeling that I had stumbled on the truth. Lake, crimson lake, surely that wasn't poisonous? Emerald green was poisonous. When we were children we were only allowed to use emerald green if we did not suck the brush. But couldn't poison have been put into the lake? What was it that the vicar's wife had said about Dr Clarke? 'I don't know anyone more capable of laying a false trail or concealing the issue.'

It took me several days of hard thinking before I saw things as I believed they happened, and even then what evidence there was was wholly circumstantial. Of my suspects Dr Clarke was the only one I had seen with Mrs Carstairs while she was sketching; if she were in the habit of sucking her brush he would have had the opportunity of noting it. Miss Clarke and Mrs Waldron were not in the least interested in their aunt's sketches. On that afternoon at Stonegate Lodge when he was carrying the cushions and all the rest of the paraphernalia into the house (and I had thought him so polite and kind) Dr Clarke had dropped the paint-box into a gorse bush, of all places. It was an easy thing to lose some of the paints, and the most natural thing to offer to replace them. And it was his wife, too, I remember him telling me, who would make the purchases. He discouraged his aunt from gardening; he recommended her to go on with her sketching, and as a reminder sent the folding chair. Then we went down to Bradgate Manor. The weather was wet, and Mrs Carstairs had had no opportunity of using her paint-box. Surely I was at fault there. She *had* used it. She had painted those rare moths to illustrate Mr Waldron's paper. But the moths were inconspicuous in their colouring. There was no trace of red about them, not even a trace of grey in which red might have been blended. Time passes, and Dr Clarke begins to wonder if the old lady has given up sketching. He doesn't write to remind her – he is an adept at covering up his traces – but he suggests to his little boy that his aunt would like to get a letter from him. Small boys of nine always ask what they shall say in a letter, and Dr Clarke is very helpful. 'Ask her to paint you a picture of the lake and the rhododendrons. How do you spell rhododendrons? Oh, you must tackle that yourself. It's *your* letter, you know.' And then comes a fine day. The rhododendrons are at their best, great banks of flaming crimson, and Mrs Carstairs remembers her little nephew's request. She uses the new pan of crimson lake for the first and last time.

It would be perfectly easy for a doctor to get hold of a crystalline alkaloid soluble in water – I know of at least two that would serve the purpose – and having reduced it to a fine powder to introduce it into the upper layer of the paint. As little as a fiftieth of a grain might cause death in a healthy woman. In an invalid a far smaller dose might be effective; the minutest dose might cause her to fall, and the shock of falling would be sufficient. If any undissolved particles clung to the brush, what more natural than that she should suck the brush? And no one would ever suspect. Hadn't he advised me to get the Waldrons' doctor to examine Mrs Carstairs so that there would be no hesitation about a death certificate? Supposing, and the chances were one in a hundred, that there had been any suspicion of poisoning, wouldn't it fall on Mr Waldron, with his killing bottles and preservatives and his queer plants? And who after a month, if an exhumation order were made, would detect a fiftieth of a grain of an alkaloid that would have disappeared long before in the ordinary course of decomposition? It could be detected, of course, in the pan of crimson lake, but I remembered that Dr Clarke had taken away the paint-box with him as a memento for Roger of his aunt.

Roger, he had said, was very fond of paints.

That was my case against Dr Clarke. It looked to me damning.

I had an increasing desire to see Dr Clarke again and make him give himself away, if that were possible. I could write and ask for an interview – and what more natural than that I should like some little thing to remember Mrs Carstairs by? Some plants perhaps from the rock garden at Stonegate Lodge.

I wrote my letter, and in reply received a polite note from Dr Clarke saying that he would be glad to see me on the following Thursday at six. He might be detained – he knew that I appreciated the difficulty a doctor has to keep appointments – but Roger would entertain me if he was late.

I rather hoped he would be late, and made a special point of catching an early bus into Yarminster so that I should be at the house well before six. I was shown into the study, where Roger, who was busy with his homework, welcomed me as an ally. I told him the correct answers to his sums – children nowadays have far too much homework – and then he got out a tracing of the map of England which he proceeded to colour. It gave me a little thrill to see him using Mrs Carstairs's paint-box. It gave me a big thrill to see that the pan of lake was missing.

'Daddy's got it,' he said, 'but he's promised to give me a new one. I use vermilion. It's a nicer colour, I think, but you can't mix it very well, can you?'

'You know,' I said, 'you oughtn't to suck your brush like that.'

'Oh, it's quite all right,' Roger said. 'Great-aunt Mary always used to suck her brush.'

It looked as if my visit had produced something, at any rate. I tried to keep calm and collected for my interview. It was going to need courage.

At last the doctor came. I had my little say, he gave me full permission to take what plants I wanted from the rock garden at Stonegate Lodge, and came with me to the door. Somehow I managed to avoid shaking hands.

At the door I fired my parting shot.

'I've been watching Roger do his homework,' I said. 'He was colouring a map of England quite nicely. I told him that it was a dangerous habit to suck the brush, and I noticed that he hadn't got any crimson lake.'

I looked him straight in the face, and for a fraction of a second I saw him with the mask off. It was not a pleasant sight.

'You are wonderfully observant, nurse,' he said. 'As a matter of fact I am preparing a paper with coloured diagrams. Black and red I find show up well. The subject – you will be interested in the subject, or ought to be – has to do with the increase in the mortality rate in certain age groups in women over forty-five. And now I mustn't keep you.'

So I am fairly sure that I am right after all, and if so Dr Clarke knows I know. It's because I am afraid that he will use his knowledge that I want this story published. He is divorced now, and lives the life of a cultured gentleman in some south coast watering-place.

If this story appears in print – the names, of course, are all fictitious – I shall send him a copy. And I shall send a copy, too, to my solicitor with the real names in an envelope which he will open at my death. There, Dr Clarke, if you did commit that crime I think any little plans you are making for your greater safety are forestalled.

If only the editor publishes it!

Chemist and Druggist

This is not the sort of story that gets printed in magazines. It is not cheerful and people are supposed to want cheerful stories in these dark days; it is not exciting, and it lacks the right sort of love interest. If you read on you mustn't expect to find the lip-stick, slap-stick, golf-stick (no, club – I'm sorry) type of heroine and hero who model themselves on film stars. My heroine and hero were a dingy middle-aged couple who had been married thirty years and who, with the exception of holidays spent at Clacton, Yarmouth, and Margate, had lived in the same dingy, middle-aged suburb all their life. Their love is not the type to interest the modern flapper.

A good editor would, of course, turn down this story for other reasons. His advertisers would be offended; Christian Scientists, who I believe are increasing every year in number and influence, might be hurt, and though of course they think that there is no such thing as pain, it doesn't pay to hurt a Christian Scientist. Worst of all, the story of Mr Peckover and his wife might well be deemed to be a cause of offence, an occasion of stumbling, to all right-minded religious people. The number of right-minded religious people who find inspiration in our popular illustrated magazines has got to be reckoned with.

Why then do I trouble to write this story? Partly for the sake of what I am still determined to call its love interest – old-fashioned I will allow you – partly as an example of a curious coincidence, partly for the drama, in which the stage was a chemist's shop.

And it's a story, too, that makes you want to ask very searching questions.

Mrs Peckover had had a severe operation, how severe she, happily, did not know. She was just able when I first went to nurse her, to be moved from her bed to the couch by the window which looked out on to a patch of garden, bounded by the red brick wall of a new garage. A very kind and patient little woman was Mrs Peckover, always apologising for the trouble she thought she was giving. I wished for her own sake that she was less sensitive.

Mr Peckover was the proprietor of a large chemist's shop. He and his wife lived over the business premises. They had one servant, a very capable middle-aged widow who was a Seventh-Day Adventist. Mr Peckover was tall and thin, with a long drooping moustache. In fact the general impression he gave was one of drooping. If he had been a pot-plant you would have felt like tying him to a stick, watering him twice daily, and putting him out on the window-sill in the sun. Perhaps you would have sponged his leaves occasionally in soap and water, not because he wasn't scrupulously clean but because he looked so grey and faded and pot-bound.

But poor Mr Peckover hadn't much opportunity of getting out into the sun. All morning and afternoon and between twelve and one and five and six on Sundays, he was busy in the shop, serving customers or dispensing medicines, his long thin fingers making up the neatest parcels, which he would seal with a dab of red sealing-wax at a little gas-jet.

I imagine that at one time Mr Peckover must have had a very flourishing business, but there was now a branch of a multiple chemist's only a hundred yards down the road. It had an imposing front of glazed tiles, and a lending library with manicured young ladies whose time was occupied in trying to persuade people to be content to take books that were not on their list. And two hundred yards down the road on the other side of the street another chemist had recently set up business. It was quite a small shop, but he had obtained the sole agency of Vibriola, the beauty specialists, and their products made a pleasing display in an inner shrine behind the plate-glass window. Mr Peckover, I am afraid, was slowly going downhill, and if it hadn't been for his savings from more prosperous days, I am quite sure that he would never have been able to have afforded a nurse.

I had come to the High Street, Bawlston, from a place in the country where a staff of ten indoor servants ministered inefficiently to the needs of a crotchety old dowager and her dogs, but I was far happier in those dingy little rooms above the shop. Mr Peckover treated me as a professional colleague; he discussed with me the many new proprietary drugs that he found necessary to stock, he lamented in a very deprecatory fashion the increasing simplicity of the prescriptions he was called upon to dispense, holding up as a pattern to all physicians the example of a Dr Catchpool who had attended the best families in the district in the long-distant days before the war. He lent me copies of the *Pharmaceutical Journal*, which I never read, and I in turn passed on to him the *Nursing Mirror*.

And Mrs Peckover, too, was kindness itself. She was always apologising for my mattress which she was afraid was rather lumpy, and when my hot-water bottle leaked I was presented next day with a new one from the shop, done up in a neat brown-paper parcel and sealed by Mr Peckover himself with red sealing-wax.

As for Mrs Greg, the Seventh-Day Adventist, who came at half past seven in the morning and left reluctantly at half past eight at night (on Saturdays, when her tenets forbade her to work, an inefficient backsliding niece called Flossie took her place), there was nothing that she would not do to help me help her mistress.

One word about Mrs Peckover's doctor, who is concerned, though only indirectly, with this story. Dr Bentwick was a busy and capable practitioner. I once heard him say that he had not had a day in bed since an attack of German measles in his boyhood. This was a great pity, for he was a hard man; he was interested in diseases but not in people. He was far too ready to accept pain as a necessary evil, and though of course pain is a very useful symptom, there comes a time when its relief should be a primary and not a secondary consideration.

It was natural for poor Mrs Peckover to suffer a lot of pain, and most doctors would have done more than Dr Bentwick did to relieve it. After I had been a fortnight at Number 102 High Street, Bawlston, I felt as if I had known Mr and Mrs Peckover for years. When I was alone with Mr Peckover he was always talking about his wife and what a wonderful little woman she was. He told me about the romance of their first meeting on the sea-front at Clacton, of their early married life when his old mother lived with them, of how for years his wife played the harmonium in the chapel. 'And when,' said Mr Peckover, 'they installed a new organ and some of the choir thought that the music mistress at the High School should be asked to play it, Mrs Peckover didn't make any fuss at all but took her place with the other sopranos in the choir. And once,' he proudly added, 'she sang in the Hallelujah Chorus at Wimbledon.'

When Mr Peckover began to talk about his wife it would have been difficult to stop him – not that I wanted to, for it was a beautiful subject. I have always been interested in biography, and this was one

that would never be written. And so I learnt of Mrs Peckover's skill
as a housekeeper, of her kindness to stray cats, and her concern for
seeing that Mr Peckover's assistants should be introduced to some of
the really nice thoughtful girls who taught in the Sunday school.

It was at meals which I shared with Mr Peckover, and in the little
sitting-room in the evenings when his wife lay restlessly dozing, that
I became, bit by bit, acquainted with the story of her life.

During the long hours spent alone with her it was of her husband
that she would talk. I marvelled at the clearness of her understanding
of his character. She had none of Mr Peckover's sentimentality; she
saw him as he really was: a plain, honest, kindly, inoffensive man who
had made a failure of life.

At the end of my first fortnight, when they had taken me into their
friendship, each in turn began to speak of themselves. I became, not
altogether willingly, the depository of their secrets.

One afternoon, after a brief visit paid by one of her friends, I found
Mrs Peckover reading a Christian Science pamphlet. She asked me
to sit down beside her, as she had something on her mind about
which she wanted to talk to me. It appeared that for some months
past she had become more and more interested in Christian Science.

'It began,' she said, 'with the pain. You mustn't breathe a word
of this to Mr Peckover, nurse. He doesn't know. This is a secret
between ourselves. But the pain was very bad and I did so want him
not to see that I was suffering. Dr Bentwick is a very good man and
I am sure he acts for the best; he gave me medicines, as you know,
but they didn't seem to do much to take the pain away. Then Mrs
Jackson, who has just called – such a kind bright woman' – as bright
and hard, I thought, as a copper kettle – 'talked to me about
Christian Science. It all seems to me very complicated, and I don't
follow their arguments at all. I am quite sure, too, for some people
medicine and drugs are the right thing. I am always telling Walter,
when he gets discouraged, that his is a noble profession, apart of
course from the soaps and sponges and toothbrushes, and they are
real necessities. But there must be such a thing as faith healing. I
know there is, because though I have only a little faith, I've put it to
the test. Do you know, nurse, that the pain has been getting less and
less? It's easily bearable now. Perhaps I may not get better, but I'm
not unhappy. I've got such a lot to be thankful for.'

She was silent for a minute and then went on: 'You won't say a
word of all this to Mr Peckover? He sometimes gets very impatient
with Christian Scientists and he finds it very difficult to get on with

Mrs Jackson. Whatever happens I don't want him to know that I suffered all that pain.'

A few days later I received a second unexpected confidence, but this time from Mr Peckover. It was evening. We were in the little sitting-room; I was knitting in an armchair by the fire and he was busy writing at the table.

I knew what he was writing; some time before he had explained to me all about it. He was taking a correspondence course in methods of modern salesmanship. He referred to it rather deprecatingly as a refresher course. One or two doctors in the district, he told me, and busy men too, found time for post-graduate study. It was up to him to follow their example and keep abreast of the times. Poor Walter was pathetically transparent. It was obvious that he was making a last gallant fight to keep his business and that he had found something that might at least take his thoughts away from the future. So he wrote weekly exercises on all the problems whose understanding Mr Hardcastle of the Imperial Institute, 55 Regent Street, Liversedge, considered essential for the successful conduct of a modern business, and the answers came back corrected, probably by a badly paid clerk, with sheets of hectographed instructions on the next lesson.

Mr Peckover sealed up the envelope with a sigh of satisfaction.

'It certainly does force one to concentrate,' he said. 'I believe Hardcastle is quite right when he says in lesson two that concentration is the big secret of a big personality, and that if the personality is there business will come. I don't know if you've noticed the new window display, nurse. I think it's rather original myself, something that will catch the public's eye. I'm wondering now whether those big glass jars of coloured water oughtn't to go – they have been there twenty-five years. Children used to like them years ago, but children change with the rest of us, and it's the customer we've got to cater for,' and he gave a rather dreary smile.

'You look tired, Mr Peckover,' I said. 'Why not let me make you some tea?'

'It's very kind of you, nurse, but I had my usual cup with Mrs Peckover an hour ago. It's a strain, you know, a very great strain, more than you would ever guess. Do you know, nurse, that three months ago, when I first began to suspect what was the matter with the wife, I had to take to stimulants to carry me through the day's work? I had always been a most abstemious man though never an abstainer, but with being up at night and so on I just couldn't go on burning the candle at both ends without something to help me.

I believe the habit was growing on me, indeed I was getting quite alarmed, but thank God I was able to pull myself up in time. I hadn't put sufficient faith in the power of my own personality. This correspondence course helped there. Personality does tell. When I went to the service at the chapel on Easter Sunday I determined that I would make a clean break in what might for others have proved a very dangerous habit. It was hard at first, but I've won through, and I've gained, if I may say so, a new self-respect. I had to keep a very tight grip on myself. I don't expect you have made a study of psychology, nurse. It is a subject that touches life at many points and is very ably dealt with in the third lesson of this correspondence course. There was one quotation from Mr William James that struck me very much at the time and which I copied out.'

He took a leather case from his pocket and proceeded to read the extract which he had written on a half-sheet of note-paper.

Some day if he only perseveres in little things, he can count on waking up to find himself one of the competent ones of his generation, in whatever pursuit he may have singled out.

' "In whatever pursuit he may have singled out",' Mr Peckover repeated, wiping his spectacles. 'That is my creed, and I am trying to follow it. Of course you won't repeat what I have said to Mrs Peckover. She knows nothing of all this and is herself an abstainer. I think in the matter of alcohol she is just a little prejudiced. It may be because I am a chemist, but I myself have always regarded alcohol as a valuable drug to be used but not to be abused. I have kept all this from Mrs Peckover because it would only worry her more if she saw that I was worrying. We must all keep a brave face and make things just as easy for her as we can.'

Poor Mr Peckover! From the way he spoke they might be surrounded with friends. As a matter of fact there were very few people who took the trouble to climb the narrow stairs to the flat above the shop – Dr Bentwick, the busy minister of the Methodist Chapel, and two or three middle-aged ladies who either talked too much or, maintaining a gloomy silence, stared out into the untended back garden that once had been so gay with flowers.

Mr and Mrs Peckover were both very orderly people whose days were governed by a strict routine. After the midday meal, at half past four and again at eight, he would go to his wife's room where they would have a cup of tea. I would bring in the tray and then leave them together. It was almost a ritual. Mr Peckover poured out the tea, since his wife was too weak to hold the pot, but she told me that she always insisted on putting the sugar into her husband's cup. It was one of the few little things left which she could do for him. Mr Peckover's sugar was kept in a special sugar basin, a lovely little bit of old china: it was really sugar intended for coffee, coloured crystals that somehow had taken his wife's fancy.

Then one afternoon I saw something that I was not intended to see. If I had not seen it this story would never have been written. It was a very hot afternoon. Mrs Peckover's bed was by the window. I had placed the tray on the table beside her and close to it was the chair where Mr Peckover was sitting. As I went out of the room she asked me to leave the door open. I then went to my own room. It too was stifling; there was not a breath of air and the sun was blazing in at the window. I shut the window, drew down the blind, and went out again into the passage.

At the end of Mrs Peckover's bedroom was a large wardrobe with a mirror. In the mirror I saw reflected not the faces of Mr and Mrs Peckover but their hands. Mrs Peckover was putting sugar into her husband's tea, but she was putting in something else as well, something that dropped into his cup from the crook of her little finger as she stirred the spoon. Then I saw Mr Peckover's right hand raise the teapot and pour out his wife's cup of tea. He held a little strainer in his left which partially concealed what those long fingers of his were doing. He too was putting something into the tea.

'I'm afraid you have found this hot afternoon very trying, my dear,' I heard him say. 'It's far cooler down in the shop than it is up here. I shouldn't wonder if we have thunder before night.'

I went into the parlour and sat down. What did it mean? Had my eyes deceived me? I felt certain that they had not. If I had not known Mr and Mrs Peckover so well I might have thought that they were trying to poison one another or that they had made a suicide pact; but I had lived with them for six weeks. The idea was preposterous. I told myself that I ought to know what was happening. I would ask them each separately the meaning of what I had chanced to see. I tackled Mr Peckover that evening. Without any beating about the bush I asked him what it was that he had put into his wife's tea.

For a moment he looked very embarrassed, and then, getting up from his chair, he began to pace up and down the room.

'I wondered,' he said, 'if you would ever notice anything. I hoped you wouldn't, because I know that, professionally speaking, my conduct is most irregular. I should certainly condemn it in another. It was

Barconal, one of these new analgesics of the barbitone group. You see, I realised from the first how much Mrs Peckover was suffering. She is very sensitive to pain, and though she tried to conceal it from me I was not deceived. I ventured on several occasions to suggest to Dr Bentwick, and it was very difficult, that more might be done in the way of sedatives. I am afraid he resented very much my interference, and so I just took the matter into my own hands. For over two months now she has been taking the drug, and I feel that I have been justified.

'But you mustn't speak of this to Mrs Peckover. If she knew, she wouldn't like to feel that she was acting in any way contrary to the wishes of her doctor and there is a special reason too. Mrs Peckover has become interested in faith healing and Christian Science. I believe that it has been a great source of comfort for her to feel that this increasing absence of pain has come as an answer to her faith. You won't interfere, will you? There is so little I can do for her; she has been just everything to me.'

Poor Mr Peckover was almost in tears. I did what I suppose nine people out of ten would have done: told him that he was perfectly right and spoke my mind about Dr Bentwick in language that was meant to shock.

I asked Mrs Peckover no questions next day, for I was busy asking myself if I had any right to question her. It wasn't to satisfy my curiosity but with the feeling that I might possibly be able to help two friends of whom I had got very fond that I eventually asked her what it was I had seen her put into her husband's cup of tea.

She looked at me with a sad little smile. 'Perhaps it's just as well,' she said, 'that you saw me do it. It is difficult to keep a secret; it weighs on your mind, and I've sometimes even envied the Roman Catholics their confessional. Of course our minister is very kind. I'm so glad he is wrapped up in the League of Nations – it's a noble cause; and all these efforts he is making to get hold of the young people and show them that religion means something, I feel it quite a privilege to be a member of his church. But of course he is a very busy man with all these committees and the sale of work for the Boys' Club coming off in a fortnight's time. You won't tell Mr Peckover if I speak to you about what had been on my mind? He is not, you know, a very strong character. It may be that it is because he is so scrupulous and conscientious that he has become too much a man of habits. Just take as an example the way in which for the last two months he hasn't once missed taking his cup of tea with me three times a day. When I first began to be ill I could see how worried poor Walter was. He used to get up at night and make me hot drinks, then he had trouble with his assistants, too, and I could see the strain was beginning to tell on him. He began to use stimulants. He said nothing to me about it, of course, but I knew, and I knew that they were getting a stronger hold on him than he realised. Then one day I saw an advertisement in a paper about' – and here Mrs Peckover blushed – 'about a cure for drunkenness. It could be taken in your tea without anyone knowing anything about it. Of course, if Walter could have had faith, even if he could have believed in himself a little more, I know from my own experience that he could have conquered. Well, I wrote up to the address given and got the medicine. At first I was afraid it was just one of those quack remedies that Walter is always declaiming against. But it has come up to all my expectations. Walter is a different man altogether, as you can see by the way he has taken up this correspondence course. Dear Walter. It has been a real pleasure to him. Last week the principal wrote personally to say that his work was full of promise and suggested that he might like to take a supplementary course on applied psychology at a reduced fee. It was a most kind letter. Oh, I'm a lucky woman. I think of Walter and Mrs Greg and you, and all our friends, and every day when I think I've counted all my blessings I find a new one.'

I am a case-hardened, unemotional, middle-aged nurse, but I was almost crying when Mrs Peckover had finished.

Three weeks later she died very peacefully in her sleep. When I said goodbye to Mr Peckover he asked me to be sure to give him a call whenever I happened to be in Bawlston and I said I would, though I knew how little likelihood there was of my ever seeing that now completely desolate suburb again. He had stood the shock of his wife's death, for which of course he had long been prepared, far better than I expected, but I dreaded the reaction. A week after I left I wrote to him enclosing a box containing tablets of the remedy Mrs Peckover had used. He wasn't an analytical chemist. I said they were an excellent tonic recommended to me by a very distinguished doctor, and I besought him for his wife's sake to give them a good trial. I told him, too, how they were to be taken. I got a very grateful letter in reply. He told me that he was thinking of selling the business, and going to live with a niece who kept a general store in a village near Colchester. His knowledge and experience, he said, would come in very useful to her, and though he had no intention of starting business again as a chemist, he thought there was an opening for patent medicines. He was taking my tonic regularly. It had done him good and somehow he had begun to look forward once again to his cup of tea.

I don't want an experience like that again; it's too shaking. Poor Mrs Peckover and her belief in faith that was no faith; poor Walter and his pride in attaining a self-mastery that was only an illusion.

But when the world and all that's behind it and in it seem black, I tell myself that self-respect and self-mastery are not everything, that faith and belief in the power of prayer are not so wonderful as what we call the ordinary love of two apparently very ordinary people.

Euphemia Witchmaid

I can't make out his handwriting,' said Miss Cruikshanks. 'It's a most difficult hand. It looks like Mrs Witchmaid and the name of the house The Mussets, or is it Murrels? The place is Colton Bramloe. All impossible names. You had better take the letter – I have made a copy of it. A medical case evidently, but why couldn't Dr Pennyfather be a little more explicit? He wants a really experienced nurse – I don't often pay compliments, as you know, so make the most of that – and he will meet you at Goldstone station and give you his instructions. If you catch the 12.10 from Liverpool Street,' she added, turning over the pages of the time-table, 'you will arrive at Goldstone soon after four – two changes. Oh, and about Dr Pennyfather. He is an old St Christopher's man, and swears by our nurses. He is well over seventy, a little cantankerous but very wide awake. Goodbye, nurse; you'll have to hurry with your packing.'

Altogether a nice beginning to a birthday. I shouldn't be able to go with Nurse Harrison to see Maisie Todhunter and Barney O'Gorman draw laughter and tears and incredible salaries in the new film at the Pompeian. I shouldn't be in for the midday post by which I hopefully expected to receive letters from my three nieces (you can't count on nephews), the laundry wouldn't have come back, and nearly every pair of stockings I possessed wanted mending.

But I'm an old campaigner and by twelve o'clock I had secured a corner seat in the train at Liverpool Street, some ham sandwiches, and a copy of the *Prattler* to warm me with righteous indignation at the busy lives of idle people. It was a fine October day with a touch of frost in the air, and soon after my first change the country became interesting. I knew very little of Essex.

We were only five minutes late at Goldstone. There was no one resembling the mental picture I had made of Dr Pennyfather on the platform, so I got my trunk out of the van, and gave up my ticket to the porter, hoping to find him in his car outside.

There was a solitary car drawn up at the station approach containing two churns of milk, a farmer, and a farmer's wife. There was a groom with a dogcart who had evidently called for some parcels and whom the porter addressed as Jim, but nowhere was there anyone resembling an elderly cantankerous doctor in search of a really experienced nurse.

I went back into the station and asked the station-master if he had seen Dr Pennyfather. He knew him, of course; he had seen him only that morning. If I were waiting for Dr Pennyfather, and if Dr Pennyfather had promised to call for me, he would advise my sitting down in the waiting-room for a bit. No, there wasn't a fire, but I should have the place to myself. I preferred the less depressing solitude of the station approach.

Ten minutes passed, a quarter of an hour, and there was no sign of Dr Pennyfather. My patience was exhausted. I asked the station-master how far it was to Colton Bramloe. It appeared that it was a matter of from five to six miles. Could I get a car? There was a garage, he told me, just round the corner, where I could inquire.

Ten minutes later I was seated in an antiquated saloon car with my trunk strapped perilously on the luggage carrier, and with a driver who knew Colton Bramloe but had never heard of Mrs Witchmaid, or The Mussets.

We reached the village, a pretty little place with a fine old church that seemed to be in the grounds of the Hall, where the driver stopped to make inquiries. We had to go back the way we had come for half a mile, take the first turning to the right, and then follow a narrow lane, again to the right, and The Mussets would be the second house we should meet.

It looked as if it had once been a small farmhouse, but whoever had restored it knew his business. The driver unstrapped my trunk and carried it up the stone-flagged path. 'That will be eleven shillings, miss,' he said. 'It's been a lovely day.' That made it twelve shillings.

Reluctantly I parted with them, rang the bell, and watched the driver manoeuvre his car round, taking advantage of an open gate that led into a field of stubble. When I had rung a second time the car was disappearing down the lane. The Mussets was undoubtedly very charming, but The Mussets was also most annoyingly deaf. I was just about to ring for the third time when I heard steps approaching from the path that led to the garden, and turned to greet a lady who was carrying a big bunch of white Japanese anemones.

She looked at me and my trunk – capacious but not a thing of beauty – as if she were rather surprised to see us, and I lost no time in introducing myself.

'But this is very queer,' she said with a smile. 'This is The Mussets and I am Mrs Witchmaid. There's nothing whatever the matter with me though. I'm as fit as a fiddle. Dr Pennyfather must have made a mistake. But come inside; you must be cold and hungry after your ride, and I'm sure you'd like a cup of tea.'

Mrs Witchmaid left me in the drawing-room. I felt that my luck was entirely out. When members of our profession get low-spirited we console ourselves in the belief, generally true, that at any rate we are wanted. In the present circumstances this hardly seemed to be the case. I wished that general practitioners in country districts would retire at the age of seventy before their memory failed. In the meantime it seemed that I should not be without my cup of tea, and I was thankful for what my old mother calls journeying mercies.

Mrs Witchmaid was back in less than five minutes with the tray.

'My daily help has gone,' she said, 'but she left everything ready,' and then she burst out laughing. 'I can't help it,' she said, 'you must excuse me. I haven't got over my surprise at seeing a nurse in uniform – you are from St Christopher's, aren't you? – standing with an immense trunk on the door-step. Now, do tell me – I'm longing to know – was I a confinement?'

I joined her in laughing. The ice was broken.

'You were intriguingly vague,' I answered, drawing Dr Pennyfather's letter from my handbag. 'A medical case about which he would enlighten me, presumably when he met me in the car, which,' I concluded, 'he never did.'

'Oh, do let me see!' she said, and I gave the letter to her. 'What an abominable hand he writes! Of course, I know Dr Pennyfather well. He treated me for a sprained ankle six weeks ago, and only last Monday he dropped in with a present of aubretias for the rock garden and stayed for tea. What can the old dear have meant?'

She sat there with the paper in her hand, frowning; a charming figure, fair-haired, dressed in black which set off her bright yellow hair – yes, yellow, not golden – which she wore in thick coils about her ears.

'I can only think,' she said, 'that he has made some perfectly absurd blunder. I can assure you, nurse, that there is absolutely nothing the matter with me, except a cough which I have had the last ten days and which is yielding to treatment. That sounds professional.

'Feel my pulse,' she went on, putting my hand in hers. 'No, go on, feel it. There's no dot and carry about that. I won't put out my tongue at a guest – it would be rude. But you will notice that I have eaten two slices of cake while you have been eating one, and it's an excellent cake, too. I made it myself. Nor am I a secret drug addict. Look at my eyes. You can see my arms if you like – there are no telltale puncture marks. You can percuss me and auscultate me and get me to whisper ninety-nine. The fact remains, I am as sound as a bell and that you have come to the wrong house. Not that I am going to drive you away. You can't possibly go at this hour of the evening. You must spend the night here – that's obvious. I shall be glad of your company.'

Of course I demurred. 'The only thing it seems to me I can do,' I said, 'is to get in touch with Dr Pennyfather. Are you on the telephone?'

'I wish I was. But there's a telephone in the village at the post office, and the postmistress by good fortune happens to be very deaf. We will walk down together when you have had a second slice of cake – it *is* good, isn't it? – and we shall catch Dr Pennyfather before he sees his surgery patients. You'll have to give me a hand with the trunk though – we can't leave it reposing on the doormat.'

In the autumn dusk we made our way to the village, following this time a footpath that skirted the stubble fields. I was glad of the walk and found Mrs Witchmaid an entertaining companion. At the post office, by shouting into the ear of the old lady behind the counter she managed at last to make her understand that I wished to telephone, and I was shown into a stuffy little back room. I hunted out Dr Pennyfather's number in the directory and soon got my call through.

An agitated voice – that of a maid, I gathered – replied to my request to speak to Dr Pennyfather.

'If you please, ma'am,' she said, 'you can't. The doctor had an accident this morning; he was run into by a motor coach and they've taken him to the cottage hospital at Kelvington. They say he's fractured his skull. Mrs Pennyfather left two hours ago.'

Here was a pretty kettle of fish. I asked if he had an assistant or partner. They were non-existent. I asked if by any chance she could tell me if Dr Pennyfather had been expecting a nurse that day for any of his patients. She did not know. Finally I asked her who would be looking after his patients while he was in hospital. Again she could not tell me, but supposed it would be either Dr Dodd of Goldstone or Dr MacLaren of King's Abbot.

When I rejoined Mrs Witchmaid I thanked my lucky stars that I was not in charge of Dr Pennyfather's telephone that night.

'Good night, Mrs Buxton,' said my companion to the postmistress. 'And try that embrocation for the lumbago. It cured mine.'

'Good night, Mrs Witchmaid,' she answered, 'and thank you kindly for the information.'

Outside in the street I told her the result of my conversation.

'But how awful!' she said. 'Poor old Dr Pennyfather! The buses shouldn't be allowed on these narrow roads. He is a most careful driver. And dear old Mrs Pennyfather, what will she do? She's only just recovering from a serious operation.'

We had gone nearly a quarter of a mile when I stopped.

'I ought to have phoned for a car to take me back,' I said.

'Nonsense,' Mrs Witchmaid replied. 'You are spending the night with me. I thought that had been all fixed up. Besides, it would be too late to get back tonight in any case, unless you wanted to arrive at Liverpool Street on the stroke of midnight. I'll send my daily maid down to the village first thing after breakfast and you can catch the ten o'clock train from Goldstone.'

Well, if Mrs Witchmaid was willing to have me I was willing enough to stay.

'The mattress in the spare bedroom is aired,' she said, 'and to show that you are really not putting me out, you shall make up the bed while I get supper ready.'

We had a simple but excellent supper. Mrs Witchmaid described to me in detail how her establishment was run.

'When strangers come along the lane,' she said, 'they naturally admire The Mussets and think how lucky the people who live there must be. I am lucky because I shouldn't be able to carry on if it were not for a little house behind the orchard at the bottom of the garden, where my gardener lives. He had the sense to marry an excellent cook, who has brought up a family of three daughters, exceedingly plain but very capable girls. Mrs Jackson comes in every day to do for me. She brings a daughter with her when I have guests or if any extra work has to be done. It would be difficult to keep resident maids in a place like this. As it is, I consider the arrangement perfect. I'm not nervous, I don't mind sleeping alone, I enjoy housework, as every educated woman should do – it's really a matter of careful planning and a well-thought-out routine – and I'm practically a vegetarian, which simplifies things enormously. In the end, however, it all comes back to the Jacksons. The house should be called The Jacksons if it did not sound so ugly. No, there's no need to wash up. We'll just stack the things in the kitchen. Mrs Jackson will see to them in the morning.'

After supper we sat in the drawing-room and talked. I found myself deep in gossip about St Christopher's which Mrs Witchmaid seemed to find highly entertaining, and she told me all about the inner work- ings of the village institute, which according to her furnished a most valuable vent for intrigue, malice, and all uncharitableness.

Then she played some Handel, to purge herself, as she expressed it, of all cynicism, and at ten o'clock lighted me to bed, bringing with her a hot-water bottle. I shall always think kindly of Mrs Witchmaid. She is the only 'patient' I have ever had who thought of providing her nurse with a hot-water bottle in the month of October.

I got into bed, thinking that after all I had spent a very happy birthday. It was entirely due to Mrs Witchmaid. Charming women are rare; thoroughly capable women are rare. Mrs Witchmaid was both, and I, at any rate, was capable of acknowledging it. The house was very still after the endless noise of the East End. A few bouts of coughing from Mrs Witchmaid's room at the far end of the corridor, a few hoots from owls searching for their food by night, and the rustle of poplars in the wind. I fell asleep before half past ten, slept like a top, and was only woken by Mrs Witchmaid's knocking at the door.

'It's half past seven, nurse,' she said. 'Breakfast will be ready at eight. Tell me, do you like tea or coffee?'

We were not quite so talkative at breakfast.

'I need warming up,' said Mrs Witchmaid, 'like the car I used to have. I suppose it's because there's Scotch blood in me. Scotch people, I've noticed, always improve as the day grows older, just as they ripen with age. I've sent Mrs Jackson down to the village to see about the car. It ought to be here in half an hour. You must let me pay for it, of course.'

I pointed out to her that my expenses would be paid through the hospital. Miss Cruikshanks would have just the sort of problem she enjoyed in deciding under what heading to enter them. Probably she would have to open an entirely new account in her ledger which the auditors would challenge.

'This,' I added, 'will take her mind off her work, and when her mind is off her work we nurses live in peace.'

'You must come down and see me again,' said Mrs Witchmaid, when the car had arrived and the trunk had been strapped on. 'Come down not with a trunk but with a large suitcase. Goodbye, and make my abject apologies to the sheepshanks lady.'

Arrived back at St Christopher's I made my report to a bewildered superintendent, not so bewildered, however, that she did not consult the timetable and verify, in the politest and most natural way, my statement about the impossibility of catching a train that arrived before midnight. [She always tells herself that she is responsible for the moral welfare of over two hundred girls.]

'Altogether most extraordinary,' she said. 'I can't understand it. And I don't know how I can charge your services to Mrs Witchmaid. It will require a lot of thinking about. Poor Dr Pennyfather; I'm most sorry to hear about his accident. I can't help thinking that his mind must have been a little confused. You ought, you know, to have telephoned to me for instructions from the post office, but we'll say no more about that. You will report for night duty this evening. I think that's all.'

St Christopher's is one of those hospitals where the outside staff work in the wards in the intervals between cases. The idea, entirely erroneous, is that it keeps them fresh.

But none the less, thanks to Mrs Witchmaid, I had had a happy birthday.

Three days later I read the notice of Dr Pennyfather's death. I never heard from Mrs Witchmaid again; I hardly expected to, nor did I ever revisit The Mussets.

But after an interval of seven years I did see Colton Bramloe. I had been nursing an old gentleman who lived in that part of the country. He was interested in archaeology, and one afternoon we went over in the car to Colton Bramloe to see the church. While he was discussing with the vicar some mural paintings that had recently been brought to light, I wandered about the churchyard. It was there that I unexpectedly came across a simple headstone that set me wondering. This was the inscription:

Sacred to the Memory

of

EUPHEMIA WITCHMAID

who departed this life on October 22, 1923,

aged 72 years

I wondered, because 22nd October was my birthday, and on 22nd October 1923 I had spent the night at The Mussets, alone, as I thought, with Mrs Witchmaid.

An old man was busy in one corner of the graveyard, raking up the leaves.

'Mrs Witchmaid,' I said to him. 'I have just been looking at her grave. I knew a Mrs Witchmaid once who lived at The Mussets, but she wasn't an old lady.'

'Ah,' he said, 'she would be young Mrs Witchmaid, old Mrs Witchmaid's daughter-in-law, the widow of Captain Witchmaid. We were all sorry when she left to go to America. She hadn't what you might call an easy job living with the old lady. Tempers don't improve with age,' he added with a smile. 'And I'm a married man myself.

'Yes, the old lady went off quite sudden at the end, though she'd been ill for a long time. It was just about the time Dr Pennyfather died. A very clever man was Dr Pennyfather.'

I should have liked to listen to his gossip, but my patient had come out of the church and was shaking hands with the vicar. He must have found me a silent enough companion during the drive back, for I was trying to picture what exactly had happened.

I pictured a disagreeable old woman standing in the way of a comparatively young woman whose life was still before her. She is ill, and the doctor is at a loss to understand why she is not making the progress she should make. As a matter of precaution and to set his mind at rest, he arranges that the nursing shall be taken out of young Mrs Witchmaid's hands. He himself will meet the nurse and put her quietly on her guard. Then in the early afternoon of the day of my arrival young Mrs Witchmaid hears that Dr Pennyfather has had an accident that will almost certainly prove fatal. She doesn't want a nurse in the house, but how can she get rid of her? And what exactly did Dr Pennyfather say when he wrote to engage the nurse? Obviously she must find out. It wouldn't do to turn the nurse away on the doorstep. Far better to be friendly to her and gain her confidence. There are no gossiping neighbours at The Mussets, no gossiping maids.

Mrs Jackson, if there was a Mrs Jackson, need never see the nurse, and old Mrs Witchmaid's room is in a different part of the house. She is usually quiet enough and she has hardly any cough. So she receives me with open-hearted kindness; she reads Dr Pennyfather's letter, which to her relief she finds is entirely noncommittal; she goes with me to the post office, and feigns complete surprise when she hears of his accident.

And some time in the night old Mrs Witchmaid dies. I depart first thing in the morning. If Mrs Jackson knows I have slept the night there, and of course she need never have known, it won't matter. There is no point in having a nurse to look after a dead woman.

There is a case against Mrs Witchmaid, but I have no intention of inviting anyone to follow it up. Personally I liked the woman and I am quite prepared to believe that old Mrs Witchmaid died a natural death, that her daughter-in-law's absence of grief was natural, that she had a natural genius for romancing. It is natural, too, that a charming and efficient woman should have the benefit of the doubt.

Still, of course, one wonders.

Ripe for Development

My nephew, the journalist who tells me that if I follow his instructions I shall soon be able to write a really good story, is quite emphatic that this tale of Mr Gossington's macaw is not the sort of thing an editor wants.

According to him it is altogether too vague. The setting is wrong, there are too many loose ends, and it lacks a fitting climax. I have made too much of the bird. His advice is to put it away in a drawer for two years and then to write it again with a view to the introduction of some love interest. He ends up his letter by enclosing an article of his that has just been accepted, *Should Footballers Marry?* 'It's tripe, of course,' he says, 'but the point is that it's what the public wants, especially when a wide-awake editor publishes it on the day after Sandy MacAlister, the centre-forward of Oldingham Wanderers, was divorced.'

Well, I'm not going to follow his advice. My story may be vague; so are sunsets, and I find nothing wrong with them. The setting of which he complains is perfectly natural, and as to my making too much of the bird, the poor young man fails to see that Mr Gossington's macaw is as essential to the story as the albatross to the *Ancient Mariner*.

An outer suburb, well served by frequent trains and Green Line buses, a village that once had charm, but whose streets had been pulled about to make room for new shops and garages that elbowed out the last century, a big new housing estate and a stately mansion in a park ripe for development – such was Bragenham, where Mrs Oldershaw, ill with double pneumonia, still preferred to live. Her house was called Winterset. It was in Clarendon Glade in the middle of the Clarendon Park estate, and was surrounded by houses that anyone would have said were very like Winterset before it was pointed out to them by the agent that each being specially designed by the estate architect had an individuality of its own. Nearly all the trees had been spared, though nearly all the trees had been lopped, and none of the houses were numbered. They all had garages and lawns and sunk gardens and bird-baths. They were easily run. Unless, of course, you had double pneumonia and two nurses, who, according to the cook, made more trouble than they were worth.

I hadn't been on a case with Cardew before, but we were old friends who got on well in double harness. She took day duty, I night. The two hours every day in the open air which St Christopher's insists that its nurses must take, did not mean, as it so often does, expostulating with harassed girls over books at the circulating library or the exercise of an objectionable dog. Mrs Oldershaw was too ill to read and she had no pets. The shops in Bragenham had no attractions, so when Cardew and I took our walks abroad it was either along the admirably laid-out roads of the Clarendon Park Estate, Clarendon Drive, Clarendon Avenue, Clarendon Close, and all the other roads called after trees, which, as I have said before, were always lopped, or into the still lovely woods of poor doomed Bragenham Place.

We soon came to the conclusion that Bragenham was not the sort of district in which we should ever want to live. When I retire I want to get my roots into something. It doesn't matter a bit about having light sandy soil or a high church vicar, nor do I want a place from which you can easily run up to town for the sales. Give me somewhere where the local milkman knows everybody, where four different laundry vans don't call for the washing of four adjoining houses on the same afternoon, where Cedar Grove doesn't deal with the Home and Empire Stores, Brocklehurst with John Plenty & Sons, and Rookery Nook with Universal Providers. No one living in Bragenham could have had any roots. It was neither fish, flesh, fowl, nor good red herring. Cardew summed up her impressions of the place by saying that everybody seemed to be shut in. They all lived their own lives behind hedges which they watched every day to see if they were growing taller, and didn't seem to care to know who their neighbours were, nor what happened to them. New houses were being built; houses that last year or the year before were new, had notices up that they were for sale. You came and you went. Since nearly everybody had a car, their friends weren't just round the corner, but at Wimbledon, or Esher, or Kew, or Weybridge.

There was one house, The Laurels, that we often used to pass on our walks, that was unlike all the others. It had originally been the stables of Clarendon House. Clarendon House itself had been pulled down, but the stables had been rather cleverly converted. A long, narrow strip of garden, bounded on one side by a high brick wall and on the other by a tall holly hedge, separated it from the road. At the back there seemed to be another garden, walled too, doubtless the old kitchen garden of the mansion. Rather an attractive place, a little gloomy perhaps, but with a character of its own.

Cardew discovered it and told me about it, but it was I who first saw the macaw. The sun was shining brightly, and someone had thoughtfully placed the cage on a stool a few yards from the gate in full view of passers-by.

It was a magnificent bird with plumage of blue and green with a touch of orange, and I stopped to admire it. A talker, too.

'I can't get out,' he said pathetically, his head cocked on one side. 'I can't get out. Scratch poor Poll.'

I should have liked to oblige, but if he couldn't get out, I couldn't, with politeness, come in, and so we parted. I told Cardew to look out for my parrot when she took her afternoon walk, to admire his colour scheme, and to tell me whether our hideous blue uniform wouldn't be improved with a touch of orange or green, but she reported that the bird was no longer there, only a very stout, bald-headed gentleman, rather like Count Fosco in *The Woman in White*, perched precariously on a pair of steps doing something to a crimson rambler.

Of course next day I had to see whether Cardew's mental picture of Wilkie Collins's superb villain corresponded with mine. To my surprise it did, provided that one can imagine Count Fosco in plus-fours. He was giving a lump of sugar to a fierce-looking Alsatian, and the macaw, no longer a prisoner, but still protesting 'I can't get out!' was perched on the handle of the garden roller to which he was attached by a thin silver chain.

After that we often used to meet Fosco when we took our solitary walks; sometimes he was unaccompanied, more often the Alsatian was with him, and occasionally he was to be seen with a lady with an aquiline nose – she was not unlike the macaw – whom we presumed to be his wife.

Cardew, who is really an exceedingly pretty girl and in consequence receives from the superintendent more than her fair share of pneumonia cases where she has to concentrate on nursing practically unconscious patients, told me that when she met Fosco by himself he always gave her a look that made her conscious of the fact that she was an Angel of Mercy. When his wife was with him it was more expressive of sympathetic and earnest regard.

'In my opinion,' she added, 'he is a really dangerous man. He may be stout, but I shouldn't be a bit surprised if he dances divinely, and he has a very fine forehead.'

'Which he was mopping with a blue silk handkerchief the only time I saw it,' I said; 'I should describe it as a teapot dome.'

From Miss Hillyard, the good-natured, ineffective little lady who from her cradle had been destined to be a companion-help, and who for years had been attached to Mrs Oldershaw, we learnt that Count Fosco's name was Mr Gossington. That and the fact that he was a recent resident formed the extent of her knowledge. Mrs Oldershaw had thought of calling on Mrs Gossington for a subscription to the League of Nations Union, but her illness had prevented it.

The next thing that happened was the wholly unexpected death of Mr Gossington's macaw, and in tragic circumstances, too, of which Cardew was an unwilling spectator. She was walking down the road behind a lady who was exercising a bad-tempered Irish terrier that refused to answer to the name of Patrick, when, as she passed The Laurels, the dog pushed open the gate and proceeded to investigate the garden. The macaw was on his perch to which he was attached by his silver chain. The bird evidently resented intruders, and began to expostulate. The dog leapt up at the perch, knocked it over, the macaw nipped its tail, there was an exhibition of what the fanciers call fur and feather, and by the time Cardew was running up the path, Mr Gossington was out of the house and down the path, and on the lawn between them lay the dead body of the parrot.

There followed an unholy row. Mr Gossington asked the lady why she did not keep her vicious beast under control. She replied by saying that Patrick, though high-spirited, was extraordinarily gentle, and that if garden gates were not properly shut it was only natural that dogs should come in. Both appealed to Cardew, whose sympathies were entirely with Mr Gossington.

When she left them he was holding the poor bird in his hand, trying to smooth the feathers of green and blue and orange while he gave vent to a stream of impassioned invective.

'I'd like to have heard what the upshot was,' said Cardew, 'but I was afraid that they would ask me for my name and address in view of legal proceedings. It was a wholly unprovoked attack on the part of the dog. That poor bird, always saying "I can't get out", and then to be worried to death when it was enjoying its liberty in the sunshine!'

When I saw Mr Gossington on the following day he was walking along rapidly with his Alsatian at his heels. He looked up as I passed and gave me an ugly scowl. I was a woman and I probably reminded him of the owner of the dog.

Three days later I was to meet him again. As I passed by The Laurels I noticed two little boys standing disconsolately at the gate. It seemed that the ball they had been playing with had gone into the garden and that they were afraid to go after it, because the old gentleman who kept the parrot didn't like little boys. It was all the more provoking because they were practically certain that they could see it in a bed of wallflowers five yards or so from the house. I offered to get it for them, and so for the first and last time entered the garden of The Laurels.

I walked straight to where the ball was lying and had just picked it up, when from somewhere within the house, I heard repeated over and over again those words with which I had become so familiar, 'I can't get out, I can't get out.' I could have sworn that it was the parrot that was speaking, but the parrot was dead.

Thoroughly startled, I looked up at the windows to see the bald-headed, smooth-faced Mr Gossington gazing down at me. He looked as surprised as I must have appeared to him. I only saw him for a moment, and then he vanished. I wasted no time in picking up the ball and making a dignified retreat. When people criticise the St Christopher's uniform, I always maintain that when viewed from behind it at least possesses dignity.

I saw Cardew that evening before going on duty and told her what had happened. She is not very quick at grasping a point. She said, 'How queer', but wherein the queerness really lay she did not fully understand until I explained it to her.

The macaw had said, 'I can't get out', and the macaw was dead. But I had heard the same words repeated in the same intonation coming from somewhere inside The Laurels.

Now, though there may be a certain amount of evidence for ghosts, I have never heard of the ghost of a bird. It was exceedingly unlikely that Mr Gossington possessed a second parrot which we had never seen. When parrots talk, they are either taught to talk or they mimic what they have heard.

They mimic what they have heard. That would explain a good deal. Suppose there really was somebody in The Laurels who couldn't get out. The parrot would learn to say what that somebody said. And moreover, just supposing that Mr Gossington didn't want attention drawn to the somebody, the macaw's intelligence would come in very useful. Neighbours and passers-by would soon get to associate anything they heard with that delightful bird. He was almost thrust on their notice, on his perch or in his cage, placed so conveniently near the gate of that long, secluded garden.

We told each other how shut-in that garden was and that there seemed to be a walled-in garden at the back too. The whole impression that Bragenham had made on us came back with renewed force, a place where no one had any roots, where people did not know each other, where houses were constantly changing hands, where there was no gossip because nobody minded other people's business or, indeed, cared to know what it was.

It looked very much as if we two were not alone in Bragenham in feeling shut in. But what could we do about it? There was a time when Cardew and I, in our desire to know what was passing behind those all too solid walls, propounded a wild scheme of writing to the window-cleaners under the forged signature of Mr Gossington, and seeing what happened if and when arriving punctually at the hour appointed, they were turned away. I almost wish we had done. And yet Mr Gossington might be a perfectly humane man, acting in a perfectly humane manner; he probably was. One is apt to forget the well-concealed tragedies of the middle class.

Try, however, as I would to regard the matter in the light of a cheerful sunny aspect facing south (Bragenham had taught me to see everything through a house-agent's eyes), whenever I passed The Laurels it appeared to me sinister.

Then one day something happened that made it even more so. A motor-hearse was drawn up outside The Laurels, and down the path four men in black were carrying a coffin. There was only one closed car, into which stepped Mr and Mrs Gossington.

Who had died at The Laurels? Nobody at Winterset knew. They were not patients of Dr Conon or his partners, and when Cardew, happening by chance to meet Nurse Brampton who was looking after an appendix for the opposition firm, asked her to make a few discreet inquiries (as if poor old Brampton was ever anything else but discreet), we found that Drs Leslie, Hawthorne, and Witherspoon knew nothing about the people who lived and died at The Laurels.

There was no burial at the local cemetery.

Mr and Mrs Gossington were back next day, but a week later, my last week with Mrs Oldershaw, who was now well on the high road to recovery and St Leonards, the Gossingtons were gone.

Yet another notice-board appeared to say that this highly desirable residence was to be sold.

Was that all? Not quite.

About a year later I was sitting in a dentist's waiting-room, turning over the pages of that silly society paper, *Dry Point*, when a photograph chanced to catch my eye. It appeared under the heading 'Lucky Mortals who have found the Sun', and underneath in smaller type were the words: 'Mrs Binney Hartigan and friend have found it at Cannes.'

Mrs Binney Hartigan, of whom of course I had never heard, was an elderly lady seated in a magnificently appointed-bath-chair. By her side was walking a little woman who might or might not have been Mrs Gossington. But there could be no doubt about who it was who was pushing the bath-chair. That tall stout gentleman so distinguishedly dressed, whose charming smile the camera had caught as he made some remark to a passing friend, was Count Fosco, was Mr Gossington of The Laurels.

That was clear, and it was equally obvious that Mrs Binney Hartigan (she began to take on the features of a parrot) couldn't get out.

On silent wheels another victim was being pushed along, by a gentleman who knew exactly where he wished to take her.

Well, that is the story which my nephew wishes me to rewrite in two years' time. Of course there are any number of loose ends, and it can well be argued that what the parrot says isn't evidence. But as it is, I find it extraordinarily suggestive. And if anyone who reads it happens to live in a place like Bragenham, I beseech them to use their imagination. For they are living not in ordinary surroundings but, if they only knew it, in extraordinary surroundings where almost anything might happen.

Let them start a townswomen's guild, let them start a revolution. Anything is better than being shut in.

Atmospherics

That commonest of phrases in a nurse's vocabulary, 'the sick-room', is a rather curious one. You think of it as meaning the room where your patient lies ill, a room that has to be kept carefully ventilated and warmed, that has its daily toilet to be performed, until it almost seems that the room itself is ill. Its eyes, the windows, are not opened so widely as they would be in health. There are bright flowers on the table, carefully removed at night, but there is the flush of fever about the roses, the pallor of disease in the hyacinths and tulips. Books and clothes are carefully put away. A thermometer hangs on the wall, and when you enter you move quietly and talk softly because it is a sick-room.

Just as such a room differs from an ordinary bedroom, so a house in which there is illness shows subtle changes, felt rather than observed, which come from the character of the people who dwell in it. There are restless houses, peaceful houses, houses that embody a spirit of heroism or of fear. Sometimes one senses the atmosphere as soon as one has set foot on the threshold.

I had come to the Red House to nurse Mrs Darling. She was an old lady who had recently undergone a serious operation, more serious indeed than she knew. She lived with her son, Philip Darling, and his wife Mary, whose name was the same as her own. The fourth member of the household was old Mrs Darling's daughter Miriam.

The first impression I received was that whatever else the Darlings might be they were in every sense of the word a united family.

The head of the household was indeed a remarkable woman. The operation she had undergone had left her physically weak – she could hardly walk beyond the garden – but mentally she was wonderfully alert; far more interested in the doings of the outside world than either her daughter or daughter-in-law, and at the same time far more interested in individuals.

She made little attempt to disguise her pride in her son. Philip Darling was a solicitor. He was a man of about forty, distinguished-looking rather than handsome, with beautiful manners and a rather attractive half-cynical smile. He was a well-known antiquarian, so old Mrs Darling informed me, and his history of the town, the first volume of which had recently appeared, had been acclaimed by the discerning as a model of its kind.

Miriam Darling, his sister, lacked the family's good looks but none of their good nature. She ran a troop of Girl Guides and managed the committee of the Townswomen's Guild, where her slight deaf-ness stood her in good stead since criticism had to be outspoken if it were to receive attention.

I have kept the younger Mrs Darling to the last because it was she who seemed least at home in the Red House. I don't think I had ever seen a lovelier woman, with her tall figure and face of classical beauty crowned with red hair. Her husband was obviously devoted to her; it was equally clear that old Mrs Darling and Miriam thought the world of her, but while responding to their kindness she some-how succeeded in keeping herself gently aloof. That glorious excuse, the artistic temperament, may have been responsible for it, for I was given to understand that the younger Mrs Darling was an exception-ally good musician.

And now to describe the background of the picture, the Red House. It stood in a quiet street in a sleepy little market town, a beautiful Queen Anne house with a long, walled garden at the back and a lawn overshadowed by a cedar. Beyond the garden an orchard and a small paddock sloped down to a sluggish stream. Three generations of Darlings had lived in the house and had left their imprint in the furniture and the pictures which hung on the walls. In nearly every room one was conscious of a restful feeling of continuity, as if the generations were all at home. The old cook had been with Mrs Darling for forty years; the elderly parlourmaid was the daughter of Mrs Darling's nurse, and the young housemaid was the niece of Dimmity the gardener. All were devoted to Mrs Darling.

Illness, as I have said, attacks houses as it does people, but the strange thing was that though old Mrs Darling herself greeted pain with a smile and accepted her disabilities as if they were old friends instead of new and disagreeable acquaintances, though affection and consideration for one another was shown by every member of the family, the house was not a peaceful one to live in. Not to me at least. I had not been there three days when I felt that there was something

queer about the atmosphere of the place; at the end of the week, I
was sure that whatever it was that was queer was also wrong. Somehow the Red House didn't ring true. Perhaps it was just because it
was too good to be true. Anyhow I told myself that I had plenty to do
without bothering about vague impressions which to be indulged in
need a good income derived from tangible securities.

I have spoken of old Mrs Darling's kindness and consideration for
others. Let me give one or two examples, trivial in themselves but
significant in view of what happened later. There was the incident of
the gardener's cat. It was a wet morning. Young Mrs Darling and
Miriam had taken the car to call on a friend, and old Mrs Darling,
debarred from her usual walk in the garden, announced that she was
expecting two visitors to whom she had promised to show the house.
Imagine my surprise when Gertrude, the parlourmaid, ushered into
the morning-room a nervous little girl who was clasping in her arms
a big tortoiseshell cat.

Mrs Darling had a happy way with children. She stroked and
fondled the cat and tried to get it to lie down in a nest she made for it
among the cushions, talking all the while to the little girl until she
began to feel at ease in her strange surroundings. She explained
to me that Eva had never seen over the house, though of course
since her cousin worked there she had heard a great deal about it.
And though she, Mrs Darling, was always hearing about Eva's cat,
she had few opportunities of seeing it. The gardener's cottage was
beyond the range of her walks; her son and her daughter and her
daughter-in-law were all bird-lovers and had no use for cats at all.

'So I'm giving myself a pleasure,' she said, 'because I have always
been devoted to them, and I hope I'm giving Eva pleasure too. Now
come along, Eva, and I'll show you both the house. Some day,
perhaps, when you leave school and if your mother can spare you,
you might come and help Mrs Hawker in the kitchen, and learn how
to make wonderful cakes with icing on them.'

Of course I offered to accompany Mrs Darling, but the old lady
evidently wanted to be alone with the child. They made a charming
picture as they slowly climbed the stairs, Eva with one hand in Mrs
Darling's and the other clasping the cat. They were gone longer
than I expected, and even then the little girl was not allowed to
depart before she had eaten a large slice of sponge cake and drunk a
glass of milk.

'Some other day when we are by ourselves you must come again,
Eva,' she said as she bade her goodbye. 'And now, nurse,' she added,

turning to me, 'I must rest a little. I have walked rather more than I usually do, and I don't want the young people to see that I am tired. I don't think you had better say anything about our visitors.'

She was indeed a game old lady. She had been the perfect hostess to the little girl, who had obviously had the happiest of mornings. I couldn't help contrasting her next day with her daughter-in-law, who, despite the fact that she had been motoring in a closed car, came down to breakfast with streaming eyes and what looked like the beginning of a bad cold. It was all 'Mary dear' and 'darling Mary' until I could almost have shaken the woman. They were quite serious in suggesting that she ought to have stayed in bed for breakfast, while the presence of old Mrs Darling, who to my own knowledge had been awake half the night, was taken as a matter of course.

Despite her physical handicap, I hardly ever saw her idle. Young Mrs Darling was fond of doing *The Times* crossword puzzles last thing at night. Old Mrs Darling would stay up long beyond the time she ought to have been in bed in order to help her. There, I suppose, I was remiss, but with her strong will she was a difficult patient to manage, and I thought the obvious pleasure she took in making other people happy did her more good than a rigid conformity to hours. She took the same sort of pleasure in helping young Mrs Darling with a wonderful piece of embroidery until it became almost as much her handiwork as her daughter-in-law's, who seemed completely oblivious of the progress made whenever she was out of sight. It reminded me of my own mother's tact in teaching me how to embroider my first kettle-holder, when each morning I would wake up agreeably surprised at the amount of work I had put in on the preceding evening.

By the time I had been a fortnight at the Red House I had come to the conclusion that young Mrs Darling was being thoroughly spoiled. She was the centre of the picture, everything in the end was referred to her for approval or disapproval, and she stood there – sat there would be a more appropriate metaphor – and received their general obeisance with a gracious smile. I have no use for languishing tiger-lilies, but no sooner had I coined the phrase than I knew what was the disturbing element I had sensed in what ought to have been the peaceful atmosphere of the Red House. It centred in the younger Mrs Darling. It entered the room with her; it left when she left the room. And the spirit was one not of selfishness, of jealousy or pride, but of active malevolence.

There was, indeed, selfishness too. Old Mrs Darling was fond of music, young Mrs Darling was something more than an accomplished musician, yet she rarely played on the grand piano which her husband's mother had given her as a wedding present, though she would spend hours in the music-room of an elderly widow who lived in the town. It would have been the easiest thing in the world to have gratified the old lady. Young Mrs Darling apparently took no delight even in doing easy things.

It was the same, too, with young Mrs Darling's garden. I was given to understand that she was passionately devoted to gardening; her interest, however, was not in bright young annuals and hardy perennials but in the rearing of delicate and backward Alpines, in the higher education, as it were, of privileged plants. She had her special nurseries on the sloping ground at the top of the orchard which she visited in the manner of a critical inspector of schools. Everything was labelled; nothing was out of place, but it was her mother-in-law, unknown to her, who did the weeding, seated in a folding stool which I used to move about from one spot to another.

And now to describe the events of that memorable Thursday which illuminated the Red House with the sudden unexpectedness of a flash of lightning.

Miriam Darling had gone up to town by the early morning train to attend some committee meetings. Young Mrs Darling had on the previous day expressed her intention of spending Thursday in completing some water-colour drawings she was preparing for a local exhibition and in planting out a new consignment of Alpine plants. Old Mrs Darling, too, had made her plans. It appeared that she was very anxious that I should see the Norman church at Umbersley some fifteen miles away. She would take her rest before instead of after lunch, motor over to Umbersley in the afternoon, see the church, and then call on Mrs Rathbone, the wife of the vicar of Swidlington, who she felt sure would be delighted to give us tea, and would see that she had a little rest before returning. The expedition would be the longest she had undertaken since her operation. Mr Darling tried at first to dissuade her but she was evidently bent on going, and he gave a rather reluctant consent on condition that she should go to bed as soon as she got back. The weather at least was all that could be wished, a perfect October day with a keen nip in the air and an unclouded sky. We got to Umbersley soon after three. Mrs Darling proved to be exceedingly well informed about its history and took real delight in explaining to me the peculiarities of its architecture. We were on our way back to the car when she complained of a sudden pain.

'It's nothing serious,' she said, 'just a queer sort of feeling; I shall be better in a minute or two. I will just sit quietly in the car for a while and then we will think what we had better do.'

Mrs Darling was a most sensible old lady. Without any fuss she let me arrange the cushions and the rugs and, closing her eyes, allowed herself to relax. At the end of ten minutes she spoke.

'I am afraid we must give up the rest of our programme,' she said, 'and get back home as soon as possible. Morgan can stop at the first post office that has a telephone, so that you may ring up Mrs Rathbone and convey my apologies. I am sure she will understand. And I should like you, too, to ring up Mr Darling at the office, so that he will be at the Red House when we arrive. Don't alarm him. Just say that I found myself rather more tired by our little expedition than I expected to be and should be glad to see him as soon as possible when we get back, but only if it is convenient.'

We found a call office without difficulty, and I delivered my messages. I could hear that Mr Darling was alarmed, for it was unlike his mother to ask for even a slight attention. I did my best to reassure him, and he said that he would go round to the Red House straight away.

Mrs Darling spoke little on the drive back. I watched her carefully, uncertain what was the matter with her. There was a curious glint in her eye, her lips were firmly pressed together. Undoubtedly she was excited, but I do not think she suffered pain; it was more as if she were expecting some inevitable stroke.

We got to the Red House soon after four.

A car was drawn up outside.

'Mary must be having visitors,' said Mrs Darling when I had helped her out. 'That's a good thing. I was afraid she might feel we had all abandoned her. Who are the visitors, Gertrude?' she went on as the parlourmaid opened the door. 'Dr Sutherland? And when did Dr Sutherland arrive? Over an hour ago? And where is Dr Sutherland now? In the garden with Mr and Mrs Darling? Then kindly inform Mr Darling that I have come back and that I shall be waiting for him in the morning-room.'

'Don't you think you had better go upstairs and let me make you comfortable in bed?' I asked.

'Of course not, nurse. I am quite capable of gauging my own capabilities.'

She spoke almost in anger; her cheeks were flushed. Dr Sutherland, of whom I had never heard, was evidently not a congenial visitor. A couple of minutes later the door opened and Mr Darling came into the room. It was the first time that I had seen him appear flurried.

'Tell me you are feeling better, mother,' he said. 'I blame myself for ever allowing you to go.'

'Nonsense, Philip,' she replied. 'I am all right now, and my coming back at all events seems to have been opportune. Where is Mary and this Sutherland man? I may as well have a word with him now he is here.'

Again the door opened. Mary Darling entered the room, followed by one of the handsomest men I had ever seen.

'Mother, dear,' she said, 'I am so sorry you are not feeling so well. Dr Sutherland, I think, you have met before. He wanted just to pay his respects to you before leaving.'

'I am glad that he found someone to entertain him, at all events. You should have let us know, Dr Sutherland, that you were coming.'

There was a curiously strained atmosphere in the room. No one, with the possible exception of old Mrs Darling, seemed at ease. All, with the exception of her, were standing.

Then young Mrs Darling spoke, and as her mother-in-law turned towards her I received a shock. It was as if a veil had suddenly fallen from the older woman's face. Never had I seen a glance of such concentrated hatred.

'Dr Sutherland's visit was not unexpected,' said Philip's wife. 'I haven't been well lately; my asthma has been bothering me again. I didn't want to worry you, and knowing you would all be out I wired to Dr Sutherland asking him to call. And now, dear, hadn't nurse better see you safely upstairs?'

Was there or was there not an echo of Mrs Darling's malice in that last remark? It was a sensible one, at all events. At a sign from Mrs Darling I went over to the old lady. I could feel her arm tremble as she laid it in mine.

Late that evening young Mrs Darling and I sat talking by the drawing-room fire. My patient was comfortably asleep, for Mr Darling had insisted on calling in the doctor, who, finding her unusually excited and restless, had given her a hypnotic. The train by which Miriam was returning from town had no connection beyond Bletchingley Junction, and Mr Darling, instead of sending the chauffeur with the car, had offered to meet her himself, but before he left soon after tea he had taken me aside and asked if I would mind sitting up with his wife until they returned.

It was the first long talk I had had alone with Mrs Darling. As she sat in the big armchair opposite me, the firelight shining on her hair, I thought I had never seen a lovelier woman.

After talking trivialities for a while she threw aside her embroidery and lit a cigarette.

'I am going to unburden myself to you, nurse,' she said. 'We are not friends; somehow, despite the fact that you have been here over three weeks, we haven't had the opportunity of becoming friends. That may make it easier for me to talk. I value your judgment, and you will be able to consider things absolutely dispassionately. I don't know what you made of this afternoon's happenings. Would it be asking too much to tell me absolutely frankly what you thought of it all?'

This was indeed a facer. There are many occasions when I should have been overjoyed to say exactly what I felt about my patients and their relations, but this was hardly one.

'You have asked me a very difficult question,' I said at last, 'and, if I may say so, not a very fair one. But if you really want to know, I thought Mrs Darling was for some reason disagreeably surprised to find Dr Sutherland here.'

'Yes,' said young Mrs Darling, 'go on.'

I took the plunge.

'It looked as if you had taken advantage of the absence of the rest of us to arrange a meeting. What you said about consulting him about your asthma did not ring very true, and you certainly all seemed ill at ease.'

'As a matter of fact it wasn't true,' said Mary Darling. 'I told two lies this afternoon. That was one of them. The other was when I said that I had sent a telegram to Dr Sutherland. I never sent any telegram at all. Wait a minute,' she went on, 'and I'll try to explain. I saw a good deal of Dr Sutherland before I married Philip. If I hadn't fallen in love with Philip it's just conceivable that I might have married him. Philip knows all about it. He knows well enough that Hugh Sutherland could never come between us. The one who came between us is that awful old woman. Oh yes, I know it sounds absurd. Dear old Mrs Darling, kind old Mrs Darling, whose whole life is devoted to others, and who hates me like poison.

'She never wanted me to marry Philip, who of course is the apple of her eye. But Philip has something of his mother's obstinacy. She had to make the best of a bad job, and so she decided to kill me by kindness. The Red House ought to have been the happiest of homes. I'm awfully fond of Miriam, we understand each other thoroughly, and we each go our own way. I like the neighbourhood and I love the house and garden. It oughtn't to have been difficult for me to fit in. Heaven knows I tried. At first, not realising her hatred, I was rather touched at the way the old lady was always helping me, and since it seemed to give her pleasure I let her work at my embroidery, finish my crosswords, mend my stockings even. Then I found that I was gradually being squeezed out of everything, and that unless I took care I should soon be reduced to a mere cipher. Not a very pleasing prospect, you must admit. You know that horrible feeling when you have got asthma of fighting for air to breathe. It was like that. She helped me in the garden, though I don't believe she is really fond of flowers. I was squeezed out of the garden and started one of my own for Alpines at the top of the orchard, giving her to understand that this, at least, was to be mine. It isn't much of a garden, is it? How can it be when Mrs Darling so carefully weeds the wrong things – not, I imagine, when you were with her the other morning; she probably contented herself then with a general stirring up of the gentian roots. I expect you think that I am selfish because I never play the piano at home, when old Mrs Darling is so fond of music. But the piano – she gave it to me for a wedding present – is always getting out of tune. I found a damp duster inside it one day. I didn't say anything about it, for I knew that none of the maids could have left it there. Mrs Darling is quite a good enough musician to know the sort of music a good musician hates to play. That was the stuff she would ask me to reel off if she caught me alone in the drawing-room. She said it revived forgotten memories. For the sake of peace I put up with her petty persecutions; with a little practice one can make oneself insensitive to pinpricks. Then she hit upon another plan. Last Christmas she presented me with a magnificent fur coat. I have never worn furs, partly because I hate to think of trapped animals, partly because I have always believed that furs bring on my attacks of asthma. These did, in any case, but I had in common politeness to wear them, at least for a time. Then when it seemed folly to go on sacrificing my health I gave my reason, was fussed over and treated as a highly-strung neurotic, and Philip came in for a great deal of quiet understanding sympathy. Quiet understanding sympathy for your husband, nurse, cuts like a knife. Old Mrs Darling would have been an adept in that form of Chinese torture, death from a thousand cuts. Some chance remark of mine made soon after I had come to the Red

House, in the days when I believed in her sympathy, unexpectedly gave her another hold on me. I dislike cats. If I am in a room with cats or where cats have been, my chest gets wheezy and my eyes begin to stream. I expect you have met people like that. Well, there were no cats in the Red House, thank goodness, but on one occasion before she was ill I saw Mrs Darling inveigle the gardener's little daughter into the house. She had her cat with her. I believe she has often done it since.'

'As a matter of fact,' I said, 'the little girl and her cat were shown all over the house only ten days ago.'

'And I expect she would be perfectly charming to both of them. But to come to the events of today. I know now that her hatred for me has become an obsession. In a way it is a relief to realise that she is only partly responsible for her actions. I had just settled down to my painting, looking forward to a long afternoon free from interruption, when the maid brought me this telegram. You had better look at it for yourself.' She handed me a buff envelope addressed to Mrs Darling.

DELIGHTED TO COME [I read] EXPECT ME SOON AFTER THREE.

'I hadn't the slightest notion,' Mrs Darling went on, 'as to whom it was from. For all I knew it might be intended for my mother-in-law. You can imagine, then, my surprise when less than an hour later Hugh Sutherland was shown into the room. I was glad enough to see him, of course. However, we soon found that we were at cross purposes. He produced a telegram that he had received this morning; I got him to give it to me, and here it is.

CAN YOU COME OVER THIS AFTERNOON SHALL BE ALONE AM ANXIOUS TO SEE YOU SEND WIRE IN REPLY TO ARRIVE HERE NOT BEFORE 2.30 MARY DARLING.

'For a minute or two I was completely puzzled. Then I remembered that I had seen Mrs Darling talking to little Eva Dimmity in the garden this morning, and in a flash I saw through the plot she had laid. She still imagined that I was in love with Hugh Sutherland; she had no notion that Philip knew of that old affair, that he was the last person in the world to suspect me of disloyalty. Obsessed by her mad hatred of me, she thought she could poison his mind against me. In the garden Hugh Sutherland and I discussed what we should do. It seemed to us obvious that Mrs Darling would make an excuse of coming back before she was expected. She would count on our keeping the matter of the telegram quiet, you know. She would expect me to deny all knowledge of it. Then she in her turn would express complete ignorance. It would be her word against mine, the word of an old lady who has been trusted all her life, who could not tell a lie, against that uncertain quantity, the artistic temperament. So, since our telling the truth was part of the lying scheme on which she depended, I determined that I too would lie, that I would openly acknowledge the sending of the telegram. As for the rest, what you didn't see you can guess. Not quite all, perhaps. For I spoke to Eva Dimmity after supper. Mrs Darling had asked her to go to the post office for me, to send off a telegram. It was in a plain sealed envelope so that she did not read it, but when she handed it to the clerk at the counter who opened it, she saw that the words were written in block capitals. That's all,' said Mary Darling. 'I'm not the stuff that heroes are made of, nurse, and I didn't want you to misjudge me. The old lady and I understand each other now. I used to hate her. I have always admired her, and I have no doubt we shall establish some sort of armed truce.'

Next morning old Mrs Darling declared that she had had an excellent night, but the sparkle had gone from her eye and her movements too were listless. In the days that followed, however, her general health continued to improve, and when soon after that memorable Thursday I left, Mrs Darling and Miriam had made their arrangements for wintering in Torquay, where in the following spring she died. I often think of the old lady. I believe I really liked her better than young Mrs Darling; it was impossible not to admire her vitality and courage; she was a staunch friend to those she liked, and a good mistress.

And I often think of the Red House when people begin to talk in a tiresome manner of being psychic and able to sense the atmosphere of a place. I do not doubt they can. The spirit of hatred pervaded the Red House. I had felt it whenever young Mrs Darling entered a room. But I, who was old Mrs Darling's constant companion, had forgotten that the fire of hatred might be smouldering all the time by my side, to be kindled into a scorching flame by the coming of youth and beauty.

The Vicar's Web

A patient asked me the other day whether I was interested in psycho-analysis, and seemed quite surprised when I told her that I was not.

'That,' she said with an exasperating smile, 'is probably because you yourself need analysing,' and then she changed the subject. You can't argue with people like that, or I should have asked her if her dislike for cocktails implied that she had a hidden craving for stimulants.

What absurd conceit! Why in the name of goodness should her little tin gods with feet of clay be always right? And yet I know people who regularly every week for years continue to send these women their dirty linen to be laundered. They lose innumerable articles in the wash, get back things that don't belong to them which they don't know what to do with, run up huge bills, and all the time most of them could have done the job for themselves at home, with the vicar or the family doctor to lend a hand with the mangle.

Of course I know that people's minds work in a very curious way, that dirty cellars are as likely to contain valuable things as rubbish, and that we are all the better for an occasional spring-cleaning. But why make such a song and dance about it? Anyhow, there is no psychoanalyst in this story, though of course the game we played was really their game. I don't particularly want to play it again, the results may be dangerous, and in this case they certainly were disturbing.

Dr Lushington was the vicar of Willeston St John. He was a great naturalist, the author of a two-volume treatise on British spiders, and though according to Mrs Lushington he had had many offers of preferment he had declined them all because Willeston Fen is in his parish, and Willeston Fen is one of the few remaining breeding grounds of two species of butterfly that are rapidly becoming extinct. I fancy that she considered the reason inadequate.

Dr Lushington was nearly sixty. He was inclined to be garrulous in anecdote, he was hopelessly absentminded, and had it not been for his wife's good management he would have been lost in cobwebs.

She it was who insisted that he should keep up his tennis, and surprisingly enough he was a remarkably good player, though when one saw him crouching in a corner of the court with the iron netting behind him it was impossible not to think of him as a human spider, incredibly patient, waiting to entangle the inevitable fly.

The Lushingtons had one child, Felicity, whom I had nursed through a bad attack of rheumatic fever. She was a delightful girl, with a disarming frankness about her that won my heart. Two days before I left she had her eleventh birthday. In the ordinary course of things there would have been a children's party to celebrate it, but Mrs Lushington, in her anxiety that Felicity should not get over-excited, had persuaded her to postpone the party proper until she was able to join in the games, and to substitute for it an invitation to her grown-up friends.

Most children would have thought the suggestion dull. Not so Felicity. Though she delighted in climbing trees and hunting rats with the boys in Captain Dawson's tithe barn, she had a remarkable social sense and really enjoyed entertaining guests, provided only that she chose them. The party consisted entirely of men. There was Mr Greatorex from the sugar-beet factory at Fenchurch, Dr Philpots, Captain Dawson, who had lost a leg in the war and was a special favourite, and Mr Cholmondley of Oldbarnhouse. Felicity hesitated a little over Mr Cholmondley. He was, she explained, a newcomer to the district and never came to church. Her father didn't even know him by sight, but then, he wasn't very good at remembering faces. Some people thought Mr Cholmondley was stuck-up, but Felicity didn't believe it. She thought he was shy, and the party would be a very good opportunity for him to make friends. So Mr Cholmondley received his invitation with the others on note-paper that was not only tinted but scented and almost entirely free from blots, and the present that he sent her with his letter of acceptance won Felicity's heart.

The guests arrived at half past three, Captain Dawson bringing his bull terrier with him by special request. We played robber croquet, Felicity keeping the score for her father to see that he neither cheated nor was cheated, and clock golf. Then, as none of the gentlemen declared that they were capable of acting adverbs and as it seemed impossible to fit Captain Dawson into a three-legged race, we sat on deck-chairs under the mulberry-tree to play at Unwinding.

'It's perfectly simple,' said Felicity, 'and great fun. You think of something like bull-terriers, that reminds someone else of bulrushes, and then you go on to Moses and the Jews and Hitler. We'll wind until tea is ready, and then after tea we will unwind. You have three lives each, but you'll soon see. You start, Mr Greatorex. I'll help you. Start with sugar-beet.'

'Sugar-beet,' said Mr Greatorex gloomily, 'reminds me of losses.'

'Losses,' said Dr Philpots, with a twinkle in his eye, 'remind me of profits.'

'Prophets,' said the vicar, carefully removing a caterpillar from his sleeve and replacing it on a leaf of the mulberry-tree, 'of silkworms, of course – I mean Moses.'

'Now, dad,' said Felicity, repeating a phrase that her mother was constantly using, 'do bring your mind to bear on the matter in hand. It's an awful pity you said Moses, because that's almost certain to bring us back to bulrushes again. However, I suppose it can't be helped. Your turn, nurse.'

Slowly we went on winding. Somehow we got to Irving and from Irving passed to Hamlet, and from Hamlet to Champainbury, a little village on the other side of the parish. That led us on through champagne to luxury.

Dr Philpots, who was a Socialist, declared that luxury reminded him of first-class railway carriages. Again the vicar had not been listening and had to be called to book by Felicity.

'What is it?' he asked. 'Oh, first-class railway carriages! First-class railway carriages remind me of murder. Surely it's time, my dear, that we were going in for tea?'

Everybody burst out laughing. Of course we all wanted to know the connection in the vicar's mind between the two things, and whether a spider had got anything to do with it.

'The association is perfectly reasonable,' he said. 'I'll explain it after tea, though the story is not a very suitable one for Felicity to hear. On the whole, I think it unsuitable. She is hardly old enough.'

How like the vicar, amiably indecisive, thinking his thoughts aloud, the easiest and most exasperating man for a woman or child to manage! But Felicity managed him all right. Tactfully she said nothing. We adjourned to the house and gazed with proper amazement at the huge birthday cake with its eleven candles. Then when the last candle had flickered out, just as Dr Philpots was finishing his fifth cup of tea, we pulled crackers and read aloud our mottoes.

'Now, ladies and gentlemen,' said Felicity, 'the vicar of Willeston St John, the notorious and dearly beloved Dr Lushington, will tell us the story he promised us about the murder. Daddy, fire away!'

'Did I really promise?' asked the vicar. 'It happened so many years ago that I've almost forgotten. It was a Saturday night and I had to travel down from London by the last train. The day had been tiring, and as I had thoughtlessly delayed preparing my Sunday sermon, I departed from my usual habit and took my seat in an empty first-class compartment. I wrote undisturbed for an hour and a half until we reached Marshington Junction, where a number of people got into the train. The guard had blown his whistle and we had begun to move when the train from Saunchester drew up. I put my head out of the window to see whether anyone had been rash enough to risk the connection. Yes, almost before the train had stopped, a door was thrown open, and a man rushed across the platform. The carriage I was in was the last in the train. He had just time to open the door of my compartment, where he flung himself down in the corner seat, panting.

' "That was touch and go," I said. "It was lucky for you that the door was not locked." He assented, and I went on with my work, noting that the man looked very pale. When I had finished the page I was writing I chanced to look on the floor. "If you don't mind," I said to my companion, "I will raise the window – the rain seems to be getting in." It was trickling across the floor along a crack in the oilcloth. But though I closed the window the little stream still ran on. I am short-sighted, and it took me twice as long as it would have done another to realise that what I saw was not water but blood dripping from a wound in the hand of the man who sat opposite me.

' "It's a nasty cut," he said, as his eyes caught mine. "Could you bind it up for me? You will find a handkerchief in my coat pocket and I have a scarf somewhere. There was a drunken man in my carriage who fell to fighting with his companion over a broken bottle of whisky. It was all I could do to separate them." I am afraid I made a very indifferent job of the bandaging, but the stranger was grateful and declared that the bleeding would soon stop. We engaged in desultory conversation until we were approaching the next station when he lowered the sash before the train stopped and looked out upon the platform.

' "My brother ought to be here to meet me," he said, "but I don't see him anywhere. Good night, sir, and many thanks."

'I must say I was relieved to see him go. He had sadly interrupted my train of thought and I had still to draw the threads, as it were, of my sermon together. Haste is always upsetting, and the stranger's exit was almost as hurried as his entrance.

'I am not at all a careful reader of the daily papers, and it was some days before I read the account of a horrible murder that had been committed on the line. The body of an old gentleman, bearing all the signs of a desperate struggle, had been found under the seat of a compartment on the 8.30 train from Saunchester. He had been identified as a well-known moneylender in Lincoln, but there was no clue to the identity or the whereabouts of his assailant.

'I thought little of the matter at the time, and it was not until a day or two later that I realised that the crime had been committed on the Saturday evening, and that it was the 8.30 from Saunchester that had steamed into Marshington Junction just as my train was leaving. Immediately following this came the thought that the stranger who had entered my carriage was the murderer. I dismissed the idea as preposterous, as unjust to a man of whom I knew no ill, but, try as I would, it came back again and again, until finally I had to receive it and to weave some sort of story around my fellow-traveller.

'As the weeks went by I felt at times that I ought to communicate my experience to the police, but they had already traced the man to the station at which I had seen him alight and I felt quite incapable of recalling his features. Moreover, I have always been opposed to capital punishment, with that awful limiting to a brief interval of weeks or months of the possibility of repentance. But whenever I think of first-class railway carriages I think of murder. They are as closely linked together in my mind as two things can be.

'And now,' said the vicar, 'I have redeemed my rash promise. I think, Felicity, you had better entertain your guests for a little in the drawing-room while I show Mr Greatorex and Mr Cholmondley those spiders which arrived last week from Brazil. They are in the study, Mr Greatorex. Captain Dawson and Dr Philpots have already seen them. We shan't be gone very long.'

'And that's the telephone!' exclaimed Mrs Lushington. 'I'll call you, Dr Philpots, if it is a message for you.'

'Now,' said Felicity, as soon as we had adjourned to the drawing-room, 'I hope you all have got comfortable chairs, because it is time we began to unwind. Daddy said he would only be gone a few minutes, but he is very bad at reckoning time and the study clock has stopped. And it's no use waiting for mother if she is talking to Mrs Bentwick.'

We started with three lives each, but Felicity, like her father, was no believer in capital punishment, and when Dr Philpots was killed he was mercifully allowed another chance.

With many jocular interruptions we pursued our devious way. So intent were we on our unravellings that we hardly noticed that the others had come back into the room.

'The Tower of London,' I said, 'reminds me of Richard the Third.'

'Richard the Third,' said Captain Dawson, 'reminds me of murder.'

'Murder,' said Dr Philpots, now confidently assured of his life, 'reminds me of first-class railway carriages.'

The vicar was standing by the window, turning over the pages of *Nature*.

'Wake up, daddy!' Felicity explained. 'It's my turn and you must come to my rescue. You shall have one of my lives. What do first-class railway carriages remind you of?'

'Mr Cholmondley,' said the vicar without raising his head:

'Now, daddy, do play properly and give attention to the game. You can have until we count ten. What do first-class railway carriages remind you of?'

Slowly Captain Dawson began to count.

The vicar took off his spectacles and wiped them carefully. Then with the little nervous smile he had when he thought that his daughter was not treating him with the respect that was his due before company, he replied.

'Murder.'

'Oh, I'm afraid he is hopeless,' she exclaimed as we burst out laughing. 'It's the Brazilian spiders; when he once sees them he can't remember anything else.'

'Cholmondley, you must deal with the vicar,' said Captain Dawson.

'But he's not here,' Mrs Lushington explained. 'It seems that his sister has been undergoing a serious operation in town and he thought a message might have come through to Oldbarnhouse, so he asked me after tea if he could use the telephone. They had just received one; bad news, I am afraid, for he said he ought to motor up at once, and wished me to make his apologies. He did not want to cast a gloom over the party.'

'She was down for a few days before Easter, I think,' said Captain Dawson. 'Rather an attractive-looking girl. Hallo, here comes the rain.'

'And all the chairs and croquet things out. No, Felicity, of course you must stay where you are. Nurse and I will see to them.'

Mr Cholmondley's sudden departure had succeeded after all in casting a shadow over the party. Dr Philpots declared that he had still some visits to pay before the evening surgery, and soon after the things had been brought in from the garden Mr Greatorex announced that it was time that he was getting back to Fenchurch, and offered to give a lift to Captain Dawson.

'They all seem to be in a hurry to leave,' said Felicity rather wistfully. 'We hadn't even time for a paper game, and I had sharpened all the pencils. And there is daddy sitting crouched up in the summerhouse like an old black spider waiting for a fly. It was funny about him and Mr Cholmondley, wasn't it, nurse? But he always does get things so mixed up.'

I lay awake longer than usual that night thinking of many things, partly of Felicity – hoping that Dr Philpots would keep a careful eye over her convalescence – partly of the game that we had played and whether the vicar's answers meant anything at all. He had said that first-class railway carriages reminded him of Mr Cholmondley and then of murder; and Mr Cholmondley, who was a comparative stranger to everyone, had left hurriedly after he had heard the vicar's story. Unless I was greatly mistaken, no doubt had crossed the mind of any of the guests. But what was the vicar thinking of as he sat brooding in the summerhouse? Would Mr Cholmondley come back to Oldbarnhouse? Had he really a sister who had undergone a serious operation? Had he by any chance a scar on hand or wrist?

It was not likely that I should ever be able to answer these questions. Perhaps it was just as well.

But I have come to the conclusion that Unwinding is not a very profitable game to play unless you are a psychoanalyst. Then, of course, it pays to find things out.

Dark Horses

'The young and inexperienced nurse,' our matron would say, 'has much to learn.'

A platitude, of course, but it would be a mistake to judge Miss Carruthers by this text of one of those Sunday evening talks which she gave all too rarely to the staff of St Christopher's. She explained with a touch of the acid humour which endeared her to the discerning that she was quoting from a sermon delivered by her father the bishop.

'I disliked it at the time,' she said, 'but it contains a valuable truth, applicable, you may note, to curates as well as nurses.' She went on to explain that by the time a girl is entitled to call herself a nurse she is only relatively young, and as for inexperience, she has probably seen more of life and death than most bishops. Then, having put her father in his place, she proceeded to say many wise things.

I wish now that I had taken notes of those talks, but of the one on the inexperience of nurses I remember two things.

She said that when we went out to private cases we were too apt to imagine that we should be welcomed with open arms. As likely as not the first thought that came into the minds of those who employed us would be: 'Can we really afford a nurse, and how long will she have to stay?' The second would be a haunting fear that we should upset the whole of the domestic staff and create yet more work in the house.

'A very natural and proper fear,' Miss Carruthers would say. 'Good cooks are as hard to find, and far harder to keep than good nurses, and a cold rice pudding is even worse than a cold linseed poultice.'

That was the first point. The second was that the patient would often be unwilling to receive our services. The presence of a nurse assured him of the fact that he was ill, and that he had to do what he was told.

'Get rid,' she said, 'of the idea of the ministering angel. I have been told myself by a responsible churchwarden with sciatica that I was an interfering devil. You will find that a certain proportion of your patients hold that opinion. Your duty is to see that they are not right, to carry on and to maintain the high tradition that invariably accompanies a low salary.'

I remembered that Sunday evening talk of Miss Carruthers when I went to Kiddington Parva as a night nurse to old Mr Weston. It was not that the family didn't welcome me with open arms: they could not have been kinder, and the staff, an old woman and a half-witted boy, would have been upset by nothing short of an earthquake. My quarrel was with Mr Weston, or, to put it more accurately, Mr Weston's quarrel with me.

I had been met at Newbury by a jolly-looking girl who introduced herself as Agatha Weston. In a workmanlike way she strapped my box on to the luggage-carrier of a disreputable-looking car into which a number of bulky packages had already been stowed.

Then, lifting a protesting bull-terrier by the scruff of his neck, from the front seat, she handed me a rug. 'You'll need it before we get there,' she said, 'and don't be alarmed if we backfire. The car is one of the family, you know. We've all seen happier days, and we can't help making a noise about it. It's lucky for us that we were able to get you, for at the moment we are in rather a hole. To begin with there is my uncle, your patient. He has had pleurisy and his heart is pretty dicky, and to make matters worse he hates being looked after. Happily my sister Meg is a trained nurse. She was at home when he was taken ill, recuperating after an attack of quinsy. You'll like Meg. She is a thorough sportswoman, but of course it's been a bit of a strain on her, more than she can manage single-handed. Then father's down with his usual winter cough, and I've got my hands full in looking after the farm. Mother is more or less of an invalid, and in any case she doesn't hit it off too well with my uncle.'

I enjoyed my ride with Agatha Weston on that bright March morning. We came all too soon to Kiddington Parva, a long straggling village. I told her that it reminded me of a place I knew in Lincolnshire.

'Lincolnshire?' she said. 'Good Lord! I wonder if that is an omen.'

'Why, what are you thinking of?' I asked.

'Oh, you wouldn't understand; some day perhaps I'll tell you, if our luck holds. And I'm inclined to think it will.'

The Manor House stood some little way back from the road. It was a big rambling house with no pretensions to style; at the back was a long range of farm buildings and stables.

'We'll leave the things in the car,' said Agatha; 'the boy will fetch them in later. Let's find mother and she'll show you your room. It's all very rough and ready here, but we're a good-natured crowd. We can't afford not to be.'

Mrs Weston was a frail, anxious-looking woman of sixty, with what most people would call a sweet smile. Women with sweet smiles are, in my experience, usually selfish – the something for nothing type – but Mrs Weston was to prove an exception. My bedroom was at the end of the east wing. She had chosen it, she explained, because it was the quietest in the house.

'You'll be able to sleep here undisturbed in the daytime,' she said. 'It's not a room that we often use, but the bed has been well aired. We shall be having lunch in a quarter of an hour.'

It was a charming room. From the window I looked out over lichen-covered roofs on to the downs, across which the shadows raced. The midday sun caught a bowl of polyanthus that Mrs Weston had placed on the old-fashioned dressing-table. The flowered wallpaper was stained and faded, but it seemed just right for that quiet room with its faint aroma of apples.

At lunch I met Meg Weston.

From the first she struck me as a remarkable woman. She must have been a good ten years older than her sister; her features were more strongly marked, but she had the same attractive smile. When nurses who work in double harness meet each other for the first time they display, from reasons of self-interest, a more than usual amount of tact. Each knows that the other will criticise her methods, and, since patients unfortunately are rarely speechless, that comparisons, more or less invidious, are almost certain to be made. Nurses, too, have an unreasonable loyalty to their own hospitals. They will champion a second-rate surgeon just because he happens to be upon the staff, uniting only in their denunciation of matrons, prunes, and rice pudding, and the complete lack of imagination displayed by mere men who sit on boards of management and think of us as fledgling Nightingales.

I liked Meg Weston from the first. She was obviously a thoroughly capable woman, who not only looked after her patient but seemed to be the one who ran the house as well.

As soon as the meal was over she took me off to her den, installed me in the most comfortable chair, and offered me a cigarette.

'We've time for a ten minutes' talk,' she said, 'before I go back to my uncle. I left him dozing. He's a difficult patient, and crotchety, but at present he's too ill to give much trouble, though sparks may begin to fly when he is on the mend. He has a left-sided pleurisy and his heart is none too strong. Dr Corrigan saw him this morning and thought him rather better. Not that I attach much weight to what he says. Horses are his first and last love, and broken collar-bones his speciality. My poor old dad is ill too, but he knows how to look after himself, and has the patience of Job.'

She went on to discuss arrangements. She proposed that I should get what sleep I could before coming on duty at eight. Supper would be at seven, and after that she would introduce me to Mr Weston and see that I had everything I wanted for the night.

'Just one word about the servants,' she added. 'There aren't any. No, don't be alarmed. I don't mean it literally, but they are not what you are accustomed to and they are not presentable. Mrs Worboys is an excellent cook who'll give you anything you want, but she has a cleft palate which makes conversation difficult. Her boy is a little wrong in the head-piece, and though he can turn out a room far better than most housemaids, he has to whistle while he does it and doesn't know what it is to walk quietly. So we've made it a rule that he keeps downstairs. My mother and sister look after the upper rooms. And if you see any bells, don't ring them because the wires are all broken.'

My previous case had been a hard one, and on coming back I had been put on night duty in one of the surgical wards, so I was glad enough to get a few hours' sleep.

The room was certainly wonderfully peaceful. There was no clanking of trams, no clattering of lorries, only the monotonous cawing of rooks in the elms and the cheerful droning of a bee that had been on night duty all winter and was now rejoicing in the March sunshine. When I fell asleep I had no fault to find with Kiddington Parva.

A hot bath at half past six, supper at seven in the dining-room – for the first time I noticed that nearly all the pictures on the walls seemed to be sporting prints – and then came my introduction to Mr Weston.

His room, I found, was next door but one to mine, a big room with a four-poster bed. It was the first time I had ever nursed anyone in a four-poster. I hope it will be the last.

'Here's Nurse Wilkie, uncle,' said Meg Weston. 'You remember I told you yesterday that Dr Corrigan thought it would be a good thing to have some additional help for a few days. You get more difficult to manage, you know, as you get stronger, and you are apt to think that you are entitled to get your own way with your niece.'

The man in the bed glared at me. He looked about sixty; he had a black, pointed beard and thick eyebrows. I could imagine him as a captain on a quarterdeck, or wherever it is that captains are to be found, raising Cain to scare some inoffensive Abel out of his wits.

'Good evening, nurse,' he said. 'I don't know why you should have come. All I want is someone to give me my medicine, not that any stuff of Corrigan's will do me any good; all he does is to strap me up like a portmanteau.'

'Now, uncle,' said Meg, 'you must not talk or you will start coughing. You are going to have a good night, and when I see you again in the morning, you will be much better.'

He closed his eyes wearily, and she beckoned me behind a screen.

'I think there's everything here that you will require, nurse,' she said. 'I've taken his temperature. Dr Corrigan wanted him to have a sleeping-draught at nine – it's on the table. He likes a good fire kept up. There are two kettles, one for hot-water bottles, and the other for your tea. I apologise for the reading-lamp: I've seen that it's filled with oil, and if you want candles by any chance, you will find a supply in the cupboard. That's all, I think. You know my room and don't hesitate to call me. But I think we shall all have good nights. I know I want one.'

At nine o'clock I gave Mr Weston his sleeping-draught. Apart from an occasional dry cough he seemed comfortable. His pulse, when I felt it, was rather rapid, but his colour was good, and when I looked at the chart I saw that his temperature had fallen since midday.

The night passed uneventfully. The fire burned cheerfully and I had provided myself with an interesting book. There were mice busy behind the skirting-boards, there were owls that called perpetually to each other, boards in the old house creaked, and the other Mr Weston, Meg's father, whose room must have been at the opposite end of the house from the one in which I was, had certainly a most distressing cough. A soft rain began to fall about dawn when the birds broke into song.

It was extraordinarily peaceful.

And then Mr Weston woke up and peace vanished. He had slept badly, he said, if he had slept at all. The room was too hot, there were far too many clothes on the bed, the pain in his side was worse. Mr Weston was as cantankerous as he could be; it was obvious that he was better, and there could be no doubt that he thoroughly enjoyed his breakfast. I was quite ready for my own.

Mrs Weston, Meg, and Agatha were taking part in an animated discussion when I entered the dining-room. There are different ways of punctuating a conversation. My role on this occasion was that, not of the comma or semi-colon, but of the full stop, followed by a new paragraph. But the new paragraph proceeded jerkily. Something was very much on the minds of the Weston family. Meg looked if anything more tired for her night in bed, Agatha was on edge, her mother still smiled sweetly, though it was an obvious effort for her to stir the sugar.

She asked after my patient, but she did not seem to be particularly interested in my reply. Then she suddenly changed the conversation to the beauties of the countryside and the stimulating quality of the downland air. This seemed to give the cue to Meg. Agatha, it appeared, had to interview a farmer some miles away about a bunch of heifers – it was the first time that I had ever heard of a bunch of heifers – and there would be room for me in the car if I cared to go. It looked as if my morning had been planned for me. The rain had ceased. In the ordinary course of things I should have gone for a solitary walk along muddy lanes. I preferred Agatha's company, and for the car to collect the mud.

We called first at Dr Corrigan's house in a village some miles away to return an electric torch which he had left behind when he had looked in on Mr Weston in the late afternoon of the previous day. Agatha seemed to have a good deal to say to him, and when she came out the doctor accompanied her to the gate. He was a good-looking young fellow, who seemed thoroughly pleased with himself, the world, and Agatha.

She introduced me.

'Glad you were able to come, nurse,' he said. 'I think we shall be able to pull the old gentleman through all right, but Miss Weston badly wanted someone to relieve her. It's been a bit of a strain. He had a good night? Well, that's splendid. I shall be looking in this morning. The very best of luck, Agatha; you won't have long to wait now.'

'A phlegmatic disposition,' said Agatha, as she waved goodbye, 'must be a gift above rubies. I haven't got it. We are all rather on edge this morning, as I expect you've noticed. Now if only you and I could get away for a few days, run down to the sea, go anywhere, do anything. I'm fed up to the teeth with Kiddington Parva.'

I looked at her more closely. What was the matter with Agatha Weston? Then as suddenly her mood changed. The sun came out and she was the same girl who had driven me from the station on the previous day.

We found our farm, and after a leisurely inspection of some disagreeable-looking young cows, Agatha suddenly discovered that she had nothing to do for the rest of the morning and that I might as well see as much of the country as I could. By the time we got back to Kiddington Parva we must have covered nearly fifty miles. It did not take me long to go to sleep that afternoon. There were certain things about the Westons that I did not understand. They combined in a strange degree frankness with secretiveness, but, after all, one of the functions of a family is to act as a ring fence. It was no business of mine to peer through the palings. I slept the sleep of the uninquisitive. But when I met the Westons before going on duty I could not help asking myself what had happened to them in the course of the afternoon. They hardly seemed the same people. Mrs Weston looked as if she had been happily weeping. Meg was laughing, and Agatha's eyes were dancing with suppressed excitement.

I only hoped that the curmudgeonly old gentleman in bed upstairs would show a different side to his nature as well. But I was to be disappointed. Mr Weston was obviously better than on the preceding night, his pulse slower, his temperature, which at four o'clock had been a hundred, was now normal.

His temper, however, was worse. Nothing that I could do for him was right. He complained of pain, but he refused to lie still. Birds and beasts and flowers soon would be asleep, but the brute in my keeping was determined to keep awake. At twelve o'clock, at one, he was still glaring at me malevolently. His remarks had become more and more personal. From criticism of my nurse's uniform he passed by stages to complaints about what he called my heavy tread.

In vain I tried to live up to all those excellent copybook maxims which deal with the theme that a nurse's first and last care should be the welfare of her patient. 'Feed the brute' was not one of them, and if it had been, the brute would have been certain to disagree with his food. At last Mr Weston fell asleep. He slept soundly for five hours, woke up with a start, and almost at once gave vent to a stream of invective. I listened in silence, which only seemed to infuriate him the more. At last my patience was exhausted.

'Mr Weston,' I said, 'I know you are ill, but I have done my very best for you. You are behaving exactly as if you wanted to get rid of me.'

'Your perspicacity, nurse,' he replied, 'is wonderful. That is exactly what I wish to do. I never asked for your help, I have no intention of paying for it. My niece was, and is, perfectly capable of looking after me. As far as I am concerned, the sooner you go the better.'

So that was that.

As soon as I came off duty, I asked to see Mrs Weston and her elder daughter. I told them what had happened and what Mr Weston had said, adding that his animus against me was so great that it seemed to me obvious that I was doing him more harm than good. They listened to me in silence. Then Meg got up from her seat and put her hand on my shoulder.

'It's perfectly abominable,' she said, 'and I know just what you are feeling. It's no use apologising for uncle. He has always been a mannerless autocrat. It isn't fair to ask you to go on, but it would be still more unfair to you if you went back to St Christopher's before your week was up.'

'Couldn't nurse stay on here as our guest?' said Mrs Weston. 'I am sure we would all try to give her as good a time as possible.'

'I don't see how I could do that,' I answered, 'though it's awfully kind of you to suggest it. Why shouldn't I nurse the other Mr Weston? Would that be any help?'

They were silent for a moment.

'Father is really much better,' said Meg. 'Indeed I think he ought to be downstairs tomorrow. But you have given me an idea. Agatha, mother. Why shouldn't she and Nurse Wilkie go off for the rest of the week together? She has been doing far too much and I've wondered the last few days if she hasn't been on the verge of a nervous breakdown. Yes, that is an excellent idea. I'll get her to run me over to Dr Corrigan's and explain matters to him. All it means is that you go from one patient to another, and an altogether nicer one. You needn't say anything to the hospital authorities about it. It's really none of their concern. They will get their cheque all right – in any case uncle wasn't going to pay it – Dr Corrigan will sign the chit saying that you have given complete satisfaction, as indeed you have, and you will have four or five delightful days with Agatha to make up for uncle's abominable conduct.'

The plan certainly had much to commend it from my point of view. True, it would involve me in a little innocent dissimulation with the hospital authorities, but my conscience is not queasy, and I very much disliked the idea of being returned to store after failure to give satisfaction. I don't think it is to be wondered at that I agreed.

The Westons were a queer family but their womenfolk undoubt-edly knew how to make decisions, and to act on them promptly. By half past eleven Agatha and I were once again in her battered car. The tank was full of petrol, England lay before us, and Kiddington Parva was only a name on a map.

The days that followed were some of the happiest I have ever spent. We had no plan and no timetable. If we saw an attractive turning we took it. Berkshire, Wiltshire, Hampshire, were full of attractive turnings. Every evening Agatha reported her whereabouts by telegram – a rather extravagant procedure, I thought – and twice on the following morning she got telegrams in reply.

On the morning of our last day together we ate our sandwiches in a clearing in the New Forest. Agatha lay stretched on the heather, smoking a cigarette.

'Well, Wilkie,' she said, 'we've had a perfectly gorgeous time. I hate to think of going back tomorrow. But there's one thing I should like to ask you. You must be perfectly honest, and don't answer in a hurry. Are you bothered with a conscience?'

I couldn't help but burst out laughing.

'I know it sounds absurd,' she went on. 'What I meant to say is, can you condone or compound, or whatever it's called, a felony?'

'Certainly not,' I replied.

'I believe,' said Agatha, 'that you could, if it was only a little felony, and you liked the people who had committed it. Come, Wilkie, I'm sure you could if you tried. In fact, you have got to, because other-wise I shall have it on my conscience. Well, I'm going to trust you, and unless I'm greatly mistaken, you will forgive me.

'To begin with, Wilkie, I can't congratulate you on your powers of observation. You spent two days in and around Kiddington Parva and you made no remark about the racing stables only a quarter of a mile from our house, which you passed at least four times. You have had an opportunity of seeing the newspaper every day and yet you are in entire ignorance of the fact that the Lincolnshire Handicap was run on the day after you arrived, and that the winner was Back-fire, by Brooklands out of Carburettor. Don't you ever have sweeps at St Christopher's?'

'Only when the chimneys smoke. We, unfortunately, are not all-owed to.'

'Wilkie, you are extraordinarily innocent. It will be news to you that Backfire was a rank outsider, but we are coming nearer to the heart of the mystery when I tell you that that really noble horse is owned by Mr Algernon Weston of Kiddington Parva, and trained at Kiddington by Perriman. Is any vestige of light beginning to dawn? I don't expect you to have heard of Perriman; he hasn't made any name for himself as yet.'

'Not a glimmering,' I replied with complete truth. 'Who is Algernon Weston? Was he my patient?'

'Now we are coming to the part where you condone the felony, or what might have been one. Algernon Weston is my uncle. You never saw him. He was frightfully ill, pleurisy and a dicky heart. Meg was nursing him night and day. No wonder she was nearly worn out.'

'But I thought my patient was your uncle?'

'That is what we wanted you to think, but as a matter of fact he was my father, and anything but a curmudgeon. He was acting a part; he hated doing it – in fact he never would have done it if Uncle Algernon had not insisted. It's like this. We are an impoverished family, land mortgaged up to the hilt, but we all of us, mother and Meg included, know a good horse when we see one. Backfire – uncle bought him as a two-year-old for eighty guineas – was a bit of a disappointment at first and seemed to share in the family's bad luck. But we never lost faith and Perriman has worked wonders with him.

'When I was at Sunday school I learnt all about faith without works being dead. We all of us put pretty well our last penny on Backfire, and if you read your papers you would see what the odds were. Then suddenly uncle became seriously ill. If he died before the race was run, Backfire would be a non-starter. There's neither sense nor equity in a rule like that, and I can't think why someone hasn't introduced a bill in Parliament to do away with such silliness. Well, poor old uncle, who is a sportsman if there ever was one, got worse and worse. It looked as if there would be quite a chance that he would never hear the result of the Lincolnshire. Then we came to the conclusion that if he died within twenty-four hours of the race being run it would be quite possible to fix things up. My father, who was himself a bit seedy, would pose as the patient, Meg would strap him up, make out one of those temperature charts that look like the foothills of the Himalayas and give him something that would temporarily affect the action of his heart. Meg is a very capable nurse. Then we would get in a nurse from outside. Unfortunately she had to be on night duty because she couldn't meet the doctor when he called to see his patient without giving the show away.

'If things had gone badly, this is how it would have worked out. Supposing uncle had died in the night following your arrival. I should have run you round in the car to Dr Corrigan's in the morning and introduced you. You would have reported the fact that your patient was comfortable and was going on well. Then we should have had to have found some excuse for Dr Corrigan to postpone his visit to the late afternoon or evening. Some hours after the race had been run, Meg would send round a note announcing the fact that he had had a sudden relapse and had died. Dr Corrigan is a fairly busy man. He knew that there were two trained nurses in the house and would not be at all likely to hurry over to see a corpse. We should have found some reason for getting you out of bed, say at three o'clock, after the race was over, to see my father, who of course would be alive and well. And if ever any questions were raised, your testimony would be all-important. Then – and I am awfully sorry about this, Wilkie, but it couldn't be helped – we should have had to get rid of you. Father would have to manage that somehow, in the way that you know. We should have packed you off next morning and all would have been well. Of course I admit it was a sort of conspiracy. It sounds cold-blooded, but you know the younger generation *is* cold-blooded, and Uncle Algernon would have hated to think that he had let us down. As it was our faith was justified – our old Sunday school teacher always said it would be if we had enough. Uncle rallied on the morning of the race, Backfire won by two lengths, and the good news acted like a tonic. But we had to get you out of the house as quickly as possible. There was always a chance of your discovering that you had got hold of the wrong patient, father had had more than enough of bed and he would not have been able to deceive you much longer. His appetite is enormous and he is very dependent on his glass of toddy last thing at night. Uncle Algernon is now well on the way to recovery, and what is more – I mean, what is almost as good – by backing Peckover in the Grand National he has brought off the double. My fancy was Locum Tenens, who came down at the first fence. But isn't it a wonderful world? There we are, a devoted family, no longer impoverished. We haven't committed or compounded any felony. Mother will be able to go on a spring cruise to the Mediterranean and take on all sorts of people's troubles. Meg will probably start a nursing home and I – '

'You, Agatha,' I said, 'will put your money not on Locum Tenens but Irish Doctor. I sincerely hope that Dr Corrigan won't come down at the first fence.'

Agatha actually blushed.

'Wilkie,' she exclaimed, 'I withdraw all that I said about your not being observant. I think you would make an excellent nurse for heart cases. You may like to know, too, that my father was most impressed by your capabilities. He told mother that he should insist on having you whenever he was seriously ill. She was quite annoyed about it. Tell me you forgive us all and wish us well.'

'I don't think the question of forgiveness comes in. You are quite the most extraordinary family I have ever met and your powers of persuasion are a danger to the community. But tell me, Agatha, was Dr Corrigan aware of what was going on?'

'I don't know. I thought it better not to ask. I think you could describe him as an innocent party. I shall probably tell him some day. He is rather sentimental, and I do like men to be realists.'

'Agatha, you are a wonderful girl. I wonder where you received your education.'

'At home and at the Sunday school,' she said, 'and when vicar's daughter is a non-starter I still occasionally lend a hand with the infants. I think it most important not so much that they should know all about Moses in the bulrushes, but that they should learn to be good sports. That is what I try to teach them. But I'm glad to say that the vicar's daughter isn't often ill. It's not really my line of country, you know.'

I felt perfectly convinced that Agatha Weston was right.

The Arm of Mrs Egan

Few people nowadays believe in spells and curses and witches. I wish that I, too, was an unbeliever, for I like comfort, physical comfort, and what the parsons would call spiritual comfort, too. I like my world to be orderly, to know that there is a definite relation between cause and effect, and to be assured that the power of malevolence is limited.

But I've lived long enough to know that we don't get what we like. Reluctantly I have to confess that I do believe in curses. I believe that Mrs Egan was to all intents and purposes a witch. She didn't ride on broomsticks, she was incapable of disappearing up the chimney, but had she lived four hundred years ago the chances of her dying in bed would have been remote.

The story of Gilbert Lennox proves that a curse today can be as horrible a thing as ever it was, more horrible indeed since for its efficacy it depends on its victim possessing certain qualities, such as conscientiousness, which are good rather than bad.

Gilbert Lennox and I were brought up together in the same country town. He was an orphan and lived with a wealthy old aunt who was exceedingly anxious to do the right thing by her nephew. My doctor uncle was one of his guardians.

I didn't particularly like Gilbert. He was far too much the model child, very serious, very intense, and without a particle of humour. He collected butterflies and moths and postage stamps and subscriptions for the Guild of Young Helpers. Before he went to his prep school his ambition was to become a missionary. When he left his prep school he had determined to be a medical missionary. Then he went to what was considered to be a good public school where he was put on his honour not to smoke or swear or to let down in any way the high moral standard of his house. By the time he had become a prefect and won a leaving scholarship he had made up his mind about his future career: he would become a doctor.

My uncle thought that the boy had made a wise decision. His aunt had died, leaving him well provided for. Gilbert was young for his years, and a good deal of a prig. If he took up medicine, he would get an insight into life that would be of permanent value, and once qualified he would be in a position to choose what branch of the profession he wished to follow. Most people would have said that he had in him the makings of a good doctor. He had an orderly mind, he was an accurate observer, he hated everything that was slipshod, and he was most conscientious.

Gilbert Lennox got through his medical exams without any difficulty. He even won a prize in anatomy. But somehow he never seemed to acquire a knowledge of people, and his professional manner, worn like a badly fitting jacket, only accentuated his boyishness. He was a poor mixer, he didn't play games, and his only interest outside his books seemed to be in moths and butterflies. By the time he had taken his house appointments he was still in the chrysalis stage. I doubt whether he had ever even emerged to flirt with a nurse.

If Gilbert had listened to my uncle's advice he would have gone in for some branch of research. He had means of his own and if at first he only got a minor post he could afford to wait. But for some reason or other he chose what he was least fitted for and set up in general practice without even a period of probation as an assistant. I can only think that it was a new manifestation of the old medical missionary idea, and that he hadn't outgrown the pernicious teaching of his former housemaster that the job which least attracted you was the one that it was your duty to do.

So Gilbert settled down in his country practice twenty miles away from the town where my uncle lived, and all the women with marriageable daughters said what a nice open face he had and what an improvement he was on old Dr Brown. For a year or so he seemed to be doing well and then he met Mrs Egan.

It was from my uncle that I learnt later what had happened. Gilbert had motored over one Sunday evening, his nerve gone all to pieces, to tell him the dreadful story. Mrs Egan was a wealthy widow with an only child on whom she doted. Ten days before she had rung Gilbert up about an eruption she had noticed on the nurse's hands. When he came over to see her he found a strapping wench who complained of nothing. She said she had a sensitive skin and had been using a new brand of soap. Two days later the little boy was violently sick. He had eaten several slices of a rich cake, and Gilbert, who was rushed off his feet with an influenza epidemic, assured the anxious Mrs Egan that it was nothing more than a slight digestive upset. The sickness, however, continued. Mrs Egan, unable to get in touch with Gilbert, called in another doctor who found that the boy had scarlet fever contracted from his nurse, an ambulant case, and that she had most likely picked up the infection at the home of the young man with whom she was walking out.

The boy died. Gilbert never saw him again, for the case was taken out of his hands, but on the day after the funeral Mrs Egan sent for him. It was then that she cursed him. She called him a licensed murderer, and said that as long as she lived Gilbert could count on one enemy who would not rest until she had got even with him.

As little by little the whole miserable story came out, my uncle found that the two things which were troubling him the most were the realisation of his own incompetence and this curse of Mrs Egan. There was no getting away from the fact that he had blundered badly. His examination of the nurse had been perfunctory, he had accepted her own diagnosis, and in the case of the boy he had jumped to the first obvious conclusion. My uncle, seeing that his self-confidence had been badly shaken, tried to talk him into a more reasonable state of mind.

He told him that the result would probably have been the same whatever he had done, that these things were part of the price the public paid for the education of a doctor. Gilbert reminded him that the boy was dead and that it was no consolation to Mrs Egan to know that he was living and learning. Then he tried to tackle the problem from another angle. He told Gilbert that a good doctor treats his patients as individuals and not as cases, but that when he thinks of his work he is wise if he thinks of it in terms of cases. He must in retrospect depersonalise it if he is to maintain his mental balance and keep a scientific point of view.

'As to Mrs Egan,' he said, 'there is no reason why you should have anything more to do with her. She'll talk, of course, but people will soon get tired of listening to her. Your practice may suffer for a bit; then someone else will make a mistake in judgment and the gossip will move on.'

Gilbert refused to be comforted. He said that my uncle did not know Mrs Egan, that her curse wasn't just the despairing cry of an overwrought woman, but that it was the deliberate expression of a malevolence which killed all pity.

My uncle had done what he could. It was little enough. He couldn't give Gilbert a lion's heart in the hide of a rhinoceros, but at all events he made him realise that he had a friend before whom he could unload his troubles.

During the next six months my uncle made a point of seeing as much of Gilbert as possible. He got him to give anaesthetics for him. His work was thoroughly competent, he made no reference to Mrs Egan, and my uncle gathered that his practice still kept him busy. Then one evening when he was dining out my uncle met Mrs Egan herself, and, as luck would have it, sat next to her at dinner.

She was a woman of about forty-five, dark and handsome, a witty and vivacious talker, and obviously a good judge of character. He found that they had several interests in common, and had to revise completely the impression of her that he had received from Gilbert. She struck him as thoroughly sane, with a sense of humour that seemed entirely out of keeping with the malevolence that Gilbert had described.

In the late autumn of that year the wife of the bank manager in Cornbury died in childbirth. My uncle heard about it from the vicar's wife. Mrs Egan had told her only that morning – a tragic case, the third baby, everything apparently normal, but a new doctor whom the poor woman had insisted on having, though Mrs Egan had begged her not to, the same man – she had forgotten his name – who had made such an awful mess of things when Mrs Egan's boy had died.

Poor Gilbert! It looked as if he would have a hard enough time of it to live things down. My uncle made an excuse for running over to see him. At first he didn't seem anxious to talk, but little by little his reserve broke down. Mrs Egan's curse, he said, had begun to work. He had always known that she was in earnest when she said she would not leave him alone. Things would have gone all right had it not been for her, but contrary to his orders about visitors she had insisted on seeing his patient. She had excited her, told her that she was behaving like an invalid when there was nothing the matter with her, and then when things had gone wrong had fussed round and put the woman in a panic.

Gilbert's nerve was badly shaken, and to make matters worse, in the months that followed he had a run of more than ordinary bad luck. In each case it was an error of judgment that might have happened to anyone, but people began to talk. The mothers of the marriageable daughters who had found him so attractively boyish now declared that it was a pity he was so lacking in experience. Someone told my uncle that Lennox was a well-meaning old woman who should have been a parson, and seemed quite astounded when my uncle said that in his opinion Gilbert was far better qualified than

most country practitioners. I wasn't surprised when I heard that
Gilbert had left Cornbury; after all, when he had a certain amount of
means of his own, why should not he leave a neighbourhood that
was, to say the least of it, becoming less and less congenial? My uncle
advised him to take a long holiday, and after spending a fortnight
with a friend on a walking tour in Scotland, he set out on a Mediterranean cruise.

The company was very select. There were archdeacons and elderly
professors who were given ample opportunity for delivering lay
sermons and lectures. There was a colonial governor too, with his
wife and daughter. I don't know if Grace Carstairs was a moth or a
butterfly, but she evidently attracted Gilbert. All went well until the
ship's surgeon went down with appendicitis and had to be put ashore
at Palermo to be operated on in the local hospital. That left the
Cantara without a doctor and Gilbert was approached by the captain,
who asked him to carry on with duties which he assured him would
be purely nominal. Reluctantly Gilbert agreed. He really had no
option. The passengers, most of whom would have said that they had
come on the cruise for reasons of health, were a remarkably healthy
lot. They suffered from over-exposure to the sun, they ate too much,
they could not sleep, and knew exactly the sort of drug that their
doctor at home was in the habit of prescribing for them. But Gilbert
had reckoned without the crew, and the fat was in the fire when he
was asked to see a Lascar who showed every sign of suffering from a
mild form of smallpox. For twenty-four hours Gilbert was kept busy
vaccinating everybody. A party of Americans from Detroit suddenly
announced that they were Christian Scientists. They had to be dealt
with. A lady and her daughter from Leicester, who were ardent anti-
vivisectionists and who seemed to know more about statistics than
anyone on board, had also to be dealt with. Gilbert was dictator and
hero, and the colonial governor was loud in his praise – until they
came into quarantine, where the port authorities, after much hum-
ming and hawing, decided that a mistake had been made, and that
the mild form of smallpox was really a severe form of chickenpox.
To the layman it looked as if Gilbert had been guilty of gross
incompetence. That was what the passengers thought, though my
uncle told me later that even the great Sir William Osler had diag-
nosed smallpox as chickenpox in an outbreak that had occurred
in a coloured ward. The only people who were cheerful were the
Christian Scientists; they had been proved right, even if one of the
archdeacons had a very sore arm. The ladies from Leicester, too,

were pleased at what they regarded as a conclusive demonstration of their theories. Despite the efforts of the shipping company to hush it up, news of the tragicomedy of the ill-fated pleasure cruise found its way into the papers. My uncle wired to Gilbert to come down and stay with him. I was there at the time, and I think he found some consolation in pouring out his woes to me. He even showed me a letter he had received from one of the passengers suggesting that he should take up chicken farming in some district where there was a competent veterinary surgeon to give him advice.

'Bee-keeping would have been more appropriate,' he suggested bitterly. 'At least I could reckon on being stung.'

But the thing that really disturbed Gilbert, that undid all the work that my uncle and I had been trying to do, was a piece of information he sent in a letter a month after he left us. Miss Carstairs, the daughter of the colonial governor, was engaged to be married to a Captain Egan of the Indian Army, a cousin of Mrs Egan of Cornbury. 'She's dogging my footsteps all right!' he said. 'I knew she would, but my career isn't wrecked yet. I've got a job as demonstrator in anatomy' – he mentioned a northern university – 'I can't kill my patients; the subjects are dead already. I ought to have known before that research was my bent. I've been fortunate to hit on some very comfortable rooms, and I've invested in a new car.'

That was the first of many letters I received from Gilbert. He was far more of an interesting letter-writer than I should have imagined; I think he forgot to whom he was writing and just used the vehicle of correspondence as a means of unburdening himself in the same way that some people keep an intimate diary. Only when you have posted a letter you can't recall it. You can't tear out a page and burn it; you can't re-read what you have written a week later and think what a fool you were. You forget, in fact, what you have written.

But I kept those letters from Gilbert, and reading them over, joining them together, it did look as if something queer was happening to his mental make-up. Take his new car, for example. He evidently enjoyed driving it, in fact he said that he rather fancied himself as a driver, and then he added this curious footnote:

The worst of it is, that when once you have become a skilled motorist, the more you drive and the longer you go on driving the more likely you are, by the law of averages, to meet with an accident, not due, of course, to your skill, which all the time should be increasing, but to the increasing probability of your coming in contact with one of the limited number of fools who should never be allowed on the road.

Now the curious thing was that though Gilbert was never involved in an accident, on several occasions he was a witness of them and was called upon to give first aid.

'It's rotten bad luck,' he wrote, 'that a man can't get away from the worries of general practice when he wants to. I don't wish to go about prepared for emergencies, but I've just got to, since the emergencies seem to come my way. It isn't only on the roads, either. The other evening I was at a cinema when the manager asked if there was any doctor present in the audience. Of course I had to go since nobody volunteered. An oldish man had collapsed. I hadn't the faintest notion of what was the matter with him, and he had no one with him. While they were phoning for an ambulance he died. I only hope to goodness there won't be an inquest.'

But there was an inquest. There had to be, for the man had had no regular medical attendant and very little seemed to be known about him except his name: Gann, Edward Gann. E. Gann, in short.

It was only a little thing, but the coincidence was for Gilbert disastrous. Once again he got the idea firmly fixed in his head of the reality of the curse of Mrs Egan. She wasn't going to allow him to live quietly as a demonstrator of anatomy. He had wanted to retire from general practice, from the possibility of making any more fatal mistakes and irremediable decisions, and all the time she was arranging that a man with a broken nerve who had lost all confidence in himself should be tested again and again and be found wanting.

By this time my uncle was beginning to get alarmed. He made a hurried visit to the north, where he saw Gilbert and had a long talk with his chief. It ended by Gilbert being given leave of absence for six months. He went up to town and saw a psychologist who allowed himself to become a rubbish-tip for Gilbert's outpourings, and proceeded to examine the contents of his mental dustbins with a muckrake. The man's aim, I believe, was to get Gilbert to face reality. It must have been as difficult as to get a sheep to look a tiger squarely in the eyes. To Gilbert Mrs Egan and her curse were too horribly real. He preferred to run away, leaving the psychologist to deal with the litter of memories he had so carefully unpacked.

But where was he to flee to? He chose at last a little cottage in Sussex. The bare ridge of the down rose steeply at the back of the garden. He felt the protection of the hills, and yet in twenty minutes after a stiff climb he could stand on top of the windy world and see for thirty miles.

He had arranged to buy the cottage when Witchling Down – why hadn't he been warned by the name? – began to be used by a gliding club. It seemed that its situation in the matter of air-currents and take-off was one of the best on the south coast. The dilapidated farm which used to supply Gilbert with eggs and milk was taken over as a club-house. The members were pleased to find that there was a retired doctor living so near. Gliding, of course, was the best sport in the world, but it wasn't everybody's game, and if an accident did happen there was this doctor fellow actually on the spot to patch you up.

Gilbert soon got to know what sort of weather was best for gliding. He looked forward to gales, to blinding rain, to the soft and kindly sea mists that blotted out the landscape; he hated the gentle breezes and the sun that caused those currents of air on which men climbed on wings into the sky. Those were the days that he chose to go in his car to Lewes or to take long walks, but he usually chose the car, because when he walked the gliders seemed to hover over him, to follow him, to swoop down on him.

It was when he was in Lewes that the club's first fatal accident occurred. People said later that it was a pity that Dr Lennox was not at home, because it had been over two hours before they had been able to get a doctor, and it looked as if the man's life might have been saved had skilled attention been at once available. It was bad luck, but nothing more. They tried to make an arrangement with Gilbert to become doctor to the club and be on duty when gliding was taking place. Gilbert had to tell them that he was sorry, but that he was leaving the district almost at once.

Neither my uncle nor I heard from Gilbert in the next twelve months, though we found out that he had definitely resigned from his teaching post for reasons of health. Then I got a long and rambling letter from him. There was no address and the postmark, he said, had no connection with the place where he was living, which he wanted to keep a secret to himself. He said that he had requested that his name should be taken off the medical register, because he no longer had any wish either to practise or to be known as a doctor. 'It hasn't,' he went on, 'brought any peace to my mind. I have forgotten a lot of what I knew, but I still know more than the ordinary individual, and I see no way of ridding myself of the responsibility of knowledge. If I went abroad or to the colonies, unless I kept to the towns, I should constantly find myself faced with situations where I ought to help, issues perhaps of life and death which I just cannot face. It would be Witchling Down over again. And where am I to live in England? Perhaps, you say, some country town where there is a good doctor. But what happens when the good doctor is out and the butcher's cleaver slips and cuts an artery? That has happened to me. A larger town, you say then. But more things are likely to happen in a larger town. Think of all the motor traffic. I hate to drive a car nowadays. I don't even like going on a train journey if the train is a corridor one; I see the guard walking down the corridor and looking into every compartment in turn. I hear him saying: "Does any of you gentlemen happen to be a doctor?" Though I am no longer on the register and can't sign death certificates, I am still a doctor of medicine. If they couldn't find anyone else, I should be bound to go. If I could only get myself to believe the things they believe in I would join a religious community. I could be quite happy in prison; indeed I tried to join the army as a ranker, but they told me my heart was dicky. I don't mind being shot. I shouldn't mind so much trying to shoot people if war broke out. I should be almost certain to miss them, and they would live as a result of my failure. Now as a result of my failure they die when I am trying to help them.'

Enclosed in the same envelope was a second letter, written on the following day. In it he gave the address of a firm of London solicitors who would forward my letter to him.

'I want you,' he wrote, 'to find out if Mrs Egan is still living in Cornbury, and if she is in the habit of leaving home from time to time. I don't expect you know where she goes, but if you could find that out, too, I should be immensely obliged. I want to check dates and happenings. Is she well? And do you by any chance know if she is interested in spiritualism?'

Some of his questions, with my uncle's help, I was able to answer. Mrs Egan was still in Cornbury, though she was often away visiting friends. Once or twice he had met her, but she had never spoken to him of Gilbert. Then my uncle had a brilliant brainwave. The British Medical Association was meeting that year in Canada. He suggested that he and Gilbert should go together. They would travel with any number of doctors, and under no conceivable circumstances could his professional help be required.

But the letter Gilbert wrote back, the last that we ever received from him, regretfully turned the proposal down. He had resigned his membership of the association some time ago – that was a minor matter as he could still have travelled with the party – but his heart was weak and rest and quiet were essential.

And now for the conclusion of my story. On August the 25th of the following year a saloon car containing four people was travelling along an unfrequented road in Lincolnshire. The road was perfectly straight; the car, driven by a woman, was proceeding at a normal pace, when something apparently went wrong with the steering, and, crashing into a pile of road metal, it overturned into a ditch. The driver was killed, two others of the passengers were seriously injured, and it was only with great difficulty that the fourth, a young man, managed to extricate himself from the wreckage. He it was who later told my uncle what had happened. There was no one in sight, but at a little distance away was a house to which he hurried for help. He knocked at the door without making anyone hear. Then, going round to the back, he found the kitchen door open and entered the house. He was met in the hall by a tall man in a dressing-gown, whom he described as looking very ill.

'I'm sorry, sir,' he said, 'but there has been a ghastly accident. Can you tell me where the nearest doctor is living?'

The face of the occupier of the house became suddenly pale. He swayed, tried to steady himself, and then collapsed on to the floor.

The nearest doctor was not living but dead.

It was only at the inquest that Gilbert's identity was revealed, for he had been living under a different name. The woman driving the car was Mrs Egan.

Do you wonder at my belief in spells and curses and witches? Belief, perhaps, is too strong a word. Fear of witches is really what I mean, a stupid unreasoning fear that omits to take into account the psychology of the unconscious, that makes it impossible to weigh evidence calmly and unemotionally.

The long arm of coincidence? Yes, I know that explains a lot.

But what if the long arm of coincidence were really the long arm, the outstretched hand, the clutching fingers, of Mrs Egan?

Old Masters

Mr Christie Elphinstone of Barham Lodge near Guildford suffered from a weak heart.

From a nursing point of view he was not an interesting patient. For many years he had lived the life of an invalid, and being, like most elderly bachelors, a creature of habit, he was perfectly content with the routine prescribed for him by his London specialist and supervised by Dr Cumberbach, the local practitioner.

He had his little setbacks, of course, and it was on account of these that his sister, Miss Cornelia Elphinstone, who lived in Hammersmith, had persuaded him to have a nurse, for though his housekeeper was in other ways efficient she could do little more in an emergency than telephone for the doctor and wring her hands.

From Mrs Garnet I was assured of a warm welcome, for not only did I relieve her of a responsibility which she had quite determined was beyond her powers to shoulder, but my coming meant that she was able to confide her troubles to another woman, to someone else besides her husband who acted as butler, valet, and general factotum to Mr Elphinstone. Mrs Tredgold, the good-natured and scatterbrained daily help, did not count. It seems a waste of opportunity when you are living in the country to regulate your life by a routine more rigid than is necessary. Mr Christie Elphinstone, however, enjoyed rules. If they were not made for him, he made them for himself.

He got up punctually on the stroke of eleven. When the weather was fine he would then walk with me round the garden of Barham Lodge in a clockwise direction, resting for not more than five minutes on three seats placed at equal distances from each other. The first faced east, the second north, the third west. Before coming in he would sit on the veranda and admire the glorious view to the south.

This little ritual he called 'boxing the compass'. He was then ready for his glass of malted milk.

When the compass had been boxed he would deal with his correspondence, steaming off the penny-halfpenny stamps on the reply-
paid envelopes which were enclosed in the many charitable appeals
he received and returning penny stamps in halfpenny envelopes to
the senders. By this means, he explained to me, he was able to make a
dignified protest against modern methods of publicity. He would
then work for a little on the cataloguing of his pictures until half past
twelve, when he rested before lunch. The remainder of the day was
as carefully planned out: a little physical exercise, a little rest, a little
mental exercise, and again a little rest. Mr Elphinstone was very
happy in his quiet search for health. Had he found it, I believe he
would have been miserable.

The most noticeable feature of Barham Lodge was the pictures.
From an uncle Mr Elphinstone had inherited a valuable collection
of Dutch and Flemish masters which he himself had added to by
discriminate purchase. He had strong views about the hanging of
pictures, and the amount of wall space that should be allotted to
each, and since Barham Lodge was not a large house many of his
smaller canvases were carefully stored in one of the upstairs rooms.
Every Monday morning two, three, or four, according to the size of
the pictures, would be removed from the store-room and hung on
the walls of the study, and one picture, which he called the picture of
the week, would be placed on an easel beside his bed. By this means,
he said, he not only secured a constant change of view, but he was
able really to know his pictures. They became at the same time
familiar friends and eagerly expected visitors.

The plan, which I thought an excellent one, showed all Mr Elphinstone's love of detailed routine. He had two typewritten lists, one for
himself and one for Garnet, which showed exactly which pictures
would appear each Monday morning.

'Five weeks from now,' he would say, 'provided my life is spared, I
shall be looking at a van der Heyden canal scene, a charming little
Eglon van der Neer, an unfinished study of cows' heads by Cuyp,
and a not wholly unsatisfactory example of van Huysum's flower
pieces. I believe that there is more in the composition than first
meets the eye, though it is not a painting that I should have bought
myself. The picture of the week will be the self-portrait of Schalken
lighting his pipe at a candle, an admirable and wholly characteristic
piece of work.'

The picture by van Huysum to which he referred, I only saw once,
when I thought that it was a rather good epitome of Mr Elphinstone

himself, stiff, precise, a little fussy, and yet at the same time with a kindly innocence about it that had a somewhat unexpected charm.

And now for Garnet, butler, valet, and general factotum. There could be no doubt who was the predominating partner of the couple who ran Barham Lodge so efficiently. To Mrs Garnet his word was law, his opinions were her beliefs, his beliefs her facts. I felt at times like shaking her, so incapable did she seem of forming even a simple judgment of her own.

Undoubtedly Garnet was a paragon. He could put washers on taps, he fixed up an electric bell from Mr Elphinstone's room to mine, he could overhaul a typewriter, and on one occasion was allowed by Mr Elphinstone to try his hand at french polishing a bureau in one of the bedrooms. The result was a complete success. He had been with Mr Elphinstone for three years. When he came he knew nothing about pictures. He had made the best of his opportunities, however, and fired by Mr Elphinstone's enthusiasm had picked up not only a great deal of miscellaneous information but had acquired, too, a certain critical sense of his own.

'It's like this, nurse,' he once said to me. 'I'm a handy man; I like mechanical things, and I have always been interested in photography. I'm a good observer too, and when I see something well done I appreciate it, even if it is only the laying of a table. Now there is no nonsense about most of these Dutch painters. Every picture tells a story, as the saying is, and tells it well. If the artist paints satin it is satin, and his mahogany is mahogany. As a butler I like to see the bloom on grapes and a nicely served dish of dessert. And if it's a picture of a young girl polishing a table, I like to see the sunlight shining on the dust where she hasn't polished. Of course the Dutch were unfortunate in their types of female beauty, but they were eminently homely. Their taste may not have been ours, but only semi-occasionally have I been able to detect a mistake in fact.'

I found my stay at Barham Lodge pleasant though monotonous. Once I accompanied Mr Elphinstone up to town when we spent the night at his sister's in Hammersmith Terrace, and twice Miss Elphinstone came down to Guildford for the day. She was, I understood, a great church-worker and had all her brother's love of a life lived to a programme. For some years past she had regularly visited Barham Lodge once a fortnight on a Thursday. The alternate Thursdays had been reserved for Mr Elphinstone's visits to her until ill health had made his journeys less frequent. When he now went up to town it was still on the same day which his sister always kept free from engagements, and he invariably spent the night away from home. Though their tastes were dissimilar – Mr Christie Elphinstone was as uninterested in ritual as she in painting – they were obviously attached to each other in a quiet, undemonstrative sort of way.

Some three weeks after my coming to Barham Lodge Mr Elphinstone consulted me about a letter he had received that morning.

'It's from a fellow I've never heard of,' he said, 'signs himself Charles Osborne, and writes from an address in Chelsea. He wants to know if he can come over one day this week to look at my pictures. He calls himself a humble connoisseur, whatever that may mean, but for all I know to the contrary he may be just one of these gentlemen dealers out to plunder the innocent provincial. I have no objection to showing my pictures to accredited strangers. On the other hand, there is a type of person who though you neither wish to sell nor buy will not take no for an answer. To treat them with courtesy is excessively fatiguing. Now am I well enough to see this man Osborne? If he comes I ought to ask him to stay for lunch, and that will mean that I shall have to sacrifice my afternoon's nap.'

I had been with Mr Elphinstone long enough to know that nothing interested him so much as to talk about his pictures. Despite his seeming reluctance he appeared quite animated at the prospect of a visitor. What he really wanted was an assurance that an invitation to lunch was not necessary and that his rest would be undisturbed.

It was finally arranged that Mr Osborne should be invited to inspect the pictures on Wednesday afternoon, between the hours of three and six. 'I should be much obliged, nurse,' he added, 'if you will be present while he is here. If I show signs of wishing to get rid of the man you must come to my rescue. Ill health and old age alike have their prerogatives.'

Soon after three on Wednesday a large car driven by a chauffeur deposited Mr Charles Osborne at the door of Barham Lodge. I could see from the first that Mr Elphinstone did not like him and that their temperaments clashed. There was the same sort of difference between them as between a delicate water-colour drawing and a clever sketch dashed off in oils. Mr Osborne was a great talker, save for the moments when he stood in a silence that was evidently meant to be profound before a picture, lost either in admiration or in an attempt to find the fitting phrase in which to sum up his verdict.

Garnet of course was in his element, lifting the pictures which were not already hung, on and off the easel, and adjusting blinds and curtains so as to get the best of the afternoon light. He had the customary mask of indifference of the well-trained servant, but once his eye caught mine when Mr Osborne was examining a small canvas with portentous solemnity. Garnet's look was eloquent. 'This man is not quite our class,' it seemed to say. 'He has the jargon but he lacks taste. Mr Elphinstone is wasting his time.'

Mr Osborne, however, gave every sign of appreciative satisfaction.

'Now this little Gerhard Dow, Mr Elphinstone,' he said, at last breaking silence. 'To me it is particularly interesting. The coincidence indeed is remarkable, most remarkable. I wonder if I might have the easel a little, just a very little nearer, the window.'

The picture he was so carefully examining I had only once seen before. It showed a young girl leaning out of a window framed by a vine, about to pick a bunch of grapes. A red admiral butterfly had alighted on the sill. In the shadow of the room an old lady stood polishing a copper pot.

'And might I ask why you find the picture so interesting?' said Mr Elphinstone.

'Because,' replied Mr Osborne, 'I have an exactly similar one in my own collection. Of course I'm not suggesting for a minute that this is not an original. It most obviously is. But I've lived with mine for nearly five years. I regard it as one of the gems of my collection, and only a month ago no less an authority than Willoughby Manton congratulated me on possessing such a lovely little masterpiece. I can only suggest that the picture was painted in duplicate.'

'That of course is possible,' said Mr Elphinstone. 'It is more likely though, to be quite frank, that yours is a copy by one of Dow's pupils. You see,' he went on, 'this particular picture has been in my family for nearly fifty years. Its history can be traced. It was part of a larger collection from which the Musée Bernard at Montpelier was formed in 1875.'

'As far as pedigree goes you have the advantage over me, Mr Elphinstone. I bought my picture in Scotland for a matter of a few guineas. It had been shamefully neglected. The people from whom I bought it came of an old family who had connections with Russia, and I need not remind you of the vogue of the Dutch school in that country in the eighteenth century.'

Mr Elphinstone was evidently not convinced.

'I should like to see it,' he said.

'And so you shall, my dear sir!' Mr Osborne exclaimed. 'I can't expect you to come down to my little place in Pembrokeshire, but that won't be necessary. I have a *pied-à-terre* in Chelsea with just a few of my favourite pictures to keep me in touch with the dear Dutch masters. My Dow – you see, I still insist on calling it a Dow – is one of them. Look me up some day, if you ever come to town. I am afraid I am usually occupied until about five, but almost any evening will suit me. All I ask is twenty-four hours' notice. And now I must give my mind to this charming little Moucheron.'

At last Mr Osborne took his departure, but not before he had renewed his invitation to Mr Elphinstone to visit him in Chelsea when he was next in town.

To my surprise Mr Elphinstone seemed little the worse for what had proved to be a rather tiring afternoon. He slept badly, and in consequence extended the periods of his daily rest by half an hour until the balance was adjusted, when he resumed his ordinary routine. He made no comments on Mr Osborne's visit, and I thought that gentleman had been completely forgotten, when the following week he announced his intention of spending Thursday night with his sister in order that he might have an opportunity of judging for himself the genuineness of Mr Osborne's picture.

'He is not a man,' he said, 'in whose taste and judgment I should put any confidence. If, however, Willoughby Manton accepted the picture as genuine, I confess that I should like to have an opportunity of examining it. I still believe that it is an excellent copy by a pupil, but I shall not be satisfied until I have seen for myself.'

So we went up to town on Thursday morning, after Mr Osborne had been duly notified. We lunched with Miss Elphinstone in Hammersmith Terrace, Mr Elphinstone rested in the afternoon, and then after tea I accompanied him in a taxi to Chelsea where we were welcomed by the effusive Mr Osborne.

The room in which he received us was large and overcumbered with furniture, good furniture, old furniture, valuable furniture. Books were everywhere, piled on chairs and even stacked on the floor, and there in the centre of the wall, dwarfed by the larger canvases which surrounded it, was the picture we had come to see.

'Now where will you sit?' said Mr Osborne fussily. 'What seat would be best for Mr Elphinstone, nurse? Perhaps this armchair; it is not too low. I will take the picture down so that we can examine it together at close quarters.'

Mounting a low stool he carefully removed the picture and placed it on a chair before Mr Elphinstone, who, spectacles on nose, sat gazing at it for a minute or two in silence. When he spoke it was to ask a question.

'Why, Mr Osborne,' he said, 'did you have it glazed?'

'It was a matter of perhaps rather foolish prejudice on my part,' he replied. 'I distrust London smoke and the damp air from the river, and my good landlady has a passion for dusting. The glass is an additional protection in travelling, for when I go down to Pembrokeshire I take it and that little study of a head by Greuze – I call her my guardian angel – with me. But you are right, Mr Elphinstone, and only confirm what Willoughby Manton said the other day when he told me about this new method of sealing pictures in wax. I should like to try the experiment. It could be cleaned at the same time. You will have noticed, of course, that it would be vastly improved by judicious cleaning.'

'Yes,' said Mr Elphinstone, 'provided that the man to whom you entrusted the work knew exactly when to stop. I congratulate you, Mr Osborne. I confess that I expected to find nothing more than a copy by a contemporary. I am not an expert, but if you really want to know my opinion, I should say that beyond doubt this is a genuine Gerhard Dow. I wish we had the two pictures together for comparison. Have you a photograph of yours, by any chance? I have only an engraving of mine by de Launey that I picked up some years ago in Paris.'

'You have come up against yet another of my foolish prejudices,' Mr Osborne exclaimed. 'I have never had my pictures photographed. But really, I do not see why I should not make an exception: I will send you a proof for comparison with pleasure, and perhaps you might be able to arrange with a local man to photograph yours.'

Mr Elphinstone explained that that would be an easy matter; he had an Admirable Crichton in his butler, who had done similar work for him before. Then, after expressing his thanks to Mr Osborne, he took his leave.

'I don't know what to make of that man, nurse,' he said to me as we drove back to Hammersmith Terrace. 'On the whole, I am inclined to think that he is not so genuine as his pictures. I should not be surprised if he has marked me down as a possible purchaser for his Dow. Well, we shall see.'

On our return to Barham Lodge Mr Elphinstone had to take things very quietly for a few days, but this did not prevent him from giving detailed instructions to Garnet about the photograph he wanted taking. I had had previous proof of Garnet's skill as a craftsman, but the result surprised me. In the photograph every detail of the picture was clear; indeed I saw in it things that I had never noticed in the original. A proof was sent to Mr Osborne and a few days later he returned one of his. Mr Elphinstone showed me the two together.

'He had the glass removed, he tells me, but whoever took the photograph did not know his job so well as Garnet. A good deal of the detail is lost, as you see; which would probably come out in cleaning. You can barely distinguish the outline of the wicker-cage in the background. But I think we may safely say that this is a genuine replica. Twins, as you know, nurse, do not like to be separated. We must see what we can do about it.'

So Mr Elphinstone was thinking of buying the picture. That, at least, was a sign that he was feeling better.

The following day, however, he took a turn for the worse, and for the first time since my arrival at Barham Lodge I was kept really busy. Dr Cumberbach, who took the view that this was only a temporary setback, suggested that I might like a woman he knew who had had some nursing experience to help at night, but Garnet offered to sleep in Mr Elphinstone's room and I preferred the known to the unknown. No one could have looked after him better, he knew exactly how to make the old gentleman comfortable, and we soon had him sitting up again demanding of his doctor a really good tonic, since he had quite made up his mind to spend the following Thursday in town.

'I have told him that I have an important business engagement,' he said. 'As a matter of fact, I intend to pay Mr Osborne a second visit and to walk away with his picture. Or rather, that you shall walk away with his picture. I have made him an offer, and after some beating about the bush he is prepared to accept it. He wants me, however, to take delivery in person.'

Dr Cumberbach hummed and hawed a little, but Mr Elphinstone was bent on getting his own way, and so satisfactory was his progress that the doctor eventually gave him leave, stipulating only that in order to avoid all unnecessary fatigue he should make the journey by car. He wished first to go straight to Mr Osborne's rooms in Chelsea. Garnet, however, got me to persuade him that it would be less tiring if he repeated the procedure of the previous visit, lunching at Miss Elphinstone's and having a long rest there in the afternoon. Routine, as I have already said, regulated Mr Elphinstone's life, and as soon as he realised that he would only be doing what he had done before he fell in with our proposal without demur.

Thursday happily was a fine day. We took with us in the car a large empty suitcase into which the picture could be packed. Though I had already seen that Mr Elphinstone was comfortably settled, Garnet insisted on adjusting the rugs and Mrs Garnet was on the steps of Barham Lodge, a rather pathetic, wistful-looking Mrs Garnet, to wish us goodbye.

'Oh, Mr Elphinstone,' she said. 'You will take care of yourself, won't you? I wish you weren't going, sir.'

'She has had bad news about her mother,' Garnet explained. 'The poor old woman was taken ill with pneumonia and had to be taken to hospital yesterday.'

'I'm sorry to hear that,' said Mr Elphinstone. 'You must make arrangements for your wife to see her, Garnet, if it seems desirable. I dare say we could manage for a day or two with Mrs Tredgold, if you can fix matters up with her.'

Soon after five that evening, Mr Elphinstone and I found ourselves again in Mr Osborne's sitting-room.

It had undergone a remarkable change since our last visit, for most of the furniture and nearly all the books had been removed.

'I must apologise a thousand times for receiving you like this, Mr Elphinstone,' he exclaimed. 'The fact of the matter is that we are in the process of spring cleaning and that the painters and paper-hangers begin their work tomorrow. It ought to have been done long ago, but I couldn't face the upheaval. You will be pleased to know that I was able to find the original receipt for the picture. I shall miss my little Dow, of course, more than I care to think about, but it is a satisfaction to realise that it will be in the safe keeping of a connoisseur like yourself. If I may express one wish, it is that the picture should not eventually find its way to America.'

'I do not think that you need fear that,' Mr Elphinstone replied. 'When I die my collection will be offered to one or other of the provincial galleries.'

He walked over to the table on which the picture had been placed and looked at it lovingly. 'After all this lapse of time,' he said, 'it is perhaps only fitting that the two should be together again.' I saw him fumbling in his pocket and, guessing the purpose, pretended to take an intelligent interest in an engraving that hung to the right of the door. Mr Elphinstone and Mr Osborne moved over towards a desk at the other end of the room. I caught a few words about a cheque and a receipt, Willoughby Manton, and a really capable restorer. Then, the transaction completed, Mr Osborne set about the business of packing the picture into the large empty suitcase which we had brought with us.

We had been gone less than an hour by the time we got back to Hammersmith Terrace. Mr Elphinstone, who showed no signs of undue fatigue, retired early to rest, but not before he had got me to unpack the picture and place it in such a position that he could see it from his bed, and enjoy the company of the little Dutch girl and her mother at breakfast.

There arrived on the following morning a letter from Garnet to say that his wife had received a telegram with worse news of her mother. She had availed herself of Mr Elphinstone's permission to leave. Garnet had had some difficulty in securing the help he had expected as Mrs Tredgold could not come until late in the day. He ventured to suggest that under the circumstances Mr Elphinstone might find it most convenient if he delayed his return until the evening. He would have telephoned, but the line was out of order.

Mr Elphinstone accepted the slight alteration to his plans – though no alteration to plans which he had made could ever appear to him as slight – with equanimity. His visit to London had been eminently successful; at whatever hour he returned he was bringing with him the spoils of war.

Owing to delay caused by a punctured tyre we did not arrive at Barham Lodge until nearly seven. We were greeted not by Garnet but by a flustered Mrs Tredgold, who appeared completely overwhelmed by the bad news she had to tell. Poor Mrs Garnet had been run over in London on her way to see her mother in hospital. Garnet had been called up by the police the night before, since it had been impossible to get through to him on the telephone. He had left a note for her which she had found when she had let herself in with her key that afternoon. There was a note for Mr Elphinstone too. The man had not come with the fish, so she had heated up some soup and made a nice rice pudding. And something had gone wrong with the electric light. If Garnet had been there he would have seen to it, of course, but she hadn't been able to get through to the electricians because the telephone was out of order.

Here was a pretty kettle of fish. It was impossible to think of every-thing at once or I should have sent back word with the chauffeur to see that at least we should have light on our troubles. Mr Elphinstone, however, was my first care. He stood in the hall, the unopened letter in his hand, a pathetic picture of indecision. I managed, finally, to persuade him that he would be best in bed, and in less than an hour he was enjoying his soup in his own room, warmed by a cheerful fire, and lighted, not so cheerfully, by four candles, a third of the total supply available for the house.

'You may as well see poor Garnet's letter,' he said to me, 'though it adds little to what Mrs Tredgold told us and gives no indication of when we may expect to see him.'

> I deeply regret to inform you [I read] that Mrs Garnet has met with a serious accident while proceeding to the hospital where her mother had been taken. As it was impossible for me to obtain your permission I thought it only right to proceed to London immediately. I have given Mrs Tredgold full instructions and trust she will give satisfaction during my enforced absence.

The letter, concise, stiff, and to the point, was typical of Garnet. How I wished he were back! Unless he returned early in the morning I looked like having an unusually busy day. For the moment there was nothing I could do except to see that Mr Elphinstone had everything he required for the night, to unpack his picture, and to place it on the easel by his bed.

I was early astir next morning preparing Mr Elphinstone's breakfast. The scatterbrained Mrs Tredgold was obviously incapable of making herself understood on the telephone, so I walked to the village post office and put through a call to the electricians, asking them to see at once to the electric light, and another to the telephone people at Guildford. I then thought of ringing up the hospital to inquire about Mrs Garnet, only to remember that Garnet in his hurried note had omitted to mention the name of the hospital to which his wife had been taken. However, the police at Guildford would know, since the message had come through them. I rang them up. To my utter amazement they informed me that they knew nothing about the matter. Briefly I informed them of what had happened and was told that someone would come over in the course of the morning. Then I hurried back to Barham Lodge, while my mind tried in vain to disentangle the events of the last twenty-four hours. It looked, of course, like a put-up job, but what was the job and who were involved in it? Garnet had obviously lied. Had Mrs Garnet lied too? The telephone and the electric light were out of order. Had that been arranged, and if so for what purpose? And then I thought of the pictures. That was what they had been after. Garnet had secured for himself a clear field and a clear start while Mr Osborne leisurely played his fish. It was certainly a matter for the police.

Poor old Mr Elphinstone! He blamed me at first for being precipitate, for he liked comfort, and a charitable disposition acts as a
buffer to reality, but as soon as I mentioned the word pictures he
became a different man. He insisted on dressing immediately in
order to take stock of his collection. With his typed catalogue in
hand he went the round of the house, checking the contents of each
room. When we came to the room where the smaller canvases were
stored Mrs Tredgold was summoned from the kitchen to assist.

'I believe,' said Mr Elphinstone at last, 'that we have been entertaining unworthy suspicions about Garnet.' Then his face suddenly
clouded. 'The Gerhard Dow!' he exclaimed. 'There is only one! Of
course there should be two. That man Osborne has sold me a fake
and Garnet has gone off with the original picture. We will have the
glass removed at once; I must examine it again.'

I have been told that for a woman I am handy with tools. It was
not a difficult matter to remove the screws, in fact they came out
very easily. Mr Elphinstone asked for a silk handkerchief and soap
and water. With infinite care he began to sponge the surface, while
I gazed at him enthralled as the colours became more brilliant and
the details of the background less obscure. I already knew the
verdict, but tact demanded that Mr Elphinstone should himself
pronounce it.

'It seems,' he said, with a wintry smile, 'that I have bought my own
picture!'

To trace the stages in the Garnet-Osborne fraud was not difficult.
Much had depended on the known regularity of Mr Elphinstone's
habits about which he prided himself so much, and on his keeping
his smaller pictures unhung in a special room; much had depended
on the fact that when he paid his fortnightly visits to his sister
he always spent the night away from home. It must have been a
comparatively easy matter for Garnet to run up to town with the
picture and, after it had been treated with whatever preparation he
and Osborne used, to place it in the glazed frame ready for Mr
Elphinstone's inspection. Osborne had managed matters in such a
way that Mr Elphinstone himself had asked for a photograph. The
capable Garnet, working at leisure at Barham Lodge then took
his photographs, a good photograph of the picture as it was known
to Mr Elphinstone, a poor photograph of the same picture in a
different frame after it had been touched up. He must, I imagine,
have had a shock when Mr Elphinstone's temporary setback had
made it seem unlikely that he would keep his engagement with Mr

Osborne. I recalled his anxious solicitude. I remembered, too, that it was Garnet who suggested that he should leave Barham Lodge on Thursday morning instead of motoring direct to Osborne's rooms in Chelsea. That gave him the time he needed for the faking of the picture and for getting it up to London.

All that remained was to cut the telephone wire and to put the electric light out of order, for it was more than possible that on his return Mr Elphinstone would want to remove from the store-room his Gerhard Dow in order to compare it with his new purchase. He could, of course, have done it by candlelight, but the old gentleman had a dread of fire.

Altogether it was a plot worthy of an old master. It deserved to succeed, and as far as I know it did. The police never traced him, or Mrs Garnet, or the glib Mr Osborne. They had more than twenty-four hours to make their getaway, and they got away. I don't know what the sum was that Mr Elphinstone paid for his experience; I doubt very much if he has learnt that regular habits and a life governed by strict routine have grave disadvantages. I myself am the richer by his gift of an excellent photograph of a girl leaning out of a window in the act of picking a bunch of grapes. And I have learnt a good deal, too, about pictures. Sometimes when I have a day off I form one of that oddly assorted group that trails after the gentleman who gives such interesting talks in the National Gallery. I even once ventured to ask him a question, just as children delight to encourage a disheartened teacher by airing their intelligence. The picture of a poulterer's shop was by Gerhard Dow. And thanks to Mr Elphinstone, to Garnet, and to Mr Osborne, I shall always be interested in Gerhard Dow.

No Body

Angram-on-Sea. I'm not likely to forget it or The Moorings or Mr Sandeman; how he lost his temper and how we lost his body when it disappeared into thin air. On dark wet nights I even dream that I am there again, a confused dream in which there is a police inspector and a black poodle; silly little Miss Sandeman goes off into hysterics and Mr Harrison Grebe tries to cope competently with an emergency, while in and out of all the dream rooms passes the figure of Peterson, the butler, just as he used to pass in real life, so noiselessly that you never knew that he had come – or gone.

It was at the beginning of 1919 that I went to The Moorings to nurse Miss Sandeman. Which shall I describe first? The house, I suppose, because though it was as ordinary as my patient it was more significant. To reach The Moorings you passed the faded false front of the esplanade – it always reminded me of Miss Sandeman's toupee – to an estate that had developed rapidly in the ten years before the war, when the golf-course had begun to rival yachting as Angram's chief attraction.

The Moorings was a large two-storeyed house of red brick, with a glaze that made it look younger than it really was – again I was reminded of Miss Sandeman – red tiles, warranted not to weather, and white paint everywhere, from the doors of the garage to the great white flagstaff on the flat roof where Mr Sandeman had mounted a telescope. He was not interested in the stars, but he liked to pick out the details of the yachts as they lay at their moorings in the estuary. From the roof too he could command the golf-course, and since he must have been the most unpopular member of the club, I have no doubt that he enjoyed commanding it.

Miss Sandeman was a woman of about sixty, vain and vulgar and intensely selfish. I had nursed her through a bad attack of influenza, her heart was weak, and she was subject to asthma. In her place I should have tried the experiment of banishing the poodle and the parrot, but she was devoted to them both. Whenever I gave her her medicine she always asked me if I had shaken the bottle. I wish I could have shaken the woman instead; it would have done her all the good in the world.

At weekends her brother, Mr Sandeman, would come down with his secretary, Mr Harrison Grebe. Mr Sandeman, I gathered, had many irons in many fires; the job of poor little Grebe was to help him pull them out at the right time, to play golf with him, or rather to be beaten at golf by him, and to act as a smiling, resilient buffer between himself and the world. Grebe had held some post in the milk controller's department during the war. Nothing seemed to sour him, the cream was always on the surface, a most polite young man.

A nurse is of course expected, and rightly expected, not to gossip, but in a thoroughly uncongenial household when you are sandwiched between two stale slices of life, it is only natural to appreciate a little mustard. Gossip is mustard, and I confess that I listened to the gossip of Mrs Peabody, the efficient and loquacious charlady who was always in and out of The Moorings, with a considerable amount of interest.

From her I learnt that Angram-on-Sea had its doubts about Mr Sandeman. They said that a partner of his had been interned during the war and that he ought to have gone with him. They distrusted the gentlemen who used to visit him at weekends in high-powered cars with improperly controlled headlights. He had been forced to take down the Union Jack which he had flown from his flagstaff in the early days of 1914 ('Wrong way up, too,' said Mrs Peabody), and people didn't think the vicar had done right in taking his subscription for the Armistice Day celebration. Of course, during the war he hadn't been allowed to use his telescope, but Mrs Peabody implied that before the war he had used it in an improper fashion to watch the war coming on. It was all what she called 'camerflage', done to make a show.

'Don't tell me, nurse,' she said, 'that a man whose neck runs up into his head like that isn't a naturalised German. He ought to be alienated, that's what he ought to be.'

Miss Sandeman, Mr Sandeman, Mr Harrison Grebe – I've introduced you to them all. But you haven't met Peterson, the butler. I liked him the best of the bunch. He knew his work, he was quiet and polite, and nurses always appreciate politeness in servants. The housemaid had a way of leaving my bedroom undusted, the parlourmaid was determined not to be put upon, the cook resented my knowledge of invalid cookery, but Peterson, who came and went so silently, treated me as he would have treated any other guest.

So much for the prologue. And now for the drama itself.

It was Saturday evening and the four of us were seated at dinner. Mr Sandeman was in one of his worst moods, for he had insisted on playing a second round at golf and Mr Grebe had forgotten himself and had beaten his employer on the last green. Miss Sandeman kept harping monotonously on her fear that her brother had been over-taxed, a beautifully expressive phrase when applied to Mr Sandeman. The man was spoiling for a quarrel. He snapped at Mr Grebe, he snubbed his sister, he gazed at me as if I were a peculiarly dangerous bunker obstructing the fairway, and when the parrot gallantly tried to open a conversation, he ordered Peterson to 'remove that bird' as if it had been a cold boiled fowl that had disagreed with him.

Of course it would be that evening of all evenings when the perfect service on which Sandeman prided himself failed. Probably there had been some sort of a row in the kitchen. There was an unaccountable delay between the soup and the fish, and to make matters worse, Peterson, in removing the plates, stumbled over the poodle which had been hiding under the table. There was a crash of crockery and an explosion from Mr Sandeman. Harrison Grebe blinked nervously behind his rimless glasses.

'You clumsy-footed, wooden-fingered effigy!' Sandeman bawled. 'I'm hanged if I know what is the matter with you tonight!'

Peterson, his neck a deep crimson, picked up the broken pieces of china, while the dog nosed at the food, his tail between his legs, and one eye turned furtively to the door.

'Poor Ponto,' said Miss Sandeman, 'it wasn't your fault, darling, was it? Come and lie down by me.'

Her brother glared at her in silence.

But the worst was still to come. As the butler handed a dish of trifle to Mr Sandeman his hand shook.

'Ah, that's what it is!' Sandeman cried, his face purple with rage. 'You've been drinking!'

'I have not, sir.'

It was evident to Mr Grebe and myself as we fidgeted in our chairs that the man would need all his self-control. Mr Sandeman was unbearable.

'You've been drinking,' he went on, 'and I've myself to blame for engaging a half-bred Swiss who as likely as not was a German spy. You can take your notice, and the sooner you leave the better. Pay the man what's owing to him, Grebe, and don't let me see him again.'

Peterson drew himself up to his full height. He was a big powerful man, the only real man present in the room.

'Madam,' he said, turning to Miss Sandeman, 'and you too, Mr Grebe, are witnesses of what has happened; it is as well to have witnesses, since my occupation is dependent on my character. I am not a half-bred Swiss, and as for being a spy, Mr Sandeman knows more – '

He never finished the sentence. The red-faced bully at the head of the table looked up suddenly, a glass of wine half raised to his lips. He sprang to his feet with a loud cry, his fists clenched in anger, and then fell sprawling across the table.

'Good Lord! The man's in a fit!' said Mr Grebe.

It was soon obvious that the man was dead.

Miss Sandeman, however, was alive and in hysterics. I could do something for her when it became evident I could do nothing for her brother. Grebe seemed incapable of grappling with the emergency.

'I think Mr Grebe and I can get him up to his room,' said Peterson, 'and then, sir, it would be perhaps as well if you were to phone for the doctor.'

For the next hour I had my hands full in looking after Miss Sandeman, in trying to quieten her and in getting her to bed. It was nearly nine when a maid knocked at the door and in an awestruck whisper told me that the doctor would like to speak to me for a minute before he came up. I found him talking to Harrison Grebe in the hall.

'A bad business,' he said to me. 'Mr Grebe and I thought it would be as well if you were to tell me just what happened at dinner.'

He heard me without interrupting.

'Yes,' he went on, 'that bears out Mr Grebe's story in every particular. It's a couple of months since I last examined Mr Sandeman, and gave him advice which, of course, he refused to take. Today he played two rounds of golf, drank rather freely at dinner, I gather, and then had this fracas with the butler. I forget who it was who said that his life was at the mercy of any scoundrel who chose to insult him. I've no reason for supposing that the butler was a scoundrel. The point is that a man with a heart in the condition of Sandeman's can't afford to fly into a towering passion when he's tired out, and has eaten and drunk too well into the bargain. There'll be no difficulty about the death certificate, Grebe. And now, nurse, about your patient? She'll tell me all about herself in a minute, I know, but I thought I'd have a word with you first.'

I had a lot to do when Dr Collins left, but by ten o'clock Miss Sandeman had had her sedative draught and asked to be left alone after giving me a message that she would like to see Mr Grebe first thing in the morning.

I found Mr Grebe in the study, the telephone beside him on the table.

'That's the fourth trunk call,' he said. 'This has come at a rather unfortunate time for Mr Sandeman's firm. I don't think they realised that he might peg out at any moment.'

It was interesting to see a new and more self-assertive Harrison Grebe emerging out of his silky chrysalis. Evidently he had no regrets for his late employer. I should have been surprised if he had.

'Things have been happening,' he went on, 'while you have been upstairs. Peterson has gone – went off in a cab half an hour ago. He said Sandeman' – it was like Harrison Grebe to omit the Mr as soon as the man who bullied him was dead – 'had told him to clear out, that he had been treated like a dog and had no intention of spending another night under this roof. I tried to dissuade him, but it was no use. Sandeman had certainly given him his dismissal. I couldn't detain him. So I paid him what was owing, got an address to which letters could be forwarded, and off goes Peterson in the pouring rain with three suitcases and a justifiable grievance. I suppose at this moment he is in the train nursing it. A queer fellow. He made a point of my going through all his baggage to make certain that he had not gone off with the spoons. But I mustn't keep you, nurse. You'll be going up to his room, I suppose. It was lucky we had you here. I've got letters that will keep me busy till midnight and I ought to draft an obituary notice.'

Before I went to Mr Sandeman's room I looked in to see that Miss Sandeman was all right. The sedative had taken effect and she was already asleep – a pathetic little object in the big curtained bed. Then I went down the corridor to Mr Sandeman's room, and, opening the door, switched on the light.

The room was empty. I was not dreaming. I had full possession of my senses. The room really was empty, and Mr Sandeman's body gone. It was neither on the bed by the window nor underneath the bed. But it must have lain on the bed, or, to be exact, someone's body had lain on the bed, which showed marks of pressure. I looked about the room. On the dressing-table were the contents of Mr Sandeman's pockets: his wallet and notebook, his massive gold watch and chain. I stifled a stupid feeling of reluctance and opened the wardrobe and cupboards, where Mr Sandeman's clothes hung in an orderly array that struck me as more horrible than confusion. Where on earth was the body? Then I told myself that, after all, there might not be the slightest call for alarm. It had probably been removed for some reason into one of the spare rooms, but before I went farther I thought it best to go down to the study and report to Mr Grebe.

He was sipping a glass of whisky and water when I entered the room.

'Is there anything I can do for you, nurse?' he said.

I told him my dilemma, watching the expression of complete bewilderment on his face.

'But this is absurd!' he said. 'When I left Mr Sandeman's room with Dr Collins, the room at the end of the corridor, his body was lying on the bed by the window. There must be some mistake. He can't have vanished.'

I told him that he had better come and see for himself, and together we went upstairs, tiptoeing like two conspirators for fear of waking Miss Sandeman.

Of course he saw that I was right and that the body had gone.

'What are we to do?' he said helplessly.

'Search the house from top to bottom,' I replied, 'and since we may as well do the job thoroughly, we'll begin with the roof.'

Mr Grebe climbed the low flight of stairs, I following him. He opened the door and looked out. It was raining cats and dogs. There was nothing to be seen but the clumsy tripod of the telescope and three white flower vases gleaming in the rain. We made a hurried search of the box-room, of the spare bedrooms, of Mr Grebe's bedroom, of my bedroom. The bath-rooms were empty, and all the downstairs rooms. We even looked into the kitchen.

'I suppose,' he said at last, 'that there is nothing for it but to telephone to the police.'

He put through the call, while I stood by him.

'And if I might make a suggestion,' he added when he had told his story, 'it would be as well to bring Dr Collins along with you. He and I were the last people to see the body.'

We sat in the study awaiting their arrival.

What could have happened? Was Mr Sandeman not dead after all? Had Peterson spirited away the body? Harrison Grebe was certain that no one had left the house from the time of the doctor's departure in his car to when Peterson had walked down the path carrying his suitcases to an empty cab. A body could not be hidden in three suitcases, and the suitcases had been searched.

An inspector of police arrived with an angry-looking Dr Collins at a quarter to eleven.

We all went into the study.

'This is a queer kettle of fish,' said the inspector, as he took out his note-book. 'Dr Collins has told me about his part in the business, but I'd like you, Mr Grebe, to begin by describing just what happened at dinner.'

Harrison Grebe gave a surprisingly coherent account of the evening's incoherence, which I confirmed. Then the telephone bell rang. The inspector took the call.

'Peterson,' he said, 'caught the 9.50 all right. He had three suitcases with him. And now,' he went on, turning to Dr Collins, 'let's establish the fact of Mr Sandeman's death. You're prepared to swear to that, doctor?'

'Of course I am; dead as a doornail.'

'And the cause of death?'

'Angina, I have no doubt. I told him my diagnosis months ago, but he was not the sort of man to listen to advice, let alone to act on it.'

'Mr Sandeman jumped up suddenly. He had been drinking a glass of wine before he collapsed,' the inspector went on.

Dr Collins looked at him curiously; he seemed to me to be not quite so confident.

'If you are thinking of poison,' he said, 'I saw not the slightest indication of it. Though,' he added, 'if the butler had poisoned him there would be every inducement to get rid of the body.'

'My job is to find out where the body is,' the inspector answered. 'You and Mr Grebe were the last to see it about eight forty-five. You, doctor, left soon after nine. At nine-thirty Peterson leaves with his suitcases for the station. And you are sure,' he went on, turning to Mr Grebe, 'that no one else left the house in the interval?'

'Absolutely certain, unless they went out through the kitchen, where the maids would have seen them.'

The inspector closed his note-book.

'And now,' he said, 'I'd like to have a good look round the house.'

Dr Collins begged to be excused. He was expected at a confinement. It was still raining hard when he left. The inspector asked me to accompany him and Grebe, and together we went up to Mr Sandeman's bedroom. But the room, like the rest of the house, which we searched in the same order as we had done before, had no secrets to disclose. The inspector, it is true, was more thorough; I had not thought of looking into the cistern or the coal-cellar, but after all I'm not paid for that sort of thing, and Mr Sandeman was no patient of mine. A strong-minded woman has to take care that she is not always being put upon. The inspector, however, earned his pay, for he went out into the steady downpour with his flash-lamp to see if there were any telltale footprints on the flower-beds or if something besides water was in the water-butts.

'It's a queer case, this,' he said when he returned, obviously as unenlightened as when he had left. 'Of course I haven't searched the whole of the house; there is Miss Sandeman's room and the maids' room. But I think they had better wait until the morning. And between ourselves,' he added with a smile, 'I'd like to know a little more about the legal position. Who owns a man's dead body? What's the charge that is going to be preferred? I don't see that we can do anything more tonight. See that the outside doors are all locked, Mr Grebe, and remove the keys. I'll be round first thing in the morning.'

It was after midnight when I went to bed. Of course I couldn't get to sleep; I didn't expect to. What was the clue to the disappearance of Mr Sandeman? Again and again I went over the happenings of the last six hours. Then I passed in review the chief actors in the drama. What did I know about them? Poor Miss Sandeman I ruled out. She was really too silly. Harrison Grebe, if I was any judge of character, was a very ordinary man, capable perhaps of carrying through a shady business deal, but lacking in imagination. I could not associate him with anything bizarre.

Peterson was different. Mr Sandeman had called him a German spy. I had always thought of him as English, though not perhaps as typically English. He certainly would make a very good spy; he was resourceful, he was silent, and he knew how to control his temper.

And Mr Sandeman himself? According to Mrs Peabody, the charlady, Angram-on-Sea had been suspicious of him for a long time, but in those days to suspect anyone you disliked was both fashionable and patriotic. Supposing, however, that rumour for once was right, that Mr Sandeman had a German partner, that he had been playing a double game? From what Peterson had said, it sounded as if he suspected something of the sort. But Sandeman could hardly be a German spy. He looked too much the part for one thing, and weekend residents on the east coast during the war were likely to be pretty carefully scrutinised by the authorities.

On the other hand, there was nothing to have prevented his being a British spy, a stalking-horse allowed to roam at large on condition that he passed on the information he received. If that were the case and Peterson knew that there had been double-crossing, there would be a deeper if less obvious source of enmity between the two men than Sandeman's overbearing temper.

At last I fell asleep only to enter a world of dreams as confused as the world of reality.

When I woke up it was half past four and the rain had ceased. Lying on my back in bed with my eyes shut, I turned again to the solution of the problem. Where was Mr Sandeman's body?

'If I were Peterson,' I thought, 'and Peterson was a German who realised that that beast Sandeman had sold his country, what should I like to see done to him? What would justice have meted out had the man but had his due?' ·

Then like a flash I saw the answer. I got out of bed and dressed, and, taking my electric torch, went along the corridor and up the flight of stairs that led on to the roof.

I opened the door. There was nothing to be seen on the roof but what we had seen before: the tripod of the telescope and the three white flower vases. But this time I was looking above the roof to where, hung high from the flagstaff, a black body blotted out the stars.

That was the end of the story, as far as I was concerned. When the inspector arrived, he and Harrison Grebe got the body down and carried it to the bed by the window. Then, after thanking me for the help I had given and after telling me that it would be as well for the present to say nothing of what had happened, I was politely given to understand that my services were no longer required. How like men! Why shouldn't I have been asked to make a third when they talked things over in the study? I had found their body for them, unravelled their skein. It was only natural that I should have liked to see the thread of the story neatly wound up.

But I know this much. The inspector stayed for an hour. He had evidently much to say to Mr Harrison Grebe. And there was no inquest on Mr Sandeman.

Nor did I ever hear again of Peterson. Whatever his nationality was, I hope he has got a situation, though it may not be as a butler, where his politeness and efficiency are properly appreciated.

Butlers with a strong sense of poetic justice are, I imagine, at somewhat of a discount.

Account Rendered

'Medical ethics,' said my uncle, 'is a very curious subject. If my plate were four times its present size, or if the lettering were in scarlet instead of black, my conduct might be judged unethical. I remember once a distinguished surgeon getting hot and bothered over what he called the ethical principle involved if qualified chiropodists were permitted to treat bunions. Any condition, he maintained, involving any structure below the level of the true skin was outside their province. It was a deep, not a superficial question, and a question of principle.'

He took down the tobacco jar from the mantelpiece and, though it was eight o'clock in the evening, filled his first pipe of the day.

'Here's a case in point,' he went on. 'A man came to me this morning with a request, a very queer request. He seemed rather surprised that I did not immediately accede to it in view of the fee he offered. He wanted me to give him an anaesthetic the day after tomorrow at twelve o'clock at night.'

'They chose a most inconvenient hour for the operation,' I said.

'But there wasn't to be an operation. That was the curious thing. All he wanted was to be fully anaesthetised between 11.45 and 12.15. As soon as I had recovered from my natural astonishment I put as tactfully as I could some of the difficulties which my caller had overlooked. I reminded him that I knew nothing whatever about him. For all I knew he might be contemplating suicide. At 11.30 he might swallow a dangerous drug and then when he expired half an hour later I should have been responsible for a death under an anaesthetic.

'Mr Tolson (I'm not guilty of unethical conduct in telling you his name because you, too, may be concerned in the matter) rather naturally took offence at this idea. He explained to me that he could produce unimpeachable references to his character, that his health was excellent, and that he was perfectly prepared to submit to a rigorous medical examination. The reason for his request, which, he now admitted, might appear strange, was that he was engaged upon a piece of research, partly mathematical, partly psychological, into what might be called the relation of space-time and the unconscious.

'He went off the deep end and I soon gave up all attempts to follow him. The gist of the matter was that he wished to verify certain scientific conclusions he had come to by recording his impressions before and after being anaesthetised. That put rather a different light on things. I am not prepared to give an anaesthetic to any Tom, Dick, or Harry who thinks that all he has got to do is to stop me and buy one. On the other hand, there is no reason why I should not co-operate in a piece of research. Tolson evidently saw that I was hesitating and produced from his pocket a telegram. He told me that he had previously arranged with the honorary anaesthetist to the County Hospital at Wilchester to do the job on the day and hour mentioned, but only that morning a wire had come to say that he was ill. He showed it to me. I have met Dr Hancock once or twice. He is a shrewd man and I told myself that if he was satisfied with Tolson's bona fides there was no reason why I should not be. The matter finally ended like this. I told Tolson that I would give him a definite answer tomorrow. If I then decided to do his job of work, I should give him a thorough overhaul and I should bring my niece, a trained nurse, along with me. I explained to him that the after-effects of an anaesthetic are sometimes unpleasant, but I really wanted to have you there to safeguard my interests as much as his. He hummed and hawed a bit but finally agreed, and there the matter rests. That is our little problem in medical ethics. What are we going to do about it?'

I think my uncle had already made up his mind, but he is an old bachelor who likes to have the support of his womenfolk.

'I should certainly anaesthetise Mr Tolson,' I said.

All this happened many years ago. I was young and inexperienced. It is hardly to be wondered at that I gave the wrong answer. I see now that my uncle would have been probably better advised to have nothing to do with Mr Tolson, but his sense of curiosity was very strongly developed – that was partly what made him so good a doctor – and he liked his own way – that was partly what had kept him a bachelor.

At a quarter past eleven on 17th December my uncle's car stopped outside the door of Lebanon Lodge, a square, old-fashioned resid-ence that stood out white behind the solitary cedar that had given to the house its name. We were not kept long waiting. Hardly had the bell ceased ringing when the door was opened by Mr Tolson himself. He was a man of nearer fifty than forty, short and wiry in build, dark hair tinged with grey, and dark, restless-looking eyes. He was wearing a dressing-gown.

'I'm glad to see you, doctor,' he said. 'I was afraid you might be late. I have everything ready, so we can go straight upstairs. I told my old housekeeper to go off to bed an hour ago, so we shall be quite undisturbed.'

The room on the first floor into which he led us had almost as much the appearance of a study as of a bedroom. It was lined with books. At the opposite end from the bed a fire was burning brightly. Heavy crimson curtains were drawn across the bow windows that looked out on to the cedar, while a *portière* of the same colour screened the door.

My uncle wasted no time. He had overhauled his patient on the previous day and had instructed him as to what preparations he should make. By the time the hands of the clock on the mantelpiece pointed to a quarter to twelve Mr Tolson was completely unconscious.

'There's this at least to be said,' remarked my uncle, 'the man knows how to take an anaesthetic.'

Outside the night was still. The only sound in the room was the deep, regular breathing of the man in the bed and the ticking of the clock. It struck twelve. And then, about five minutes past the hour a curious thing happened. Without any warning the door opened and an old man looked into the room. I could only see his head and shoulders. He wore a little black skull-cap, and as he stood there, his lean scraggy neck peering forward, his toothless mouth half open, he gave me the impression of a timid but inquisitive tortoise slowly intruding itself into a hostile world.

'Ah, you are busy, Charles,' he said. 'You can't see me now. But there is no hurry, no need for hurry at all. Another time will do.' Then he closed the door as quietly as he had opened it and disappeared.

'Who the devil was that?' said my uncle. 'There, hold his legs; he's not so deeply under as I thought he was. Steady now, my hearties. That's better,' as the deep, regular breathing began again. 'Who was that, Margaret? I wasn't watching. The housekeeper?'

'It may have been the housekeeper's husband,' I said. 'He seemed quite at home. We'll ask Mr Tolson when he comes round.'

At a quarter past twelve my uncle stopped the anaesthetic and began to put his things together. And then in the hall below we heard the telephone ring. No one seemed to answer the bell; the house-keeper, or whoever it was who had looked into the room a quarter of an hour before, must either have been very deaf or have gone to bed.

'I'll go,' said my uncle. 'It's probably an emergency call for me. My luck's out tonight.'

He was back again in a few minutes.

'Yes,' he said, 'that young ass Jerry Polegate has collided with a lamp-post again and will probably need a couple of stitches. He's round at the surgery. The only comfort is that the motor-bicycle is a complete wreck. What are we to do with you, my dear? Do you mind being left alone here for an hour or so? Of course Tolson is all right, but I should be easier in my mind if there was someone with him. I'll call for you as soon as I have finished branding that young road-hog.'

Naturally I agreed. Tolson was sleeping quietly, the fire was burning brightly. I drew up a chair and settled down to read. The book I took down from the shelf was a beautifully bound copy of *John Buncle*. The fly-leaf was inscribed 'Ex-libris Jarvis Effington'. The name had a slightly familiar ring and I tried in vain to place it, until I remembered that I had once gathered primroses at a place called Effington in Kent. The book itself, however, was as unfamiliar as it was delightful and I read on, regardless of the time.

As the clock struck one Mr Tolson stirred uneasily and began to mutter to himself. A little later he opened his eyes.

'Where am I?' he asked. 'Where has he gone to?'

'Dr Parkinson has been called out to a case,' I replied. 'He will be back very soon.'

'It's all over then,' he said, 'it's all safely over,' and he closed his eyes with a weary sigh of satisfaction, only to open them a few minutes later.

'Tell me,' he said, 'did anything happen when I was under?'

'You took the anaesthetic splendidly. The only thing that surprised us was when an old man came up the stairs a little after twelve and looked into the room without knocking. I think he, too, was surprised to see us and said something about seeing you another time.'

Mr Tolson glanced at me in a curious way. I saw fear, dismay, and a suggestion of something else, of wily satisfaction that gave one the impression that he was well pleased to have escaped from a tiresome visitor.

'That would be my old uncle,' he said at last. 'He ought to have been in bed hours ago.'

'That's where *my* uncle ought to have been,' I thought to myself, but I had not very long to wait before I heard his steps on the stairs.

'Sorry to run off and leave you like that, Mr Tolson,' he said as he came into the room. 'You see, there is no end to a doctor's day. You will be going off to sleep now, I expect. Is there anything I can do for you before we go?'

Apparently there was nothing. Tolson thanked him for his services and handed him an envelope from the table by his bedside.

'I won't keep you waiting,' he said, with a rather attractive smile, 'not even for your fee. I think you will find it is right. Again many thanks, and to you too, nurse.'

As we got into the car we could see that the lights were still burning in Mr Tolson's room in Lebanon Lodge.

'A rum sort of cove,' my uncle remarked. 'He is probably going to write up his notes on what I hope will have proved a satisfactory experiment.'

Some three years later I was nursing a doctor in the midlands. Clergymen and doctors are, in my experience, far the most unsatisfactory patients to deal with, but Dr Gilkes was an exception. He was an excellent talker – his fractured thigh was no impediment – and he had knocked about all over the world. Something or other had made me tell him about the strange case of the man who wanted to be anaesthetised. He listened with, I thought, unusual interest and then he burst out laughing.

'That's a funny thing,' he said. 'I've met Mr Tolson. At least, I think I have, though Drewit was the name he went by. How long ago would it be? Five years, perhaps. At any rate, I hadn't started in general practice. I was ship's surgeon in the *Valumeria*, a venerable survivor of pre-war days that used to make the trip to Australia by way of the Cape. Four days out from Hobart something went wrong with the propeller, and though things were patched up – the weather, thank goodness, was fine – it meant our proceeding in whatever was the nautical equivalent of bottom gear and we were three days behind our schedule. We all put as cheerful a face on things as we could with the exception of this Drewit fellow, who seemed to think that the fates had personally insulted him. He had, it appeared, a most important engagement in Hobart. We did our best to console him, partly because a man with a most important engagement in sleepy Tas (that's Tasmania, you know) is a rare bird, but I never knew its actual nature until the day before we were due in port. No, it wasn't time-space and its relation to the psychology of the unconscious. The dope he dealt out to me had to do with telepathy. Drewit, it seemed, was writing a treatise on telepathy which was to include the results of some entirely new experiments. He and a friend in England had arranged to be put under an anaesthetic at the same hour. A third friend – what curious friends some people do seem to have! – was then to broadcast on the appropriate brain wave-length and the other two, on coming round, would record their impressions. You see the idea? Telepathy and the unconscious mind. Unmitigated nonsense!

'Well, Drewit had fixed everything up with a doctor he knew in Hobart, when this unforeseen delay occurred. He was most anxious that I should do the job. Anxious, indeed, is hardly the word to describe his dithering importunity. I didn't know what to do, but when he produced a letter from his friend in England to convince me of his bona fides and mentioned a twenty-guinea fee without turning a hair, I hesitated no longer. I was human and I was stony broke.

'The time Drewit had chosen for his experiment, between 11.45 and 12.15 at night, suited me well, since it was unlikely that we should be disturbed. Some of the bright young sparks among the passengers had fixed up a fancy-dress ball. I slipped away soon after eleven and got my things ready. I had rather expected that Drewit would have been nervous. Not a bit of it. When I examined his heart he took it as a matter of ordinary routine, and when I started to anaesthetise him he made not the slightest effort to resist, but went on breathing away as if he enjoyed it. It was the easiest twenty guineas that I had ever earned or was likely to earn. I could feel myself in Harley Street. The only thing that happened was that when I was half-way through, the door of the cabin opened and someone popped in his head. Then, seeing what was going on he apologised, said something about look-ing in again later, and withdrew. I thought at the time it was Dow, the third engineer, dressed up as one of our ancestors. I taxed him with it next day, but he said the only time he had worn fancy dress was at his sister's wedding, when he had a gardenia in his buttonhole. He had, moreover, an alibi. At the time I mentioned, it appeared that he was endeavouring to point out the glories of the Southern Cross – they need a lot of searching – to a girl from Dulwich.

'Of course I never heard of Drewit again. You are the first person I've met who ever came across him, because obviously it must be the same man masquerading under another name. I suppose you don't remember the date?'

'It was the seventeenth of December,' I said, 'the day before my uncle's birthday.'

Dr Gilkes asked me to hand him his diary.

'I'll make a note of that,' he said. 'It would be about the middle of December that we got to Hobart. I can't be sure of the actual day, but I'll look it up as soon as I'm on my pins again. I should dearly like to know what has happened to Drewit, if he still indulges in this annual stunt and why he does it. It makes a good story, but we want the closing chapter. There's one thing that's certain. The man's medical attendants are pretty certain to remember him; it is the sort of case, too, about which they might easily talk. If I hear anything that will throw light on our mysterious patient, I will let you know, and I expect you to do the same to me.'

Dr Gilkes, I am glad to say, made an excellent recovery from his accident. I did not expect to hear from him again, and the letter I received two years later came as a surprise.

'I haven't forgotten my promise,' he wrote, 'to let you know if anything more turned up about our friend Tolson-Drewit. Three weeks ago I was staying with a doctor, an old University College man, who told me a story almost precisely similar to the one we could tell. It happened on the same date in December, and the patient was evidently the same, though on this occasion he passed under the name of Royce. He persuaded my friend into giving him an anaesthetic by propounding an ingenious theory about the nature of memory. Soon after twelve there was the usual interruption, but Handysides had kept his patient only very lightly under, and when the door opened and the old fellow poked his head in, it was all he could do to hold Drewit down. When he came round he was extremely indignant and declared that he had been conscious half the time, and poor old Handysides had to be content with only ten guineas. As he is a Scotsman he naturally remembers the incident very well. That's the story in brief; the same in all the principal features as ours. If I ever hear more, I'll let you know.'

Then there was silence for four years, but I was to hear once more from Dr Gilkes.

'I have just come across this extract,' he wrote, 'from a three months' old copy of a local paper. I wonder if it is the sort of explanation that satisfies you. If you care to do so, you will be able to look up the case in greater detail by consulting the newspaper files. To me it seems that Drewit was for once speaking the truth when he told my friend on the last occasion on which we heard of him that he was investigating the nature of memory. Reading between the lines I can guess who and what it was he wanted to forget.'

And this was the cutting:

SUDDEN DEATH OF A WADDISLOW VISITOR
Mystery of a famous poisoning case recalled

On Monday last an inquest was held at the Crown Inn, Waddislow, upon the body of Mr Charles Spenser Newcombe, who had for some weeks been a resident in the district. Mr Newcombe, who was a victim of insomnia, was found dead in his bedroom. Medical evidence showed that the deceased died from an overdose of laudanum. A curious feature of the case was brought forward in Dr Edwards's evidence. He said that he had been attending the deceased gentleman for the last ten days, and had arranged at his express desire to administer a general anaesthetic on the night of his death, but that owing to his being called away in connection with a motor accident, he had been unable to fulfil his engagement.

The deceased gentleman, who was travelling under the name of Fuller, came prominently before the public in the early nineties in what was known as the Sulphonal Case. He acted as librarian and confidential secretary to the eccentric Sir Jarvis Effington, who died under rather curious circumstances in Naples from an overdose of that drug, leaving his entire property to Mr Newcombe. The will was contested by the family, and many of the leading counsel of the day appeared in the case. The jury's decision in favour of the defendant caused general surprise in view of the comments of the presiding judge.

Portraits of Sir Jarvis Effington and Mr Newcombe will be found on another page.

Dr Gilkes had cut out the two portraits. Tolson's face I recognised at once. The other, though I had seen it only for a moment on a night more years ago than I cared to remember, I recognised too. There were the dark eyes, the long scraggy neck, the thin lips, mocking and cruel. I can well believe that to one man at least it would be a face to forget.

The Flying out of Mrs Barnard Hollis

I have always been fond of old ladies, partly because as a girl I was brought up by a grandmother who taught me that it was possible to bridge the generations with kindliness and grace, partly because as a nurse I have been especially fortunate in my patients. They are, I think, younger in many ways than the old men, their contemporaries, less conservative, more hopeful of the future; often they are endowed with a courage and gaiety that have to be seen to be believed.

Such a woman was Mrs Barnard Hollis. To say that she was a perfect old dear did her less than justice. There is a touch of patronage about the phrase, as if good nature can be achieved by anyone who is prepared to be imposed upon and to surrender their independence of judgment. There are old dears who spend their lives knitting in their comfortable armchairs by the fire while the traffic of the world rolls by, but Mrs Barnard Hollis emphatically was not one of these. She belonged rather to the company of saints, humble, courageous in experiment, and with something about her that filled the room she was in with vitality.

I don't know how old she was. She looked as if she might be eighty or more; her body was frail and bent and she wore widow's weeds. Mr Barnard Hollis, whose portrait faced her as she sat at the end of the dining-room table at Mickleham Grange, had been killed in a carriage accident three years after their marriage, but though the school buildings in the village, erected to his memory, were already covered with ivy, his walking-stick still stood in the stand in the hall.

The Grange had been a house of refuge to many. In the early days of the war Mrs Barnard Hollis had offered hospitality to two families of Belgian refugees for a week. They had stayed for four years. There was a constant succession of guests, overworked parsons and their wives from the East End, lonely deaconesses, governesses waiting for a job, decayed gentlefolk – how I loathe the expression! – who nobody wanted to entertain because they were so unentertaining.

The old lady's correspondence was enormous. She carried her writing-case with her wherever she went, and her cheque-book was always in it.

One of the interesting things about Mrs Barnard Hollis was that she was seldom imposed upon. A casual observer might have put her down as a timid, kind-hearted little woman who would easily fall a prey to sharks, but the casual observer would have been wrong. She was, indeed, a remarkably shrewd judge of character.

For six weeks I had nursed her through an illness that had puzzled the doctors. At one time it seemed as if an operation would be necessary, and all the preparations for it had been made when she made an unexpected rally, and from that time never looked back.

It was a hot August afternoon. Tea had been served in the shade of the cedar on the lawn. Mrs Smith, Mrs Cole, and Miss Tangye were the callers. They were all old friends and they had plenty to talk about, for the village was all agog with the news of the disappearance of Mrs Cator Byng.

'I hope she won't be found!'

Mrs Barnard Hollis put down her cup on the little table that Mrs Smith had so thoughtfully placed by her chair. She spoke with emphasis and her black eyes gleamed.

'I hope she won't be found!' she repeated. The three ladies burst out laughing. They had known Mrs Hollis all their lives. Never had they heard her say an unkind thing, and now this little old lady was expressing unashamedly a desire which probably each of us consciously or unconsciously shared. Mrs Cator Byng was not popular in the district. She was the owner of Basset House, but she did nothing for the village, and her occasional weekend parties introduced what the vicar called a distinctly undesirable element into the parish. And now Mrs Cator Byng, flying her aeroplane, the *Green Streak*, in an attempt to beat the record from England to the Cape, had disappeared. It seemed probable that she had been forced down in crossing the Sahara. Anyhow she was lost. There were no traces of her whereabouts, and Mrs Smith, Mrs Cole, Miss Tangye and most surprising of all Mrs Barnard Hollis, were glad that she had not been found.

'But this is too delightful,' said Mrs Cole. 'Unless I actually heard you myself, nothing in the wide world would have made me believe that you could have expressed such a wish. I like to know that you are completely human. I had my doubts, Mrs Hollis, I really had my doubts.'

'Don't waste time in flattery, Emily,' Mrs Hollis answered. 'I'm a wicked old woman ever to have said such a thing. But Mrs Cator Byng is – no, I can't trust myself to speak of her with charity. She has ruined the lives of two good men, she is vain and cruel in her frivolity, she has no pity or love for little children. Nurse Wilkie and I met that little girl of hers walking out with the governess when we were in the village this morning. She was ill when her mother left to make her final preparations. Did that make any difference? Of course not. I expect that even now gallant French officers, men with wives and children of their own, are risking their lives searching for her. I hope the woman won't be found. Dear me! That is the third time I've said it. And now, Julia, let us change the conversation. Tell me about this German girl whom you have engaged as cook. Are you seeing that she is making suitable friends?'

Reluctantly the three ladies abandoned the subject of Mrs Cator Byng.

At half past five Mrs Smith took Miss Tangye off in her car to attend a committee, and when soon afterwards Mrs Cole left, Mrs Hollis suggested that I too might like to walk to the village.

'She really is the most wonderful old lady I know,' said Mrs Cole. 'She puts our generation to shame with that rare combination of charity and candour.' We had turned back to look at the little black figure of Mrs Barnard Hollis, leaning on the ebony cane she always carried, as she passed slowly along the yew walk towards the house.

'Wasn't it extraordinary,' Mrs Cole went on, 'the way she blazed up over Mrs Cator Byng? I am told that attractive great-nephew of hers was seeing a good deal of the woman after her second divorce, which might partly explain it. She is a poisonous little thing. Was, I suppose I should say. Upton Basset won't miss her.'

The evening was too hot for me to wish to extend my walk beyond Mrs Cole's garden gate. I remembered, too, that the news bulletin would be due at six. It would be interesting to hear whether anything more had been found out of the whereabouts of that much-disliked woman, Mrs Cator Byng.

When I entered the library I found that Mrs Hollis had already switched on the wireless.

' . . . and it is feared,' the announcer was saying, 'that the loss of life must be very great.

'*The Missing Airwoman*. No news, as yet, has been received of the whereabouts of Mrs Cator Byng, who left Croydon on Tuesday in an attempt to set up a new record for the solo flight from England to the

Cape. Her aeroplane, the *Green Streak*, was last seen flying over Reggan, two hundred miles south of Beni Abbas. French military machines are searching for Mrs Cator Byng, who, it is feared, may have been forced down in difficult country.

'*The Disarmament Conference*. Speaking at a luncheon . . . '

Mrs Hollis, who despite her years knew more of the work of the Disarmament Conference than anyone I had met, switched off the wireless. She had evidently heard all that she wished to hear.

'I wonder,' she said, 'if I might trouble you to get the atlas. These names, I am afraid, mean so little to me.'

I fetched the atlas which she had bought four weeks before in order to be able to follow better the informative talks of Professor Caldecotte on 'New Frontiers and Old', and together we traced the route. Somewhere in that ochre-coloured expanse so devoid of names was Mrs Cator Byng.

'And now,' said Mrs Hollis, 'I have one or two important letters to write. I shall place them when they are finished in a sealed envelope in my desk addressed to Dr Cole. I don't want him to receive it before, shall we say, midday tomorrow? It may not be necessary for him to receive it at all. But if for any reason I'm not here tomorrow afternoon, will you hand the envelope over to him?'

The request was a curious one, and I wondered what was at the back of Mrs Hollis's mind. Was she feeling unwell? She showed no sign of it. Had she planned some expedition for the morrow? That, again, was hardly likely in view of the intense heat.

At supper that evening Mrs Barnard Hollis was unusually silent. Clearly she was oppressed by something, but whatever it was it did not prevent her from making a good meal. She even drank a glass of wine. But when we went to the drawing-room her manner changed. She got me to draw her armchair to the open window, where she could see the full glory of the sunset behind the cedars.

'Come and sit beside me, nurse,' she said. 'I shall be going to bed early tonight, but there is still time for a good talk. Tell me about your future.'

I couldn't help but laugh. The future of a middle-aged nurse is not an interesting topic for conversation. I don't often think about it myself, and here was Mrs Hollis taking it as much for granted as she would my past.

Perhaps there was something in the atmosphere of that hot August evening with its threatening of thunder, perhaps it was the mere presence of the magnetic personality of the old lady by my side, but whatever it was I felt a curious feeling of stimulation, of exhilaration. I found myself talking more freely than I had ever done before of long-concealed ambitions and frustrated hopes. I found myself listening to Mrs Hollis too. She seemed to know me far better than I knew myself. That talk with her was the only experience I have ever had of what the confessional may mean.

When the clock struck nine she rose to go to bed.

'Would you come to my room in half an hour,' she said, 'and read to me my evening portion? It was kind of you to speak so frankly. I have often found strength in frankness. No, don't trouble to come with me upstairs. You see, I am becoming quite independent.'

Half an hour later I knocked at her bedroom door and was told to come in.

Mrs Barnard Hollis lay in her bed facing the windows, which were wide open. The curtains had not been drawn. On the table by her side were a reading-lamp, a tumbler half full of water, and a Bible.

'Leave the curtains as they are,' she said. 'The light is poor, but your eyes are stronger than mine. I want you to read me the first chapter of Ezekiel.'

I drew up a chair to the table and found the place. When I lifted up my eyes from the page I looked south through the open window, to where toppling thunderclouds had already begun to gather. The words I read were unfamiliar to me. I could not understand their meaning, but I was conscious of a power about them that was strangely disturbing.

' "And I looked, and, behold, a whirlwind came out of the north, a great cloud, and a fire infolding itself, and a brightness was about it, and out of the midst thereof as the colour of amber, out of the midst of the fire." '

I read of the four living creatures.

' "And they had the hands of a man under their wings on their four sides. . . . Their wings were joined one to another; they turned not when they went; they went every one straight forward. . . . And they went every one straight forward: whither the spirit was to go, they went; and they turned not when they went.

' "As for the likeness of the living creatures, their appearance was like burning coals of fire, and like the appearance of lamps: it went up and down among the living creatures; and the fire was bright, and out of the fire went forth lightning. And the living creatures ran and returned as the appearance of a flash of lightning." '

The long-expected storm had come at last. The leaves of the aspen in the garden chattered in terror as flash succeeded flash, great jagged scimitars of light cutting the southern sky.

I looked at Mrs Barnard Hollis. She lay perfectly still in the big bed, her eyes wide open.

' "And when the living creatures went, the wheels went by them: and when the living creatures were lifted up from the earth, the wheels were lifted up. Whithersoever the spirit was to go, they went, thither was their spirit to go; and the wheels were lifted up over against them: for the spirit of the living creature was in the wheels. When those went, these went; and when those stood, these stood; and when those were lifted up from the earth, the wheels were lifted up over against them: for the spirit of the living creature was in the wheels. . . .

' "And when they went, I heard the noise of their wings, like the noise of great waters, as the voice of the Almighty, the voice of speech, as the noise of an host. . . . " '

I finished the chapter and closed the book.

'Good night, nurse,' said Mrs Barnard Hollis. 'You may put out the light now; I have all that I require.' I went over to the bed. She put her hand for a moment in mine, and then – I don't know why – I knelt for a moment beside her and kissed it while flashes of lightning illumined the darkness. Quietly I moved to the door. I was opening it when Mrs Barnard Hollis spoke. There was a curious tremor in her voice.

'Mrs Cator Byng!' she said, and then again: 'Mrs Cator Byng!'

It was long before I fell asleep. For more than an hour the thunder continued with drenching rain. Then the storm passed over to the west, and from the flowerbed beneath my window came the scent of stocks.

I went into Mrs Hollis's room next morning soon after seven. Usually she awoke early, but finding that she was still fast asleep, I left instructions with the maid not to bring her customary cup of early morning tea.

I breakfasted alone at eight. At half past eight I again went to Mrs Hollis's room. To my surprise she was still sleeping. There was something about her breathing that made me begin to wonder whether it were wholly natural. I felt her pulse; it was slow and regular, but she gave no sign of stirring as my fingers touched her wrist. Then my eye fell on the glass on the table beside her bed. I thought I saw a slight sediment at the bottom. Was it possible that unknown to me Mrs Hollis had taken some sort of sleeping-draught?

I remembered a conversation that had taken place some weeks before, when Miss Tangye, who suffered from a painful form of neuralgia and had a horror of becoming a drug addict, had sought the advice of Mrs Hollis. She said some very sensible things, and then told us of an experience of her own which I remembered because it was so typical of the woman.

Mrs Hollis, who at the time was suffering from sleeplessness, was staying with a niece, the wife of a doctor. At her suggestion she had been induced to try the effect of a new drug that had recently come on the market, called Barbinol. The result had been exactly the opposite to what she had expected. Instead of sleep coming quickly it had been delayed. She had become conscious of an unusual quickening of the senses, of a rather alarming feeling of awareness. She had not repeated the experiment, so startling were the results, but before she left she had taken three tablets from the bottle for use in case of emergency. She had not asked leave because she knew that leave would not have been given her; to equalise the account, however, she had left behind a bottle of aspirin.

Miss Tangye and I had laughed together over Mrs Hollis. There was something extraordinarily droll in the innocent way she told the story of her pilfering. Her scruples seemed to act in a manner as unforeseen as the drug.

The recollection of the incident, however, did make me wonder if her sleep was natural. From the time of her outburst against Mrs Cator Byng on the previous evening she had not been her usual self, and it was quite possible that unknown to me she might have taken a dose of Barbinol. For an hour or so I was rather anxious.

Soon after ten she opened her eyes and then she spoke. Evidently she was only half awake.

> 'They wept like anything to see
> Such quantities of sand,'

said Mrs Barnard Hollis. 'And of course you can't sweep sand like that away. Terrible, terrible. But I'm very glad indeed to be back. Surely I know your face. Why, of course, it's Nurse Wilkie! Good morning, nurse. I have overslept myself, and I am afraid I am very tired. I think, if it's not being too lazy, that I will stay in bed this morning.'

I suggested that she might like to see Dr Croft, but Mrs Hollis was emphatic that there was nothing seriously the matter with her.

'Just a little dazed, my dear,' she said, 'and a curious drumming in my ears. But I should very much appreciate a strong cup of tea.'

For two days Mrs Barnard Hollis took things very quietly. Dr Croft, when he paid his routine visit, could find nothing the matter with her. He told her that she had been over-exerting herself and prescribed a simple tonic. But she had lost her usual vivacity. Even the brief announcement on the wireless of the unexpected rescue of Mrs Cator Byng failed to arouse anything more than a quiet expression of satisfaction. She took it almost as a matter of course. And so apparently did the intrepid airwoman. The papers were full of her exploits.

I still have a cutting of what she said to the representative of the United Press who interviewed her in Oran. It has been folded and unfolded so many times (when you read it the reason will be apparent) that some of the lines are almost indecipherable.

I had practically given up hope. The dear old *Green Streak* was done for; I hadn't the ghost of a notion of my whereabouts except that I was somewhere about five hundred miles south of Reggan. On the day before my rescue, when night came on I had half a cup of coffee left in my thermos and only two cigarettes. It looked like the end, and I don't mind admitting that I would have given my soul for a cocktail, certainly for two. The injury to my ankle prevented me moving from the spot where I was forced down, a wide and shallow saucer. I felt like a half-swatted fly, quite incapable of dragging myself to the brim. Like the Walrus and the Carpenter, I could have wept to see such quantities of sand.

When the moon rose over the saucer's edge I had one moment of ecstatic hope. There was a little old woman in black wearing one of the long veils of the country, and obviously she had seen me, for she waved her stick. But all my expectations were dashed. She had seen me all right, but she was jeering at me. I suppose I was one of the white devils she had heard about. I lit my last cigarette but one, and then, while I looked – and I was cursing the old lady for all I was worth – her twin sister appeared out of nowhere, proceeded to remonstrate with her. What she said evidently had no effect, so old lady number two went on to tackle her in a thoroughly workmanlike manner while I looked on. I don't quite know what happened next. It ended in the disappearance of the first wizened hag, and with my friend number two waving what were unmistakably signals of encouragement to me with her stick. In the moonlight I could see her quite distinctly.

She might have passed for a European, and reminded me with her black veil of a slightly ridiculous and very conventional old widow I once met at a garden party. Anyhow, it must have been she who informed the head man, big noise, or whatever you call them, of the nearest village, for they all turned out a couple of hours later and swarmed over the *Green Streak* like flies. They brought their children with them, adorable little creatures. I have always adored children, so that you can understand that I'm just aching to see my own little girl.

By the way, I managed to retrieve the instruments. I'm pretty certain from what they show that until I crashed I was well within the record.'

When I first read that interview it made no great impression on me. After what I had been told I was revolted at the way Mrs Cator Byng spoke of adoring children. 'Aching to see her own little girl'. I didn't believe it for a minute. Her own pet Pekinese, perhaps; but her daughter, no. All she wanted for those aches was a couple of aspirins and a tub of hot water with plenty of bath salts. From Dr Cole I gathered that he was of the same opinion, but a remark of his made me re-read the newspaper account, and after re-reading it to cut it out.

'Our intrepid airwoman,' he said, 'knows how to draw the long bow. I doubt very much whether in the part of Africa where she landed little old women wear long black veils like our good friend Mrs Barnard Hollis. They do not speak of white devils – she is mixing up China with Africa – and twin sisters are probably not allowed to exist. Mrs Cator Byng should take up fancy embroidery. She seems to have a gift for it.'

There are two ways in which this story may be regarded. Nine people out of ten, I suppose, would say that Mrs Barnard Hollis was a kind, sensitive old lady who was quite unnecessarily disturbed by the expression of an uncharitable wish and had in consequence taken a rather dangerous dose of a sleeping-draught to make certain of a good night's rest. She had been thinking of Mrs Cator Byng when she fell asleep. When she awoke her thoughts still centred in the airwoman's awful plight. That is an easy and plausible explanation.

But just suppose for a moment that Mrs Barnard Hollis was a most extraordinary woman, the sort of extraordinary woman that centuries ago we should have called a witch, with the faculty, only half guessed at, of liberating the living spirit from the living body. She had thrice vehemently expressed a wish that Mrs Cator Byng should not be found. She, to use a colloquialism, had flown out. Later that same evening she flew out again, but this time deliberately. She was prepared for all risks. In case of death her final instructions would be received by her solicitor. I remembered the envelope to which she had drawn my attention and the words she had used – even then they had struck me as curious – 'if for any reason I'm not here tomorrow'.

I remembered what Mrs Barnard Hollis had said about the effect Barbinol had had in quickening the senses. I believe that in the East, Indian hemp is used by devotees to induce a special psychic state. Mrs Hollis was quite capable of doing the same thing.

But what about the time factor? Mrs Hollis's evil spirit 'flew out' soon after half past four in the afternoon and appeared before Mrs Cator Byng in Africa, somewhere on the meridian of Greenwich, at midnight. Mrs Hollis herself left her body probably before midnight and arrived there approximately at the same time. These time comparisons are interesting.

Sometimes I wish that I had the courage to visit Mrs Hollis at Mickleham Grange and ask for her version of the story. Would she give it to me? I hardly think she would. Sympathy, yes, understanding, yes, but her confidence, no.

There are secrets which saints and witches never tell.